U0146925

NEW TOEIC®

趙 御 筌

南陽街多益天后
美國威斯康辛州立大學麥迪遜分校
英研所應用語言學組碩士

TOEIC®

字彙資優班

一次學會字彙、聽力、口語

眾文圖書股份有限公司

感 謝

　　這本書的順利付梓，首先要感謝眾文圖書公司所有辛苦同仁的專業付出。謝謝家人與好友們無條件的愛與關懷；感謝 Prof. Charles T. Scott, Prof. Sandra Arfa, Julio, Marcela, Miranda, Ethan Chang, Felicia Lin 以及朱奉學先生和陳宏岳先生分享的智慧與溫暖；謝謝思祁、森渙、俐尹、婉容與音葳同學的協助與鼓勵。最後，要感謝所有用最大努力，以永不放棄的求知精神，一路提醒、挹注我教學熱忱的可愛同學們——真心感激你們在追尋理想的過程中，讓老師有幸盡一份心力。

趙御筌

兩個問題與一個願望

◎ 第一個問題總是……

在教授及研究 TOEIC 考題的這幾年中，不管在教室裡或演講後，同學們常問我兩個問題，第一個常常是：「TOEIC 可不可以自己準備？」在回答之前，我總是會先問他們：「你想考幾分？你需要考幾分？你覺得考幾分之後才可以不必再考一次？」同學們總是一臉困惑，沉吟半刻後回答：「喔，當然是愈高愈好！」或「最少要超過 800 分吧……」於是，我會問：「那你打算花多少時間準備？」面對這個問題，同學思考的時間更久，而答案通常是：「嗯……也還好耶……就……儘量讀就是了。」或「啊？當然是愈快準備好愈好呀……」這些對話，跟聽力測驗的錄音帶內容一樣，老師耳熟能詳，而那一張張困惑的臉龐，也一樣歷歷在目……。

→ 「高分素人」還是「高分達人」？

必須在短時間內考取高分的 TOEIC 考生，他們的目標有可能達成嗎？答案是 "Yes and No."。No 的原因在於，英文底子不錯的同學，在投入足夠的時間下，光靠自修確實有可能拿到 600-700 分的及格分數，但想當「素人高分考生」，光是砸時間猛讀，而能成功掠取紫金色高分證書的人卻是少數。

TOEIC 取材實用，絕不代表它的範圍狹隘或程度粗淺，這點從歷年台灣地區考生的平均成績在亞洲排名中落後就可一窺究竟。撇開答題技巧的重要性不談，光是它的頻考單字要蒐羅完整，就不是光靠揣測，或亂槍打鳥的準備方式就可以做到的。的確，時間投資愈多，愈有可能「接近」完整，但光靠一個「接近」，往往使得大部分的考生都只能落在功敗垂成的高分邊緣。

➜「高分考生」還是「高分陪考生」？

或許你會問 "Where is the silver lining?"（希望在哪？）希望，就在你認清了 TOEIC 高分考生的特質是：1. 會考試，2. 讀到的都會考。高分考生都是投資報酬率達到最飽和狀態的「考試達人」，而非盲目浪費時間在錯誤練習方式與失焦素材的純真「陪考生」。考生若能在一進入備考階段，就題題切中焦點、背誦的單字個個命中核心，短期之內要考出高分，絕非夢想！那些我所教過的同學的成績顯示，若準備方式正確，即使面對令人聞之色變的聽力測驗，能考出 420 分以上好成績的，早已不是個案，而是通例，更有同學們屢屢挑戰 495 滿分成功！

英文實力強不保證 TOEIC 分數高。ETS 向來擅長的就是狂電沒有對症下藥、囫圇吞棗或習慣輕敵的考生。從開始準備到進入最後衝刺階段，加上報考一到兩次的時間，正確的備考策略與素材應該能讓考生在四到六個月之間拿到漂亮的分數（即使是在下班後以幾近爆肝的狀態去準備）。真正的決勝關鍵，不只在比較分數的多寡，更在收割每一單位的投資報酬率高低。

◎ 第二個問題常常是……

我最常被問到的另一個問題是：「老師，我模考平均在 ××× 分左右，妳覺得我真正考試能拿幾分？」

TOEIC 出題水準成熟，題庫的質量與完整度優，加上複考率超高這三個利多，即使備考時間與體力有限，懂得怎麼考試的同學，一樣能成功「鑲紫鍍金」。在長期觀察、接觸了數萬名考生之後，我發現所有的高分考生除了會考試、懂得準備，更有一項共通的特質：他們都是深信與其花時間擔心、懷疑，甚至抱怨或裹足不前，不如趕緊追隨高分前輩的足跡，套用成功的公式於己身的積極人士。而這個特質，不是在校生、在職人士或

英語程度高超的考生的專利，而是一項只要你願意，就能選擇擁有的「超能力」。

於是，面對這個問題，我總是回答：「第一，你絕對會進步很多；第二，以數據上來推，要猜能進步幾分可以，但，請努力讓老師猜不中──因為你努力的最大值一定會突破平均數值，創造出專屬你個人的奇蹟。」通常從笑開了的臉龐，老師看到真正的答案──是的，在短期內要考出 TOEIC 高分的機率是 "Yes and No."，但從這個笑容裡，我看到的是一個大大的、令人安心的 "Yes"。

◎ 一個願望

TOEIC 高分證書是職場加分的最佳利器之一。分數的高低，有時可以決定你拿到的是前排的坐票還是角落的站票。準備方式正確，願意相信並投資自己的人，肯定能在揮汗向前後，置身於美麗人生 party 的搖滾特區中。原來，考試不只是考試，而是一次認識自己的機會；一張高分證書也不只是證書，而是一張嶄新視野的邀請函。

希望這本書能成為你的 VIP Pass，在激烈的職場競爭中，帶你輕快地抵達最想要的位置。

Contents

感謝 ii

作者序 iii

趙御筌 TOEIC 簡介及發音規則

TOEIC 簡介 2

本書使用說明 9

重要發音規則 12

趙御筌 TOEIC 字彙 A~Z

A-B 20

Check List 1 62

C-D 64

Check List 2 104

E-F 106

Check List 3 144

G-M 146

Check List 4 182

N-P 184

Check List 5 220

P-Q 222

Check List 6 256

R 258

Check List 7 298

S 300

Check List 8 334

S 336

Check List 9 372

T-Z 374

Check List 10 418

趙 御 筌
TOEIC®
簡介及發音規則

TOEIC 簡介

⌘ 何謂 TOEIC ？

TOEIC（Test of English for International Communication，多益測驗）為 ETS（Educational Testing Service，美國教育測驗服務社）針對英語非母語的人士所設計的英語能力測驗，用以評估受測者在國際職場上的英語溝通能力。TOEIC 最初由日本企業委託 ETS 設計研發，過去一直盛行於東南亞各國，而近年來 TOEIC 的影響力急速擴大，歐洲企業也紛紛採用 TOEIC 作為其測試員工英語能力的檢定測驗。

⌘ NEW TOEIC 測驗形式

TOEIC 目前為紙筆測驗，測驗形式分為聽力與閱讀兩大類，共 200 題選擇題，測驗時間為 2 小時。臺灣地區自 2008 年 3 月起，採用新制 TOEIC，下半年則將增設口說與寫作測驗為選考項目。考生要特別注意，新制的 TOEIC，不再只是美式英語的口音，可能會有來自英國、澳洲、加拿大的各國口音。

I. 聽力測驗

聽力測驗分為 4 大部分，共 100 題單選題，測驗時間為 45 分鐘。

Part 1：照片描述（10 題）
邊看試題冊上的照片，邊聆聽播放的 4 個選項，然後選出最符合照片內容的選項。

Part 2：應答問題（30 題）
聆聽播放的問題及 3 個可能的答句，選出正確的選項。

Part 3：簡短對話（30 題）

聆聽播放的簡短對話，閱讀試題冊上的問題及答案選項，然後選出正確的選項。每段對話會搭 3 個問題。

Part 4：簡短獨白（30 題）

聆聽播放的演講或發言，並閱讀試題冊上的問題及答案選項，然後選出正確的選項。每段獨白會有 3 個問題。

II. 閱讀測驗

閱讀測驗分為 3 大部分，共 100 題選擇題，測驗時間為 75 分鐘。

Part 5：單句填空（40 題）

從 4 個答案選項中，選出一個最符合句子空白處的選項，以完成一個完整的句子。

Part 6：短文填空 （12 題）

每段短文搭配 4 個填空選擇題，短文內容為商業信件、公告等。

Part 7：閱讀測驗（48 題）

包括單篇文章測驗（7-10 篇共 28 題）及雙篇文章測驗（4 組共 20 題）。單篇文章為一篇文章搭配 2~5 個問題；雙篇文章為兩篇有關聯性的文章搭配 5 個問題。文章取自報紙或雜誌的短篇報導、廣告、公告或商業文件。

◎ TOEIC 計分方式（聽力與閱讀測驗）

考生用鉛筆在電腦答案卷上作答（需自備 2B 鉛筆及橡皮擦）。分數由答對的題數決定，答錯不倒扣。將兩大類（聽力類、閱讀類）答對題數轉換成分數，每大類分數範圍在 5 到 495 分之間。兩大類加起來即為總分，範圍在 10 到 990 分之間。成績單將於考試完約 15 個工作天後寄發，考生也可以於網路進行成績查詢 (www.toeic.com.tw/reginfo13.htm)。

◎ TOEIC 成績與英語能力對照（聽力與閱讀測驗）

TOEIC 成績	英語能力	證書顏色
905~990	對任何主題的談話都能清楚地理解，可運用正式及非正式的語言進行溝通。英語能力已相當接近英語為母語者，能親自主持以英語進行的會議。	金色 (860~990)
785~900	對於各種專業、社交甚至抽象的談話都能大致理解。在會議的討論中表達流暢，除非過於緊張，用英語進行溝通時少有停頓及遲疑的情況。	藍色 (730~855)
605~780	在熟悉的主題下，能了解及進行基本對話，故可應付例行性的業務會議。仍侷限於使用簡單且常見的字彙及句型。	綠色 (470~725)
405~600	可以主動進行簡單的對話，對話的內容也不侷限於日常生活場景。已經可以從事須使用簡單英語的相關工作。	棕色 (220~465)
255~400	能理解日常生活中特定場合的簡單對話，可用簡單英語表達詢問、打招呼及自我介紹等。	
10~250	能說出日期及時間等簡單的字彙，以及背誦簡單的句子，但尚無法自行造句進行溝通。	橘色 (10~215)

⌘ TOEIC 口說與寫作測驗

據 TOEIC 官方表示，TOEIC 測驗將於 2008 下半年增設口說與寫作測驗，考生可自行選擇是否加考這部分測驗。TOEIC 口說與寫作測驗的施測方式不同於聽力與閱讀測驗的紙筆測驗，所採用的是電腦網路測驗 (internet-based test, iBT) 的形式。

口說與寫作測驗的測驗時間約為 80 分鐘。

I. 口說測驗

口說測驗共有 11 題，包括 6 種測驗內容，測驗時間約 20 分鐘。

題數	測驗內容	作答時間	說明
1-2	Read a text aloud （朗讀短文）	45 秒（準備時間） 45 秒（每題的時間）	朗讀一篇短文
3	Describe a picture （描述照片）	30 秒（準備時間） 45 秒（答題時間）	依據提供的照片，詳細描述照片內容
4-6	Respond to questions （回答問題）	各 15 秒（第 4-5 題） 30 秒（第 6 題）	根據題目設定的情境，回答 4-6 的問題
7-9	Respond to questions using information provided （根據題目資訊應答）	各 15 秒（第 7-8 題） 30 秒（第 9 題）	根據題目提供的資訊及設定的情境，回答 7-9 的問題
10	Propose a solution （提出解決方案）	30 秒（準備時間） 60 秒（答題時間）	根據題目提供的資訊及設定的情境，提出解決方案
11	Express an opinion （陳述意見）	15 秒（準備時間） 60 秒（答題時間）	根據題目指定的議題，表達看法並陳述意見

II. 寫作測驗

寫作測驗共有 8 題，包括 3 種測驗內容，測驗時間約 60 分鐘。

題數	測驗內容	作答時間	說明
1-5	Write a sentence based on a picture （看圖造句）	8 分	使用題目指定的兩個單字或片語，造出一句符合照片內容的句子
6-7	Respond to a written request （書面回覆）	10 分	讀取一篇電子郵件，並依據其內容回覆
8	Write an opinion （論說文）	30 分	根據題目指定的議題，表達看法並陳述意見

◎ TOEIC 口說及寫作測驗評分依據

口說測驗			
題數	測驗內容	評分依據	評分級距
1-2	Read a text aloud （朗讀短文）	• 發音及語調	0-3
3	Describe a picture （描述照片）	• 發音及語調 • 字彙、文法及組織	0-3
4-6	Respond to questions （回答問題）	• 發音及語調 • 字彙、文法及組織 • 內容的一致性與完整性	0-3
7-9	Respond to questions using information provided （根據題目資訊應答）	• 發音及語調 • 字彙、文法及組織 • 內容的一致性與完整性	0-3

10	Propose a solution（提出解決方案）	• 發音及語調 • 字彙、文法及組織 • 內容的一致性與完整性	0-5
11	Express an opinion（陳述意見）	• 發音及語調 • 字彙、文法及組織 • 內容的一致性與完整性	0-5

寫作測驗			
題數	測驗內容	評分依據	評分級距
1-5	Write a sentence based on a picture（看圖造句）	• 文法正確性 • 是否符合照片內容	0-3
6-7	Respond to a written request（書面回覆）	• 句子的難易度及多變性 • 字彙的選擇 • 組織性	0-4
8	Write an opinion（論說文）	• 論點是否有充分的理由或例子 • 文法正確性 • 字彙的選擇 • 組織性	0-5

◎ **TOEIC 口說及寫作測驗得分說明**

　　TOEIC 口說及寫作測驗以級距評分，再將所得級距轉換爲相對應的分數及能力等級。考生收到的成績單上將會有得分以及能力等級的分析說明。

口說測驗		寫作測驗	
得分	能力等級	得分	能力等級
190-200	8	200	9
160-180	7	170-190	8
130-150	6	140-160	7
110-120	5	110-130	6
80-100	4	90-100	5
60-70	3	70-80	4
40-50	2	50-60	3
0-30	1	40	2
		0-30	1

⌘ **進一步資訊**

　　有關 TOEIC 考試日期、地點或申請證書等相關資訊，可以親自向 TOEIC 臺灣地區代表忠欣股份有限公司查詢（電話：02-2701-7333，網址：http://www.toeic.com.tw）。

本書使用說明

◎ 說出聽力滿分‧聽出閱讀滿分

快速累積複考率最高的單字字庫量，是取得 TOEIC 高分的首要之務。雖然考生普遍對這點有所認知，但在實際執行時通常會遭遇以下幾個問題：

1. 取材失焦，背過的字不會考
2. 背過的單字只有眼睛會認，耳朵卻聽不懂
3. 背過就忘

的確，想把單字背熟，並同時在聽力與閱讀測驗都獲得理想的投資報酬率，一定要先克服方法錯誤及取材失焦所造成時間上的虛擲。

本書為了幫助考生在最短的時間內充分備妥必考字彙，不僅詳細比對歷年 TOEIC 考題題庫（含 2008 年考題最新用字），彙整複考率最高的字彙及其同義字，還特別針對考生盲點，錄製字彙的「一般正常速度」與「ETS 全真速度」，佐以坊間同類書籍所沒有的「音變作用解析」，讓考生不但聽得懂考試用字的一般速度發音，更能在 ETS 飆速時，即時聽懂單字，不受美式發音的獨特連音、消音或變音牽制。

其次，為解決考生背過就忘的問題，作者特別提供「本書最佳使用方法」，幫助考生以正確的練習步驟，達到最高的學習效率。考生不必受到時間及地點的限制，均能以「聽說雙併」的互動方式，讓背過的字彙過目不忘、每聽必認得。

最後，本書特別收納「考古題應用」的必考短句，除了讓考生更熟稔重點字彙、片語及句型的使用，獨家設計的口語互動練習，不但能強化字彙的記憶，更是 TOEIC 全面改制後，提升考生口說能力的一大利器！

◎ 本書最佳使用方法

範例

abandon (v.t) 捨棄	一般正常速度 [ə`bændən]	考古題應用 His heavy workload forced him to abandon his family trip.
同 desert, dispose of, get rid of, abolish	ETS全真速度 [ə`bæn＿n] ➡ [d] 在 [n] 前消音	沉重的工作量迫使他放棄家族旅行的計畫。
		口試練習題 Why did he look so upset? 考生回答處

練習步驟

1. 先決定每日的單字量。

2. 細讀該單字的所有重點，請特別注意「➡ 音變作用解析」。

3. 利用 MP3 互動練習：

❶ 一中二英：當 MP3 播放中文時，請說出相對英文單字；若來不及，請仔細聽 MP3 播放單字的「一般正常速度」，並在 MP3 播放「ETS 全真速度」時（兩遍），同步朗讀該字

> MP3：捨棄 → [ə`bændən] → [ə`bæn＿n] → [ə`bæn＿n]
>
> 考生同步說出：→ [ə`bændən] → [ə`bæn＿n] → [ə`bæn＿n]

❷ 請聽 MP3 播放「考古題應用」的例句

> MP3：His heavy workload forced him to abandon his family trip.

❸ 聽完「口試練習題」的問句，在提示音後回答

> MP3：Why did he look so upset?
>
> 考生回答：His heavy workload forced him to adandon his family
> trip.

4. 練習完該單字後，再接著記下 關（相關字）及 回（頻考同義字）的字彙。請注意，頻考同義字的先後順序是依照於歷年考試出現的頻率高低排列，考生可依準備時間的長短先從第一個同義字背起。

5. 左頁的左上角會列出該頁的五個單字，單字前面會有兩個方格（如：□□ abandon），請在第一次練習該單字後，於第一個方格內打勾。當練習完全書再次複習時，若確定該單字已完全熟練，再於第二個方格內打勾；若第二次複習時，該單字依然不熟練，請等完全熟悉該單字後再於第二個方格內打勾。

備註

1. 請切記：將字「背熟」跟把字「背完」同等重要。每回規定自己細讀的單字數量可以不拘，但字義與發音弄清楚後，請盡可能反覆進行 MP3 互動練習。

2. 跟著 MP3 複述單字或進行口試練習題時，發音可唸成一般速度或 ETS 全眞速度（以後者爲佳）。

重要發音規則

　　「發音解析」是本書的一大特色，在開始背單字、矯正發音及提升單字辨識能力前，我們先來看看一些重要的發音規則。這裡針對的是台灣學生比較容易混淆及覺得較困難的發音做說明，包括「ETS 發音 vs. 台式發音」以及「美式英語變音規則」兩部分。

ETS 發音 vs. 台式發音

I. 子音
A. 與國語注音近似的發音

子音	單字	ETS 發音	台式發音	與國語注音近似的發音
[w]	web	[wɛb]		有聲子音。發音方式近似國語注音的「ㄨㄛ」
[h]	hose	[hoz]		無聲子音。發音方式近似國語注音的「ㄏ（無聲版）」
[r]	hear	[hɪr]		有聲子音。發音方式近似國語注音的「ㄦ」

B. 常見的台式錯誤發音

子音	單字	ETS 發音	台式發音	用力過度
[p]	top	[tap]	[tapə]	無聲子音。在字尾／音節尾出現時請勿加 [ə]
[b]	lab	[læb]	[læbə]	有聲子音。在字尾／音節尾出現時請勿加 [ə]
[f]	beef	[bif]	[bifu]	無聲子音。在字尾／音節尾出現時請勿加 [u]

[v]	of	[ə(v)]	[əv]	有聲子音。在字尾／音節尾出現時輕唸即可
[s]	miss	[mɪs]	[mɪ厶]	無聲子音。在字尾／音節尾出現時，請勿唸成國語注音「厶」
[z]	please	[pli(z)]	[pliz]	有聲子音。在字尾／音節尾出現時輕唸即可
[g]	rug	[rʌg]	[rʌgə]	有聲子音。在字尾／音節尾出現時請勿加 [ə]
[ʃ]	fresh	[frɛʃ]	[frɛㄒㄩ]	無聲子音。發音時 1) 嘴唇輕噘即可，2) 在單字字尾時請勿唸成國語注音的「ㄒㄩ」
[ʒ]	garage	[gəˋraʒ]	[gəˋradʒ]	有聲子音。發音時 1) 嘴唇輕噘即可，2) 勿用力過度而唸成了 [dʒ]
[tʃ]	watch	[watʃ]	[waㄑㄩ]	無聲子音。發音時 1) 嘴唇輕噘即可，2) 勿用力過度而唸成了國語注音的「ㄑㄩ」
[dʒ]	bridge	[brɪdʒ]	[brɪㄐㄩ]	有聲子音。發音時 1) 嘴唇輕噘即可，2) 勿用力過度而唸成了國語注音的「ㄐㄩ」

子音	單字	ETS 發音	台式發音	口型錯誤
[θ]	something	[ˋsʌmθɪŋ]	[ˋsʌmsɪŋ]	無聲子音。發音時請務必吐舌
[ð]	bathe	[beð]	[bez]	有聲子音。發音時請務必吐舌
[m]	someday	[ˋsʌm‚de]	[ˋsʌn‚de]	有聲子音；在字尾／音節尾出現時請務必緊閉雙唇
[l]	double	[ˋdʌbl̩]	[ˋdʌbㄛ]	有聲子音。發音時務必 1) 頂舌，2) 切勿噘嘴唸成國語注音的「ㄛ」

子音	單字	ETS 發音	台式發音	母語發音轉移
[n]	Monday	[ˋmʌnde]	[ˋmʌŋde]	有聲子音。請勿唸成 [ŋ]
[r]	rose	[roz]	[ꓘoz]	有聲子音。在單字字首時請勿唸成國語注音的「ㄖ」
[j]	year	[jɪr]	[ir]	有聲子音。發音時舌根要往上頂並摩擦，否則會聽起來像 [i]

II. 母音

A. 與國語注音近似的發音

母音	單字	ETS 發音	台式發音	與國語注音近似的發音
[i]	treat	[trit]		發音方式近似國語注音的「ㄧ」，無須刻意拉長聲音
[ɛ]	bet	[bɛt]		發音方式近似國語注音的「ㄝ」
[u]	food	[fud]		發音方式近似國語注音的「ㄨ」
[ɔ]	bought	[bɔt]		發音方式近似國語注音的「ㄛ」
[ɑ]	pot	[pɑt]		發音方式近似國語注音的「ㄚ」

B. 常見的台式錯誤發音

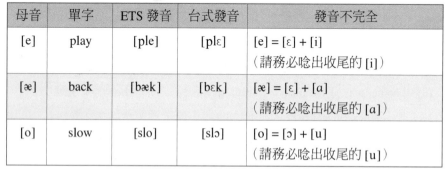

母音	單字	ETS 發音	台式發音	發音不完全
[e]	play	[ple]	[plɛ]	[e] = [ɛ] + [i]（請務必唸出收尾的 [i]）
[æ]	back	[bæk]	[bɛk]	[æ] = [ɛ] + [ɑ]（請務必唸出收尾的 [ɑ]）
[o]	slow	[slo]	[slɔ]	[o] = [ɔ] + [u]（請務必唸出收尾的 [u]）

母音	單字	ETS 發音	台式發音	口型錯誤
[ɪ]	kiss	[kɪs]	[kis]	發音時舌頭位置要比 [i] 下降一點
[ʊ]	book	[bʊk]	[buk]	一發出 [ʊ] 後雙唇馬上鬆開，不必噘嘴（如台語「鬱卒」的「鬱」）
[ʌ]	bus	[bʌs]	[bɑs]	一開始口型為 [a]，固定後用 [a] 的口型唸出 [ə]（嘴巴一樣要張大）

美式英語變音規則

I. 連音

1. 母子連音：

兩音相鄰，當前者為子音，後者為母音時，會造成「前子後母」的連音組合。

- disorder [dɪs`ɔrdɚ]
- an order [æn `ɔrdɚ]
- He has just placed an order. [plest æn `ɔrdɚ]

> 註：[t] 的變音詳見 p.16 的「子音強化」

2. 母母連音：

兩音相鄰，當兩者皆為母音時，會出現類母音（[j] 或 [w]）串連此二母音。

a. 兩音相鄰，當第一個音為 [i], [ɪ], [ɛ], [æ], [aɪ] 時，會出現類母音 [j] 串連兩個母音。

- Seattle [si`ætl̩] → [si`jætl̩]

b. 兩音相鄰，當第一個音為 [u], [ʊ], [o], [ɔ], [aʊ] 時，會出現類母音 [w] 串連兩個母音。

- TOEIC [`tɔɪk] → [`towɪk]

15

II. 變音

1. 子音強化：

位於輕音節的無聲子音，若其後接母音，常被強化為有聲子音。

- paper [ˋpepɚ] → [ˋpebɚ]
- wrap it [ræp ɪt] → [ræb ɪt]

2. [t] → [ɖ]：

位於輕音節的 [t]，在前後有母音包夾時會變音為 [ɖ]。

- letter [ˋlɛtɚ] → [ˋlɛɖɚ]
- light up [laɪt ʌp] → [laɪɖ ʌp]
- Peter shut it down. [ˋpitɚ ʃʌt ɪt daʊn] → [ˋpiɖɚ ʃʌɖ ɪt daʊn]

> 註：[ɖ] 的發音方式
> 發 [d] 的時候，舌尖是以點觸的方式，彈擊上排門牙背面，力道較強；唸 [ɖ] 時舌尖則像扇子一樣，輕輕拍過 (flapping) 門牙背面，比 [d] 輕柔，速度因此更快。請仔細比對上面的錄音示範。

3. [s] + [p]/[t]/[k]：

當字首或音節首的 [s] 遇到 [p], [t], [k] 任一音時，[p]/[t]/[k] 須變音為有聲子音 [b]/[d]/[g]。

- spell [spɛl] → [sbɛl]
- stood [stʊd] → [sdʊd]
- skirt [skɝt] → [sgɝt]

III. 消音

1. 字尾子音：

位於單字字尾的無聲子音可輕唸或消音；有聲子音則輕唸即可。

- sight [saɪt] → [saɪ(t)]
- notebook [ˋnot.bʊk] → [ˋno(t).bʊ(k)]

2. [t]/[d] 遇到 [n]：

[t]/[d] 遇到 [n] 時，[t]/[d] 常省略不發音。

a. [t]/[d] 在 [n] 前：

- mountain [ˋmaʊntən] → [ˋmaʊn__n̩]
- suddenly [ˋsʌdənlɪ] → [ˋsʌ__nlɪ]

b. [t]/[d] 在 [n] 後（注意：[t] 消音後，其前後兩音可連音）。

- internet [ˋɪntɚˏnɛt] → [ˋɪn__ɚˏnɛt] → [ˋɪnɚˏnɛt]
- advantage [ədˋvæntɪdʒ] → [ədˋvæn__ɪdʒ] → [ədˋvænɪdʒ]

3. 副詞子音：

-ly 副詞原字根字尾若為 [t] 或 [d] 時，則 [t]/[d] 均可消音；消音處稍停一拍。

- definitely [ˋdɛfɪnɪtlɪ] → [ˋdɛfɪnɪ__lɪ]
- hardly [ˋhɑrdlɪ] → [ˋhɑr__lɪ]

趙御筌
TOEIC®
字彙A~Z

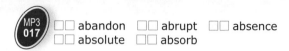

Ab-

abandon (v.t) 捨棄

同 desert, dispose of, get rid of, abolish

一般正常速度 [əˋbændən]

ETS全真速度 [əˋbæn＿＿n]

➡ [d] 在 [n] 前消音

abrupt (adj.) 突然的

同 sudden, unexpected

一般正常速度 [əˋbrʌpt]

ETS全真速度 [əˋbrʌp(t)]

➡ 字尾無聲子音 [t] 輕唸即可

absence (n.) 缺席

關 absent (adj.) 缺席的

一般正常速度 [ˋæbsn̩s]

ETS全真速度 [ˋæbsn̩(s)]

➡ 字尾 [s] 輕唸即可

absolute (adj.) 絕對的

關 absolutely (adv.) 絕對地
同 total, sheer, pure, whole

一般正常速度 [ˋæbsəˌlut]

ETS全真速度 [ˋæ(b)səˌlu(t)]

➡ 1) 形容詞與副詞的 [b] 均輕唸即可
　 2) 形容詞的 [t] 輕唸即可，副詞的 [t] 必須消音

absorb (v.t) 吸收

關 absorption (n.) 吸收；專注
　 absorbent (adj.) 有吸收力的
同 take in, receive, consume, assimilate

一般正常速度 [əbˋsɔrb]

ETS全真速度 [ə(b)ˋsɔr(b)]

➡ 所有詞性的 [b] 均輕唸即可

考古題應用 His heavy <u>workload</u> forced him to abandon his family trip. **A**
沉重的<u>工作量</u>迫使他放棄家族旅行的計畫。

口試練習題 Why did he look so upset?
考生回答處

考古題應用 They were surprised at the abrupt change of policy.
他們對於政策急轉彎感到驚訝。

口試練習題 How did everyone respond to the CEO's speech?
考生回答處

考古題應用 Jorge took a two-week leave of absence.
Jorge 請了兩週的假。

口試練習題 Where has Jorge been?
考生回答處

考古題應用 We have absolute faith in our <u>updated product line</u>.
我們對於<u>新系列產品</u>有絕對的信心。

口試練習題 What do you have to say about your updated product line?
考生回答處

考古題應用 We decided to absorb the smaller <u>rivals</u>.
我們決定吸收規模較小的<u>競爭對手</u>。

口試練習題 What is your plan to expand the market share?
考生回答處

abstract (adj.) 抽象的

關 abstraction (n.) 抽象
同 deep, complex, unpractical

一般正常速度 [`æbstrækt]
ETS全真速度 [`æ(b)sdræk(t)]

→ 1) [b] 均輕唸即可
2) 第一個 [t] 須變音為 [d]
3) 形容詞字尾 [t] 輕唸即可

absurdly (adv.) 誇張地

關 absurd (adj.) 誇張的
同 crazily, illogically, meaninglessly

一般正常速度 [əb`sɜdlɪ]
ETS全真速度 [ə(b)`sɜ__lɪ]

→ 1) 形容詞與副詞的 [b] 均輕唸即可
2) 形容詞的 [d] 輕唸即可，副詞的 [d]
必須消音

abundant (adj.) 充沛的

關 abundance (n.) 豐富，充沛
同 rich, full, plenty

一般正常速度 [ə`bʌndənt]
ETS全真速度 [ə`bʌn__n(t)]

→ 1) [d] 可以消音
2) 形容詞字尾 [t] 輕唸即可

abuse (v.t) 濫用

關 abuse (n.) 濫用
abusive (adj.) 濫用的
同 damage, harm, misuse, mistreat

一般正常速度 [ə`bjuz]
ETS全真速度 [ə`bjuz]

accelerate (v.t) 加速

關 acceleration (n) 加速
同 speed up, hurry, forward,
advance

Ac-

一般正常速度 [æk`sɛlə,ret]
ETS全真速度 [æ__`sɛlə,re(t)]

→ 1) 動詞與名詞的 [k] 均停一拍即可，
無須發音
2) 動詞字尾 [t] 輕唸即可

A

考古題應用 Action is more important than abstract discussion.
行動比空談重要。

口試練習題 Do we need to call another emergency meeting?
考生回答處 _____

考古題應用 No one wants to buy our absurdly priced PDAs.
沒人想買我們貴得要命的 PDA。

口試練習題 Why were our profits down this quarter?
考生回答處 _____

考古題應用 The shelter has abundant food and electricity.
避難所裡提供足夠的食物跟電力。

口試練習題 Why do we have to transport the residents to the shelter?
考生回答處 _____

考古題應用 The R&D manager was demoted for abusing his power.
研發部門的經理因濫用職權被降職了。

口試練習題 Why was the manager's title changed?
考生回答處 _____

考古題應用 Good policies accelerated the growth of sales.
好的政策加速了業績的成長。

口試練習題 Why was our first quarter highly profitable?
考生回答處 _____

accent (n.) 口音

同 pronunciation, tone, intonation

一般正常速度 [ˋæksɛnt]
ETS全真速度 [ˋæ(k)sɛn(t)]
➡ [k] 與字尾 [t] 均輕唸即可

access (n.) 入口

關 accessible (adj.) 易取得的
同 road, path, entry, admission

一般正常速度 [ˋæksɛs]
ETS全真速度 [ˋæ__sɛs]
➡ 1) 重音在第一音節
2) [k] 停一拍即可，無須發音

accessories (n.pl.) 配件

同 extra, addition, decoration,
expansion

一般正常速度 [ækˋsɛsəriz]
ETS全真速度 [æ__ˋsɛsəriz]
➡ [k] 停一拍即可，無須發音

accommodation
(n.) 住宿

關 accommodate (v.t) 能容納
同 housing, lodging, settlement,
sheltering

一般正常速度 [əˌkɑməˋdeʃən]
ETS全真速度 [əˌkɑməˋdeʃən]

accomplish (v.t) 完成

關 accomplishment (n.) 成就
同 achieve, finish, complete, finalize,
manage

一般正常速度 [əˋkɑmplɪʃ]
ETS全真速度 [əˋkɑmplɪʃ]

A

考古題應用 She speaks English with a French accent.
她說起英文來有法文腔。

口試練習題 How does Monique's English sound?

考生回答處 _____

考古題應用 We need easier access to the library.
我們需要能方便進入圖書館。

口試練習題 Why are you adding a large entrance to the library?

考生回答處 _____

考古題應用 One of its accessories is a strong roof bar.
堅固的車頂架是它的配備之一。

口試練習題 What's so special about your new SUV?

考生回答處 _____

考古題應用 I have asked the travel agency to arrange our accommodations.
我已經請旅行社安排我們的住宿。

口試練習題 Have you made any travel arrangements?

考生回答處 _____

考古題應用 We accomplished a great deal on our trip to Prague.
我們的布拉格之旅成果非凡。

口試練習題 How was your trip to Prague?

考生回答處 _____

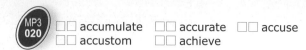
accumulate (v.t) 累積

關 accumulation (n.) 積累
accumulative (adj.) 累積的
同 store, grow, build up, pile up

一般正常速度 [ə`kjumjə.let]

ETS全真速度 [ə`kjumjə.le(t)]

➡ 1) 動詞字尾 [t] 輕唸即可
2) 形容詞的 [t] 可變音為 [d]

accurate (adj.) 正確的

關 accuracy (n.) 正確性
同 right, correct, precise

一般正常速度 [`ækjərɪt]

ETS全真速度 [`ækjərɪ(t)]

➡ 形容詞字尾 [t] 輕唸即可

accuse (v.t) 控告

關 accusation (n.) 控告
accused (adj.) 被控告的
同 charge, blame

一般正常速度 [ə`kjuz]

ETS全真速度 [ə`kjuz]

➡ 動詞與形容詞的重音都在第二音節

accustom (v.t) 習慣於

關 accustomed (adj.) 習慣的
同 get used to, be familiar with,
adapt to

一般正常速度 [ə`kʌstəm]

ETS全真速度 [ə`kʌsdəm]

➡ 動詞與形容詞的 [t] 均可變音為 [d]

achieve (v.t) 達成

關 achievement (n.) 成就
同 accomplish, bring about, carry
out, finish

一般正常速度 [ə`tʃiv]

ETS全真速度 [ə`tʃi(v)]

➡ 動詞與名詞的 [v] 均輕唸即可

考古題應用　We encourage our staff to accumulate experiences in every related field.
我們鼓勵員工在所有相關領域累積經驗。

試練習題　What do you do to improve your staff's performances?
考生回答處　_____

考古題應用　This report isn't accurate enough.
這份報告不夠正確。

試練習題　Why are you still working on the report, Officer?
考生回答處　_____

考古題應用　His secretary was accused of theft.
他的祕書被控偷竊。

試練習題　Why did Mr. Jimenez sound so worried?
考生回答處　_____

考古題應用　I am still trying to get accustomed to the new work environment.
我還在努力適應新的工作環境。

試練習題　How is everything at work?
考生回答處　_____

考古題應用　You must work harder to achieve your goals.
你需要更努力才能達成目標。

試練習題　Why isn't my plan working?
考生回答處　_____

acidity (n.) 酸性

關 acidify (v.t) 使變酸
acid (adj.) 酸的
同 sourness

一般正常速度 [əˋsɪdɪtɪ]

ETS全真速度 [əˋsɪđɪđɪ]

➡ 1) 名詞與動詞的重音都在第二音節
2) 名詞與動詞的 [d] 均須變音為 [đ]
3) 名詞字尾 [t] 須變音為 [đ]

Ad-

additional (adj.) 額外的

關 addition (n.) 附加
同 extra, added, other

一般正常速度 [əˋdɪʃən]]

ETS全真速度 [əˋdɪʃən]]

➡ 形容詞與名詞的重音都在第二音節

address (v.t) 發表演說

關 address [ˋædrɛs] (n.) 地址
addressee (n.) 收件人
同 give a lecture to, deliver a
speech to

一般正常速度 [əˋdrɛs]

ETS全真速度 [əˋdrɛs]

➡ address 當動詞時，重音落在第二音
節，當名詞時則在第一音節

adjacent (adj.) 鄰近的

同 close, near, next-door,
neighboring

一般正常速度 [əˋdʒesənt]

ETS全真速度 [əˋdʒesən(t)]

➡ 字尾 [t] 輕唸即可

administration (n.) 行政

關 administer (v.t) 管理
administrative (adj.) 管理的
同 control, government,
management

一般正常速度 [ədˌmɪnəˋstreʃən]

ETS全真速度 [ə__ˌmɪnəˋstreʃən]

➡ 1) 字首 [d] 停一拍即可，無須發音
2) 形容詞的第二個 [t] 可變音為 [đ]

A

考古題應用 | The researchers have <u>adopted a new approach</u> to reduce the soil acidity.
研究人員已<u>採用新方法</u>來降低土壤的酸性。

試練習題 | Will the soil acidity damage your harvest this year?
考生回答處 | _____

考古題應用 | Is there an additional charge if we <u>share a cab</u>?
<u>共乘一部計程車</u>要多付錢嗎？

試練習題 | Do you have any questions before we call a taxi?
考生回答處 | _____

考古題應用 | Our CEO is about to address the entire staff.
我們執行長即將對所有員工發表演說。

試練習題 | Why is everyone in the conference hall?
考生回答處 | _____

考古題應用 | The <u>staff cafeteria</u> is adjacent to the lecture hall.
<u>員工餐廳</u>在演講廳的旁邊。

試練習題 | Where can I get something to eat?
考生回答處 | _____

考古題應用 | You must have some experience in administration.
你得具有行政方面的經驗。

試練習題 | What is the job requirement?
考生回答處 | _____

admire (v.t) 欣賞

關 admiration (n.) 欽佩，讚賞
admirable (adj.) 令人欽佩的
同 appreciate, adore, think highly of

一般正常速度 [əd`maɪr]

ETS全真速度 [ə__`maɪr]

➡ 所有詞性的 [d] 均停一拍即可，無須
發音

adopt (v.t) 採納

關 adoption (n.) 採納
adoptive (adj.) 採用的
同 accept, choose, take on

一般正常速度 [ə`dɑpt]

ETS全真速度 [ə`dɑ(pt)]

➡ 字尾 [pt] 輕唸即可

advance (n.) 預付款

關 advance (v.t) 預付
同 payment beforehand

一般正常速度 [əd`væns]

ETS全真速度 [ə__`væns]

➡ 1) 名詞與動詞的唸法相同
2) [d] 停一拍即可，無須發音

Af-

afford (v.t) 經得起

關 affordable (adj.) 經得起的
同 stand, sustain, be able to buy

一般正常速度 [ə`ford]

ETS全真速度 [ə`for(d)]

➡ 1) 動詞字尾 [d] 輕唸即可
2) 形容詞字尾 [d] 可變音為 [ɖ]

Ag-

agency (n.) 機構

關 agent (n.) 代理商
同 office, department, organization

一般正常速度 [`edʒənsɪ]

ETS全真速度 [`edʒənsɪ]

A

考古題應用 We should take time to stop and admire the view.
我們得找時間停下來欣賞風景。

口試練習題 Why are we going to make a brief stop at the park?
考生回答處 _____

考古題應用 The commissioners adopted my suggestions.
委員們採納了我的建議。

口試練習題 How did the meeting go with the commissioners?
考生回答處 _____

考古題應用 My company will pay me an advance of 300 dollars.
公司會預付我 300 塊美元。

口試練習題 How are you going to pay for the rent this month?
考生回答處 _____

考古題應用 We can't afford to lose a client like him.
我們經不起失去他這種客戶。

口試練習題 Why do we always do what Mr. Bradley says?
考生回答處 _____

考古題應用 We hire people through an employment agency.
我們經由職業介紹所來雇用員工。

口試練習題 How do you hire people?
考生回答處 _____

agenda (n.) 討論事項

同 list, plan, schedule, timetable, calendar

一般正常速度 [ə`dʒɛndə]
ETS全真速度 [ə`dʒɛndə]
➡ 第二個 a 發 [ə] 的音

aggressive (adj.) 積極的

關 aggressiveness (n.) 積極進取；侵略性
同 pushy, energetic, forceful

一般正常速度 [ə`grɛsɪv]
ETS全真速度 [ə`grɛsɪ(v)]
➡ 形容詞字尾 [v] 輕唸即可

agreement (n.) 合約

關 agree (v.i) 同意
　　agreeable (adj.) 同意的；宜人的
同 contract, lease

一般正常速度 [ə`grimənt]
ETS全真速度 [ə`grimən(t)]
➡ 1) 所有詞性的重音都在第二音節
　　2) 名詞字尾 [t] 輕唸即可

Al-

alimony (n.) 贍養費

一般正常速度 [`ælə͵monɪ]
ETS全真速度 [`ælə͵monɪ]

allergic (adj.) 過敏的

關 allergy (n.) 過敏
同 susceptible, sensitive

一般正常速度 [ə`lɝdʒɪk]
ETS全真速度 [ə`lɝdʒɪ(k)]
➡ 1) 形容詞的重音在第二音節，名詞的重音在第一音節
　　2) 形容詞字尾 [k] 輕唸即可

A

考古題應用 The question of cutting salaries is on the agenda.
減薪的問題有排在討論事項裡。

口試練習題 What's on the agenda for tomorrow's meeting?
考生回答處 _____

考古題應用 We have to organize an aggressive <u>marketing campaign</u>.
我們得策畫積極性的<u>行銷活動</u>。

口試練習題 How should we promote the spring collection?
考生回答處 _____

考古題應用 You'd better read the terms of the agreement beforehand.
你最好先看過合約條款。

口試練習題 I think I am ready to sign the contract.
考生回答處 _____

考古題應用 They are still arguing over the alimony <u>settlement</u>.
他們對贍養費的<u>安排</u>仍有爭議。

口試練習題 Why were you so surprised?
考生回答處 _____

考古題應用 I am allergic to seafood.
我對<u>海鮮</u>過敏。

口試練習題 Would you like to try some of our crab salad?
考生回答處 _____

allotted (adj.) 指派的

關 allot (v.t) 分配
allotment (n.) 分配
同 assigned, allocated

一般正常速度 [əˋlɔtɪd]
ETS全真速度 [əˋlɔđɪd]

➡ 1) 所有詞性的重音都在第二音節
2) 形容詞的 [t] 須變音為 [đ]
3) 動詞與名詞字尾 [t] 均輕唸即可

allowance (n.) 允許額度

關 allow (v.t) 允許
allowable (adj.) 可容許的
同 share, quota, allotment

一般正常速度 [əˋlauəns]
ETS全真速度 [əˋlauəns]

➡ 所有詞性的重音都在第二音節

ally (n.) 親信

關 ally (v.t) 結盟
同 friend, helper, associate

一般正常速度 [ˋælaɪ]
ETS全真速度 [ˋælaɪ]

➡ 名詞的重音在第一音節，動詞的重音在第二音節

alternative (n.) 替代方案

關 alter (v.t) 更改
alteration (n.) 修改
alternate (adj.) 交替的
同 other choice, option, substitute

一般正常速度 [ɔlˋtɜnətɪv]
ETS全真速度 [ɔlˋtɜnəđɪ(v)]

➡ 1) alternative 的第二個 [t] 須變音為 [đ]
2) alternative 的 [v] 輕唸即可

altitude (n.) 高度

同 height, peak, summit

一般正常速度 [ˋæltə‚tjud]
ETS全真速度 [ˋældə‚tju(d)]

➡ 1) 第一個 [t] 須變音為 [đ]
2) 字尾有聲子音 [d] 輕唸即可

考古題應用 They failed to finish the job in the allotted time.
他們無法在規定時間內完成工作。

A

□試練習題 Why did they have to work overtime?
考生回答處 _____

考古題應用 A single man's tax allowance is 77,000 NT dollars.
單身人士的免稅額是新台幣七萬七千元。

□試練習題 How much is a single man's tax allowance?
考生回答處 _____

考古題應用 Ms. Atkins is one of the President's closest allies.
Atkins 小姐是總經理的親信之一。

□試練習題 Why does the President often consult with Ms. Atkins?
考生回答處 _____

考古題應用 We had no alternative but to lay off some people.
除了解雇幾名員工外，我們別無選擇。

□試練習題 Did you make any decision on the emergency meeting this
morning?
考生回答處 _____

考古題應用 The airplane is flying at an altitude of 35,000 feet.
飛機目前的飛行高度是三萬五千英尺。

□試練習題 What is the altitude we are currently flying at?
考生回答處 _____

alumnus (n.) 校友

關 alumni (n.) 校友（複數）

一般正常速度 [əˋlʌmnəs]
ETS全真速度 [əˋlʌmnəs]

➡ 複數名詞的母音字母 i 唸 [aɪ] 的音

Am-

amateur (adj.) 業餘的

同 inexpert, unskilful, unprofessional

一般正常速度 [ˋæmə͵tʃʊr]
ETS全真速度 [ˋæmə͵tʃʊr]

➡ 字母 t 發 [tʃ] 的音

ambience (n.) 環境

關 ambient (adj.) 周遭的
同 surroundings, settings, atmosphere

一般正常速度 [ˋæmbɪəns]
ETS全真速度 [ˋæmbɪəns]

➡ 名詞與形容詞的重音都在第一音節

ambiguous (adj.) 不明確的

關 ambiguity (n.) 模稜兩可的話
同 not clear, uncertain, vague

一般正常速度 [æmˋbɪgjʊəs]
ETS全真速度 [æmˋbɪgjʊəs]

➡ 1) 形容詞的重音在第二音節，名詞的重音在第三音節 (-gu-)
　 2) 第一個 u 均發 [jʊ] 的音

amendment (n.) 修改

關 amend (v.t) 修正
同 change, correction, revision, alteration

一般正常速度 [əˋmɛndmənt]
ETS全真速度 [əˋmɛn__mən(t)]

➡ 1) 名詞與動詞的重音都在第二音節
　 2) 名詞的 [d] 停一拍即可，無須發音
　 3) 名詞字尾 [t] 輕唸即可

A

考古題應用 The alumni association is holding a <u>fundraiser</u> this weekend.
校友會將在本週末舉辦<u>募款活動</u>。

口試練習題 Why does the alumni association need the auditorium this Friday?

考生回答處 _____

考古題應用 It's difficult for an amateur photographer to win that award.
一名業餘攝影師要贏那個獎很難。

口試練習題 Do you think he will win that award?

考生回答處 _____

考古題應用 The ambience in that hotel is very <u>elegant</u>.
那座飯店的環境非常<u>高雅</u>。

口試練習題 Hotel Azul is very popular among European tourists, isn't it?

考生回答處 _____

考古題應用 This ambiguous agreement still needs <u>a lot of revisions</u>.
這份不夠明確的合約書仍需<u>大幅修改</u>。

口試練習題 Is there any problem with this agreement?

考生回答處 _____

考古題應用 This <u>project</u> needs some amendment.
這份<u>企畫書</u>需要修改一下。

口試練習題 What do you think of my project?

考生回答處 _____

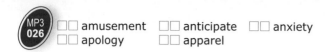
amusement (n.) 娛樂

關 amuse (v.t) 娛樂
同 entertainment, recreation

一般正常速度 [əˋmjuzmənt]
ETS全真速度 [əˋmjuzmən(t)]

➜ 名詞字尾 [t] 輕唸即可

 An-

anticipate (v.t) 預期

關 anticipation (n.) 預期
同 expect, look for, hope for

一般正常速度 [ænˋtɪsəˌpet]
ETS全真速度 [ænˋtɪsəˌbe(t)]

➜ 1) 動詞與名詞的 [p] 均可變音為 [b]
　 2) 動詞字尾 [t] 輕唸即可

anxiety (n.) 焦慮

關 anxious (adj.) 焦慮的
同 worry, care, nervousness

一般正常速度 [æŋˋzaɪətɪ]
ETS全真速度 [æŋˋzaɪəɖɪ]

➜ 名詞的 [t] 可變音為 [ɖ]

Ap-

apology (n.) 道歉

關 apologize (v.i) 道歉
　 apologetic (adj.) 表示歉意的
同 excuse, explanation

一般正常速度 [əˋpalədʒɪ]
ETS全真速度 [əˋpalədʒɪ]

➜ 1) 名詞與動詞的重音都在第二音節，
　　 形容詞的重音在第四音節
　 2) 形容詞的 [t] 須變音為 [ɖ]

apparel (n.) 衣著配備

關 apparel (v.t) 穿著
同 clothing, gear, outfit, equipment

一般正常速度 [əˋpærəl]
ETS全真速度 [əˋpærəl]

➜ 名詞與動詞的唸法相同

考古題應用 The company picnic will be held near the amusement park.
公司野餐將在遊樂園附近舉辦。

口試練習題 Where will the company picnic be held?
考生回答處 _____

考古題應用 We hadn't anticipated any problems with the new machine.
我們沒想到新機器會出問題！

口試練習題 Why were you so surprised?
考生回答處 _____

考古題應用 There's a lot of anxiety among the staff about cutting salaries.
員工們對減薪的事感到很焦慮。

口試練習題 How do people feel about the new policy?
考生回答處 _____

考古題應用 We received a letter of apology.
我們收到了一封道歉信函。

口試練習題 Did he say sorry for your loss?
考生回答處 _____

考古題應用 Our women's apparel is offered in one size.
我們的女裝只有一種尺寸。

口試練習題 What sizes do you have for women's apparel?
考生回答處 _____

appeal (v.i) 訴請

關 appeal (n.) 請求
同 ask, beg, call upon

一般正常速度 [əˋpil]
ETS全真速度 [əˋpil]

➔ 動詞與名詞的唸法相同

appetite (n.) 慾望

關 appetite (n.) 食慾
　　appetizer (n.) 開胃菜
　　appetizing (adj.) 促進食慾的
同 hunger, desire, longing

一般正常速度 [ˋæpə.taɪt]
ETS全真速度 [ˋæbə.taɪ(t)]

➔ 1) 所有詞性的 [p] 均須變音為 [b]
　 2) appetite 字尾的 [t] 輕唸即可

applaud (v.i) 鼓掌

關 applause (n.) 鼓掌，喝采
同 cheer, give a big hand, praise

一般正常速度 [əˋplɔd]
ETS全真速度 [əˋplɔ(d)]

➔ 1) 動詞與名詞的重音都在第二音節
　 2) 動詞字尾 [d] 輕唸即可

apply (v.i) 申請

關 application (n.) 申請
　　applicant (n.) 申請人
　　applicable (adj.) 適用的
同 request, put in, appeal

一般正常速度 [əˋplaɪ]
ETS全真速度 [əˋplaɪ]

➔ applicant 與 applicable 的重音都在第
　 一音節

appraise (v.t) 評鑑

關 appraisal (n.) 鑑定
同 judge, review, assess

一般正常速度 [əˋprez]
ETS全真速度 [əˋprez]

➔ 1) 動詞與名詞的重音都在第二音節
　 2) s 均須發音為 [z]

A

考古題應用 He appealed to the <u>union</u> to give up on the <u>strike</u>.
他請求<u>工會</u>停止<u>罷工</u>。

試練習題 Why did the CEO call the union?
考生回答處 _____

考古題應用 He has no appetite for <u>fame</u>.
他對<u>出名</u>沒興趣。

試練習題 Why didn't he accept the TV interview?
考生回答處 _____

考古題應用 The audience cheered and applauded at the end of the show.
表演結束時觀眾們歡呼鼓掌。

試練習題 How did the audience like the performance?
考生回答處 _____

考古題應用 He applied to the committee for a <u>scholarship</u>.
他向委員會申請<u>獎學金</u>。

試練習題 How did Antoine pay for his tuition and fees?
考生回答處 _____

考古題應用 The director will appraise our <u>job performance</u>.
主管會評鑑我們的<u>工作表現</u>。

試練習題 Who will be doing the performance reviews?
考生回答處 _____

appreciate (v.t) 感激

關 appreciation (n.) 感激;鑑賞
appreciative (adj.) 感激的
同 be thankful for, be grateful for

一般正常速度 [əˋpriʃɪˌet]
ETS全真速度 [əˋpriʃɪˌe(t)]

➡ 1) 動詞與形容詞的重音都在第二音節
2) 動詞字尾 [t] 輕唸即可
3) 形容詞的 [t] 須變音為 [đ]

apprentice (n.) 新手

關 apprentice (v.t) 成為學徒
同 student, learner, trainee, pupil

一般正常速度 [əˋprɛntɪs]
ETS全真速度 [əˋprɛnđɪs]

➡ 1) 名詞與動詞的唸法相同
2) [t] 須變音為 [đ]

approach (v.t) 接近

關 approach (n.) 方法
同 come near, move forward,
advance

一般正常速度 [əˋprotʃ]
ETS全真速度 [əˋprotʃ]

➡ 動詞與名詞的唸法相同

approve (v.t) 准許

關 approval (n.) 批准
同 agree, allow, permit, give the
green light to

一般正常速度 [əˋpruv]
ETS全真速度 [əˋpru(v)]

➡ 1) 動詞與名詞的重音都在第二音節
2) 動詞字尾 [v] 輕唸即可

aptitude (n.) 性向

同 tendency, inclination

一般正常速度 [ˋæptəˌtjud]
ETS全真速度 [ˋæ__təˌtju(d)]

➡ 1) [p] 停一拍即可,無須發音
2) 字尾 [d] 輕唸即可

A

考古題應用　She never appreciates her hard-working staff.
她從未對認眞工作的員工心懷感激。

試練習題　Why do people always complain about her?
考生回答處　_____

考古題應用　Some of our department heads started off as apprentices.
我們有些部門主管是從新手開始做起的。

試練習題　I really don't think apprentices can accomplish anything.
考生回答處　_____

考古題應用　The crowd grew silent when he approached the podium.
當他走近講台時，群眾安靜了下來。

試練習題　How did the crowd react to Mr. Fang's sudden appearance?
考生回答處　_____

考古題應用　The building commission finally approved our building plans.
建管局終於批准了我們的興建計畫。

試練習題　Why is everybody celebrating?
考生回答處　_____

考古題應用　I had to take an aptitude test before the interview.
面試前我必須做性向測驗。

試練習題　Did they ask you to do anything before the interview?
考生回答處　_____

Ar-

articulate (adj.) 口才好的

關 articulate (v.t) 明確地表達
　articulation (n.) 清楚的發音
同 clear, meaningful,
　understandable

一般正常速度 [ɑrˋtɪkjəlɪt]

ETS全真速度 [ɑrˋtɪgjəlɪ(t)]

➜ 1) 字尾 [t] 輕唸即可
　 2) 所有詞性的 [k] 均可變音為 [g]

artificial (adj.) 人工的

同 man-made, non-natural

一般正常速度 [ˌɑrtəˋfɪʃəl]

ETS全真速度 [ˌɑrđəˋfɪʃəl]

➜ [t] 須變音為 [đ]

As-

assembly (n.) 組裝

關 assemble (v.t) 聚集
同 putting together, setting up,
　building up

一般正常速度 [əˋsɛmblɪ]

ETS全真速度 [əˋsɛmblɪ]

➜ 名詞與動詞的重音都在第二音節

assess (v.t) 評鑑

關 assessment (n.) 評鑑
　assessor (n.) 評鑑者
同 judge, estimate, rate

一般正常速度 [əˋsɛs]

ETS全真速度 [əˋsɛs]

➜ 所有詞性的重音都在第二音節

asset (n.) 資產

同 money, property

一般正常速度 [ˋæsɛt]

ETS全真速度 [ˋæsɛ(t)]

➜ 1) 重音在第一音節
　 2) 字尾 [t] 輕唸即可

A

考古題應用　The new salesman is very articulate.
新來的售貨員口才很好。

口試練習題　Have you heard anything about the salesman?
考生回答處　＿＿＿＿＿＿＿＿＿＿＿＿＿＿＿＿＿＿＿＿

考古題應用　Our products contain no artificial coloring.
我們的產品不含人工色素。

口試練習題　What's so special about your products?
考生回答處　＿＿＿＿＿＿＿＿＿＿＿＿＿＿＿＿＿＿＿＿

考古題應用　Cars are being put together on that assembly line.
車子在那條生產線組裝。

口試練習題　What are they working on?
考生回答處　＿＿＿＿＿＿＿＿＿＿＿＿＿＿＿＿＿＿＿＿

考古題應用　It's too early to assess the effects of the new policy.
要評估新政策的影響還太早。

口試練習題　What do you think of the new policy?
考生回答處　＿＿＿＿＿＿＿＿＿＿＿＿＿＿＿＿＿＿＿＿

考古題應用　A sense of responsibility is your greatest asset.
責任感是你最大的資產。

口試練習題　I don't know how I am going to win the contract.
考生回答處　＿＿＿＿＿＿＿＿＿＿＿＿＿＿＿＿＿＿＿＿

assist (v.t) 協助

關 assistance (n.) 協助
　 assistant (n.) 助手
同 help, support, sustain

一般正常速度 [ə`sɪst]
ETS全真速度 [ə`sɪs(t)]

➡ 1) 所有詞性的重音均在第二音節
　 2) 動詞字尾 [t] 輕唸即可

assume (v.t) 假設

關 assumption (n.) 假定
同 think, guess, suppose

一般正常速度 [ə`sjum]
ETS全真速度 [ə`sjum]

➡ 1) 母音唸 [ju] 或 [u] 都可以
　 2) 名詞的 [p] 停一拍即可，無須發音

At-

athletic (adj.) 有運動細胞的

關 athlete (n.) 運動員
同 strong, powerful, energetic

一般正常速度 [æθ`lɛtɪk]
ETS全真速度 [æθ`lɛɾɪ(k)]

➡ 1) 形容詞的重音在第二音節，名詞的
　　　重音在第一音節
　 2) 形容詞的 [t] 須變音為 [ɖ]
　 3) 形容詞字尾 [k] 輕唸即可

atmosphere (n.) 氣氛

關 atmospheric (adj.) 有獨特氛圍的
同 feeling, environment,
　 surroundings

一般正常速度 [`ætməs,fɪr]
ETS全真速度 [`æ__məs,fɪr]

➡ 1) 名詞的重音在第一音節，形容詞的
　　　重音在倒數第二音節
　 2) 兩詞性的 [t] 均停一拍即可，無須
　　　發音

attach (v.t) 附著

關 attachment (n.) 附著；附件
同 add, link, stick, tie, connect

一般正常速度 [ə`tætʃ]
ETS全真速度 [ə`tætʃ]

➡ 動詞與名詞的重音都在第二音節

A

考古題應用 A number of consultants will assist me with the <u>negotiations</u>.
在談判方面會有一些顧問協助我。

口試練習題 Are you going to do this alone?
考生回答處 _____

考古題應用 Assuming you are right, what could we do with her?
假設你說的沒錯，我們能拿她怎麼辦？

口試練習題 I still think she is the one who should be responsible.
考生回答處 _____

考古題應用 Michael Jordan is very athletic.
Michael Jordan 超有運動細胞。

口試練習題 Can you think of anyone who's athletic?
考生回答處 _____

考古題應用 The office's atmosphere is always pleasant.
辦公室裡的氣氛一向很好。

口試練習題 What do you like about this job?
考生回答處 _____

考古題應用 The assistant attached a note to the <u>folder</u>.
助理在檔案夾上貼了一張紙條。

口試練習題 What is that piece of paper on the folder?
考生回答處 _____

attraction (n.) 吸引人的東西

關 attract (v.t) 吸引
　　attractive (adj.) 有吸引力的

一般正常速度 [əˋtrækʃən]
ETS全真速度 [əˋtræ＿ʃən]

➔ 1) 所有詞性的重音都在第二音節
　 2) [k] 均停一拍即可，無須發音

attribute (v.t) 歸功於

關 attribute [ˋætrə.bju(t)] (n.) 特徵
同 credit, refer

一般正常速度 [əˋtrɪbjut]
ETS全真速度 [əˋtrɪbjʊ(t)]

➔ 1) attribute 當動詞時，重音在第二音
　　 節，當名詞時在第一音節
　 2) 動詞的 a 唸 [ə]，名詞的 a 唸 [æ]

badge (n.) 徽章

同 sign, brand, mark, identification

一般正常速度 [bædʒ]
ETS全真速度 [bædʒ]

ballot (n.) 選票

關 ballot (v.i) 投票
同 vote, election

一般正常速度 [ˋbælət]
ETS全真速度 [ˋbælə(t)]

➔ 1) 名詞與動詞的唸法相同
　 2) 字尾 [t] 輕唸即可

bank (n.) 河堤

關 bank (n.) 銀行
同 slope, tilt

一般正常速度 [bæŋk]
ETS全真速度 [bæŋ(k)]

➔ 字尾 [k] 輕唸即可

A
B

考古題應用 The park has the biggest tourist attraction, a <u>ferris wheel</u>.
公園有最吸引人的觀光景點——<u>摩天輪</u>。

試練習題 Why does this park always attract so many tourists?
考生回答處 _____

考古題應用 He attributed his success to his family.
他把功勞歸功於家人。

試練習題 What did he say at the award ceremony?
考生回答處 _____

考古題應用 You have to present your visitor's badge at the front door.
你得在正門出示訪客證。

試練習題 How do I get into that office complex?
考生回答處 _____

考古題應用 They are still counting the ballots.
他們還在計票中。

試練習題 Who won the election?
考生回答處 _____

考古題應用 There are trees growing along the bank.
沿著河堤有一排樹。

試練習題 Where can I see trees around here?
考生回答處 _____

□□ bankruptcy　□□ bar　　　□□ bare
□□ bargain　　□□ belongings

bankruptcy (n.) 破產

關 bankrupt (v.t) 使人破產
　bankrupt (n.) 破產者
同 ruin, lack, crash

一般正常速度 [`bæŋkrəptsɪ]
ETS全真速度 [`bæŋkrə__sɪ]
➡ 所有詞性的 [pt] 均須消音

bar (v.t) 禁止

關 bar (n.) 鐵條或條狀物（如吧臺）
同 ban, prohibit, obstruct

一般正常速度 [bɑr]
ETS全真速度 [bɑr]

bare (adj.) 赤裸的

關 bare (v.t) 使赤裸
同 nude, naked, uncovered

一般正常速度 [bɛr]
ETS全真速度 [bɛr]
➡ 形容詞與動詞的唸法相同

bargain (v.i) 講價

關 bargain (n.) 物超所值的貨品
同 barter, negotiate

一般正常速度 [`bɑrgən]
ETS全真速度 [`bɑrgən]
➡ 1) 動詞與名詞的唸法相同
　2) ai 唸 [ə] 的音

Be-

belongings (n.) 個人物品

關 belong (v.i) 屬於
同 stuff, possessions, personal property

一般正常速度 [bə`lɔŋɪŋz]
ETS全真速度 [bə`lɔŋɪŋz]

考古題應用 More than five computer companies have filed for bankruptcy.
已經有超過五家電腦公司宣告破產。

B

□試練習題 Why does everyone have little faith in the market?

考生回答處 _____

考古題應用 The building was barred to the public due to police investigation.
這棟大樓因警方進行搜查而禁止民眾進入。

□試練習題 Why is the front entrance blocked?

考生回答處 _____

考古題應用 Most trees are bare then.
那時大部分的葉子都掉光了。

□試練習題 Why are there less tourists during winter time?

考生回答處 _____

考古題應用 You'd better bargain with them for a discount.
那你最好跟他們議價以取得折扣。

□試練習題 I really think this cell phone is overpriced.

考生回答處 _____

考古題應用 Don't forget to collect your belongings before you leave.
離開前別忘了收拾好個人物品。

□試練習題 I am just about to leave the library.

考生回答處 _____

benefit (n.) 補助

關 benefit (v.t) 受益
同 aid, help, assistance

一般正常速度 [ˋbɛnəfɪt]
ETS全真速度 [ˋbɛnəfɪ(t)]

➡ 1) 名詞與動詞的唸法相同
2) 字尾 [t] 輕唸即可

Bi-

bid (n.) 下標的價錢

關 bid (v.t) 出價，投標
同 offer, price, proposal

一般正常速度 [bɪd]
ETS全真速度 [bɪ(d)]

➡ 1) 名詞與動詞的唸法相同
2) 字尾 [d] 輕唸即可

---

bill (n.) 法案

關 bill (n.) 鈔票
bill (v.t) 開帳單
同 law, proposal

一般正常速度 [bɪl]
ETS全真速度 [bɪl]

➡ 1) 名詞與動詞的唸法相同
2) 字尾 [l] 請勿唸成 [ɔ]（台式發音）

---

bind (v.t) 捆綁

關 bind (n.) 困境
同 tie, attach, glue

一般正常速度 [baɪnd]
ETS全真速度 [baɪn(d)]

➡ 1) 動詞與名詞的唸法相同
2) 字尾 [d] 輕唸即可

Bl-

blame (v.t) 責怪

關 blame (n.) 過錯
同 charge, accuse, find fault with

一般正常速度 [blem]
ETS全真速度 [blem]

➡ 動詞與名詞的唸法相同

B

考古題應用 Do you have unemployment benefits?
你有失業補助嗎？

試練習題 I was laid off last month.
考生回答處 _____

考古題應用 We placed a bid of 20 dollars for the used book.
我們下標 20 元買那本二手書。

試練習題 How much did you bid for the used book?
考生回答處 _____

考古題應用 The government has yet to pass the related transport bill.
政府還沒通過相關的交通法案。

試練習題 When will they build the new expressway?
考生回答處 _____

考古題應用 We used the red tape to bind the files.
我們用紅色的膠帶把檔案捆綁住。

試練習題 What did you do with the files?
考生回答處 _____

考古題應用 I won't blame you for any losses.
我不會因為有損失而責怪你。

試練習題 What if my plan doesn't work?
考生回答處 _____

□□ blank □□ block □□ blueprint
□□ bonus □□ boom

blank (adj.) 空白的

關 blankness (n.) 空白
　　blankly (adv.) 完全地；茫然地
同 empty, vacant, bare

一般正常速度 [blæŋk]
ETS全真速度 [blæŋ(k)]

➡ 形容詞與名詞的 [k] 均輕唸即可，副詞的 [k] 須消音

block (v.t) 阻擋

關 block (n.) 街區
同 bar, obstruct

一般正常速度 [blɑk]
ETS全真速度 [blɑ(k)]

➡ 1) 動詞與名詞的唸法相同
　　2) 字尾 [k] 輕唸即可

blueprint (n.) 藍圖

同 plan, design, layout

一般正常速度 [`blu͵prɪnt]
ETS全真速度 [`blu͵prɪn(t)]

➡ 字尾 [t] 輕唸即可

bonus (n.) 紅利

同 benefit, plus, commission

一般正常速度 [`bonəs]
ETS全真速度 [`bonəs]

➡ 重音節母音發 [o] 的音，不是 [ɔ]（請仔細聽 MP3 的發音）

boom (n.) 暴漲

關 boom (v.i) 激增
同 increase, progress, advance,
　　growth, development

一般正常速度 [bum]
ETS全真速度 [bum]

➡ 名詞與動詞的唸法相同

考古題應用　Please fill in your name on the blank space.
請在空白處填寫名字。

B

口試練習題　What do I do with the form?
考生回答處　＿＿＿＿＿＿＿＿＿＿＿＿＿＿＿＿＿＿＿＿

考古題應用　Their houses are blocked by oak trees.
他們的房子被橡樹擋住了。

口試練習題　Why don't I see their houses from here?
考生回答處　＿＿＿＿＿＿＿＿＿＿＿＿＿＿＿＿＿＿＿＿

考古題應用　The blueprints are being carefully examined by the architect.
建築師正仔細地檢視藍圖。

口試練習題　Have you seen the blueprints?
考生回答處　＿＿＿＿＿＿＿＿＿＿＿＿＿＿＿＿＿＿＿＿

考古題應用　We'll be receiving significant portions of our bonuses before
Christmas.
耶誕節前我們會領到一大筆的紅利。

口試練習題　Has the committee made any decision about our bonuses?
考生回答處　＿＿＿＿＿＿＿＿＿＿＿＿＿＿＿＿＿＿＿＿

考古題應用　The boom in PDAs' popularity has brought us a lot more
customers.
PDA 人氣的暴漲為我們帶來更多顧客。

口試練習題　Which has brought you more customers, PDAs or cell phones?
考生回答處　＿＿＿＿＿＿＿＿＿＿＿＿＿＿＿＿＿＿＿＿

boost (n.) 促進
關 booster (n.) 推進器

一般正常速度 [bust]

ETS全真速度 [bus(t)]

➡ boost 字尾 [t] 輕唸即可，booster 的 [t] 則須變音為 [d]

border (n.) 邊界
關 border (v.t) 畫出界限
同 edge, boundry, limits

一般正常速度 [ˋbɔrdɚ]

ETS全真速度 [ˋbɔrđɚ]

➡ 1) 名詞與動詞的唸法相同
2) 字尾 [d] 可變音為 [đ]

bounce (v.t) 彈回
關 bounce (n.) 反彈
同 jump, leap, spring

一般正常速度 [bauns]

ETS全真速度 [bauns]

➡ 動詞與名詞的唸法相同

Br-

brand (n.) 品牌
關 brand (v.t) 印商標於…
同 label, mark, trademark

一般正常速度 [brænd]

ETS全真速度 [bræn(d)]

➡ 1) 名詞與動詞的唸法相同
2) 字尾 [d] 輕唸即可

breach (n.) 違反
關 breach (v.t) 違反
同 violation, disobedience, infringement

一般正常速度 [britʃ]

ETS全真速度 [britʃ]

➡ 名詞與動詞的唸法相同

B

考古題應用　His words gave our morale a large boost.
他的話讓我們的士氣大振。

□試練習題　How did everyone react to the VP's speech?
考生回答處　_____

考古題應用　That French village is near the German border.
那個法國村落靠近德國邊境。

□試練習題　Where is the village you visited last spring?
考生回答處　_____

考古題應用　We called off the deal because of the bounced check.
我們因為支票跳票而取消了交易。

□試練習題　I thought you had a deal with their company.
考生回答處　_____

考古題應用　My favorite brand of salad dressing is "Kraft".
我最喜歡的沙拉醬品牌是「卡夫」。

□試練習題　What is your favorite brand of salad dressing?
考生回答處　_____

考古題應用　His action was a breach of the consumer protection law.
他的行為有違消保法。

□試練習題　Sam refused to make a full refund to his customer.
考生回答處　_____

breakthrough (n.) 突破

回 development, advance, improvement

一般正常速度 [ˋbrekˌθru]
ETS全真速度 [ˋbre___ˌθru]
➡ [k] 停一拍即可，無須發音

bribe (v.t) 賄賂

關 bribery (n.) 賄賂
回 get at, buy off

一般正常速度 [braɪb]
ETS全真速度 [braɪ(b)]
➡ 動詞字尾 [b] 輕唸即可

brief (v.t) 做簡報

關 brief (n.) 簡報
　 brief (adj.) 簡短的
回 prepare, advise, inform

一般正常速度 [brif]
ETS全真速度 [bri(f)]
➡ 1) 所有詞性的唸法相同
　 2) 字尾 [f] 輕唸即可

browse (v.i) 瀏覽

關 browse (n.) 瀏覽
回 look through, scan, go over

一般正常速度 [brauz]
ETS全真速度 [brauz]
➡ 動詞與名詞的唸法相同

Bu-

built-in (adj.) 內建的

回 in-built, included, inseparable

一般正常速度 [bɪltˋɪn]
ETS全真速度 [bɪɖˋɪn]
➡ 1) 重音落在 in
　 2) [t] 須變音為 [ɖ]
　 3) [ɖ] 與 [ɪ] 須連音

考古題應用　His team made a major breakthrough in biotechnology.
他的團隊在生化科技上有重大的突破。

口試練習題　Why did you ask Joshua to give the opening speech at the convention?

考生回答處　_____

考古題應用　He lost his job for bribing the building commissioners.
他因爲賄賂建管局委員而丟了工作。

口試練習題　Why was he fired?

考生回答處　_____

考古題應用　I need to brief the consultants before the negotiation begins.
我得在談判開始前向顧問們做簡報。

口試練習題　Why are you in such a hurry?

考生回答處　_____

考古題應用　I spent the whole afternoon browsing through fashion magazines.
我整個下午都在翻閱流行雜誌。

口試練習題　What did you do this Wednesday afternoon?

考生回答處　_____

考古題應用　This laptop has a built-in DVD burner.
這台筆記型電腦有內建式 DVD 燒錄器。

口試練習題　What's so special about this notebook?

考生回答處　_____

bulk (n.) 大量

關 bulk (v.i) 變大
　　bulky (adj.) 龐大的
同 massiveness

一般正常速度 [bʌlk]
ETS全真速度 [bʌl(k)]

➡ 1) 名詞與動詞的字尾 [k] 均輕唸即可
　 2) 形容詞字尾 [k] 可變音為 [g]

bulldozer (n.) 壓路機

關 bulldoze (v.t) 以堆土機清除；恫嚇

一般正常速度 [`bʊl.dozɚ]
ETS全真速度 [`bʊl.đozɚ]

➡ 1) 重音落在第一音節
　 2) [d] 須變音為 [đ]

buyer's market
(n.) 買方市場（供過於求）

一般正常速度 [`baɪɚz markɪt]
ETS全真速度 [`baɪɚz markɪ(t)]

➡ 1) 重音在第一個字或第二個字均可
　 2) 字尾 [t] 輕唸即可

B

考古題應用　I sent them by bulk mail for the <u>reduced rates</u>.
我為了<u>省錢</u>寄大宗郵件。

口試練習題　Did you send the pamphlets by express mail or bulk mail?
考生回答處　_____

考古題應用　The bulldozer is <u>leveling the ground</u>.
壓路機正在<u>整地</u>。

口試練習題　Why is the garden closed to the public?
考生回答處　_____

考古題應用　<u>Real estate agents</u> say it's a buyer's market in housing now.
<u>房仲業者</u>表示目前房市供過於求。

口試練習題　Do we have a lot of choices in housing?
考生回答處　_____

Check List 1

到目前為止，我們已經學了 100 個字彙左右，現在來複習一下，看看是不是都記起來了！

☐ abandon	☐ accustom	☐ allowance
☐ abrupt	☐ achieve	☐ ally
☐ absence	☐ acidity	☐ alternative
☐ absolute	☐ additional	☐ altitude
☐ absorb	☐ address	☐ alumnus
☐ abstract	☐ adjacent	☐ amateur
☐ absurdly	☐ administration	☐ ambience
☐ abundant	☐ admire	☐ ambiguous
☐ abuse	☐ adopt	☐ amendment
☐ accelerate	☐ advance	☐ amusement
☐ accent	☐ afford	☐ anticipate
☐ access	☐ agency	☐ anxiety
☐ accessories	☐ agenda	☐ apology
☐ accommodation	☐ aggressive	☐ apparel
☐ accomplish	☐ agreement	☐ appeal
☐ accumulate	☐ alimony	☐ appetite
☐ accurate	☐ allergic	☐ applaud
☐ accuse	☐ allotted	☐ apply

☐ appraise	☐ badge	☐ boost
☐ appreciate	☐ ballot	☐ border
☐ apprentice	☐ bank	☐ bounce
☐ approach	☐ bankruptcy	☐ brand
☐ approve	☐ bar	☐ breach
☐ aptitude	☐ bare	☐ breakthrough
☐ articulate	☐ bargain	☐ bribe
☐ artificial	☐ belongings	☐ brief
☐ assembly	☐ benefit	☐ browse
☐ assess	☐ bid	☐ built-in
☐ asset	☐ bill	☐ bulk
☐ assist	☐ bind	☐ bulldozer
☐ assume	☐ blame	☐ buyer's market
☐ athletic	☐ blank	
☐ atmosphere	☐ block	
☐ attach	☐ blueprint	
☐ attraction	☐ bonus	
☐ attribute	☐ boom	

calculate (v.t) 考量

關 calculation (n.) 計算
calculated (adj.) 仔細考量過的
calculating (adj.) 工於心計的
同 consider, estimate, weigh

一般正常速度 [`kælkjə.let]
ETS全真速度 [`kælkjə.le(t)]

➡ 1) 動詞字尾 [t] 輕唸即可
2) 形容詞的 [t] 均須變音為 [đ]

candidate (n.) 候選人

同 applicant, competitor, runner

一般正常速度 [`kændə.det]
ETS全真速度 [`kændə.đe(t)]

➡ 1) 字中兩個 [d] 均可變音為 [đ]
2) 字尾 [t] 輕唸即可

capacity (n.) 容量

關 capability (n.) 能力
capable (adj.) 有能力的
同 room, size, space, extent

一般正常速度 [kə`pæsətɪ]
ETS全真速度 [kə`pæsəđɪ]

➡ 字尾 [t] 可變音為 [đ]

capital (n.) 資金

關 capital (n.) 首都
capitalism (n.) 資本主義
capital (adj.) 大寫印刷體的
同 cash, assets, funds

一般正常速度 [`kæpətḷ]
ETS全真速度 [`kæbəđḷ]

➡ 1) 所有詞性的 [p] 均可變音為 [b]
2) capital 的字尾 [t] 可變音為 [đ]

cargo (n.) 貨物

同 shipment, goods, freight

一般正常速度 [`kargo]
ETS全真速度 [`kargo]

考古題應用 The advisers have to carefully calculate the <u>possible effects</u> of the changes.
顧問們得小心考量改變的<u>可能影響</u>。

C

試練習題 Why haven't the new policies been put into effect?
考生回答處 _____

考古題應用 We'll be interviewing the presidential candidates.
我們即將採訪總統候選人。

試練習題 Who are you interviewing?
考生回答處 _____

考古題應用 This plant has a productive capacity of 300 computers a day.
這座工廠擁有一天三百台電腦的生產量。

試練習題 How many computers does this plant produce a day?
考生回答處 _____

考古題應用 We need more capital to <u>expand our factory</u>.
我們需要更多的資金才能<u>擴廠</u>。

試練習題 What are we waiting for?
考生回答處 _____

考古題應用 The <u>loading dock workers</u> are still working on the cargo.
<u>碼頭工人</u>還在處理貨物。

試練習題 Why is the ship still docked at the harbor?
考生回答處 _____

carousel (n.) 行李轉盤

同 moving belt, conveyor belt

一般正常速度 [ˌkæruˋzɛl]

ETS全真速度 [ˌkæruˋzɛl]

➡ 重音在第三音節

carpool (v.i) 共乘

關 carpool (n.) 共乘
同 take turns driving each other

一般正常速度 [ˋkɑrpul]

ETS全真速度 [ˋkɑrpul]

➡ 動詞與名詞的唸法相同

cautious (adj.) 謹慎的

關 caution (n.) 小心，謹慎
同 careful, watchful, calculated

一般正常速度 [ˋkɔʃəs]

ETS全真速度 [ˋkɔʃə(s)]

➡ 形容詞字尾 [s] 輕唸即可

Ce-

certify (v.t) 認證

關 certificate (n.) 證照
　certified (adj.) 經過認證的
同 verify, endorse, guarantee

一般正常速度 [ˋsɝtəˌfaɪ]

ETS全真速度 [ˋsɝđəˌfaɪ]

➡ [t] 可變音為 [đ]

Ch-

chart (n.) 圖表

關 bar chart (n.) 長條圖
　pie chart (n.) 圓餅圖
同 graph, diagram, table

一般正常速度 [tʃɑrt]

ETS全真速度 [tʃɑr(t)]

➡ 字尾 [t] 輕唸即可

C

[考古題應用] You need to <u>collect</u> your luggage from the carousel.
你得從轉盤上把行李<u>取下來</u>。

[□試練習題] Where do I pick up my baggage?
[考生回答處] _____

[考古題應用] We encourage our workers to carpool to save gas and space.
我們鼓勵員工共乘以節省汽油和空間。

[□試練習題] Why is carpooling encouraged?
[考生回答處] _____

[考古題應用] We are very cautious about using <u>chemicals</u> on <u>crops</u>.
我們使用<u>化學藥劑</u>在<u>農作物</u>上時非常謹慎。

[□試練習題] Don't you think it's dangerous to use chemicals?
[考生回答處] _____

[考古題應用] These foods are certified 100% natural by the <u>health inspector</u>.
<u>這些</u>是經過衛生局<u>檢查員</u>認證的百分之百天然食品。

[□試練習題] Do these foods contain artificial flavoring?
[考生回答處] _____

[考古題應用] The <u>meteorologist</u> is pointing at a weather chart.
<u>氣象專家</u>正指著一張氣象圖。

[□試練習題] What is on the chart that the meteorologist is showing?
[考生回答處] _____

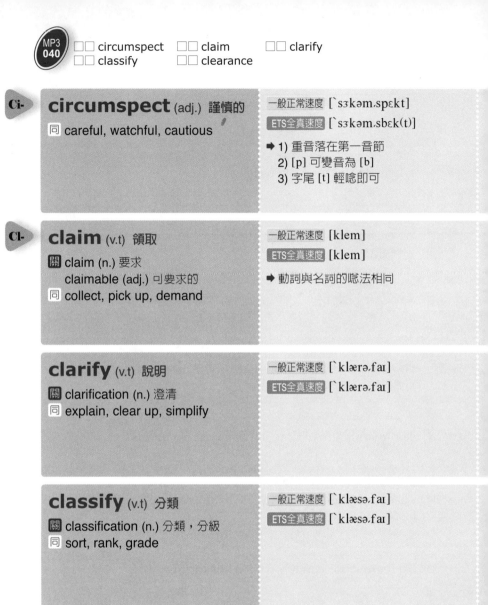

Ci-

circumspect (adj.) 謹慎的

同 careful, watchful, cautious

一般正常速度 [ˈsɜkəmˌspɛkt]

ETS全真速度 [ˈsɜkəmˌsbɛk(t)]

➡ 1) 重音落在第一音節
2) [p] 可變音為 [b]
3) 字尾 [t] 輕唸即可

Cl-

claim (v.t) 領取

關 claim (n.) 要求
claimable (adj.) 可要求的
同 collect, pick up, demand

一般正常速度 [klem]

ETS全真速度 [klem]

➡ 動詞與名詞的唸法相同

clarify (v.t) 說明

關 clarification (n.) 澄清
同 explain, clear up, simplify

一般正常速度 [ˈklærəˌfaɪ]

ETS全真速度 [ˈklærəˌfaɪ]

classify (v.t) 分類

關 classification (n.) 分類，分級
同 sort, rank, grade

一般正常速度 [ˈklæsəˌfaɪ]

ETS全真速度 [ˈklæsəˌfaɪ]

clearance (n.) 清空

關 clear (v.t) 清理
clear (adj.) 晴朗的
同 emptying, removal, withdrawal

一般正常速度 [ˈklɪrəns]

ETS全真速度 [ˈklɪrəns]

C

考古題應用 Successful bankers are circumspect in their investments.
成功的銀行家對於投資很謹慎。

試練習題 What is a successful banker like?
考生回答處 _____

考古題應用 We claimed our baggage right after arriving at our destination.
一抵達終點我們馬上去領行李。

試練習題 What did you do first thing after arrival?
考生回答處 _____

考古題應用 We would like you to clarify this financial report.
我們需要你說明這份財務報告。

試練習題 What would you like me to do?
考生回答處 _____

考古題應用 It is necessary to classify these files into different types.
這些檔案需要做不同的分類。

試練習題 What should we do with these files?
考生回答處 _____

考古題應用 They are having a clearance sale on sporting goods.
他們正在舉辦運動用品的清倉大拍賣。

試練習題 Why is that store suddenly so popular?
考生回答處 _____

Co-

code (n.) 號碼

關 area code (n.) 電話區域號碼
zip code (n.) 郵遞區號
同 number

一般正常速度 [kod]
ETS全真速度 [ko(d)]
➜ 字尾 [d] 輕唸即可

command (v.t) 命令

關 command (n.) 命令
同 order, demand

一般正常速度 [kə`mænd]
ETS全真速度 [kə`mæn(d)]
➜ 1) 動詞與名詞的唸法相同
2) 字尾 [d] 輕唸即可

commission (v.t) 委託

關 commission (n.) 佣金;委員會
commissioner (n.) 委員
同 send, order, appoint

一般正常速度 [kə`mɪʃən]
ETS全真速度 [kə`mɪʃən]
➜ 最後一個音節的母音唸 [ə] 而非 [o]

commute (v.i) 通勤

關 commuter (n.) 通勤者
同 travel regularly between one's
home and work

一般正常速度 [kə`mjut]
ETS全真速度 [kə`mju(t)]
➜ 1) 動詞重音在第二音節
2) 字尾 [t] 輕唸即可

compatible (adj.) 可相容的

關 compatibility (n.) 相容性;協調
同 adaptable, agreeable, suitable

一般正常速度 [kəm`pætəbḷ]
ETS全真速度 [kəm`pæɾəbḷ]
➜ 1) 形容詞的重音在第二音節
2) [t] 可變音為 [ɾ]

考古題應用 What's the telephone area code for Prague?
布拉格的電話區域號碼是多少？

C

口試練習題 Could you call the Prague Office?
考生回答處 _____

考古題應用 He commanded the entire staff to <u>work overtime</u> every day this week.
他命令所有的員工這週每天<u>加班</u>。

口試練習題 Why is everyone complaining about the new credit manager?
考生回答處 _____

考古題應用 He has commissioned Mr. Atwood to do his <u>portrait</u>.
他委託 Atwood 先生幫他<u>畫肖像畫</u>。

口試練習題 Why does Mr. Atwood visit him so often?
考生回答處 _____

考古題應用 They have to commute from Taipei to Taichung every day.
他們得每天從台北通車到台中。

口試練習題 Why do they get up so early every day?
考生回答處 _____

考古題應用 This software is not compatible with my computer.
這套軟體跟我的電腦不相容。

口試練習題 What's wrong with this software?
考生回答處 _____

compensation
(n.) 補償

關 compensate (v.i) 補償

一般正常速度 [ˌkɑmpənˈseʃən]
ETS全真速度 [ˌkɑmbənˈseʃən]

➡ 名詞與動詞的 [p] 均可變音為 [b]

competent (adj.) 適任的

關 compete (v.i) 競爭
　 competence (n.) 能力
同 capable, adequate, appropriate

一般正常速度 [ˈkɑmpətənt]
ETS全真速度 [ˈkɑmbətən(t)]

➡ 1) 形容詞與名詞重音都在第一音節，
　　 動詞重音則在第二音節
　 2) [p] 可變音為 [b]
　 3) 形容詞字尾 [t] 輕唸即可

compile (v.t) 編纂

關 compiler (n.) 編輯
同 gather, collect, put together, edit,
　 organize

一般正常速度 [kəmˈpaɪl]
ETS全真速度 [kəmˈpaɪl]

➡ 動詞與名詞的重音都在第二音節

compliment (n.) 稱讚

關 compliment (v.t) 稱讚
　 complimentary (adj.) 稱讚的
同 praise, tribute

一般正常速度 [ˈkɑmpləmənt]
ETS全真速度 [ˈkɑmbləmən(t)]

➡ 1) 名詞與動詞的發音相同
　 2) [p] 可變音為 [b]
　 3) 字尾 [t] 輕唸即可

conclusion (n.) 結論

關 conclude (v.t) 推斷
同 deduction, inference, judgment

一般正常速度 [kənˈkluʒən]
ETS全真速度 [kənˈkluʒən]

考古題應用 Our company would provide compensation for their loss.
我們公司會補償他們的損失。

C

口試練習題 What if a worker was injured?
考生回答處 _____

考古題應用 We've finally found someone competent enough for the job.
我們終於找到可勝任這個職務的人了。

口試練習題 How were the interviews with the applicants?
考生回答處 _____

考古題應用 It took him a month to compile this annual report.
他花了一個月的時間編纂這份年度報告。

口試練習題 He seems to have spent much time on the report.
考生回答處 _____

考古題應用 A wise supervisor always knows when to pay his workers compliments.
聰明的主管永遠知道何時該稱讚員工。

口試練習題 What is a wise supervisor like?
考生回答處 _____

考古題應用 After the trial period, I've come to the conclusion that Marge is the best assistant I have ever had.
試用期過後我得到一個結論：Marge 是我共事過最好的助手。

口試練習題 What do you think of Marge?
考生回答處 _____

□□ concrete　　□□ confidential　　□□ conform
□□ connection　□□ consensus

---

concrete (adj.) 具體的

關 concrete (n.) 混凝土
同 real, specific, substantial

一般正常速度 [ˋkankrit]
ETS全真速度 [ˋkankrit]

➡ 形容詞與名詞的唸法相同

---

confidential (adj.) 機密的

關 confidentiality (n.) 機密
同 private, secret, classified

一般正常速度 [͵kanfəˋdɛnʃəl]
ETS全真速度 [͵kanfəˋdɛnʃəl]

➡ 形容詞的重音在第三音節，名詞的重音在倒數第三音節

---

conform (v.i) 符合

關 conformance (n.) 符合，一致
　 conformable (adj.) 一致的
同 suit, agree, match

一般正常速度 [kənˋfɔrm]
ETS全真速度 [kənˋfɔrm]

➡ 所有詞性的重音皆在第二音節

---

connection (n.) 關係

關 connection (n.) 轉機
　 connect (v.t) 連接
　 connected (adj.) 有關連的
同 link, relationship, bond

一般正常速度 [kəˋnɛkʃən]
ETS全真速度 [kəˋnɛ__ʃən]

➡ [k] 停一拍即可，無須發音

---

consensus (n.) 共識

關 consent (v.i) 同意
　 consent (n.) 同意
同 agreement, concord, unanimity

一般正常速度 [kənˋsɛnsəs]
ETS全真速度 [kənˋsɛnsə(s)]

➡ 1) 所有詞性的重音均在第二音節
　 2) 名詞字尾 [s] 輕唸即可

考古題應用 Providing some <u>compensation</u> is more concrete than an apology.
比起道歉，補償是比較具體的做法。

口試練習題 What should we do with the injured workers?

考生回答處 _____

考古題應用 He lost his job for <u>leaking</u> confidential information.
他因洩露機密消息而丟了工作。

口試練習題 Why was he fired?

考生回答處 _____

考古題應用 The heater does not conform with new <u>safety standards</u>.
這台暖氣不符合新的安全規定。

口試練習題 What's wrong with this heater?

考生回答處 _____

考古題應用 Janet is very good at finding the best connections.
Janet 很會找關係。

口試練習題 Why did you recommend Janet for the job?

考生回答處 _____

考古題應用 They have already reached a consensus.
他們已經達成共識。

口試練習題 Is the board still debating over the merger?

考生回答處 _____

considerable
(adj.) 相當多的

關 consider (v.t) 考慮
consideration (n.) 考慮；貼心
considerably (adv.) 相當，非常
同 large, great, plenty

一般正常速度 [kən`sɪdərəb!]
ETS全真速度 [kən`sɪdərəb!]

➜ 所有詞性第一音節的 o 均唸 [ə] 的音

consistent (adj.) 持續的

關 consistency (n.) 一貫，一致
同 regular, steady, constant,
unchanging, persistent

一般正常速度 [kən`sɪstənt]
ETS全真速度 [kən`sɪsdən(t)]

➜ 1) 形容詞與名詞的重音均在第二音節
2) 第一個 [t] 均須變音為 [d]
3) 形容詞字尾 [t] 輕唸即可

consolidation (n.) 強化

關 consolidate (v.t) 加強
同 reinforcement, enhancement,
strengthening, fortification

一般正常速度 [kən͵salə`deʃən]
ETS全真速度 [kən͵salə`deʃən]

➜ 名詞與動詞字首的 o 均唸成 [ə]，而不
是 [a]（台式發音）

construction (n.) 施工

關 construct (v.t) 建造
constructive (adj.) 有建設性的
同 building, structure, formation

一般正常速度 [kən`strʌkʃən]
ETS全真速度 [kən`strʌ__ʃən]

➜ 1) 所有詞性的重音都在第二音節
2) 第二個 [k] 均可消音

consult (v.t) 諮詢

關 consultant (n.) 顧問
consultation (n.) 商討
同 ask, question, ask advice of

一般正常速度 [kən`sʌlt]
ETS全真速度 [kən`sʌl__]

➜ 動詞字尾 [t] 可消音

C

考古題應用　He has a considerable income.
他的收入頗高。

口試練習題　Can he afford the expensive apartment?

考生回答處　_____

考古題應用　There has been a consistent improvement in his performance.
他的表現一直有持續的進步。

口試練習題　Why did he get the raise?

考生回答處　_____

考古題應用　Calcium tablets are good for the consolidation of bones.
鈣片有助於骨骼的強化。

口試練習題　Why do you take calcium tablets on a daily basis?

考生回答處　_____

考古題應用　The gymnasium is still under construction.
體育館仍在施工中。

口試練習題　Why are there so many construction workers?

考生回答處　_____

考古題應用　We have to consult a lawyer first.
我們得先請教過律師。

口試練習題　Why haven't you signed the contract? ∨

考生回答處　_____

cooperation (n.) 合作

關 cooperate (v.) 合作
cooperative (adj.) 合作的
同 assistance, collaboration, participation

一般正常速度 [ko,apə`reʃən]
ETS全真速度 [ko,abə`reʃən]

➡ 1) 動詞與形容詞的重音在第二音節，名詞的重音則在倒數第二音節
2) [p] 可變音為 [b]

corruption (n.) 貪汙

關 corrupt (v.t) 賄賂
corrupt (adj.) 貪汙的
同 dishonesty, fraud

一般正常速度 [kə`rʌpʃən]
ETS全真速度 [kə`rʌ(p)ʃən]

➡ 1) 所有詞性的重音都在第二音節
2) [p] 均輕唸即可

coupon (n.) 折價券

同 ticket, voucher, certificate

一般正常速度 [`kupan]
ETS全真速度 [`kuban]

➡ 1) ou 唸 [ju] 或 [u] 都可以
2) [p] 可變音為 [b]

Cr-

credentials (n.pl.) 資格

關 credibility (n.) 可信度
credible (adj.) 可信的
同 certificate, qualification, diploma

一般正常速度 [krɪ`dɛnʃəlz]
ETS全真速度 [krɪ` đɛnʃəlz]

➡ [d] 可變音為 [đ]

credibility (n.) 信用

關 credit (n.) 信用
creditor (n.) 債權人
同 believability, trustworthiness

一般正常速度 [,krɛdə`bɪlətɪ]
ETS全真速度 [,krɛđə`bɪləđɪ]

➡ 1) [d] 可變音為 [đ]
2) [t] 可變音為 [đ]

C

考古題應用　We need your cooperation in developing the new product.
我們需要您的合作以研發新產品。

口試練習題　What can I do for your team?
考生回答處　_____

考古題應用　The mayor resigned because of his charges of corruption.
市長因貪汙的指控而辭職。

口試練習題　Why has the mayor resigned?
考生回答處　_____

考古題應用　You can get 20 percent off your next purchase with this coupon.
用這張折價券下次購物時可以打八折。

口試練習題　What can I do with this coupon?
考生回答處　_____

考古題應用　The first applicant has the best credentials.
第一位申請者的資格最好。

口試練習題　Which candidate is the best?
考生回答處　_____

考古題應用　We'll lose our credibility with the public.
我們會失去大眾的信任。

口試練習題　What if we don't keep our promises?
考生回答處　_____

criterion (n.) 標準

關 criteria (n.) 標準（複數）
同 standard, norm, measure

一般正常速度 [kraɪˋtɪrɪən]
ETS全真速度 [kraɪˋtɪrɪən]

➡ 單複數名詞的重音都在第二音節

critical (adj.) 危急的

關 critically (adv.) 危急地
同 urgent, serious, dangerous

一般正常速度 [ˋkrɪtɪkl̩]
ETS全真速度 [ˋkrɪɖɪgl̩]

➡ 1) [t] 均可變音為 [ɖ]
　 2) [k] 均可變音為 [g]

crucial (adj.) 關鍵的

同 decisive, critical

一般正常速度 [ˋkruʃəl]
ETS全真速度 [ˋkruʃəl]

∨

customize (v.t) 量身訂做

關 custom (n.) 習慣
　 customs (n.) 海關
同 tailor, adapt

一般正常速度 [ˋkʌstəˌmaɪz]
ETS全真速度 [ˋkʌsɖəˌmaɪz]

➡ [t] 可變音為 [ɖ]

deadlock (n.) 僵局

關 deadlock (v.t) 僵持
同 stop, standstill, tie

一般正常速度 [ˋdɛdˌlak]
ETS全真速度 [ˋdɛ__ˌla(k)]

➡ 1) 名詞與動詞的唸法相同
　 2) [d] 停一拍即可，無須發音
　 3) 字尾 [k] 輕唸即可

∨

C
D

考古題應用 Hiring a teenager is against our employment criteria.
雇用青少年違反我們的任用標準。

口試練習題 Why can't a sixteen-year-old work here as a waitress?
考生回答處 _____

考古題應用 Those injured in the accident are in critical condition.
那場事故中的傷患情況危急。

口試練習題 What happened to those injured in the car crash?
考生回答處 _____

考古題應用 The meeting tomorrow is crucial to the future of our firm.
明天的會議對我們事務所的發展是個關鍵。

口試練習題 Why is the meeting tomorrow so important?
考生回答處 _____

考古題應用 We can customize furniture to your needs.
我們可以依需求替您訂做家具。

口試練習題 Do you offer only ready-made furniture?
考生回答處 _____

考古題應用 We need to be patient with the negotiation deadlock.
當談判陷入僵局時我們要有耐心。

口試練習題 Our negotiation with the pharmaceutical company has made little progress, hasn't it?
考生回答處 _____

deal (n.) 交易

關 deal (v.i) 交易
同 trade, business, negotiation

一般正常速度 [dil]
ETS全真速度 [dil]
➡ [l] 不可發音為 [l]

debate (v.t) 爭論

關 debater (n.) 辯論家；好爭論者
同 argue, discuss, question

一般正常速度 [dɪˋbet]
ETS全真速度 [dɪˋbe(t)]
➡ 動詞字尾 [t] 輕唸即可

debt (n.) 債務

同 due, debit, liability

一般正常速度 [dɛt]
ETS全真速度 [dɛ(t)]
➡ 字尾 [t] 輕唸即可

declare (v.t) 申報

關 declaration (n.) 申報（海關，稅務）
　 declarable (adj.) 需申報的
同 make known, show, disclose

一般正常速度 [dɪˋklɛr]
ETS全真速度 [dɪˋklɛr]
➡ 動詞的重音在第二音節

decline (n.) 下滑

關 decline (v.i) 下跌
同 drop, decrease

一般正常速度 [dɪˋklaɪn]
ETS全真速度 [dɪˋklaɪn]
➡ 名詞與動詞的發音相同

考古題應用　We've decided to make a deal with the Japanese company.
我們已經決定要跟日本公司做生意。

口試練習題　Who have you decided to do business with?

考生回答處　_____

D

考古題應用　They are still debating the issue.
他們還在為這件事爭論。

口試練習題　Have they decided who's being promoted?

考生回答處　_____

考古題應用　I heard he is heavily in debt at the moment.
我聽說他目前負債累累。

口試練習題　Do you know that he's filed for bankruptcy?

考生回答處　_____

考古題應用　I told him I had nothing to declare.
我跟他說我沒有東西要申報。

口試練習題　What did you say to the customs officer?

考生回答處　_____

考古題應用　Our <u>domestic</u> sales are on the decline.
我們國內的銷售業績在下滑中。

口試練習題　Why is our sales VP so upset about the financial report?

考生回答處　_____

deduct (v.t) 扣除

關 deduction (n.) 扣除；扣除額
deductible (adj.) 可扣除的
同 take off, take from, remove

一般正常速度 [dɪ`dʌkt]
ETS全真速度 [dɪ`dʌ(kt)]

→ 1) 所有詞性的重音都在第二音節
2) 動詞字尾 [kt] 輕唸即可

defective (adj.) 有瑕疵的

關 defect (v.i) 背叛
defect (n.) 缺點；缺陷
同 broken, imperfect, out of order

一般正常速度 [dɪ`fɛktɪv]
ETS全真速度 [dɪ`fɛkdɪ(v)]

→ 1) 名詞的重音在第一音節，動詞與形
容詞的重音在第二音節
2) [t] 可變音為 [d]
3) 形容詞字尾 [v] 輕唸即可

deficiency (n.) 缺點

關 deficient (adj.) 有缺陷的
同 flaw, imperfection, defect,
shortcoming

一般正常速度 [dɪ`fɪʃənsɪ]
ETS全真速度 [dɪ`fɪʃənsɪ]

→ 名詞與形容詞的重音都在第二音節

deficit (n.) 赤字

同 shortage, loss

一般正常速度 [`dɛfəsɪt]
ETS全真速度 [`dɛfəsɪt]

→ 重音在第一音節

deflation (n.) 通貨緊縮

關 deflate (v.t) 緊縮
同 reduction, decrease, devaluation

一般正常速度 [dɪ`fleʃən]
ETS全真速度 [dɪ`fleʃən]

→ 所有詞性的重音都在第二音節

考古題應用 The fees will be deducted from your next monthly payment.
費用會從您下次的付款當中扣除。

試練習題 Do I have to pay for the fee right now?

考生回答處 _____

D

考古題應用 They have decided to <u>recall</u> all of the defective products.
他們決定要回收所有的瑕疵品。

試練習題 How did they react to the customer's complaints?

考生回答處 _____

考古題應用 The most serious deficiency in this system is its stability.
這套系統最大的缺點在於它的穩定性。

試練習題 What problem do you see in this system?

考生回答處 _____

考古題應用 Our department has been trying very hard to <u>make up</u> for the deficit.
我們部門一直很努力想補足赤字的部分。

試練習題 Why is everyone in your department working so hard?

考生回答處 _____

考古題應用 Deflation is beginning to <u>affect</u> the <u>clothing industry</u>.
通貨緊縮已經開始影響到服飾業了。

試練習題 Why was there a drop in our business last quarter?

考生回答處 _____

delegate (v.t) 委派

關 delegate [ˋdɛləgɪ(t)] (n.) 代表
delegation (n.) 委派
同 assign, authorize, designate

一般正常速度 [ˋdɛlə.get]
ETS全真速度 [ˋdɛlə.ge(t)]

➡ 1) 除 delegation 的重音在第三音節外，動詞與名詞的重音都在第一音節
2) 動詞字尾 [t] 輕唸即可

deliberately (adv.) 故意地

關 deliberate (v.i) 仔細考慮
deliberation (n.) 深思熟慮
deliberate (adj.) 故意的
同 on purpose, calculatedly, intentionally

一般正常速度 [dɪˋlɪbərɪtlɪ]
ETS全真速度 [dɪˋlɪbərɪ__lɪ]

➡ 1) 除 deliberation 外，其他詞性的重音都在第二音節
2) 副詞的 [t] 須消音

deliver (v.t) 發表演說

關 delivery (n.) 演講；交貨
同 address, give a talk, give a lecture

一般正常速度 [dɪˋlɪvɚ]
ETS全真速度 [dɪˋlɪvɚ]

deluxe (adj.) 高級的

同 special, costly, superior

一般正常速度 [dɪˋlʌks]
ETS全真速度 [dɪˋlʌ(ks)]

➡ 1) 重音在第二音節
2) 字尾 [ks] 輕唸即可

demand (n.) 市場需求

關 demand (v.t) 需求；要求
同 market, need, requirement

一般正常速度 [dɪˋmænd]
ETS全真速度 [dɪˋmæn(d)]

➡ 1) 名詞與動詞的唸法相同
2) 字尾 [d] 輕唸即可

考古題應用 Jorge is delegated to <u>host the meeting</u> in Panama.
Jorge 被派去巴拿馬主持會議。

試練習題 Who will you send to Panama to host the meeting?
考生回答處

D

考古題應用 An <u>irresponsible</u> supervisor often deliberately ignores his staff's complaints.
不負責任的主管對員工們的抱怨常會故意視而不見。

試練習題 Why didn't the president do anything about our complaints?
考生回答處

考古題應用 We've asked a famous doctor to deliver a speech to the <u>interns</u>.
我們請了一位有名的醫師來對實習生演講。

試練習題 Who will be our guest speaker?
考生回答處

考古題應用 This winery <u>is</u> very <u>proud of</u> their deluxe champagne.
這家酒廠相當以它們的高級香檳自豪。

試練習題 What would you recommend I buy from this winery?
考生回答處

考古題應用 There is still a great demand for iPods.
iPod 的市場需求量仍然很大。

試練習題 Are iPods still very popular items?
考生回答處

democracy (n.) 民主

關 Democrat (n.) 民主黨
同 republic, government by the people

一般正常速度 [dɪˋmɑkrəsɪ]
ETS全真速度 [dɪˋmɑkrəsɪ]

➡ democracy 的重音在第二音節，Democrat 的重音在第一音節

demolish (v.t) 拆除

關 demolition (n.) 破壞，毀壞
同 destroy, tear down, knock down

一般正常速度 [dɪˋmɑlɪʃ]
ETS全真速度 [dɪˋmɑlɪʃ]

➡ 名詞 demolition 的第一個母音發 [ɛ]

demonstration

(n.) 示威遊行

關 demonstrate (v.t) 示威；示範
　 demonstrative (adj.) 示範的
同 march, parade, rally, protest

一般正常速度 [ˌdɛmənˋstreʃən]
ETS全真速度 [ˌdɛmənˋsdreʃən]

➡ [t] 可變音為 [d]

demotion (n.) 降職

關 demote (v.t) 降級
同 degrade, downgrade

一般正常速度 [dɪˋmoʃən]
ETS全真速度 [dɪˋmoʃən]

➡ 動詞字尾 [t] 輕唸即可

denomination (n.) 面額

關 denominate (v.t) 命名
同 value

一般正常速度 [dɪˌnɑməˋneʃən]
ETS全真速度 [dɪˌnɑməˋneʃən]

考古題應用 The democracies in some countries are facing big challenges.
有些國家的民主正面臨重大的挑戰。

口試練習題 Do you think the spread of democracy is successful everywhere?

D

考生回答處 _____

考古題應用 One of the buildings is being demolished.
其中一棟大樓正在被拆除。

口試練習題 Why are there so many bulldozers?

考生回答處 _____

考古題應用 The police said over 1,000 ferry workers had participated in the demonstration.
警方表示有超過一千名的渡輪工人參加了示威遊行。

口試練習題 How many people were in Sunday demonstration?

考生回答處 _____

考古題應用 He said the demotion was unfair.
他認為降職不公平。

口試練習題 How did Edward react to his demotion?

考生回答處 _____

考古題應用 She paid in bills of large denomination.
她用大面額的鈔票付錢。

口試練習題 Did she buy the laptop in cash?

考生回答處 _____

depict (v.t) 描寫

關 depiction (n.) 描寫
同 outline, portray, illustrate

一般正常速度 [dɪˋpɪkt]
ETS全真速度 [dɪˋpɪ(kt)]

➡ 1) 動詞與名詞的重音都在第二音節
2) 動詞字尾 [kt] 輕唸即可
3) [k] 均輕唸即可

deposit (n.) 存款

關 deposit (v.t) 支付（保證金）
同 money, payment

一般正常速度 [dɪˋpɑzɪt]
ETS全真速度 [dɪˋpɑzɪ(t)]

➡ 1) 名詞與動詞的唸法相同
2) 字尾 [t] 輕唸即可

depreciate (v.t) 貶值

關 depreciatory (adj.) 貶值的
同 decrease, devalue, lessen

一般正常速度 [dɪˋpriʃɪˌet]
ETS全真速度 [dɪˋpriʃɪˌe(t)]

➡ 1) 動詞與形容詞重音都在第二音節
2) 動詞字尾 [t] 輕唸即可

depreciation (n.) 折舊

關 depreciate (v.t) 貶值
　　depreciative (adj.) 貶值的
同 drop, fall, slump, deflation

一般正常速度 [dɪˌpriʃɪˋeʃən]
ETS全真速度 [dɪˌpriʃɪˋeʃən]

➡ 動詞與形容詞的重音都在第二音節

deserted (adj.) 空無一人的

關 desert [dɪˋzɝt] (v.t) 遺棄
　　desert [ˋdɛzɚt] (n.) 沙漠
同 empty, unoccupied, abandoned

一般正常速度 [dɪˋzɝtɪd]
ETS全真速度 [dɪˋzɝɖɪd]

➡ 1) 名詞的重音在第一音節
2) 形容詞的 [t] 可變音為 [ɖ]

考古題應用 The article in the paper depicted him as a tyrant.
報紙上的文章把他描寫成一名暴君。

試練習題 Why was the CEO so furious upon reading the paper?
考生回答處

D

考古題應用 You should have 500 dollars as an initial deposit.
你的開戶首存金額要有五百塊美元。

試練習題 What should I do to get a bank account?
考生回答處

考古題應用 The car would be depreciated after being flooded.
車子泡過水之後就貶值了。

試練習題 What would happen to a flooded car?
考生回答處

考古題應用 You'd better take into consideration the car's depreciation rate.
你最好把車子的折舊率考慮進去。

試練習題 What do I have to pay attention to when selling a used car?
考生回答處

考古題應用 The streets are deserted when a typhoon comes.
颱風來時街道上空無一人。

試練習題 What happens when a typhoon comes?
考生回答處

designate (v.t) 指定

關 designation (n.) 任命
同 assign, choose, delegate

一般正常速度 [`dɛzɪɡ.net]
ETS全真速度 [`dɛzɪ(g).ne(t)]

➡ [g] 與字尾 [t] 均輕唸即可

destination (n.) 終點站

同 goal, end, purpose

一般正常速度 [.dɛstə`neʃən]
ETS全真速度 [.dɛsdə`neʃən]

➡ 第一個 [t] 可變音為 [d]

detect (v.t) 偵測

關 detector (n.) 探測器
同 notice, recognize, identify

一般正常速度 [dɪ`tɛkt]
ETS全真速度 [dɪ`tɛk(t)]

➡ 1) 所有詞性的重音都在第二音節
2) 動詞字尾 [t] 輕唸即可

develop (v.t) 開發

關 development (n.) 發展
同 establish, progress, promote

一般正常速度 [dɪ`vɛləp]
ETS全真速度 [dɪ`vɛlə(p)]

➡ 動詞字尾 [p] 輕唸即可

device (n.) 裝置

關 devise [dɪ`vaɪz] (v.t) 設計；發明
同 equipment, tool, apparatus

一般正常速度 [dɪ`vaɪs]
ETS全真速度 [dɪ`vaɪs]

➡ 名詞與動詞的重音都在第二音節

考古題應用 | Mr. Choi has been designated to <u>take over</u> the negotiation with us.
崔先生被指定接手與我們談判。

試練習題 | Who will be talking to us after Mr. Kim leaves?

D

考生回答處 | _____

考古題應用 | They <u>arrived at</u> their final destination two days ago.
他們在兩天前抵達終點站。

試練習題 | Are the managers still on their way to Paris?

考生回答處 | _____

考古題應用 | We've <u>installed</u> a new software to detect virus.
我們安裝了新的軟體以偵測病毒。

試練習題 | Have we done anything to prevent our computers from infection?

考生回答處 | _____

考古題應用 | Our company has decided to develop this 300 <u>acres</u> of land.
我們公司已經決定要開發這片三百英畝的土地。

試練習題 | Is this property going to be deserted forever?

考生回答處 | _____

考古題應用 | No recording devices of any kind are allowed in the <u>concert hall</u>.
各種錄音設備都不能帶進音樂廳裡。

試練習題 | Are we allowed to record his performance?

考生回答處 | _____

Di-

dig (v.t) 挖掘

關 dig-dug-dug（動詞三態）
同 excavate, break up

一般正常速度 [dɪg]
ETS全真速度 [dɪ(g)]
➤ 字尾 [g] 輕唸即可

diminish (v.i) 減弱

同 decrease, reduce, lessen

一般正常速度 [dəˋmɪnɪʃ]
ETS全真速度 [dəˋmɪnɪʃ]

diplomatic (adj.) 委婉的

關 diplomat (n.) 外交官
　 diplomatically (adv.) 圓滑地
同 politic, tactful, polite, subtle

一般正常速度 [ˌdɪpləˋmætɪk]
ETS全真速度 [ˌdɪbləˋmæđɪ(k)]
➤ 1) 形容詞與副詞的重音都在第三音
　 節，名詞的重音在第一音節
　 2) 形容詞與副詞字尾的 [t] 都須變音
　 為 [đ]
　 3) [p] 均可變音為 [b]

directory (n.) 通訊錄

關 direct (v.) 指引
　 director (n.) 主管
　 direction (n.) 方向
同 list

一般正常速度 [dəˋrɛktərɪ]
ETS全真速度 [dəˋrɛ(k)dərɪ]
➤ 1) 字中 [k] 輕唸即可
　 2) [t] 均須變音為 [d]

disaster (n.) 災害

關 disastrous (adj.) 災難性的
同 accident, trouble, ruin

一般正常速度 [dɪˋzæstɚ]
ETS全真速度 [dɪˋzæsdɚ]
➤ 名詞的 [t] 可變音為 [d]

考古題應用 It took them two months to dig under the building to <u>lay the cables</u>.
他們花了兩個月的時間在大樓下方挖洞埋設電纜線。

試練習題 How long did they work on the construction?

考生回答處 _____

D

考古題應用 The <u>PR manager</u> is worried about our product's diminishing popularity.
公關經理擔憂我們產品的人氣下滑。

試練習題 Why does the PR manager want to consult with me?

考生回答處 _____

考古題應用 She tends to work out problems in a more diplomatic way.
她傾向用比較委婉的方式解決問題。

試練習題 How does Joanne approach matters of dispute with customers?

考生回答處 _____

考古題應用 This is our updated telephone directory.
這是我們最新的通訊錄。

試練習題 There seems to be many changes in this telephone directory.

考生回答處 _____

考古題應用 The State of Louisiana has remained an official disaster area for the past three months.
路易斯安那州成為正式災區已經三個月了。

試練習題 Has New Orleans recovered from Hurricane Katrina?

考生回答處 _____

discern (v.t) 辨識

關 discernable (adj.) 可辨識的
同 distinguish, notice, recognize, detect, perceive

一般正常速度 [dɪˋsɜn]
ETS全真速度 [dɪˋsɜn]

➡ 動詞與形容詞的重音都在第二音節

discipline (n.) 紀律

關 disciplinary (adj.) 紀律的
disciplined (adj.) 有紀律的
同 control, regulation, rule

一般正常速度 [ˋdɪsəplɪn]
ETS全真速度 [ˋdɪsəblɪn]

➡ 1) 所有詞性的重音都在第一音節
2) [p] 可變音為 [b]

discount (v.t) 打折

關 discount (v.t) 不全然聽信（對某人說的話打折扣）
discount (n.) 折扣
同 lower, reduce, mark down

一般正常速度 [ˋdɪskaʊnt]
ETS全真速度 [ˋdɪsgaʊn(t)]

➡ 1) 與「金錢上的折扣」有關時，重音不論動詞或名詞都在第一音節
2) [k] 可變音為 [g]
3) 字尾 [t] 輕唸即可

discrepancy (n.) 不一致

關 discrepant (adj.) 有差異的
discrepantly (adv.) 不一致地
同 difference, conflict, inconsistency, disagreement

一般正常速度 [dɪˋskrɛpənsɪ]
ETS全真速度 [dɪˋsgrɛbənsɪ]

➡ 1) [k] 均須變音為有聲的 [g]
2) [p] 均須變音為有聲的 [b]

disorder (n.) 混亂

關 disorder (v.t) 擾亂
同 chaos, mess, confusion

一般正常速度 [dɪsˋɔrdə]
ETS全真速度 [dɪsˋɔrdə]

➡ 1) [s] 跟 [ɔ] 要唸出連音，中間不要停頓
2) 第二個 [d] 須變音為 [ð]

考古題應用 No one can discern such <u>minute differences</u>.
沒人能夠辨識出這麼<u>細微的差異</u>。

試練習題 Do you think our customers can tell these two fabrics apart?
考生回答處
_____

D

考古題應用 Order and discipline <u>are highly valued</u> in our company.
我們公司<u>非常重視</u>命令與紀律。

試練習題 Do you think discipline is important in a workplace?
考生回答處
_____

考古題應用 Only purchases over 50 dollars will be discounted.
只有超過 50 塊美金的商品才有打折。

試練習題 Will every item be discounted during the sale?
考生回答處
_____

考古題應用 There's a distinct discrepancy between their descriptions of the <u>suspect</u>.
他們對<u>嫌犯</u>的描述有明顯的出入。

試練習題 Why are the police still interrogating the witnesses?
考生回答處
_____

考古題應用 The lobby is in disorder because <u>the alarm went off</u>.
<u>警鈴大作</u>使得大廳陷入一片混亂。

試練習題 What is all the noise downstairs?
考生回答處
_____

display (v.t) 展示

關 display (n.) 展覽，陳列
同 show, exhibit, disclose

一般正常速度 [dɪˋsple]
ETS全真速度 [dɪˋsble]

➡ 1) 動詞與名詞的唸法相同
　2) [p] 須變音為 [b]

disposable (adj.) 可拋式的

關 dispose (v.t) 處置，配置
　disposal (n.) 處置
同 spendable, consumable,
　expendable

一般正常速度 [dɪˋspozəbl̩]
ETS全真速度 [dɪˋsbozəbl̩]

➡ 1) 所有詞性的重音都在第二音節
　2) [p] 可變音為 [b]

dispute (n.) 爭辯

關 dispute (v.t) 爭辯
　disputable (adj.) 有待商榷的
同 argument, debate

一般正常速度 [dɪˋspjut]
ETS全真速度 [dɪˋsbju(t)]

➡ 1) 名詞與動詞的唸法相同
　2) 所有詞性的 [p] 均須變音為 [b]
　3) dispute 的 [t] 輕唸即可
　4) 形容詞的 [t] 須變音為 [d]

distinction (n.) 差異點

關 distinguish (v.t) 辨別
　distinct (adj.) 明顯不同的
　distinctive (adj.) 特殊的
同 clear difference

一般正常速度 [dɪˋstɪŋkʃən]
ETS全真速度 [dɪˋsdɪŋ(k)ʃən]

➡ 1) 所有詞性的重音都在第二音節
　2) [t] 可變音為 [d]
　3) [k] 輕唸即可

distinguish (v.t) 辨別

關 distinguishable (adj.) 可辨識的
　distinguished (adj.) 有成就的
同 differentiate, tell apart, tell
　between

一般正常速度 [dɪˋstɪŋgwɪʃ]
ETS全真速度 [dɪˋstɪŋgwɪʃ]

➡ 所有詞性的重音都在第二音節

| 考古題應用 | We are about to display our latest product line.
我們即將展示最新的系列產品。 |

| 試練習題 | What is on display at the trade show tomorrow? |
| 考生回答處 | |

| 考古題應用 | You'll have to bring some disposable paper cups.
你得帶一些免洗紙杯。 |

| 試練習題 | What will I have to prepare for the picnic? |
| 考生回答處 | |

| 考古題應用 | The committee has been set up to <u>resolve</u> labor disputes.
委員會是爲了解決勞資糾紛而成立的。 |

| 試練習題 | Why did you set up a mediation committee? |
| 考生回答處 | |

| 考古題應用 | No one can see the distinction between them.
沒人看得出來它們之間的差異。 |

| 試練習題 | Why do I have to revise these two reports? |
| 考生回答處 | |

| 考古題應用 | He just can't distinguish right from wrong.
他就是無法明辨是非。 |

| 試練習題 | I don't understand why he always screws things up! |
| 考生回答處 | |

distribute (v.t) 分發

關 distribution (n.) 分配，分發
　　distributive (adj.) 分配的
同 spread, share, allocate

一般正常速度 [dɪˋstrɪbjut]

ETS全真速度 [dɪˋsdrɪbjʊ(t)]

➜ 1) 動詞與形容詞的重音都在第二音節
　　2) 第一個 [t] 均可變音為 [d]
　　3) 動詞字尾 [t] 輕唸即可

diversity (n.) 多樣性

關 diversify (v.t) 使多樣化
　　diverse (adj.) 多種的
同 difference, variety

一般正常速度 [daɪˋvɜsətɪ]

ETS全真速度 [daɪˋvɜsəɖɪ]

➜ 1) 所有詞性的重音都在第二音節
　　2) 名詞字尾 [t] 可變音為 [ɖ]

Do-

dominant (adj.) 主導的

關 dominate (v.t) 主導
　　dominance (n.) 主導
同 leading, ruling, controlling,
　　commanding

一般正常速度 [ˋdɑmənənt]

ETS全真速度 [ˋdɑmənən(t)]

➜ 1) 所有詞性的重音都在第一音節
　　2) 字尾 [t] 均輕唸即可

donate (v.t) 捐贈

關 donation (n.) 捐贈物品
　　donor (n.) 捐贈人
同 give, contribute

一般正常速度 [ˋdonet]

ETS全真速度 [ˋdone(t)]

➜ 1) donation 重音在第二音節 (-na-)
　　2) 動詞字尾 [t] 輕唸即可

doubt (n.) 懷疑

關 doubt (v.t) 懷疑
　　doubtful (adj.) 令人懷疑的
　　undoubtedly (adv.) 無庸置疑地
同 mistrust, suspicion

一般正常速度 [daʊt]

ETS全真速度 [daʊ(t)]

➜ 1) 所有詞性的 b 均不須發音
　　2) doubt 的 [t] 輕唸即可
　　3) 形容詞的 [t] 輕唸即可
　　4) 副詞中的 [t] 須變音為 [ɖ]

考古題應用 | All of the <u>part-time workers</u> were distributing <u>flyers</u> to the crowd.
所有<u>兼職員工</u>都在發送<u>宣傳單</u>給民眾。

口試練習題 | Where has everyone been?

考生回答處

D

考古題應用 | New York is famous for its cultural diversity.
紐約以它的文化多樣性著稱。

口試練習題 | What's so special about New York?

考生回答處

考古題應用 | He has to <u>maintain</u> his dominant position in the company.
他必須<u>維持</u>在公司的主導地位。

口試練習題 | Why does the President visit the large shareholders so often?

考生回答處

考古題應用 | Last year we donated 2 million dollars to a <u>charity foundation</u>.
去年我們捐了兩百萬美元給一個<u>慈善基金會</u>。

口試練習題 | Did you make any charitable donations last year?

考生回答處

考古題應用 | It was, without a doubt, the best seminar we've ever attended.
這無疑是我們參加過最好的研討會。

口試練習題 | What do you think of this morning's seminar?

考生回答處

 Dr-

drift (v.i) 漂流

關 drift (n.) 漂流物
同 float, be carried along

一般正常速度 [drɪft]
ETS全真速度 [drɪ(ft)]

➡ 1) 動詞與名詞的唸法相同
2) 字尾 [ft] 輕唸即可

drill (n.) 練習

關 drill (v.t) 鑽
　　drill (n.) 鑽子
同 practice, rehearsal, training,
exercise

一般正常速度 [drɪl]
ETS全真速度 [drɪl]

➡ 1) 名詞與動詞的唸法相同
2) 字尾 [l] 請勿唸成 [ɔ]（台式發音）

 Du-

due (adj.) 到期

同 owed, owing, unpaid

一般正常速度 [dju]
ETS全真速度 [dju]

duplicate (n.) 複製品

關 duplicate (v.t) 複製
　　duplication (n.) 複製
　　duplicate (adj.) 複製的
同 copy, clone, reproduction, replica

一般正常速度 [ˋdjuplə͵ket]
ETS全真速度 [ˋdjublə.ge(t)]

➡ 1) duplicate 當名、動及形容詞時，唸
法都相同
2) [p] 均可變音為 [b]
3) [k] 均可變音為 [g]

duty (n.) 責任

關 dutiful (adj.) 盡職的
同 responsibility, obligation, mission,
assignment, task, work

一般正常速度 [ˋdjutɪ]
ETS全真速度 [ˋdjuɗɪ]

➡ 兩個詞性的 [t] 均須變音為 [ɗ]

考古題應用　The boat is drifting along the stream.
船沿著小溪漂流。

試練習題　Is the boat docked in your backyard or drifting along the stream?

考生回答處　_____

D

考古題應用　We <u>perform</u> a fire drill at least once a month.
我們至少一個月<u>進行</u>一次消防演習。

試練習題　How often do you perform fire drills?

考生回答處　_____

考古題應用　The first <u>installment</u> is due this coming Wednesday.
首期<u>分期付款</u>這週三到期。

試練習題　When is the first installment due?

考生回答處　_____

考古題應用　That painting is a duplicate.
那幅畫是複製品。

試練習題　Is the painting in your office an original or a duplicate?

考生回答處　_____

考古題應用　Her job duty is <u>exploring</u> the Southeast Asian market.
她的職責為<u>開發</u>東南亞市場。

試練習題　Is Alicia's duty to explore the Australian market?

考生回答處　_____

Check List 2

到目前為止，字彙量又增加了不少，繼續學新單字之前，我們先來複習一下，看看是不是都記起來了！

☐ calculate	☐ commute	☐ corruption
☐ candidate	☐ compatible	☐ coupon
☐ capacity	☐ compensation	☐ credentials
☐ capital	☐ competent	☐ credibility
☐ cargo	☐ compile	☐ criterion
☐ carousel	☐ compliment	☐ critical
☐ carpool	☐ conclusion	☐ crucial
☐ cautious	☐ concrete	☐ customize
☐ certify	☐ confidential	☐ deadlock
☐ chart	☐ conform	☐ deal
☐ circumspect	☐ connection	☐ debate
☐ claim	☐ consensus	☐ debt
☐ clarify	☐ considerable	☐ declare
☐ classify	☐ consistent	☐ decline
☐ clearance	☐ consolidation	☐ deduct
☐ code	☐ construction	☐ defective
☐ command	☐ consult	☐ deficiency
☐ commission	☐ cooperation	☐ deficit

- [ ] deflation
- [ ] delegate
- [ ] deliberately
- [ ] deliver
- [ ] deluxe
- [ ] demand

- [ ] democracy
- [ ] demolish
- [ ] demonstration
- [ ] demotion
- [ ] denomination
- [ ] depict

- [ ] deposit
- [ ] depreciate
- [ ] depreciation
- [ ] deserted
- [ ] designate
- [ ] destination

- [ ] detect
- [ ] develop
- [ ] device
- [ ] dig
- [ ] diminish
- [ ] diplomatic

- [ ] directory
- [ ] disaster
- [ ] discern
- [ ] discipline
- [ ] discount
- [ ] discrepancy

- [ ] disorder
- [ ] display
- [ ] disposable
- [ ] dispute
- [ ] distinction
- [ ] distinguish

- [ ] distribute
- [ ] diversity
- [ ] dominant
- [ ] donate
- [ ] doubt
- [ ] drift

- [ ] drill
- [ ] due
- [ ] duplicate
- [ ] duty

□□ economical　　□□ edit　　□□ elaborate
□□ election　　□□ elementary

economical (adj.) 省錢的

關 economics (n.) 經濟學
economy (n.) 經濟
同 money-saving, cost-effective, unwasteful

一般正常速度 [ˌikəˈnamɪkḷ]
ETS全真速度 [ˌigəˈnamɪgḷ]

➔ 1) 除名詞 economy 的重音在第二音節外 (-con-)，其他詞性的重音都在第三音節
2) [k] 均可變音為 [g]

---

edit (v.t) 編纂

關 editor (n.) 編輯
edition (n.) 版本
editorial (n.) 社論
editorial (adj.) 編輯的
同 put together, compile, compose

一般正常速度 [ˈɛdɪt]
ETS全真速度 [ˈɛɖɪ(t)]

➔ 1) [dl] 均可變音為 [ɖ]
2) 動詞字尾 [t] 輕唸即可

---

elaborate (v.i) 詳細說明

關 elaboration (n.) 詳細闡述；精巧
elaborate (adj.) 詳盡的
同 add details, complicate, expand

一般正常速度 [ɪˈlæbəˌret]
ETS全真速度 [ɪˈlæbəˌre(t)]

➔ 1) 形容詞字尾的母音唸 [ɪ]
2) 字尾 [t] 均輕唸即可

---

election (n.) 選舉

關 elect (v.t) 選舉
elective (adj.) 選舉的
同 choosing, selection, voting

一般正常速度 [ɪˈlɛkʃən]
ETS全真速度 [ɪˈlɛkʃən]

➔ 所有詞性的重音都在第二音節

---

elementary (adj.) 基本的

關 element (n.) 要素
elemental (adj.) 基本的
同 basic, beginning, introductory

一般正常速度 [ˌɛləˈmɛntərɪ]
ETS全真速度 [ˌɛləˈmɛntərɪ]

➔ 形容詞的重音都在第三音節，名詞的重音在第一音節

考古題應用　It's more economical to use <u>fans</u> instead of <u>air-conditioners</u>.
開電扇比開冷氣要省。

試練習題　Why didn't you turn on the air-conditioner?
考生回答處　_____

E

考古題應用　She used to edit <u>the *Chicago Tribune*</u>.
她以前是《芝加哥論壇報》的編輯。

試練習題　Have you heard anything about our new editor?
考生回答處　_____

考古題應用　Would you like to elaborate on that?
您可以解釋清楚一點嗎？

試練習題　Building fuel-efficient vehicles is good for our business.
考生回答處　_____

考古題應用　The presidential election will be held next spring.
總統大選將在明年春天舉行。

試練習題　When is the presidential election?
考生回答處　_____

考古題應用　This job requires elementary computer skills.
這份工作需要基本的電腦技能。

試練習題　What is the requirement for this position?
考生回答處　_____

□□ embargo　□□ embark　□□ embezzle
□□ emergency　□□ emphasize

Em-

embargo (n.) 禁運

關 embargo (v.t) 禁運
同 stop, ban, prohibition, block, hindrance

一般正常速度 [ɪm`bɑrgo]
ETS全真速度 [ɪm`bɑrgo]

➡ 1) 名詞與動詞的唸法相同
2) 字尾 o 發 [o]

---

embark (v.i) 搭機；上船

關 embarkation (n.) 乘坐
同 get aboard, take on board, put on board

一般正常速度 [ɪm`bɑrk]
ETS全真速度 [ɪm`bɑr(k)]

➡ 動詞字尾 [k] 輕唸即可

---

embezzle (v.t) 盜用公款

關 embezzlement (n.) 盜用公款
embezzler (n.) 盜用公款的人
同 steal

一般正常速度 [ɪm`bɛzl̩]
ETS全真速度 [ɪm`bɛzl̩]

➡ 所有詞性的重音都在第二音節

---

emergency (n.) 緊急

關 emergent (adj.) 緊急的
同 crisis, danger

一般正常速度 [ɪ`mɝdʒənsɪ]
ETS全真速度 [ɪ`mɝdʒənsɪ]

➡ 名詞與形容詞的重音都在第二音節

---

emphasize (v.t) 強調

關 emphasis (n.) 強調
同 lay stress on

一般正常速度 [`ɛmfə‚saɪz]
ETS全真速度 [`ɛmfə‚saɪz]

➡ 動詞與名詞的重音都在第一音節

考古題應用 Our government has put an oil embargo out against them.
我國政府已經下令禁止輸出石油給他們。

口試練習題 Why is it now illegal to sell oil to that country?

考生回答處 _____

E

考古題應用 We will be embarking from Zurich in three hours.
我們會在三個小時內於蘇黎士登機。

口試練習題 When are you leaving?

考生回答處 _____

考古題應用 The secretary embezzled 50,000 dollars from the firm.
祕書從事務所盜用了五萬塊美金。

口試練習題 Why are the police asking questions about the secretary?

考生回答處 _____

考古題應用 In case of an emergency, please exit through the side door.
萬一有緊急事故，請從側門出去。

口試練習題 What do we do in an emergency?

考生回答處 _____

考古題應用 I'd like to emphasize that we are ready to take the first step.
我想強調的是，我們已經準備好要跨出第一步了。

口試練習題 What would you like to say to the committee?

考生回答處 _____

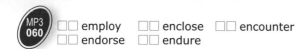
employ (v.t) 雇用

關 employment (n.) 雇用
employer (n.) 雇主
employee (n.) 員工
同 hire, commission

一般正常速度 [ɪm`plɔɪ]
ETS全真速度 [ɪm`plɔɪ]

➡ 只有 employee 重音在最後一音節
(-ee)，其他詞性的重音都在第二音節

En-

enclose (v.t) 隨函附上

關 enclosure (n.) 隨函附上的物品
同 include, put in, send with

一般正常速度 [ɪn`kloz]
ETS全真速度 [ɪn`kloz]

➡ 動詞與名詞的重音都在第二音節

encounter (v.t) 遭遇到

關 encounter (n.) 遭遇；邂逅
同 come across, bump into, run into

一般正常速度 [ɪn`kaʊntɚ]
ETS全真速度 [ɪn`kaʊnɾɚ]

➡ 1) 動詞與名詞唸法相同
2) [t] 須變音為 [ɾ]

endorse (v.t) 背書

關 endorsement (n.) 背書（支票）
同 support, recommend, promote

一般正常速度 [ɪn`dɔrs]
ETS全真速度 [ɪn`dɔr(s)]

➡ 1) 動詞與名詞的重音都在第二音節
2) 動詞字尾 [s]、名詞字尾 [t] 均輕唸
即可

endure (v.i) 支撐

關 endurance (n.) 忍耐；耐力
endurable (adj.) 耐用的
同 sustain, last

一般正常速度 [ɪn`djʊr]
ETS全真速度 [ɪn`djʊr]

➡ 所有詞性的重音都在第二音節

考古題應用 In order to <u>make the deadline</u>, we'll employ fifty more workers.
為了<u>趕上截止日期</u>，我們會多雇用 50 名工人。

口試練習題 What can we do to meet the deadline?

考生回答處

E

考古題應用 I have enclosed, with this letter, a check of 300 dollars.
我隨信附上一張三百塊美金的支票。

口試練習題 How are you going to pay the rent?

考生回答處

考古題應用 We've encountered some <u>technical problems</u>.
我們遇到了一些<u>技術上</u>的問題。

口試練習題 Is everything going well with the new system?

考生回答處

考古題應用 The manager's project is endorsed by the consultants.
經理的提案有顧問們的背書支持。

口試練習題 Do you think the manager's project will be approved?

考生回答處

考古題應用 These <u>shelters</u> won't endure much longer without power.
沒有電的話，這些<u>避難所</u>撐不了多久。

口試練習題 What problems do we have in these shelters?

考生回答處

enforcement (n.) 執行

關 enforce (v.t) 執行
enforceable (adj.) 可實施的
同 application, administration, carrying out

一般正常速度 [ɪnˋforsmənt]
ETS全真速度 [ɪnˋforsmən(t)]

➜ 1) 所有詞性的重音都在第二音節
2) 動詞字尾 [s] 與名詞字尾 [t] 均輕唸即可

engrave (v.t) 雕刻

關 engraving (n.) 雕刻
同 cut, inscribe

一般正常速度 [ɪnˋgrev]
ETS全真速度 [ɪnˋgre(v)]

➜ 1) 動詞與名詞的重音都在第二音節
2) 動詞字尾 [v] 輕唸即可

enlarge (v.t) 擴大

關 enlargement (n.) 擴大
同 blow up, make larger, expand

一般正常速度 [ɪnˋlardʒ]
ETS全真速度 [ɪnˋlar(dʒ)]

➜ 1) 動詞與名詞的重音都在第二音節
2) 動詞字尾 [dʒ] 輕唸即可

enroll (v.t) 報名

關 enrollment (n.) 登記
同 join, sign up for, register

一般正常速度 [ɪnˋrol]
ETS全真速度 [ɪnˋrol]

➜ 1) 所有詞性的重音都在第二音節
2) 動詞字尾 [l] 請勿唸成 [ɔ]（台式發音）

ensemble (n.) 組合

同 set, collection

一般正常速度 [anˋsambl]
ETS全真速度 [anˋsambl]

➜ 前兩個 e 都發成 [a] 的音

考古題應用　The police will be responsible for law enforcement.
警方會負責執法。

試練習題　Who will keep public order during the rally?

考生回答處 _____

考古題應用　These wedding rings can be engraved with your names.
婚戒上可以刻上你們的名字。

試練習題　How do we personalize these wedding rings?

考生回答處 _____

考古題應用　The school decided to enlarge its library.
校方決定擴建圖書館。

試練習題　What decision did the school come to during the board meeting?

考生回答處 _____

考古題應用　His parents had enrolled him in painting classes.
他父母幫他報名過繪畫班。

試練習題　I didn't know Aaron could paint so well!

考生回答處 _____

考古題應用　This scarf and your dress make a beautiful ensemble.
這條圍巾跟妳的洋裝搭配起來很好看。

試練習題　Do you think I chose the right scarf for my dress?

考生回答處 _____

ensure (v.t) 確保

同 make certain, make sure, guarantee

一般正常速度 [ɪnˋʃʊr]
ETS全真速度 [ɪnˋʃʊr]
➡ 重音在第二音節

enter (v.t) 參加

關 entry (n.) 參加；出賽
同 sign up, enroll, participate, take part in

一般正常速度 [ˋɛntɚ]
ETS全真速度 [ˋɛn__ɚ]
➡ 動詞的 [t] 可以消音

enterprise (n.) 企業

關 enterprising (adj.) 有事業心的
同 business, company, firm, establishment

一般正常速度 [ˋɛntɚ͵praɪz]
ETS全真速度 [ˋɛn__ɚ͵praɪz]
➡ 名詞與形容詞字中的 [t] 均可消音

entertain (v.t) 招待

關 entertainment (n.) 招待；娛樂
entertainer (n.) 藝人
同 make happy, please, amuse

一般正常速度 [͵ɛntɚˋten]
ETS全真速度 [͵ɛn__ɚˋten]
➡ 動詞與名詞的第一個 [t] 均可消音

entitle (v.t) 賦予資格

關 entitlement (n.) 應得的權利
同 allow, authorize, permit, qualify for

一般正常速度 [ɪnˋtaɪtl̩]
ETS全真速度 [ɪnˋtaɪđl̩]
➡ 動詞與名詞的第一個 [t] 均不可消音，第二個 [t] 均須變音為 [đ]

考古題應用 We do everything to ensure the quality of our services.
我們盡一切努力確保服務品質。

試練習題 How has your hotel remained so popular after all these years?
考生回答處 _____

E

考古題應用 There are fifty young ladies entering the beauty contest.
一共有 50 名佳麗參加這場選美比賽。

試練習題 How many contestants are there in this beauty contest?
考生回答處 _____

考古題應用 The government has done a lot to promote local enterprises.
政府做了很多事來促進地方事業。

試練習題 What has the government done for our economy?
考生回答處 _____

考古題應用 We've planned a party to entertain our Australian visitors.
我們籌備派對招待澳洲來的客人。

試練習題 What will we do to welcome our guests?
考生回答處 _____

考古題應用 You are entitled to use the club facilities for free.
你可以免費使用俱樂部的設施。

試練習題 What can I do with this VIP?
考生回答處 _____

environment (n.) 環境

關 environmental (adj.) 環境的
environmentalist (n.) 環保人士
同 scene, setting, atmosphere

一般正常速度 [ɪn`vaɪrənmənt]
ETS全真速度 [ɪn`vaɪrənmən(t)]

➡ 名詞字尾 [t] 輕唸即可

 Eq-

equal (adj.) 相等的

關 equal (v.t) 比得上
equal (n.) 相等的事物
equally (adv.) 相同地
同 alike, the same, identical

一般正常速度 [`ikwəl]
ETS全真速度 [`igwəl]

➡ 1) 所有詞性的重音都在第一音節
2) 所有詞性的 [k] 均可變音為 [g]

equip (v.t) 配備

關 equipment (n.) 配備
同 install, prepare, provide with

一般正常速度 [ɪ`kwɪp]
ETS全真速度 [ɪ`gwɪ(p)]

➡ 1) 動詞與名詞的 [k] 均可變音為 [g]
2) 動詞字尾 [p] 輕唸即可

Er-

errand (n.) 差事

同 job, mission, task

一般正常速度 [`ɛrənd]
ETS全真速度 [`ɛrən(d)]

➡ 字尾 [d] 輕唸即可

erratic (adj.) 不穩定的

關 erratically (adv.) 不定地
同 unstable, unsteady, variable,
irregular, unpredictable

一般正常速度 [ɪ`rætɪk]
ETS全真速度 [ɪ`rædɪk]

➡ 形容詞與副詞的 [t] 均須變音為 [d]

考古題應用　This company offers a pleasant working environment.
這家公司提供了舒適的工作環境。

口試練習題　Why do you want to stay in this company?
考生回答處 _____

E

考古題應用　The workers are demanding equal rights at work.
勞工們要求工作權利平等。

口試練習題　Why are the foreign workers going on strike?
考生回答處 _____

考古題應用　The <u>mechanic</u> equipped our car with <u>an alarm system</u>.
<u>修車師傅幫我們的車子安裝防盜裝置</u>。

口試練習題　Why was your car in the repair shop?
考生回答處 _____

考古題應用　I asked her to run some errands for me.
我請她去幫我辦點事。

口試練習題　Have you seen Katie?
考生回答處 _____

考古題應用　The erratic rainfall in March will damage the upcoming harvest.
三月份不穩定的降雨會影響到將來的收成。

口試練習題　How will the weather affect the wheat farmers?
考生回答處 _____

Es-

escalate (v.i) 攀升

關 escalation (n.) 升高
　　escalator (n.) 升降梯
同 grow, increase, rise

一般正常速度 [ˋɛskəˌlet]
ETS全真速度 [ˋɛsgəˌle(t)]

➡ 1) 動詞與名詞的 [k] 均須變音為 [g]
　 2) escalator 中的 [t] 須變音為 [đ]

escort (n.) 隨扈

關 escort (v.t) 護送
同 company, guard, protection

一般正常速度 [ˋɛskɔrt]
ETS全真速度 [ˋɛsgɔr(t)]

➡ 1) 名詞與動詞唸法相同
　 2) [k] 可變音為 [g]
　 3) 字尾 [t] 輕唸即可

essential (adj.) 必要的

關 essential (n.) 必需品
　　essence (n.) 基本要素
　　essentially (adv.) 基本上
同 important, necessary, needed

一般正常速度 [ɪˋsɛnʃəl]
ETS全真速度 [ɪˋsɛnʃəl]

➡ 只有名詞 essence 的重音在第一音
　 節，其他詞性的重音都在第二音節

establishment
(n.) 事業體

關 establish (v.t) 建立
同 building, firm, organization

一般正常速度 [ɪsˋtæblɪʃmənt]
ETS全真速度 [ɪsˋdæblɪʃmən(t)]

➡ 1) 名詞與動詞的第一個 [t] 均須變音
　　 為 [d]
　 2) 名詞字尾 [t] 輕唸即可

estimate (v.t) 預估

關 estimate (n.) 估計
　　estimation (n.) 推測
同 assess, calculate

一般正常速度 [ˋɛstəˌmet]
ETS全真速度 [ˋɛsdəˌme(t)]

➡ 1) 所有詞性的第一個 [t] 均須變音為
　　 [d]
　 2) 動詞字尾 [t] 輕唸即可

考古題應用　Oil prices are escalating as well.
油價也一直在攀升。

口試練習題　Is the price for gold the only thing that is escalating?
考生回答處　_____

E

考古題應用　The queen has arrived at Heathrow Airport under escort.
女王已在護送之下抵達了希斯洛機場。

口試練習題　Is the queen still on her way to Heathrow Airport?
考生回答處　_____

考古題應用　Water is essential to the growth of those plants.
水對這些植物的生長是必要的。

口試練習題　Why do we need to water these plants on a daily basis?
考生回答處　_____

考古題應用　This department store is a <u>well-run</u> establishment.
這家百貨公司是<u>經營得很成功的</u>企業。

口試練習題　What do you know about the Harrods Department Store in London?
考生回答處　_____

考古題應用　The builder estimates a delay of two months.
建商預估會落後兩個月。

口試練習題　Will the construction project be finished on time?
考生回答處　_____

Et-

ethnic (adj.) 民族的

關 ethnicity (n.) 種族地位
同 racial, cultural, traditional

一般正常速度 [`εθnɪk]
ETS全真速度 [`εθnɪ(k)]
→ 1) 形容詞字尾 [k] 輕唸即可
　 2) 名詞字尾 [t] 發 [đ] 的音

etiquette (n.) 禮儀

同 manners, politeness, courtesy

一般正常速度 [`εtɪˌkεt]
ETS全真速度 [`εđɪˌgε(t)]
→ 1) 字首 [t] 須變音為 [đ]，[k] 可變音
　 為 [g]
　 2) 字尾 [t] 輕唸即可

Ev-

evacuate (v.t) 撤離

關 evacuation (n.) 撤離
同 clear, move out, withdraw

一般正常速度 [ɪ`vækjuˌet]
ETS全真速度 [ɪ`vækjuˌe(t)]
→ 動詞字尾 [t] 輕唸即可

evaluate (v.t) 評估

關 evaluation (n.) 評價
同 assess, calculate, estimate, rate

一般正常速度 [ɪ`væljuˌet]
ETS全真速度 [ɪ`væljuˌe(t)]
→ 動詞字尾 [t] 輕唸即可

event (n.) 事件

同 affair, matter, happening

一般正常速度 [ɪ`vεnt]
ETS全真速度 [ɪ`vεn(t)]
→ 1) 重音在第二音節
　 2) 字尾 [t] 輕唸即可

考古題應用 They were invited to watch an ethnic dance.
他們受邀欣賞民族舞蹈。

試練習題 Why didn't Mr. and Mrs. Takano attend the meeting last night?
考生回答處 _____

E

考古題應用 To take off your hat indoors is a common etiquette.
在室內將帽子脫下是一般性禮儀。

試練習題 May I keep my hat on when entering the auditorium?
考生回答處 _____

考古題應用 The townees were evacuated because of flooding.
居民因為淹水的關係都撤離了。

試練習題 Why are the streets deserted in this town?
考生回答處 _____

考古題應用 The market situation is hard to evaluate at this moment.
目前很難評估市場狀況。

試練習題 Do you think now is the best time for investment?
考生回答處 _____

考古題應用 Wang's games with the Red Sox are the huge sporting events.
王建民與紅襪隊的比賽是重大的運動賽事。

試練習題 Why have you stayed up late watching television recently?
考生回答處 _____

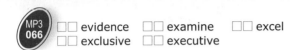
evidence (n.) 證據

關 evident (adj.) 明顯的
evidently (adv.) 明顯地
同 proof, confirmation, declaration

一般正常速度 [ˋɛvədəns]
ETS全真速度 [ˋɛvədən(s)]

→ 1) 名詞字尾 [s] 輕唸即可
2) 副詞的 [t] 必須消音

Ex-

examine (v.t) 檢查

關 examination (n.) 檢視；考試
exam (n.) 考試
同 inspect, go over, go through

一般正常速度 [ɪgˋzæmɪn]
ETS全真速度 [ɪgˋzæmɪn]

excel (v.i) 表現優秀

關 excellence (n.) 傑出
excellent (adj.) 出色的
同 be the best, be better

一般正常速度 [ɪkˋsɛl]
ETS全真速度 [ɪkˋsɛl]

→ 只有動詞的重音在第二音節，其餘詞性的重音都在第一音節

exclusive (adj.) 獨占的

關 exclude (v.t) 排除
exclusion (n.) 排除
同 private, absolute, unshared

一般正常速度 [ɪkˋsklusɪv]
ETS全真速度 [ɪkˋsglusɪ(v)]

→ 1) 所有詞性的重音都在第二音節
2) 字中 [k] 均須變音為 [g]
3) 形容詞字尾 [v] 輕唸即可

executive (n.) 主管

關 execute [ˋɛksɪˌkju(t)] (v.t) 執行
execution (n.) 執行
同 director, manager, administrator

一般正常速度 [ɪgˋzɛkjutɪv]
ETS全真速度 [ɪgˋzɛkjuɖɪv]

→ 1) 注意名詞與動詞的發音
2) [t] 可變音為 [ɖ]

考古題應用 Before the police came, the manager had destroyed all the evidence.
在警方抵達之前，負責人已經湮滅了所有的證據。

試練習題 Why didn't the police find any evidence of guilt?

考生回答處 _____

E

考古題應用 The health inspector wants to examine the fruits first.
衛生局的檢查員想先檢查一下水果。

試練習題 Why haven't these imported fruits been unpacked and put on the shelves?

考生回答處 _____

考古題應用 Derek has excelled in this position over last two years.
過去兩年 Derek 在這個位置上都表現得很優秀。

試練習題 Do you think Derek is worth the merit raise?

考生回答處 _____

考古題應用 Club members have exclusive use of the tennis court.
這個網球場只限會員獨享。

試練習題 Why isn't the tennis court open to the public?

考生回答處 _____

考古題應用 I'm sure Craig will be a very good advertising executive.
我相信 Craig 會成為很好的廣告主管。

試練習題 Is it wise to promote Craig to the position of advertising executive?

考生回答處 _____

exemption (n.) 免除

關 exempt (v.t) 免除
exempt (adj.) 免除的
同 discharge, exception, immunity

一般正常速度 [ɪgˋzɛmpʃən]
ETS全真速度 [ɪgˋzɛm＿ʃən]

➡ [p] 均停一拍即可，無須發音

exhibition (n.) 展覽

關 exhibit [ɪgˋzɪbɪ(t)] (v.t) 展覽
同 show, display, presentation

一般正常速度 [ˌɛksəˋbɪʃən]
ETS全真速度 [ˌɛksəˋbɪʃən]

➡ 注意動詞的發音

exit (n.) 出口

關 exit (v.t) 出去
同 gate, door, way out

一般正常速度 [ˋɛksɪt]
ETS全真速度 [ˋɛgsɪ(t)]

➡ 1) 名詞及動詞的唸法相同
　2) [k] 可變音為 [g]
　3) 字尾 [t] 輕唸即可

expand (v.t) 擴大

關 expansion (n.) 擴張
同 increase, broaden, widen

一般正常速度 [ɪkˋspænd]
ETS全真速度 [ɪkˋsbæn(d)]

➡ 1) 動詞與名詞的重音都在第二音節
　2) [p] 均須變音為 [b]
　3) 動詞字尾 [d] 輕唸即可

expense (n.) 開支

關 expend (v.t) 花費
同 cost, expenditure, spending

一般正常速度 [ɪkˋspɛns]
ETS全真速度 [ɪkˋsbɛn(s)]

➡ 1) 名詞與動詞的重音都在第二音節
　2) [p] 均須變音為 [b]
　3) 名詞字尾 [s] 輕唸即可
　4) 動詞字尾 [d] 輕唸即可

考古題應用 She called for the information on tax exemption.
她打電話來要有關免稅的資訊。

試練習題 Ms. Daniels called our office this morning, didn't she?
考生回答處 _____

E

考古題應用 Picasso paintings are on exhibition.
正在展出畢卡索的畫作。

試練習題 Why is the city museum so crowded?
考生回答處 _____

考古題應用 There are more than ten exits.
出口超過 10 個。

試練習題 How many exits are there in the office complex?
考生回答處 _____

考古題應用 We have to expand the size of our stock room.
我們得擴建儲藏室。

試練習題 Why is the stock room under construction?
考生回答處 _____

考古題應用 I don't think he will approve your expense account.
我不認為他會批准你的開支帳戶。

試練習題 Do you think our director will approve my proposal?
考生回答處 _____

expiration (n.) 到期

關 expire (v.i) 到期
同 end, finish, conclusion

一般正常速度 [ˌɛkspəˋreʃən]
ETS全真速度 [ˌɛ(k)sbəˋreʃən]

➡ 1) 名詞與動詞的 [p] 均須變音為 [b]
　　2) [k] 均輕唸即可

explicit (adj.) 明確的

關 explicitly (adv.) 明確地
同 clear, exact, certain

一般正常速度 [ɪkˋsplɪsɪt]
ETS全真速度 [ɪkˋsblɪsɪ(t)]

➡ 1) 形容詞與副詞的 [p] 均須變音為 [b]
　　2) 形容詞字尾 [t] 輕唸即可

exploit (v.t) 剝削

關 exploitative (adj.) 剝削的；開發的
同 abuse

一般正常速度 [ɪkˋsplɔɪt]
ETS全真速度 [ɪkˋsblɔɪ(t)]

➡ 1) 動詞與形容詞的重音都在第二音節
　　2) 動詞與形容詞的 [p] 均須變音為 [b]
　　3) 動詞字尾 [t] 輕唸即可，形容詞的
　　　 [t] 均可變音為 [ɖ]

express (adj.) 快速的

關 express (v.t) 表達
　　express (n.) 特快車
　　express (adv.) 快速地
同 quick, rapid, speedy

一般正常速度 [ɪkˋsprɛs]
ETS全真速度 [ɪkˋsbrɛ(s)]

➡ 1) 所有詞性的唸法相同
　　2) [p] 須變音為 [b]
　　3) 字尾 [s] 輕唸即可

extend (v.t) 延長

關 extension (n.) 延伸
　　extensive (adj.) 廣泛的
同 lengthen, prolong, expand

一般正常速度 [ɪkˋstɛnd]
ETS全真速度 [ɪkˋsdɛn(d)]

➡ 1) 所有詞性的重音都在第二音節
　　2) 第一個 [t] 須變音為 [d]
　　3) 動詞字尾 [d] 輕唸即可

考古題應用　The landlord has decided to <u>raise the rent</u> after the expiration date.
房東決定期限一到就要調漲租金。

試練習題　Why don't you want to renew the lease next year?

考生回答處 _____

E

考古題應用　We have to ask her for more explicit <u>instructions</u>.
我們得向她要求更明確的指示。

試練習題　Don't you think the manager's orders are too hard to understand?

考生回答處 _____

考古題應用　I heard your company exploits workers by paying low wages.
聽說你們公司以低薪資來剝削員工。

試練習題　What have you heard about our company?

考生回答處 _____

考古題應用　I've sent the package by express delivery.
我已經將包裹用快遞寄出去了。

試練習題　Do you think they will receive the package in time?

考生回答處 _____

考古題應用　You could have extended the <u>guarantee</u> by paying ten extra dollars.
你原本若多付 10 塊美金就可延長保固期的。

試練習題　I didn't realize that this guarantee expired last month!

考生回答處 _____

127

F

Fa-

fabulous (adj.) 很棒的

同 amazing, wonderful, incredible

一般正常速度 [`fæbjələs]
ETS全真速度 [`fæbjələ(s)]

➡ 字尾 [s] 輕唸即可

facade (n.) 門面

同 front, exterior, appearance

一般正常速度 [fə`sad]
ETS全真速度 [fə`sa(d)]

➡ 1) 重音在第二音節
2) 重音節的 a 發 [ɑ] 的音
3) 字尾 [d] 輕唸即可

facility (n.) 設施

關 facilitate (v.t) 幫助
同 equipment, means

一般正常速度 [fə`sɪlətɪ]
ETS全真速度 [fə`sɪləɖɪ]

➡ 名詞 [t] 須變音為 [ɖ]

fake (n.) 仿冒品

關 fake (v.t) 偽造，冒充
fake (adj.) 冒充的
同 copy, reproduction, forgery

一般正常速度 [fek]
ETS全真速度 [fe(k)]

➡ 1) 所有詞性的唸法相同
2) 字尾 [k] 輕唸即可

familiar (adj.) 熟悉的

關 familiarize (v.t) 熟悉
familiarity (n.) 熟悉
同 familiarized, informed,
knowledgeable

一般正常速度 [fə`mɪljə]
ETS全真速度 [fə`mɪljə]

➡ 1) 只有名詞的重音在第四音節 (-ar-)，
形容詞與動詞的重音都在第二音節
2) 名詞字尾 [t] 須變音為 [ɖ]

考古題應用 The <u>theme party</u> last night was absolutely fabulous!
昨晚的主題派對真是棒極了！

試練習題 How did you like the theme party last night?
考生回答處 _____

F

考古題應用 They spent a lot of time on the repairs to its facade.
他們花了很久時間整修門面。

試練習題 The front of the hotel is magnificent!
考生回答處 _____

考古題應用 The club has excellent recreational facilities.
這個俱樂部有很棒的休閒設施。

試練習題 Why does this club have so many registered members?
考生回答處 _____

考古題應用 An expert <u>confirmed</u> that it is a fake.
一名專家證實它是個仿冒品。

試練習題 Is this vase a genuine antique?
考生回答處 _____

考古題應用 Jacob may not be familiar with the <u>tax laws</u>.
Jacob 對稅務法可能不熟。

試練習題 Do you think Jacob can help me out with the tax forms?
考生回答處 _____

fare (n.) 交通費

回 ticket money, transport cost

一般正常速度 [fɛr]
ETS全真速度 [fɛr]

fasten (v.t) 綁緊

回 bind, connect, secure

一般正常速度 [`fæsn̩]
ETS全真速度 [`fæsn̩]

➡ 字中 t 不發音

Fe-

feasibility (n.) 可行性

關 feasible (adj.) 可行的
回 usefulness, workability,
　practicability

一般正常速度 [ˌfizəˋbɪlətɪ]
ETS全真速度 [ˌfizəˋbɪlədɪ]

➡ 1) 名詞與形容詞的 s 均須唸成 [z]
　2) 名詞的 [t] 須變音為 [đ]

feedback (n.) 意見

關 feed (v.t) 餵食；提供
回 remarks, comments, review

一般正常速度 [`fid.bæk]
ETS全真速度 [`fi(d).bæ(k)]

➡ 名詞的 [d] 與 [k] 均輕唸即可

festival (n.) 慶祝活動

關 festivity (n.) 慶祝活動
　festive (adj.) 歡樂的
回 holiday, celebration, feast

一般正常速度 [`fɛstəvl̩]
ETS全真速度 [`fɛsdəvl̩]

➡ 1) 所有詞性的 [t] 均須變音為 [d]
　2) festivity 字尾的 [t] 須變音為 [đ]

考古題應用 I don't have enough money for the bus fare!
我公車錢不夠！

試練習題 You left your wallet in the office!
考生回答處 _____

F

考古題應用 I've already fastened my seatbelt.
我已經繫好安全帶了。

試練習題 Please don't forget to buckle up.
考生回答處 _____

考古題應用 The commissioners have to <u>study</u> the feasibility of the proposal first.
委員們得先<u>研究</u>一下提案的可行性。

試練習題 Did Mr. Kim approve my proposal?
考生回答處 _____

考古題應用 We really need your feedback on the <u>spring collection</u>.
我們很需要你針對<u>春裝</u>提出意見。

試練習題 Why did you ask me to fill out the form?
考生回答處 _____

考古題應用 This town holds spring music festivals.
這個小鎮在春天會舉辦音樂慶典。

試練習題 Why do most tourists visit this town in the spring?
考生回答處 _____

Fi-

fiction (n.) 小說

關 fictional (adj.) 虛構的
同 story, novel, work of imagination

一般正常速度 [`fɪkʃən]
ETS全真速度 [`fɪ(k)ʃən]

➡ 名詞與形容詞的 [k] 均輕唸即可

figure (n.) 數字

關 figure (v.t) 猜想
同 number

一般正常速度 [`fɪgjɚ]
ETS全真速度 [`fɪgjɚ]

➡ 名詞與動詞的唸法相同

file (v.t) 提出

關 file (n.) 檔案
　　file (v.t) 歸檔
同 enter, put in place, record

一般正常速度 [faɪl]
ETS全真速度 [faɪl]

➡ 所有詞性的唸法相同

finalize (v.t) 完成

關 final (n.) 決賽；期末考
　　final (adj.) 最終的
同 complete, conclude, finish,
　 work out, settle

一般正常速度 [`faɪn!͵aɪz]
ETS全真速度 [`faɪn!͵aɪz]

➡ 名詞與形容形字尾 [l] 勿唸成 [ɔ]（台式發音）

financial (adj.) 財務上的

關 finances (n.) 財務
　　finance (v.t) 資助
同 money, budgeting, economic,
　 fiscal

一般正常速度 [faɪ`nænʃəl]
ETS全真速度 [faɪ`nænʃəl]

➡ 形容詞的重音在第二音節，名詞與動詞的重音在第一或第二音節均可

考古題應用 The <u>cash register</u> in the fiction section is closed today.
小說區那邊的收銀機今天沒開。

試練習題 Why isn't there a cashier in the fiction section?
考生回答處 _____

F

考古題應用 The unemployment figures are getting lower.
失業率在下降中。

試練習題 What does it say in the paper about the jobless rate?
考生回答處 _____

考古題應用 We should have filed a complaint to the committee.
我們應該要向委員會提出申訴的。

試練習題 Can you believe the construction upstairs is still going on?
考生回答處 _____

考古題應用 <u>Hopefully</u> we can finalize the contract by tomorrow.
希望明天之前我們能把合約完成。

試練習題 You've already started to run behind schedule, haven't you?
考生回答處 _____

考古題應用 We've hired Mr. Crystal as our financial adviser.
我們已雇用 Crystal 先生來擔任我們的財務顧問。

試練習題 How do we work out our financial problems?
考生回答處 _____

Fo-

forbid (v.t) 禁止

同 disallow, ban, prohibit

一般正常速度 [fəˋbɪd]
ETS全真速度 [fəˋbɪ(d)]

➡ 1) 重音在第二音節
2) 字尾 [d] 輕唸即可

forecast (n.) 預報

關 forecast (v.t) 預測
同 a statement of future events

一般正常速度 [ˋfor͵kæst]
ETS全真速度 [ˋfor͵kæ(st)]

➡ 1) 名詞與動詞的唸法相同
2) 字尾 [st] 輕唸即可

foresee (v.t) 預料

關 foreseeable (adj.) 可預見的
同 predict, forecast, anticipate

一般正常速度 [forˋsi]
ETS全真速度 [forˋsi]

➡ 1) 所有詞性的重音都在第二音節
2) 形容詞字尾 [l] 請勿唸成 [ɔ]（台式發音）

forfeit (v.t) 喪失

關 forfeit (n.) 代價
同 have something taken away

一般正常速度 [ˋfɔrfɪt]
ETS全真速度 [ˋfɔrfɪ(t)]

➡ 1) 動詞與名詞的唸法相同
2) 字尾 [t] 輕唸即可

formula (n.) 配方

關 formulate (v.t) 公式化
同 blueprint, method, recipe

一般正常速度 [ˋfɔrmjələ]
ETS全真速度 [ˋfɔrmjələ]

➡ 動詞字尾 [t] 輕唸即可

考古題應用　Our government forbids the addition of certain chemicals.
政府禁止一些特定的化學添加物。

試練習題　Why are some of the dairy products off the shelves right now?

考生回答處　_____

F

考古題應用　The weather forecast said there will be a thunderstorm.
氣象預報說會有大雷雨。

試練習題　Why will there be a delay for Flight 707?

考生回答處　_____

考古題應用　We should have foreseen the problem long ago.
我們應該老早就要預料到會發生這樣的問題。

試練習題　I don't understand why the plan didn't work.

考生回答處　_____

考古題應用　All his possessions were forfeited by the government.
他所有的財產都被政府沒收了。

試練習題　Why did Alex lose all his money?

考生回答處　_____

考古題應用　The formula for our salad dressing has leaked out.
我們的沙拉醬配方被洩露出去了。

試練習題　Why is our stock price on a decline?

考生回答處　_____

fortify (v.t) 強化

關 fortification (n.) 設防
fortifiable (adj.) 可設防的
同 strengthen, reinforce, enhance

一般正常速度 [ˋfɔrtəˏfaɪ]
ETS全真速度 [ˋfɔrđəˏfaɪ]

➡ 所有詞性的 [t] 均須變音為 [đ]

fortune (n.) 財富

關 fortunate (adj.) 幸運的
fortunately (adv.) 幸運地
同 possessions, money, riches

一般正常速度 [ˋfɔrtʃən]
ETS全真速度 [ˋfɔrtʃən]

➡ 副詞字尾 [t] 停一拍即可,不須發音

forum (n.) 論壇

同 meeting, gathering, symposium

一般正常速度 [ˋforəm]
ETS全真速度 [ˋforəm]

forward (v.t) 轉寄

關 forward (n.) 前鋒
forward (adv.) 往前
同 send, send on, transmit

一般正常速度 [ˋfɔrwəd]
ETS全真速度 [ˋfɔrwə(d)]

➡ 1) 所有詞性的唸法相同
 2) 字尾 [d] 輕唸即可

foundation (n.) 基礎

關 found (v.t) 建立基礎
foundation (n.) 基金會
同 base, basis, groundwork

一般正常速度 [faʊnˋdeʃən]
ETS全真速度 [faʊnˋdeʃən]

考古題應用　It is especially fortified with calcium.
它特別強化鈣質。

試練習題　Why has this brand of milk popular among parents?

考生回答處　_____

F

考古題應用　He won a fortune by playing the lottery.
他玩樂透中了一大筆錢。

試練習題　How could Mr. Tahara afford a trip to Europe?

考生回答處　_____

考古題應用　They will be holding a forum for financial experts.
他們將為財經專家舉辦一場論壇。

試練習題　Why is the staff decorating the conference hall?

考生回答處　_____

考古題應用　I still need his forwarding address to send him the package.
我需要他的轉寄地址才能把包裹寄給他。

試練習題　Did you give Mr. Romano his package?

考生回答處　_____

考古題應用　Her theories always have a very solid academic foundation.
她的理論一向都有非常扎實的學術基礎。

試練習題　Dr. Nyuen's latest linguistic theory is very convincing, isn't it?

考生回答處　_____

137

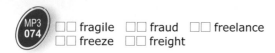

Fr-

fragile (adj.) 易碎的
關 fragility (n.) 脆弱
同 weak, fine, breakable

一般正常速度 [`frædʒəl]
ETS全真速度 [`frædʒəl]

fraud (n.) 詐欺
關 fraudulent (adj.) 詐欺的
同 deception, cheat

一般正常速度 [frɔd]
ETS全真速度 [frɔ(d)]

➡ 1) 形容詞的重音在第一音節
   2) 名詞字尾 [d] 輕唸即可

freelance (adj.) 自由工作者的
關 freelance (n.) 自由工作者
同 self-employed, independent

一般正常速度 [`friˌlæns]
ETS全真速度 [`friˌlæns]

➡ 形容詞與名詞的唸法相同

freeze (v.t) 凍結
同 hold, suspend

一般正常速度 [friz]
ETS全真速度 [fri(z)]

➡ 字尾 [z] 輕唸即可

freight (n.) 貨物
關 freight (v.t) 送貨
   freighter (n.) 貨輪
同 cargo, shipment, load, goods

一般正常速度 [fret]
ETS全真速度 [fre(t)]

➡ 1) 所有詞性的 gh 均不發音
   2) 名詞字尾 [t] 輕唸即可

考古題應用　The glass inside is very fragile.
裡面的玻璃杯相當易碎。

□試練習題　Why is this package labeled "Please handle with care"?
考生回答處 _____

F

考古題應用　They are giving out flyers against fraud.
他們在發放反詐欺的傳單。

□試練習題　What are those people giving out in the plaza?
考生回答處 _____

考古題應用　As a freelance worker, he does not have a regular income.
身為自由工作者，他沒有固定收入。

□試練習題　Why is it hard to predict Sergio's annual income?
考生回答處 _____

考古題應用　His assets were frozen by the government.
他的財產被政府凍結了。

□試練習題　Why did Zach call his lawyer for help?
考生回答處 _____

考古題應用　This train carries freight only.
這輛火車只提供貨運服務。

□試練習題　Can we take this train to Cairo?
考生回答處 _____

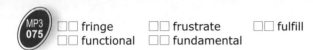
fringe (n.) 邊緣

關 fringe (v.t) 鑲邊
同 addition, margin

一般正常速度 [frɪndʒ]
ETS全真速度 [frɪndʒ]

➡ 名詞與動詞的唸法相同

frustrate (v.t) 使人沮喪

關 frustration (n.) 沮喪
同 disappoint, discourage

一般正常速度 [`frʌstret]
ETS全真速度 [`frʌsdre(t)]

➡ 1) 第一個 [t] 均可變音為 [d]
2) 動詞字尾 [t] 輕唸即可

Fu-

fulfill (v.t) 滿足

關 fulfillment (n.) 滿足；成就
同 accomplish, complete, satisfy

一般正常速度 [fʊl`fɪl]
ETS全真速度 [fʊl`fɪl]

➡ 所有詞性的重音都在第二音節

functional (adj.) 可使用的

關 function (v.i) 運轉
function (n.) 功能
同 workable, practical, useful

一般正常速度 [`fʌŋkʃən!]
ETS全真速度 [`fʌŋ__ʃən!]

➡ [k] 停一拍即可，無須刻意發音

fundamental (adj.) 基礎的

關 fund (v.t) 資助
fund (n.) 資金
同 basic, central, essential,
important

一般正常速度 [ˌfʌndə`mɛnt!]
ETS全真速度 [ˌfʌndə`mɛnḑ!]

➡ 形容詞的 [t] 可唸成 [ḑ]

考古題應用　One of the job's fringe benefits is its free <u>health insurance</u>.
免費的健保是這個工作的福利之一。

試練習題　Are there any fringe benefits for this job?
考生回答處　_____

F

考古題應用　This <u>earnings report</u> frustrated our sales team.
這份營收報告讓我們的銷售團隊覺得很沮喪。

試練習題　How did your colleagues feel about the quarterly earnings?
考生回答處　_____

考古題應用　The printer we've been working with should fulfill our requirements.
向來與我們合作的那家印刷廠應該可以滿足我們的需求。

試練習題　Do you think we should look for a new printer?
考生回答處　_____

考古題應用　The <u>smoke alarms</u> on all floors are fully functional.
每一樓的煙霧偵測器都很正常。

試練習題　The smoke detectors aren't out of order, are they?
考生回答處　_____

考古題應用　There is a fundamental difference between these two <u>security systems</u>.
這兩個保全系統基本上是不同的。

試練習題　Are these two systems identical?
考生回答處

141

furnished (adj) 附家具的

關 furnishings (n.) 裝修
　furnisher (n.) 家具商
　furniture (n) 家具
同 equipped, provided, decorated

一般正常速度 [ˋfɝnɪʃt]
ETS全真速度 [ˋfɝnɪʃt]

➡ 所有詞性的重音都在第一音節

考古題應用 We are renting a furnished apartment.
我們租的是有附家具的公寓。

口試練習題 Do we have to buy some furniture before moving in?

考生回答處 _____

F

Check List 3

到目前為止，字彙量又增加了不少，繼續學新單字之前，我們先來複習一下，看看是不是都記起來了！

- ☐ economical
- ☐ edit
- ☐ elaborate
- ☐ election
- ☐ elementary
- ☐ embargo

- ☐ embark
- ☐ embezzle
- ☐ emergency
- ☐ emphasize
- ☐ employ
- ☐ enclose

- ☐ encounter
- ☐ endorse
- ☐ endure
- ☐ enforcement
- ☐ engrave
- ☐ enlarge

- ☐ enroll
- ☐ ensemble
- ☐ ensure
- ☐ enter
- ☐ enterprise
- ☐ entertain

- ☐ entitle
- ☐ environment
- ☐ equal
- ☐ equip
- ☐ errand
- ☐ erratic

- ☐ escalate
- ☐ escort
- ☐ essential
- ☐ establishment
- ☐ estimate
- ☐ ethnic

- ☐ etiquette
- ☐ evacuate
- ☐ evaluate
- ☐ event
- ☐ evidence
- ☐ examine

- ☐ excel
- ☐ exclusive
- ☐ executive
- ☐ exemption
- ☐ exhibition
- ☐ exit

- ☐ expand
- ☐ expense
- ☐ expiration
- ☐ explicit
- ☐ exploit
- ☐ express

- [ ] extend
- [ ] fabulous
- [ ] facade
- [ ] facility
- [ ] fake
- [ ] familiar

- [ ] fare
- [ ] fasten
- [ ] feasibility
- [ ] feedback
- [ ] festival
- [ ] fiction

- [ ] figure
- [ ] file
- [ ] finalize
- [ ] financial
- [ ] forbid
- [ ] forecast

- [ ] foresee
- [ ] forfeit
- [ ] formula
- [ ] fortify
- [ ] fortune
- [ ] forum

- [ ] forward
- [ ] foundation
- [ ] fragile
- [ ] fraud
- [ ] freelance
- [ ] freeze

- [ ] freight
- [ ] fringe
- [ ] frustrate
- [ ] fulfill
- [ ] functional
- [ ] fundamental

- [ ] furnished

G

Ge-

gear (n.) 裝備

關 gear (v.t) 安裝
同 equipment, accessories, instrument, tools

一般正常速度 [gɪr]

ETS全真速度 [gɪr]

➜ 名詞與動詞的唸法相同

general (adj.) 一般的

同 common, widespread, universal

一般正常速度 [ˋdʒɛnərəl]

ETS全真速度 [ˋdʒɛnərəl]

generate (v.t) 衍生

關 generator (n.) 發電機
　generation (n.) 世代
同 cause, make, produce, create

一般正常速度 [ˋdʒɛnəˏret]

ETS全真速度 [ˋdʒɛnəˏre(t)]

➜ 動詞字尾 [t] 輕唸即可

Go-

govern (v.t) 決定

關 government (n.) 政府
　governor (n.) 主事者
同 control, handle, manage, rule

一般正常速度 [ˋgʌvən]

ETS全真速度 [ˋgʌvən]

➜ 所有詞性的重音都在第一音節

Gr-

grade (v.t) 評比

關 grade (n.) 分數；等級
同 classify, group, rank

一般正常速度 [gred]

ETS全真速度 [gre(d)]

➜ 1) 動詞與名詞的唸法相同
　 2) 字尾 [d] 輕唸即可

考古題應用　We'd better bring rain gear with us.
我們最好帶雨具出門。

口試練習題　There will be a thunderstorm this afternoon.
考生回答處　_____

考古題應用　Is the conference room for general use or only for
management?
這個會議室是供一般使用，還是只供主管使用呢？

G

口試練習題　Did you see that we've got a new conference room?
考生回答處　_____

考古題應用　The advisor said that the change in policy would generate
new problems.
顧問表示政策轉變會衍生出新問題。

口試練習題　What did the advisor say about our policy change?
考生回答處　_____

考古題應用　The price of bread is governed by the quality of <u>flour</u>.
麵包的價格是由使用的<u>麵粉</u>品質來決定的。

口試練習題　What will probably influence the price of bread?
考生回答處　_____

考古題應用　These fruits have been graded according to size and quality.
這些水果已依照大小跟品質而分級。

口試練習題　How do you grade these fruits?
考生回答處　_____

MP3 078

□□ gradual   □□ grant   □□ gratitude
□□ guarantee   □□ guidance

---

gradual (adj.) 漸進的

關 gradually (adv.) 漸漸地
同 continuous, progressive

一般正常速度 [ˋgrædʒʊəl]
ETS全真速度 [ˋgrædʒʊəl]

---

grant (v.t) 授與

關 grant (n.) 經費
同 agree, admit, allocate, give

一般正常速度 [grænt]
ETS全真速度 [græn(t)]

➡ 1) 動詞與名詞的唸法相同
  2) 字尾 [t] 輕唸即可

---

gratitude (n.) 感激

同 appreciation, thankfulness, gratefulness

一般正常速度 [ˋgrætəˌtjud]
ETS全真速度 [ˋgrædəˌɖju(d)]

➡ 兩個 [t] 均須變音成 [ɖ]

Gu-

guarantee (n.) 保證書

關 guarantee (v.t) 保證
同 warranty, guaranty, promise, assurance

一般正常速度 [ˌgærənˋti]
ETS全真速度 [ˌgærənˋti]

➡ 1) 名詞與動詞的唸法相同
  2) 重音落在最後一音節
  3) [t] 不可消音或變音

---

guidance (n.) 輔導

關 guide (v.t) 導引
  guide (n.) 導遊
同 advice, instruction, teaching, recommendation, help

一般正常速度 [ˋgaɪdns]
ETS全真速度 [ˋgaɪ__ns]

➡ [d] 在 [n] 前可消音

148

考古題應用 There's been a gradual increase in the number of our clients.
我們的客戶人數漸漸增多。

口試練習題 Do you think our marketing strategy works?

考生回答處 _____

考古題應用 We have been granted the permission to build the new city hall.
我們被授與許可建造新的市府大樓。

G

口試練習題 What kind of permission have you been granted?

考生回答處 _____

考古題應用 We will show them our gratitude by sending gift baskets.
我們會送他們禮盒來表達謝意。

口試練習題 How are we showing our appreciation to the staff?

考生回答處 _____

考古題應用 This digital camera has a one-year guarantee.
這台數位相機有一年保固期。

口試練習題 Does this camera come with a guarantee?

考生回答處 _____

考古題應用 Their agency provides people with employment guidance.
他們的機構提供人們就業輔導。

口試練習題 Does their agency find jobs for people?

考生回答處 _____

H
Ha-

hands-on (adj.) 實用的

同 useful, functional, practical

一般正常速度 [ˋhændzˋɑn]
ETS全真速度 [ˋhændzˋɑn]

➡ hands 與 on 之間要連音

harvest (v.i) 收割

關 harvest (n.) 收穫
同 collect, pick, reap

一般正常速度 [ˋhɑrvɪst]
ETS全真速度 [ˋhɑrvɪst]

➡ 動詞與名詞的唸法相同

hazard (n.) 危險

關 hazardous (adj.) 危險的
同 danger, risk, threat

一般正常速度 [ˋhæzɚd]
ETS全真速度 [ˋhæzɚ(d)]

➡ 1) 名詞與形容詞的重音均在第一音節
　 2) 名詞字尾 [d] 輕唸即可

Hi-

high-rise (n.) 摩天樓

關 high-rise (adj.) 高樓的
同 skyscraper, very tall building

一般正常速度 [ˋhaɪˋraɪz]
ETS全真速度 [ˋhaɪˋraɪz]

hire (v.t) 雇用

同 employ, appoint, commission

一般正常速度 [haɪr]
ETS全真速度 [haɪr]

考古題應用　This <u>computer workshop</u> will offer a lot of hands-on knowledge.
這個電腦研習會將提供許多實用的知識。

試練習題　How will this computer workshop help our employees?

考生回答處　＿＿＿＿＿＿＿＿＿＿＿＿＿＿＿＿＿＿＿＿＿＿＿＿＿

考古題應用　We <u>strongly recommend</u> that our farmers harvest by machine.
我們強烈建議農民用機器收割。

試練習題　Do you recommend harvesting by hand?

考生回答處　＿＿＿＿＿＿＿＿＿＿＿＿＿＿＿＿＿＿＿＿＿＿＿＿＿

H

考古題應用　Many reports suggest that smoking may be a health hazard.
許多報告表示抽菸可能會危害健康。

試練習題　I didn't know that you had quit smoking!

考生回答處　＿＿＿＿＿＿＿＿＿＿＿＿＿＿＿＿＿＿＿＿＿＿＿＿＿

考古題應用　The <u>law firm</u> is located on the twenty-third floor of the high-rise.
律師事務所位於摩天大樓的第 23 層樓。

試練習題　Do you know which floor of the building the firm is on?

考生回答處　＿＿＿＿＿＿＿＿＿＿＿＿＿＿＿＿＿＿＿＿＿＿＿＿＿

考古題應用　We've decided to hire a new <u>janitor</u> for the building.
我們已經決定要雇用新的大樓管理員了。

試練習題　Did you know that the old janitor is going to retire soon?

考生回答處　/dʒænɪtɚ/ ＿＿＿＿＿＿＿＿＿＿＿＿＿＿＿＿＿＿＿＿＿

Ho-

hospitality (n.) 殷勤款待

關 hospitable (adj.) 殷勤的
同 friendliness, warmth, welcome

一般正常速度 [ˌhɑspɪˋtælətɪ]
ETS全真速度 [ˌhɑsbɪˋtælədɪ]
➡ 1) 名詞重音在第三音節，形容詞重音則在第一音節 (hos-)
2) 名詞的 [p] 可變音為 [b]
3) 名詞中第二個 [t] 位於輕音節，要發 [d] 的音

host (v.t) 主持

關 host (n.) 主持人
hostess (n.) 女主人
同 introduce, present

一般正常速度 [host]
ETS全真速度 [hos(t)]
➡ 動詞字尾 [t] 輕唸即可

housing (n.) 住宅

關 house (v.t) 提供住宿
同 accommodation, houses, homes

一般正常速度 [ˋhauzɪŋ]
ETS全真速度 [ˋhauzɪŋ]
➡ s 要發成 [z] 的音

Hu-

humid (adj.) 潮濕的

關 humidity (n.) 濕度
同 wet, damp, moist

一般正常速度 [ˋhjumɪd]
ETS全真速度 [ˋhjumɪd]
➡ 名詞的 [d] 可發成 [d]

hurricane (n.) 颶風

同 storm, typhoon, tornado

一般正常速度 [ˋhɜɪˌken]
ETS全真速度 [ˋhɜɪˌken]
➡ a 發 [e] 的音

考古題應用　Visitors to Taiwan <u>are impressed with</u> the hospitality of the people.
來台觀光的旅客對人們的好客印象深刻。

試練習題　Why are visitors to Taiwan so impressed?

考生回答處　_____

考古題應用　Mr. Scott will be hosting a meeting for 200 people.
Scott 先生將主持一場兩百人的會議。

H

試練習題　What will Mr. Scott do this coming Friday?

考生回答處　_____

考古題應用　The <u>shortage</u> of low-cost housing in New York has become a problem.
紐約低價住宅的短缺已經造成了問題。

試練習題　Do you think the housing policies in New York worked?

考生回答處　_____

考古題應用　The <u>climate</u> in this area is too humid for our crops.
這個地區的氣候對我們的農作物來說太過潮濕。

試練習題　Do you think the climate here is ideal for our crops?

考生回答處　_____

考古題應用　The Weather Bureau has <u>issued</u> a hurricane watch.
氣象局已經發布了颶風警報。

試練習題　Why does the manager want to change our schedule?

考生回答處　_____

I

In-

inclement (adj.) 惡劣的

關 inclemency (n.) 嚴苛，惡劣
同 severe, harsh

一般正常速度 [ɪnˋklɛmənt]
ETS全真速度 [ɪnˋklɛmən(t)]

➡ 1) 形容詞與名詞的重音都在第二音節
2) 形容詞字尾 [t] 輕唸即可

insomnia (n.) 失眠

關 insomniac (n.) 失眠者
同 sleeplessness

一般正常速度 [ɪnˋsɑmnɪə]
ETS全真速度 [ɪnˋsɑmnɪə]

➡ insomniac 的 a 唸 [æ]

interpret (v.t) 翻譯

關 interpreter (n.) 翻譯人員
interpretation (n.) 翻譯
同 translate, explain, define

一般正常速度 [ɪnˋtɝprɪt]
ETS全真速度 [ɪnˋtɝprɪ(t)]

➡ 動詞字尾 [t] 輕唸即可

intervene (v.i) 介入

關 intervention (n.) 居中協調
同 involve, step in, mediate

一般正常速度 [ˌɪntəˋvin]
ETS全真速度 [ˌɪn__əˋvin]

➡ 1) 兩個詞性中的 [t] 均須消音
2) 動詞重音節母音為 [i]，名詞則是 [ɛ]

invalid (adj.) 無效的

關 invalidate (v.t) 作廢
同 disabled, not correct in law

一般正常速度 [ɪnˋvælɪd]
ETS全真速度 [ɪnˋvælɪ(d)]

➡ 形容詞字尾 [d] 輕唸即可

考古題應用 The <u>sailboat race</u> has been canceled because of inclement weather.
帆船賽因天候不佳已經取消了。

試練習題 Weren't you supposed to be joining the sailboat race now?

考生回答處 _____

考古題應用 Some insomnia pills have to be <u>prescribed</u> by a doctor.
有些安眠藥需要醫生<u>開處方</u>。

試練習題 Are all brands of insomnia pills available in the drugstore?

考生回答處 _____

考古題應用 You'd better find someone else to interpret it for us.
你最好請別人來翻譯。

試練習題 Can you read this manual written in German?

考生回答處 _____

考古題應用 Our government should intervene to <u>stabilize the market</u>.
我們的政府應該介入來<u>穩定市場</u>。

試練習題 Don't you think our market is negatively influenced by the imports?

考生回答處 _____

考古題應用 The guarantee has <u>expired</u>, so it's invalid.
保證書已經<u>過期</u>了，所以無效。

試練習題 Why isn't my car under guarantee?

考生回答處 _____

inventory (n.) 清單

同 list, catalogue, record

一般正常速度 [ˋɪnvən.torɪ]
ETS全真速度 [ˋɪnvəntrɪ]

➜ -tory 結尾可以唸成 [trɪ] 或 [drɪ]（如 factory）

invest (v.t) 投資

關 investment (n.) 投資
同 put in, devote, spend

一般正常速度 [ɪnˋvɛst]
ETS全真速度 [ɪnˋvɛs(t)]

➜ 1) 動詞與名詞的重音都在第二音節
2) 名詞的第一個 [t] 要消音
3) 字尾 [t] 均輕唸即可

investigate (v.t) 調查

關 investigation (n.) 調查行動
investigator (n.) 調查人員
同 inspect, examine, look into

一般正常速度 [ɪnˋvɛstə.get]
ETS全真速度 [ɪnˋvɛsdə.ge(t)]

➜ 1) 名詞 investigation 重音在第四音節 (-ga-)，其他兩字重音在第二音節
2) 所有詞性的第一個 [t] 都要唸成 [d]
3) investigator 的第二個 [t] 要唸成 [ɖ]

invoice (n.) 發票

一般正常速度 [ˋɪnvɔɪs]
ETS全真速度 [ˋɪnvɔɪ(s)]

➜ 字尾 [s] 輕唸即可

Ir-

irrelevant (adj.) 不相干的

關 irrelevance (n.) 不相干
irrelevantly (adv.) 不相干地
同 not connected, having nothing to do with

一般正常速度 [ɪˋrɛləvənt]
ETS全真速度 [ɪˋrɛləvən(t)]

➜ 1) 所有詞性的重音都在第二音節
2) 形容詞字尾 [t] 輕唸即可，副詞的 [t] 則一定要消音

考古題應用 You'd better take an inventory of all the stock.
你最好先盤點一下所有的存貨。

試練習題 What preparation is needed before we open the store?
考生回答處 _____

考古題應用 I'll probably invest the money in a computer company.
我可能會把錢投資到一家電腦公司。

I

試練習題 What will you do with your bonus?
考生回答處 _____

考古題應用 The police are still investigating the accident.
警方還在調查這起意外。

試練習題 Did they find out what caused the fire in the office complex?
考生回答處 _____

考古題應用 We forgot to issue an invoice for the entry fee.
報名費的部分我們忘了開發票。

試練習題 Why did so many customers file complaints?
考生回答處 _____

考古題應用 His nationality is irrelevant to his job performance.
他的國籍跟他的工作表現毫不相關。

試練習題 Do you consider Mr. Sato's nationality a problem?
考生回答處 _____

☐☐ isolate　　☐☐ issue　　☐☐ issue
☐☐ itinerary　☐☐ janitor

Is-

isolate (v.t) 隔離

圐 isolation (n.) 隔離
　　isolated (adj.) 被隔離的
回 disconnect, separate, set apart

一般正常速度 [`aɪsḷ.et]
ETS全真速度 [`aɪsḷ.e(t)]
➡ 動詞字尾 [t] 輕唸即可

issue (v.t) 發布

回 announce, release, distribute,
　　give out

一般正常速度 [`ɪʃju]
ETS全真速度 [`ɪʃju]
➡ 重音在第一音節

issue (n.) 焦點

回 point, argument, affair

一般正常速度 [`ɪʃju]
ETS全真速度 [`ɪʃju]
➡ 重音在第一音節

It-

itinerary (n.) 旅遊計畫

圐 itinerary (adj.) 路線的
回 route

一般正常速度 [aɪ`tɪnəˌrɛrɪ]
ETS全真速度 [aɪ`tɪnəˌrɛrɪ]
➡ 名詞與形容詞的唸法相同

J

Ja-

janitor (n.) 管理員

回 caretaker, custodian, concierge

一般正常速度 [`dʒænɪtə]
ETS全真速度 [`dʒænɪdə]
➡ [t] 須變音為 [d]

考古題應用　The sick workers will be isolated from other people.
生病的工人會被隔離起來。

試練習題　What will happen to those people who are infected?
考生回答處　_____

考古題應用　He issued a statement denying all <u>charges</u>.
他發表聲明否認所有的<u>指控</u>。

I

J

試練習題　What happened at the mayor's press conference?
考生回答處　_____

考古題應用　I think the meeting's key issue is <u>quality control</u>.
我想會議的重點是<u>品質控管</u>。

試練習題　Is the key issue for the meeting the need for promotion?
考生回答處　_____

考古題應用　She hasn't finished her travel itinerary.
她還沒規畫好旅遊路線。

試練習題　Will Denise visit Rome on her way to Modena?
考生回答處　_____

考古題應用　Maybe you should ask the janitor for help.
或許你應該請管理員幫忙。

試練習題　What should I do with the leaky faucet in my dorm?
考生回答處　_____

jaywalk (v.i) 非法橫越馬路

關 jaywalker (n.) 非法橫越馬路的人
同 walk across a street in a careless way

一般正常速度 [`dʒeˌwɔk]
ETS全真速度 [`dʒeˌwɔ(k)]

➡ 1) 動詞字尾 [k] 輕唸即可
   2) 名詞的 [k] 須變音為 [g]

judge (v.t) 判斷

關 judgment (n.) 判斷
同 consider, assess, examine, evaluate

一般正常速度 [dʒʌdʒ]
ETS全真速度 [dʒʌ(dʒ)]

➡ 字尾 [dʒ] 輕唸即可，請勿唸成橘子的「橘」（台式發音）

justify (v.t) 合理化

關 justifiable (adj.) 合理的
    justification (n.) 正當的理由
同 explain, excuse, support

一般正常速度 [`dʒʌstəˌfaɪ]
ETS全真速度 [`dʒʌsdəˌfaɪ]

➡ 所有詞性的第一個 [t] 都要唸成 [d]

know-how (n.) 技術

同 experience, knowledge, skill

一般正常速度 [`noˌhaʊ]
ETS全真速度 [`noˌhaʊ]

➡ 重音落在 know

label (v.t) 貼標籤

關 label (n.) 標籤
同 mark, brand, tag

一般正常速度 [`lebl]
ETS全真速度 [`lebl]

➡ 1) 動詞與名詞的唸法相同
   2) 字尾發 [l] 而非 [ɔ]

| 考古題應用 | He's received a <u>ticket</u> for jaywalking.
他因爲非法橫越馬路收到了一張罰單。 |

| 試練習題 | Why is Carson so upset? |
| 考生回答處 | |

| 考古題應用 | It'll take a few more months to judge the effect of the change.
還要再幾個月才能判斷這項改變的成效。 |

| 試練習題 | The policy change is helpful for our business, isn't it? |
| 考生回答處 | |

J

K

L

| 考古題應用 | He's <u>filed a report</u> justifying the cost.
他已經交了一份報告來解釋他的開銷。 |

| 試練習題 | Mr. Liu shouldn't have spent so much on the project, right? |
| 考生回答處 | |

| 考古題應用 | Its government is buying equipment and know-how <u>from abroad</u>.
它的政府一直向國外購買設備跟技術。 |

| 試練習題 | Can you explain why this country has a strong economy? |
| 考生回答處 | |

| 考古題應用 | He needs to label all the bottles before tomorrow.
他得在明天之前把所有的瓶子貼上標籤。 |

| 試練習題 | Why is Mike working overtime? |
| 考生回答處 | |

lack (v.t) 缺乏

關 lack (n.) 缺乏
同 miss, require, need, be short of

一般正常速度 [læk]
ETS全真速度 [læ(k)]

➡ 1) 動詞與名詞的唸法相同
2) 字尾 [k] 輕唸即可

landscape (n.) 景色

關 landscaper (n.) 庭園設計師
同 view, scene, outlook

一般正常速度 [ˋlænd.skep]
ETS全真速度 [ˋlæn___.sge(p)]

➡ 1) 兩個名詞的 [d] 均須消音
2) [k] 均須變音為 [g]
3) 字尾 [p] 輕唸即可

last (v.i) 持續

關 last (adj.) 最後的
同 continue, carry on, keep on, remain

一般正常速度 [læst]
ETS全真速度 [læs(t)]

➡ 1) 動詞與形容詞的唸法相同
2) 字尾 [t] 輕唸即可

launch (v.t) 發起

關 launch (n.) 推出，發行
同 open, start, initiate, begin, embark

一般正常速度 [lɔntʃ]
ETS全真速度 [lɔn(tʃ)]

➡ 1) 動詞與名詞的唸法相同
2) 請注意母音唸 [ɔ]（lunch 的母音則是 [ʌ]）

 Le-

lease (v.t) 租借

關 lease (n.) 租約
同 loan, rent, let

一般正常速度 [lis]
ETS全真速度 [lis]

➡ 動詞與名詞的唸法相同

考古題應用 She won the contest even though she lacked confidence.
雖然缺乏信心，她還是贏得了比賽。

試練習題 Did Brooke win the public-speaking contest?
考生回答處 _____

考古題應用 A landscape designer should work on the extension.
庭園設計師應處理擴建的部分。

試練習題 Who will take care of the extension of our garden, a landscape designer or an interior designer?
考生回答處 _____

考古題應用 Their second branch lasted for less than a year.
他們的第二家分店維持不到一年。

試練習題 How long did their second branch store last?
考生回答處 _____

考古題應用 We are planning to launch a campaign to raise funds.
我們打算發起一項活動來募款。

試練習題 Is there anything we can do for the earthquake victims?
考生回答處 _____

考古題應用 We've decided to lease it for the first two years.
我們決定前兩年先用租的。

試練習題 Did you decide to lease or buy the property?
考生回答處 _____

L

legal (adj.) 合法的
同 right, lawful, valid, legitimate

一般正常速度 [ˋligl]
ETS全真速度 [ˋligl]

level (v.t) 弄平
關 level (n.) 水平
同 make flat, even off, smooth

一般正常速度 [ˋlɛvl]
ETS全真速度 [ˋlɛvl]
➡ 1) 動詞與名詞的唸法相同
   2) 字尾 [l] 請勿唸成 [ɔ]

Li-

liabilities (n.pl.) 債務
關 liable (adj.) 有…的傾向
同 debt, debit, obligation

一般正常速度 [ˌlaɪəˋbɪlətɪz]
ETS全真速度 [ˌlaɪəˋbɪlədɪz]
➡ 1) 名詞的 [t] 須唸成 [d]
   2) 形容詞字尾 [l] 請勿唸成 [ɔ]

license (n.) 執照
關 license (v.t) 核發執照
同 permission, permit, right, certificate

一般正常速度 [ˋlaɪsn̩s]
ETS全真速度 [ˋlaɪsn̩s]
➡ 名詞與動詞的唸法相同

lifestyle (n.) 生活方式

一般正常速度 [ˋlaɪfˌstaɪl]
ETS全真速度 [ˋlaɪfˌsdaɪl]
➡ [t] 須變音為 [d]

[考古題應用] What our company did is perfectly legal.
我們公司所做的一切都是完全合法的。

[口試練習題] Aren't you afraid that the government may take legal action against you?
[考生回答處] _____

[考古題應用] The bulldozer outside is leveling the ground.
外頭的壓路機正在整地。

[口試練習題] Where is the noise coming from?
[考生回答處] _____

L

[考古題應用] If a person's liabilities exceed his assets, he may go bankrupt.
如果一個人的負債超過資產，他可能會破產。

[口試練習題] What would happen if one's liabilities exceed his assets?
[考生回答處] _____

[考古題應用] Our company will have to apply for a license from the FDA first.
我們公司得先向食品藥物管理局申請執照。

[口試練習題] Why hasn't your new drug hit the market?
[考生回答處] _____

[考古題應用] His workshop provided many tips for a healthy lifestyle.
他的研習會提供許多健康生活方式的小祕訣。

[口試練習題] Why did so many people attend Mr. Dawson's workshop?
[考生回答處] _____

165

limit (n.) 限制

關 limit (v.t) 限制
同 end, extend, breaking point

一般正常速度 [ˋlɪmɪt]
ETS全真速度 [ˋlɪmɪ(t)]

➜ 1) 名詞與動詞的唸法相同
　 2) 字尾 [t] 輕唸即可

liquidate (v.t) 清算財產

關 liquidation (n.) 清償
同 clear, pay, pay off, settle

一般正常速度 [ˋlɪkwɪˌdet]
ETS全真速度 [ˋlɪgwɪˌđe(t)]

➜ 1) [k] 須唸成 [g]
　 2) 動詞的 [d] 要唸成 [đ]
　 3) 動詞字尾 [t] 輕唸即可

lounge (n.) 休息室

關 lounge (v.i) 懶洋洋地躺臥著

一般正常速度 [laʊndʒ]
ETS全真速度 [laʊndʒ]

➜ 1) 名詞與動詞的唸法相同
　 2) 母音要唸成 [aʊ] 而不是 [ɑ]（台式
　　 發音）

low (adj.) 低落的

一般正常速度 [lo]
ETS全真速度 [lo]

loyal (adj.) 忠心的

關 loyalty (n.) 忠心
同 faithful, dutiful, true

一般正常速度 [ˋlɔɪəl]
ETS全真速度 [ˋlɔɪəl]

➜ 名詞字尾 [t] 須變音為 [đ]

考古題應用 I will tell you as much as I can, but there's a limit to what I remember.
我會盡可能跟你說，不過我記得的有限。

口試練習題 Could you tell me what you saw in the file?

考生回答處 _____

考古題應用 They plan to liquidate all their assets before Christmas.
他們打算在耶誕節之前清算所有的資產。

口試練習題 Do you know what will become of them after the bankruptcy?

考生回答處 _____

L

考古題應用 We've just had some drinks in the VIP lounge.
我們剛剛才在貴賓休息室喝過東西了。

口試練習題 Would you like anything to drink?

考生回答處 _____

考古題應用 This hotel is fully occupied even in its low season.
這家飯店即使在淡季都還是客滿的。

口試練習題 Is this a very popular hotel in Portugal?

考生回答處 _____

考古題應用 He's remained loyal even after he was demoted.
即使遭到降職，他還是忠心不二。

口試練習題 How did Mr. Carson react to his demotion?

考生回答處 _____

Lu-

luxury (n.) 奢侈品

關 luxurious (adj.) 奢華的
同 extravagance, nonessentials

一般正常速度 [`lʌkʃərɪ]
ETS全真速度 [`lʌkʃərɪ]

➤ 名詞的重音在第一音節，形容詞的重音則在第二音節 (-ur-)

M
Ma-

magnificent (adj.) 豪華的

關 magnificence (n.) 豪華
同 brilliant, elegant, grand, luxurious

一般正常速度 [mæg`nɪfəsənt]
ETS全真速度 [mæ(g)`nɪfəsənt]

➤ 1) 形容詞與名詞的重音都在第二音節
2) 兩個詞性的 [g] 均輕唸即可

maintenance (n.) 維修

關 maintain (v.t) 維修
同 care, keeping, repair

一般正常速度 [`mentənəns]
ETS全真速度 [`men__nəns]

➤ 1) 名詞的重音在第一音節，動詞的重音在第二音節 (-tain)
2) [t] 停一拍即可，無須發音

manage (v.i) 設法完成

關 management (n.) 管理
manageable (adj.) 可控制的
同 succeed, accomplish, deal with

一般正常速度 [`mænɪdʒ]
ETS全真速度 [`mænɪdʒ]

➤ 所有詞性的重音都在第一音節

mandatory (adj.) 強制性的

關 mandate (v.t) 命令
同 required, obligatory, compulsory

一般正常速度 [`mændə,torɪ]
ETS全真速度 [`mændə,torɪ]

➤ 1) 形容詞的重音在第一音節，動詞的重音在第二音節
2) 形容詞的 [d] 須變音為 [ð]

考古題應用 | I can't afford luxury food on my pay.
我的薪水買不起奢侈食品。

試練習題 | Have you ever tried this deluxe caviar?
考生回答處

考古題應用 | The ceremony will be held in a magnificent ball room.
典禮將在一個豪華的宴會廳舉行。

試練習題 | Where will the award ceremony be held?
考生回答處

L

M

考古題應用 | The old carpet was replaced during the monthly maintenance.
舊的地毯在每月例行維修時被換掉了。

試練習題 | Did you see we just got a new carpet in the lobby?
考生回答處

考古題應用 | He managed to finish the Christmas issue before its deadline.
他在截止日期前設法完成了耶誕節特刊。

試練習題 | Did Keith finish the Christmas issue in time?
考生回答處

考古題應用 | He has reached the mandatory retirement age of 65.
他已經到達 65 歲的強制退休年齡。

試練習題 | Did you know that Mr. Yoshida is retiring soon?
考生回答處

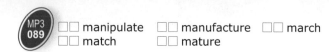
manipulate (v.t) 操弄

關 manipulation (n.) 操弄
manipulative (adj.) 好操弄別人的
同 control, influence, handle

一般正常速度 [məˋnɪpjə‚let]

ETS全真速度 [məˋnɪbjə‚let]

➡ 1) 動詞與形容詞的重音都在第二音節，名詞則在第四音節
2) 所有詞性的 [p] 均須變音為 [b]
3) 形容詞的 [t] 須變音為 [d]

manufacture (v.t) 製造

關 manufacture (n.) 製造
manufacturer (n.) 製造商
同 produce, make, assemble, build, construct

一般正常速度 [‚mænjəˋfæktʃə]

ETS全真速度 [‚mænjəˋfæ__tʃə]

➡ 1) 所有詞性的重音都在第三音節
2) [k] 均停一拍即可，無須發音

march (v.i) 前進

關 march (n.) 前進，行進
同 move, proceed, walk, parade

一般正常速度 [martʃ]

ETS全真速度 [mar(tʃ)]

➡ 1) 動詞與名詞的唸法相同
2) 字尾 [tʃ] 輕唸即可

match (v.t) 匹敵

關 match (n.) 比賽
同 compete, compare, equal

一般正常速度 [mætʃ]

ETS全真速度 [mæ(tʃ)]

➡ 1) 動詞與名詞的唸法相同
2) 字尾 [tʃ] 輕唸即可

mature (v.i) 到期

關 maturity (n.) 成熟
mature (adj.) 成熟的
同 become chargeable／collectable／payable／receivable

一般正常速度 [məˋtʃur]

ETS全真速度 [məˋtʃur]

➡ 所有詞性的重音均在第二音節

考古題應用 It is wrong to manipulate the election.
操弄選舉是不對的。

口試練習題 Jake has been lobbying the members of the board, hasn't he?
考生回答處 _____

考古題應用 Our factories don't manufacture plastic bags.
我們工廠沒有製造塑膠袋。

口試練習題 Are you the manufacturer of plastic bags?
考生回答處 _____

考古題應用 Protesters are marching along the road.
抗議者沿著馬路前進。

M

口試練習題 What's causing the traffic jam?
考生回答處 _____

考古題應用 Its magnificent ocean view can't be matched.
它壯麗的海景是無與倫比的。

口試練習題 Why does everyone highly recommend the St. Monarch Beach Resort?
考生回答處 _____

考古題應用 They will pay me when my savings plan matures.
定存到期時，他們就會付錢給我。

口試練習題 When will the bank pay you your bonus?
考生回答處 _____

maximum (adj.) 最大的

關 maximize (v.t) 擴大至最大值
同 top, utmost, peak

一般正常速度 [`mæksəməm]
ETS全真速度 [`mæksəməm]

➜ 形容詞與動詞的重音都在第一音節

measure (n.) 措施

關 measure (v.t) 測量
measurement (n.) 尺寸
同 action, procedure, proceeding,
step

一般正常速度 [`mɛʒə]
ETS全真速度 [`mɛʒə]

➜ 所有詞性的重音都在第一音節

merchandise (n.) 商品

關 merchandise (v.t) 販賣
merchant (n.) 商人
同 goods, product, stock

一般正常速度 [`mɝtʃən‚daɪz]
ETS全真速度 [`mɝtʃən‚daɪz]

➜ 所有詞性的重音都在第一音節

merger (n.) 合併

關 merge (v.t) 合併
同 combination, incorporation,
union

一般正常速度 [`mɝdʒə]
ETS全真速度 [`mɝdʒə]

➜ 名詞的重音在第一音節

merit (n.) 績效

關 merit (v.t) 值得
同 excellence, value, goodness

一般正常速度 [`mɛrɪt]
ETS全真速度 [`mɛrɪ(t)]

➜ 1) 名詞與動詞的唸法相同
   2) 字尾 [t] 輕唸即可

考古題應用 The maximum amount of money I can spend is 600 dollars.
我最多可以花六百塊美金。

試練習題 What's the maximum amount of money you can spend on the business trip?

考生回答處 _____

考古題應用 The minister was forced to take emergency measures against the protest.
部長被迫採取緊急措施以應付這場抗議活動。

試練習題 Why did the minister decide to shut down the power plant?

考生回答處 _____

考古題應用 They mostly provide merchandise to customers over the age of sixty-five.
他們大多提供商品給年過 65 歲的顧客。

試練習題 Who does Everyoung Pharmaceuticals sell their merchandise to?

考生回答處 _____

M

考古題應用 We'll be announcing the merger between two European airline companies.
我們要宣布兩家歐洲航空公司的合併。

試練習題 Why will there be a press conference in the hotel at 2 o'clock?

考生回答處 _____

考古題應用 The board gave him a merit raise and promoted him.
董事會給了他績效加薪並且讓他升官。

試練習題 Did you hear that Mike finally got his promotion?

考生回答處 _____

metropolitan

(adj.) 大都會的

關 metropolis (n.) 大都會
同 of a capital, of a city, urban, municipal

一般正常速度 [ˌmɛtrəˋpɑlətn̩]
ETS全真速度 [ˌmɛtrəˋpɑlətn̩]

➡ 形容詞的重音在第三音節，名詞的重音在第二音節 (-trop-)

Mi-

milestone (n.) 里程碑

關 mile (n.) 英里
同 landmark, milepost, breakthrough

一般正常速度 [ˋmaɪlˌston]
ETS全真速度 [ˋmaɪlˌsdon]

➡ 1) milestone 的 [t] 須變音為 [d]
2) mile 不可唸成 [maɪ]（台式發音），字尾 [l] 請務必唸出來

minority (n.) 少數

關 minor (adj.) 次要的；輕微的
同 less than half

一般正常速度 [maɪˋnɔrətɪ]
ETS全真速度 [maɪˋnɔrədɪ]

➡ 1) 名詞的重音在第二音節，形容詞的重音在第一音節
2) 名詞的 [t] 須變音為 [d]

miscellaneous

(adj.) 各式各樣的

同 various, varied, mixed, diversified

一般正常速度 [ˌmɪsɪˋlenjəs]
ETS全真速度 [ˌmɪsɪˋlenjəs]

misplace (v.t) 錯放

關 misplacement (n.) 誤放
同 put in the wrong place, place unwisely

一般正常速度 [mɪsˋples]
ETS全真速度 [mɪsˋples]

➡ 動詞與名詞的重音都在第二音節

考古題應用 The New York metropolitan area <u>is packed with</u> tourists.
整個紐約大都會區都塞滿了觀光客。

口試練習題 What is New York like during the New Year holidays?

考生回答處 _____

考古題應用 The <u>debut</u> of the cordless earphones is a milestone in our company's development history.
無線耳機的推出是我們公司研發史上的里程碑。

口試練習題 Why are we throwing a big party for the debut of the cordless earphones?

考生回答處 _____

考古題應用 Workers from Argentina are in the minority at our factory.
阿根廷來的工人在我們工廠占少數。

口試練習題 Are workers from Argentina in the majority at your factory?

考生回答處 _____

M

考古題應用 There are miscellaneous goods in the stockroom.
儲藏室裡有各式各樣的雜貨。

口試練習題 What's in our stockroom?

考生回答處 _____

考古題應用 A creative employee like him shouldn't have been misplaced in that job.
像他那麼有創意的員工不該被錯放在那個職位。

口試練習題 Was it right to have Mr. Anderson accept the job offer?

考生回答處 _____

Mo-

mobilize (v.t) 動員

關 mobilization (n.) 動員
同 prepare, activate, call up

一般正常速度 [ˋmobḷ͵aɪz]
ETS全真速度 [ˋmobḷ͵aɪz]

➡ 動詞的重音在第一音節，名詞的重音在第四音節 (-za-)

model (n.) 機種

關 model (v.t) 做模型
同 design, form, pattern

一般正常速度 [ˋmadḷ]
ETS全真速度 [ˋmadḷ]

➡ 1) 名詞與動詞的唸法相同
2) [d] 須變音為 [d]
3) 字尾 [l] 不能唸 [ɔ]（台式發音）

moderate (adj.) 適當的

關 moderate (v.t) 使…緩和
moderately (adv.) 適度地
同 controlled, mild, gentle, reasonable

一般正常速度 [ˋmadərɪt]
ETS全真速度 [ˋmadərɪ(t)]

➡ 1) 形容詞與動詞的字尾 [t] 輕唸即可，副詞的 [t] 必須消音
2) [d] 須變音為 [d]

modernize (v.t) 使現代化

關 modernization (n.) 現代化
同 remake, remodel, update, renew

一般正常速度 [ˋmadən͵aɪz]
ETS全真速度 [ˋmadən͵aɪz]

➡ 動詞的重音落在第一音節，名詞的重音則在第四音節 (-za-)

modest (adj.) 少量的

關 modesty (n.) 謙虛
同 moderate, fair, limited

一般正常速度 [ˋmadɪst]
ETS全真速度 [ˋmadɪs(t)]

➡ 1) 兩個詞性的重音都在第一音節
2) 形容詞字尾的 [t] 輕唸即可，名詞的 [t] 須變音為 [d]

考古題應用 The government has mobilized all its <u>resources</u> to support its latest policy.
政府動員了所有資源來支持它的最新政策。

口試練習題 Has the government made any effort to promote its latest policy?

考生回答處 _____

考古題應用 Our latest model will be introduced in a technology magazine.
我們的最新機種會在雜誌裡介紹。

口試練習題 Will there be any special ads for our latest model?

考生回答處 _____

考古題應用 Asking for a <u>small wage increase</u> is a moderate demand.
爭取小幅度調高工資是合理的要求。

口試練習題 What do you think of the union leader's demand?

考生回答處 _____

M

考古題應用 They modernized the old apartment by <u>installing a security system</u>.
他們安裝保全系統讓舊公寓變現代化。

口試練習題 What did they do to modernize the old apartment?

考生回答處 _____

考古題應用 There's only a modest rise in fuel prices.
油價只有輕微的調漲。

口試練習題 Has there been a sharp rise in fuel prices?

考生回答處 _____

modify (v.t) 調整
關 modification (n.) 調整
同 revise, change, adjust, alter, remodel

一般正常速度 [`mɑdəˌfaɪ]
ETS全真速度 [`mɑɖəˌfaɪ]
➤ 兩個詞性的 [d] 均須變音為 [ɖ]

monopoly (n.) 壟斷事業
關 monopolize (v.t) 壟斷
同 control, possession

一般正常速度 [mə`nɑpḷɪ]
ETS全真速度 [mə`nɑbḷɪ]
➤ 1) 名詞與動詞的重音都在第二音節
　 2) [p] 均須變音為 [b]

moral (adj.) 道德的
關 morals (n.) 操守

一般正常速度 [`mɔrəl]
ETS全真速度 [`mɔrəl]
➤ 字尾的 [l] 請勿唸成 [ɔ]（台式發音）

morale (n.) 士氣
同 spirit

一般正常速度 [mɔ`ræl]
ETS全真速度 [mɔ`ræl]
➤ 1) 重音落在第二音節
　 2) 字尾 [l] 請勿唸成 [ɔ]（台式發音）

mortgage (n.) 房貸
關 mortgage (v.t) 抵押
同 an agreement for a loan

一般正常速度 [`mɔrgɪdʒ]
ETS全真速度 [`mɔrgɪdʒ]
➤ 1) 名詞與動詞的唸法相同
　 2) t 不發音

考古題應用 We have modified the settings to improve <u>power consumption</u>.
我們已調整過設定來改善耗電量的問題。

□試練習題 What have you done to improve power consumption?

考生回答處 _____

考古題應用 Our government wouldn't approve of such a monopoly.
我們的政府不會批准這樣的壟斷事業。

□試練習題 Do you think we should buy up our main competitors?

考生回答處 _____

考古題應用 He still has a moral obligation for the loss.
對於損失的部分他仍有道德上的責任。

M

□試練習題 Mr. Woods doesn't have to pay for the loss, does he?

考生回答處 _____

考古題應用 The <u>R&D department</u> is suffering from low morale.
研發部門目前遭遇到士氣低落的問題。

□試練習題 What happened to the R&D department?

考生回答處 _____

考古題應用 Mortgage rates are <u>awfully low</u> right now.
房貸利率現在<u>超級低</u>。

□試練習題 Why are you considering buying your own place?

考生回答處 _____

Mu-

motivated (adj.) 積極的

關 motivate (v.t) 刺激
motivation (n.) 動機
同 active, spontaneous, high-spirited

一般正常速度 [ˋmotɪˏvetɪd]
ETS全真速度 [ˋmođɪˏveđɪ(d)]

➡ 1) motivated 的兩個 [t] 均須變音為 [đ]
2) 形容詞字尾 [d] 輕唸即可

multiply (v.i) 增加

關 multiple (adj.) 多重的
同 increase, build up, expand, extend

一般正常速度 [ˋmʌltəˏplaɪ]
ETS全真速度 [ˋmʌlđəˏplaɪ]

➡ 1) 動詞與形容詞的重音都在第一音節
2) 兩個詞性的 [t] 都要變音為 [đ]

mushroom (v.i) 激增

關 mushroom (n.) 蘑菇；急速成長的東西
同 increase, grow rapidly, spread

一般正常速度 [ˋmʌʃrum]
ETS全真速度 [ˋmʌʃrum]

➡ 1) 動詞與名詞的唸法相同
2) 重音節母音 u 要唸 [ʌ] 而不是 [ɑ]
（請仔細聽 MP3 發音）

mutual (adj.) 互相的

關 mutually (adv.) 互相地
同 shared, common, joint

一般正常速度 [ˋmjutʃʊəl]
ETS全真速度 [ˋmjutʃʊəl]

➡ 1) 兩個詞性的重音都在第一音節
2) 字中的 -tual 都要唸成 [-tʃʊəl] 而不是 [-tʃɔl]（台式發音）

考古題應用　Joseph has remained very motivated since day one.
Joseph 從第一天開始就表現的非常積極。

試練習題　Joseph really deserved this promotion, didn't he?

考生回答處　_____

考古題應用　Our spending on machinery has multiplied over the last ten years.
過去十年我們花在機器上的費用已經倍增。

試練習題　Do you think we need to put more money toward buying new machinery?

考生回答處　_____

考古題應用　Many food stands have mushroomed in this area.
此區的小吃攤數量激增。

試練習題　Have there been any changes in this area since the circus arrived?

考生回答處　_____

M

考古題應用　We've worked out an agreement for our mutual benefit.
我們已經完成一項對雙方都有利的協議。

試練習題　How was your meeting with the Central Bank of Ireland?

考生回答處　_____

Checl List 4

到目前為止，字彙量又增加了不少，繼續學新單字之前，我們先來複習一下，看看是不是都記起來了！

☐ gear	☐ humid	☐ judge
☐ general	☐ hurricane	☐ justify
☐ generate	☐ inclement	☐ know-how
☐ govern	☐ insomnia	☐ label
☐ grade	☐ interpret	☐ lack
☐ gradual	☐ intervene	☐ landscape
☐ grant	☐ invalid	☐ last
☐ gratitude	☐ inventory	☐ launch
☐ guarantee	☐ invest	☐ lease
☐ guidance	☐ investigate	☐ legal
☐ hands-on	☐ invoice	☐ level
☐ harvest	☐ irrelevant	☐ liabilities
☐ hazard	☐ isolate	☐ license
☐ high-rise	☐ issue	☐ lifestyle
☐ hire	☐ issue	☐ limit
☐ hospitality	☐ itinerary	☐ liquidate
☐ host	☐ janitor	☐ lounge
☐ housing	☐ jaywalk	☐ low

- [ ] loyal
- [ ] luxury
- [ ] magnificent
- [ ] maintenance
- [ ] manage
- [ ] mandatory

- [ ] manipulate
- [ ] manufacture
- [ ] march
- [ ] match
- [ ] mature
- [ ] maximum

- [ ] measure
- [ ] merchandise
- [ ] merger
- [ ] merit
- [ ] metropolitan
- [ ] milestone

- [ ] minority
- [ ] miscellaneous
- [ ] misplace
- [ ] mobilize
- [ ] model
- [ ] moderate

- [ ] modernize
- [ ] modest
- [ ] modify
- [ ] monopoly
- [ ] moral
- [ ] morale

- [ ] mortgage
- [ ] motivated
- [ ] multiply
- [ ] mushroom
- [ ] mutual

N
Na-

nationality (n.) 國籍

關 nation (n.) 國家
national (adj.) 國家的
同 nation, race, ethnic group

一般正常速度 [ˌnæʃəˈnælətɪ]
ETS全真速度 [ˌnæʃəˈnælədɪ]

➡ nationality 的 [t] 須變音為 [d]

---

native (adj.) 本地的

關 native (n.) 本地人
同 local, home-made, domestic

一般正常速度 [ˈnetɪv]
ETS全真速度 [ˈnedɪv]

➡ 1) 兩個詞性的唸法相同
2) [t] 須變音為 [d]

Ne-

neat (adj.) 整齊的

關 neatly (adv.) 整齊地
同 orderly, tidy

一般正常速度 [nit]
ETS全真速度 [ni(t)]

➡ 形容詞字尾 [t] 輕唸即可，副詞的 [t]
則必須消音

---

necessity (n.) 必需品

關 necessary (adj.) 必需的
同 essentials, needs, fundamentals,
requirements

一般正常速度 [nəˈsɛsətɪ]
ETS全真速度 [nəˈsɛsədɪ]

➡ 名詞字尾 [t] 須變音為 [d]

---

negatively (adv.) 負面地

關 negative (adj.) 負面的
同 unpleasantly, depressingly

一般正常速度 [ˈnɛɡətɪvlɪ]
ETS全真速度 [ˈnɛɡədɪvlɪ]

➡ 兩個詞性的 [t] 都要變音為 [d]

考古題應用 Experts of different nationalities are invited to this convention.
不同國籍的專家受邀參加這場會議。

試練習題 Are the experts at this convention only from the United States?

考生回答處 _____

考古題應用 The commission decided to <u>launch a campaign</u> to promote native fruits.
委員會決定<u>發起活動</u>以促銷國產水果。

試練習題 Why did the commission decide to launch a campaign?

考生回答處 _____

考古題應用 We've hired someone to keep the office neat and tidy.
我們有僱人維持辦公室的整潔。

試練習題 This office is very clean, isn't it?

考生回答處 _____

N

考古題應用 Martha always spends her money on necessities instead of <u>luxuries</u>.
Martha 一向把錢花在買必需品而非<u>奢侈品</u>上。

試練習題 Why has Martha saved so much money?

考生回答處 _____

考古題應用 Our project won't be negatively affected by his <u>resignation</u>.
我們的企畫案不會受到他<u>辭職</u>的負面影響。

試練習題 Will Mr. Kondo's resignation affect our project in a bad way?

考生回答處 _____

No-

neutral (adj.) 中立的

關 neutralize (v.t) 使中立化；中和
同 indifferent, undecided, impartial

一般正常速度 [`njutrəl]
ETS全真速度 [`njutrəl]

➔ 形容詞與動詞的重音都在第一音節

normal (adj.) 正常的

關 normalize (v.t) 正常化
同 usual, standard, reasonable

一般正常速度 [`nɔrml̩]
ETS全真速度 [`nɔrml̩]

➔ 形容詞字尾 [l] 請勿唸成 [ɔ]（台式發音）

notable (adj.) 顯著的

關 note (v.t) 注意
同 noticeable, distinguished, noteworthy

一般正常速度 [`notəbl̩]
ETS全真速度 [`noɖəbl̩]

➔ 形容詞的 [t] 須變音為 [ɖ]

notify (v.t) 通知

關 notification (n.) 通知
同 inform, tell, declare

一般正常速度 [`notəˌfaɪ]
ETS全真速度 [`noɖəˌfaɪ]

➔ 動詞與名詞的第一個 [t] 均須變音為 [ɖ]

novelty (n.) 新奇的產品

關 novel (adj.) 新奇的
同 innovation, originality

一般正常速度 [`nɑvl̩tɪ]
ETS全真速度 [`nɑvl̩ɖɪ]

➔ 1) 名詞與形容詞的重音都在第一音節
　2) 名詞字尾 [t] 須變音為 [ɖ]

考古題應用 His article makes a neutral analysis of the issue.
他的文章對這個議題採中立的分析。

試練習題 Does the author of this article take a side on this particular issue?

考生回答處 _____

考古題應用 Ferry services are now back to normal.
渡輪服務目前已經恢復正常。

試練習題 Are the ferry workers still out on strike?

考生回答處 _____

考古題應用 The corrected version has notable improvement.
訂正後的版本有顯著的改善。

N

試練習題 How is the revised financial report?

考生回答處 _____

考古題應用 Please notify the entire staff that the mayor will be here in thirty minutes.
請通知全體員工市長即將在 30 分鐘之內抵達。

試練習題 What do you want me to tell everybody, Ms. Takashi?

考生回答處 _____

考古題應用 Novelties like iPods are popular among young customers.
像 iPod 之類的新鮮貨很受年輕顧客的喜愛。

試練習題 What kind of products are popular among young customers?

考生回答處 _____

Nu-

nullify (v.t) 廢除

關 nullification (n.) 廢除
同 cancel, abolish

一般正常速度 [ˋnʌləˌfaɪ]
ETS全真速度 [ˋnʌləˌfaɪ]

➡ 重音節母音唸 [ʌ] 而非 [ɑ]（台式發音）

O
Ob-

obedience (n.) 服從

關 obedient (adj.) 順從的
　　obediently (adv.) 順從地
同 agreement, conformity, respect

一般正常速度 [əˋbidjəns]
ETS全真速度 [əˋbidjən(s)]

➡ 1) 三個詞性的重音都在第二音節
　　2) [d] 均須變音為 [ɖ]
　　3) 名詞字尾 [s] 輕唸即可

object (v.i) 反對

關 objection (n.) 反對
同 argue against, oppose, protest

一般正常速度 [əbˋdʒɛkt]
ETS全真速度 [ə(b)ˋdʒɛ(kt)]

➡ 1) 動詞與名詞的 [b] 均輕唸即可
　　2) 動詞字尾的 [kt] 輕唸即可

objective (adj.) 客觀的

關 objectivity (n.) 客觀性
同 fair, just, impartial

一般正常速度 [əbˋdʒɛktɪv]
ETS全真速度 [ə(b)ˋdʒɛ(k)dɪv]

➡ 1) 形容詞與名詞的 [b] 均輕唸即可
　　2) 形容詞的 [t] 須唸成 [d]
　　3) [k] 輕唸即可
　　4) 名詞字尾 [t] 須變音成 [ɖ]

obligation (n.) 職責

關 obligatory (adj.) 職責所在的
同 duty, requirement, responsibility

一般正常速度 [ˌɑbləˋgeʃən]
ETS全真速度 [ˌɑbləˋgeʃən]

➡ 名詞的重音在第三音節，形容詞的重音在第二音節

考古題應用 Your vote was nullified without your signature.
你的選票因為沒有簽名而作廢了。

口試練習題 Why did they say my vote didn't count?
考生回答處 _____

考古題應用 The new director asked us to show absolute obedience to his orders.
新任主管要我們對他的命令絕對服從。

口試練習題 What did the new director ask the entire staff to do?
考生回答處 _____

考古題應用 They strongly object to being demoted after the merger.
他們強烈反對在合併案之後被降職。

口試練習題 Why are the managers protesting?
考生回答處 _____

考古題應用 Mr. Morton can provide us with an objective analysis.
Morton 先生能提供給我們客觀的分析。

口試練習題 Why are we hiring Mr. Morton as our adviser?
考生回答處 _____

考古題應用 It's a citizen's legal obligation to pay taxes annually.
每年繳稅是公民的法律責任。

口試練習題 Why do I need to provide the tax office with earnings details?

考生回答處 _____

obliged (adj.) 一定得做的

關 oblige (v.t) 非得要
同 necessary, forced, required, obligatory

一般正常速度 [ə`blaɪdʒd]
ETS全真速度 [ə`blaɪdʒd]

➡ 1) 形容詞與動詞的重音都在第二音節
　 2) 字尾唸 [dʒ]，請勿唸成「橘」（請仔細聽 MP3 發音）

observation (n.) 觀察

關 observe (v.t) 觀察
　 observant (adj.) 觀察敏銳的
同 inspection, examination, watching, notice

一般正常速度 [ˌɑbzə`veʃən]
ETS全真速度 [ˌɑ(b)zə`veʃən]

➡ 1) 所有詞性的 [b] 均輕唸即可
　 2) 形容詞與動詞的重音都在第二音節 (-serv-)

obstacle (n.) 障礙

同 difficulty, block, obstruction

一般正常速度 [`ɑbstəkḷ]
ETS全真速度 [`ɑ(b)sdəgḷ]

➡ 1) 重音在第一音節
　 2) [b] 輕唸即可
　 3) [t] 須變音為 [d]
　 4) 字尾 [k] 可變音為 [g]

obstruct (v.t) 阻礙

關 obstruction (n.) 阻礙
同 block, interrupt, prevent

一般正常速度 [əb`strʌkt]
ETS全真速度 [ə(b)`sdrʌ(kt)]

➡ 1) 動詞與名詞的重音都在第二音節
　 2) [b] 均輕唸即可
　 3) 第一個 [t] 都要變音成 [d]
　 4) 動詞字尾 [kt] 輕唸即可

obtain (v.t) 取得

關 obtainable (adj.) 可以取得的
同 get, gain, acquire

一般正常速度 [əb`ten]
ETS全真速度 [ə(b)`ten]

➡ 1) 兩個詞性的重音均在第二音節
　 2) [b] 均輕唸即可
　 3) [t] 均不能消音

考古題應用 We are obliged to ship orders before the deadline.
我們一定得在期限之前出貨。

試練習題 Why have you been working overtime so much recently?

考生回答處 _____

考古題應用 The wounded are in the hospital under careful observation.
傷患目前住院仔細觀察中。

試練習題 What happened to the wounded after the car crash?

考生回答處 _____

考古題應用 Low morale remains an obstacle to our on-the-job effectiveness.
低迷的士氣一直是我們工作效率的障礙。

試練習題 Why can't our IT department be more effective?

考生回答處 _____

考古題應用 A white sedan obstructed the traffic in the intersection.
一部白色轎車阻礙了十字路口的交通。

試練習題 What is causing the traffic jam?

考生回答處 _____

考古題應用 More information about the workshop can be obtained from our website.
更多有關研習會的資料可以在我們的網站上取得。

試練習題 Where do I get more information about the computer workshop?

考生回答處 _____

obvious (adj.) 明顯的

關 obviously (adv.) 明顯地
同 clear, distinct, evident

一般正常速度 [`ɑbvɪəs]
ETS全真速度 [`ɑ(b)vɪə(s)]

➡ 1) [b] 均輕唸即可
　 2) 形容詞字尾 [s] 輕唸即可

occasion (n.) 場合

關 occasional (adj.) 偶而的
　 occasionally (adv.) 偶而地
同 moment, time

一般正常速度 [ə`keʒən]
ETS全真速度 [ə`keʒən]

➡ 所有詞性的重音都在第二音節

occupational (adj.) 職業的

關 occupation (n.) 職業
同 vocational, professional,
　 job-related

一般正常速度 [ˌɑkjə`peʃənl]
ETS全真速度 [ˌɑkjə`beʃənl]

➡ 1) 形容詞與名詞的重音均在第三音節
　 2) [p] 可變音為 [b]
　 3) 字尾 [l] 請勿唸成 [ɔ]（台式發音）

occupy (v.t) 占據

關 occupant (n.) 占有者；居住者
同 own, possess, live in

一般正常速度 [`ɑkjəˌpaɪ]
ETS全真速度 [`ɑkjəˌbaɪ]

➡ 1) 動詞與名詞的重音都在第一音節
　 2) [p] 可變音為 [b]

occur (v.i) 發生

關 occurrence (n.) 發生
同 happen, take place, come about

一般正常速度 [ə`kɝ]
ETS全真速度 [ə`kɝ]

➡ 動詞與名詞的重音都在第二音節

考古題應用 We've found some obvious mistakes in his report.
我們在他的報告裡發現一些明顯的錯誤。

口試練習題 Why did you ask Oscar to revise his quarterly report?
考生回答處 _____

考古題應用 We only need to wear ties on special occasions.
我們只有在特殊場合才需要繫領帶。

口試練習題 Is there a dress code in your company?
考生回答處 _____

考古題應用 Injuries are occupational hazards for professional athletes.
受傷是專業運動員的職業風險。

口試練習題 What are the occupational hazards for professional athletes?
考生回答處 _____

考古題應用 There are fifty food stands occupying half of the plaza.
有 50 個小吃攤占據一半的廣場。

口試練習題 How many food stands are there in the plaza?
考生回答處 _____

考古題應用 The accident occurred when they took a wrong turn.
當他們轉錯彎時意外就發生了。

口試練習題 How did the accident happen?
考生回答處 _____

Of-

offer (n.) 條件

關 offer (v.t) 提供
同 bid, proposal, proposition, suggestion

一般正常速度 [ˋɔfɚ]
ETS全真速度 [ˋɔfɚ]

➡ 名詞與動詞的唸法相同

official (adj.) 正式的

關 official (n.) 官員
同 formal, authoritative, certified, endorsed

一般正常速度 [əˋfɪʃəl]
ETS全真速度 [əˋfɪʃəl]

➡ 1) 形容詞與名詞的唸法相同
　 2) 字尾 [l] 請勿唸成 [ɔ]（台式發音）

Om-

omit (v.t) 省略

關 omission (n.) 省略
同 skip, leave out, exclude, drop

一般正常速度 [oˋmɪt]
ETS全真速度 [oˋmɪ(t)]

➡ 1) 動詞與名詞的重音都在第二音節
　 2) 動詞字尾 [t] 輕唸即可

Op-

operation (n.) 業務

關 operate (v.i) 運作
　 operator (n.) 接線生
　 operational (adj.) 操作上的
同 business, enterprise, deal

一般正常速度 [͵ɑpəˋreʃən]
ETS全真速度 [͵ɑbəˋreʃən]

➡ 所有詞性的 [p] 均要變音為 [b]

oppose (v.t) 反對

關 opposition (n.) 反對
　 opponent (n.) 反對者
　 opposite (adj.) 相反的
同 block, obstruct, prevent

一般正常速度 [əˋpoz]
ETS全真速度 [əˋpoz]

➡ 動詞與名詞的重音都在第二音節，形容詞重音在第一音節

考古題應用	He made us a very generous offer.
	他開給我們非常優厚的條件。

口試練習題	Why did you sign the contract with Mr. Rivera?
考生回答處	

考古題應用	We're still waiting for official permission from the building commission.
	我們還在等建管局的正式核准。

口試練習題	Why are we waiting to begin our construction plan?
考生回答處	

考古題應用	You'd better omit all the negative comments on this issue.
	你最好忽略這個議題的所有負面評論。

口試練習題	Do you have any suggestions for my report?
考生回答處	

O

考古題應用	Our domestic operations include clothing and accessories.
	我們國內的業務包括服飾與配件。

口試練習題	Is clothing your only domestic operation?
考生回答處	

考古題應用	The new power plant is strongly opposed by many people.
	新發電廠遭受到很多人的強烈反對。

口試練習題	Is everything going well with the new power plant?
考生回答處	

option (n.) 選擇

關 optional (adj.) 可隨意選擇的
同 choice, alternative, preference

一般正常速度 [ˋɑpʃən]
ETS全真速度 [ˋɑ(p)ʃən]

➡ 1) 名詞與形容詞的重音都在第一音節
2) [p] 均輕唸即可

Or-

ordinary (adj.) 一般的

關 ordinarily (adv.) 普通地
同 common, everyday, regular, usual

一般正常速度 [ˋɔrdənˌɛrɪ]
ETS全真速度 [ˋɔr_nˌɛrɪ]

➡ 兩個詞性的 [d] 均停一拍即可，無須發音

organize (v.t) 籌畫

關 organization (n.) 組織
organized (adj.) 有組織的
同 arrange, form, construct, establish, put together

一般正常速度 [ˋɔrgənˌaɪz]
ETS全真速度 [ˋɔrgənˌaɪz]

➡ 動詞與形容詞的重音都在第一音節

orient (v.t) 導向

關 orientation (n.) 新進員工訓練
同 direct, adjust, familiarize

一般正常速度 [ˋorɪˌɛnt]
ETS全真速度 [ˋorɪˌɛn(t)]

➡ 1) 動詞的重音在第一音節，名詞的重音在第四音節 (-ta-)
2) 動詞字尾 [t] 輕唸即可

ornament (n.) 裝飾品

關 ornament (v.t) 裝飾
同 decoration, adornment

一般正常速度 [ˋɔrnəmənt]
ETS全真速度 [ˋɔrnəmən(t)]

➡ 1) 名詞與動詞的唸法相同
2) 字尾 [t] 輕唸即可

考古題應用 Workers are given the option of going to work by company <u>shuttle</u>.
員工可以選擇搭乘公司的接駁車上班。

口試練習題 What transportation options do your workers have?

考生回答處 _____

考古題應用 Our product contains 40% less <u>fat</u> than ordinary cookies.
我們產品比一般的餅乾少了 40% 的脂肪。

口試練習題 Why are your cookies healthier than ordinary cookies?

考生回答處 _____

考古題應用 We've asked Jane to organize the <u>wedding banquet</u>.
我們已經請 Jane 籌辦喜宴。

口試練習題 Who will be organizing the wedding banquet?

考生回答處 _____

考古題應用 We provide our employees with technically-oriented learning programs.
我們提供員工技術導向的學習課程。

口試練習題 Are there any on-the-job training opportunities available for your employees?

考生回答處 _____

考古題應用 Maybe we should hang some ornaments on the walls.
或許我們應該在牆上加一些裝飾品。

口試練習題 Don't you find the walls in our lobby too plain?

考生回答處 _____

MP3 102

☐☐ outline ☐☐ outlook ☐☐ overall
☐☐ overcast ☐☐ overcome

Ou-

outline (v.t) 勾勒出

關 outline (n.) 大綱
同 depict, form, shape

一般正常速度 [`aʊtˌlaɪn]
ETS全真速度 [`aʊ__ˌlaɪn]

➡ 1) 動詞與名詞的唸法相同
2) [t] 停一拍即可，無須發音

outlook (n.) 前景

關 outlook (v.t) 外觀勝過
同 prospect, probability, future

一般正常速度 [`aʊtˌlʊk]
ETS全真速度 [`aʊ(t)ˌlʊ(k)]

➡ 1) 名詞與動詞的唸法相同
2) [t] 與 [k] 均輕唸即可

Ov-

overall (adj.) 整體的

關 overalls (n.) 連身工作服
同 general, complete, total

一般正常速度 [`ovɚˌɔl]
ETS全真速度 [`ovɚˌɔl]

➡ 形容詞與名詞的重音都在第一音節

overcast (adj.) 陰暗的

關 overcast (v.t) 變陰暗
overcast (n.) 陰暗
同 cloudy, darkened

一般正常速度 [`ovɚˌkæst]
ETS全真速度 [`ovɚˌkæs(t)]

➡ 字尾 [t] 輕唸即可

overcome (v.t) 克服

同 beat, conquer, defeat

一般正常速度 [ˌovɚ`kʌm]
ETS全真速度 [ˌovɚ`kʌm]

考古題應用　The interior designer outlined her plan to <u>remodel</u> the lobby.
室內設計師勾勒出她<u>整修大廳</u>的計畫。

試練習題　What did the interior designer say in the meeting?
考生回答處　_____

考古題應用　The report indicates that our outlook is bright.
報告指出我們的前景看好。

試練習題　What does the latest report say about your company?
考生回答處　_____

考古題應用　The board is still <u>evaluating</u> her overall performance.
董事會還在<u>評估</u>她的整體表現。

試練習題　Will Ms. Fang be appointed as the new VP?
考生回答處　_____

O

考古題應用　The Meteorologist predicts overcast skies but no rain tomorrow.
氣象專家預測明天陰天但不會下雨。

試練習題　Will it rain tomorrow?
考生回答處　_____

考古題應用　The R&D department had to overcome many difficulties.
研發部門得克服很多困難。

試練習題　Why did it take so long for the R&D department to develop the new model?

考生回答處　_____

overdue (adj.) 逾期的

同 late, behind schedule, long delayed

一般正常速度 [`ovə`dju]
ETS全真速度 [`ovə`dju]

overlook (v.t) 忽視

同 ignore, leave out, neglect, omit, skip

一般正常速度 [ˌovə`luk]
ETS全真速度 [ˌovə`lu(k)]
➡ 字尾 [k] 輕唸即可

overseas (adv.) 在海外

關 oversea (adj.) 海外
同 abroad, away

一般正常速度 [`ovə`siz]
ETS全真速度 [`ovə`siz]

oversee (v.t) 監督

關 overseer (n.) 監督者
同 supervise, watch

一般正常速度 [`ovə`si]
ETS全真速度 [`ovə`si]

overview (n.) 概述

同 description, summary, account

一般正常速度 [`ovəˌvju]
ETS全真速度 [`ovəˌvju]

考古題應用 He has to return a book that is two weeks overdue.
他得去還一本已經逾期兩週的書。

口試練習題 Why does Jason have to drop by the library on his way home?

考生回答處 _____

考古題應用 We'd better make sure we didn't overlook any typos.
我們最好確定沒有遺漏任何拼字錯誤。

口試練習題 Do you think we can send this report to the printer now?

考生回答處 _____

考古題應用 She just returned from a trip overseas.
她剛從海外旅行回來。

口試練習題 Why does Sarah need more time to prepare for the negotiation?

考生回答處 _____

O

考古題應用 We've asked Mr. Rodriguez to oversee construction.
我們請 Rodriguez 先生去監督施工。

口試練習題 Who is the overseer of the construction site?

考生回答處 _____

考古題應用 The host is giving us an overview of next presentation.
主持人正在為我們做下一場報告的概述。

口試練習題 What is the host's introduction mainly about?

考生回答處 _____

overwhelming

(adj.) 壓倒性的

關 overwhelm (v.t) 壓倒，征服
同 overpowering, irresistible, uncontrollable

一般正常速度 [`ovə`hwɛlmɪŋ]
ETS全真速度 [`ovə`hwɛlmɪŋ]

 Ow-

owe (v.t) 虧欠

關 owing (adj.) 未付清的
同 be in debt, be indebted, be under an obligation to

一般正常速度 [o]
ETS全真速度 [o]

➡ 兩個詞性的第一個母音都唸 [o] 而不是 [ɔ]（台式發音）

own (v.t) 擁有

關 owner (n.) 老闆
ownership (n.) 所有權
own (adj.) 自己的
同 keep, have, hold, possess

一般正常速度 [on]
ETS全真速度 [on]

➡ 母音都唸 [o] 而不是 [ɔ]（台式發音）

P

Pa-

pack (v.i) 打包

關 unpack (v.t) 打開（包裹）
package (n.) 包裹
同 load, package

一般正常速度 [pæk]
ETS全真速度 [pæ(k)]

➡ 1) 動詞字尾 [k] 輕唸即可
2) 名詞的 [k] 須唸成 [g]

paddle (v.i) 划槳

關 paddle (n.) 槳
同 row, propel

一般正常速度 [`pædl]
ETS全真速度 [`pædl]

➡ 1) 動詞與名詞的唸法相同
2) [d] 可變音為 [ɾ]
3) 字尾 [l] 請勿唸成 [ɔ]（台式發音）

考古題應用 She won the election by an overwhelming majority.
她以壓倒性的多數贏得了選舉。

口試練習題 How did Ms. Richardson win the election?
考生回答處 _____

考古題應用 Their company owes money to more than twenty banks.
他們公司虧欠超過 20 家銀行的錢。

口試練習題 Is their company in debt?
考生回答處 _____

考古題應用 Jake's father owns the shipping company.
Jake 的父親擁有這家貨運公司。

口試練習題 How did Jake get promoted so easily in the shipping
company?
考生回答處 _____

考古題應用 He wants you to pack up for the business trip right away.
他要你馬上打包東西準備出差。

口試練習題 What did the project manager ask me to do?
考生回答處 _____

考古題應用 They are about to paddle in a canoe.
他們要去划獨木舟。

口試練習題 Why are those American tourists wearing life jackets?
考生回答處 _____

O
P

pageant (n.) 比賽
同 contest, competition

一般正常速度 [`pædʒənt]
ETS全真速度 [`pædʒən(t)]
➡ 字尾 [t] 輕唸即可

pamphlet (n.) 小冊子
同 brochure, booklet, leaflet

一般正常速度 [`pæmflɪt]
ETS全真速度 [`pæmflɪ(t)]
➡ 字尾 [t] 輕唸即可

panel (n.) 面板
關 panel (v.t) 鑲嵌
同 board, surface

一般正常速度 [`pænḷ]
ETS全真速度 [`pænḷ]
➡ 1) 名詞與動詞的唸法相同
　 2) 字尾 [l] 請勿唸成 [ɔ]（台式發音）

parade (n.) 遊行
關 parade (v.i) 遊行
同 march, pageant

一般正常速度 [pə`red]
ETS全真速度 [pə`re(d)]
➡ 1) 名詞與動詞的唸法相同
　 2) 字尾 [d] 輕唸即可

parallel (n.) 可匹敵的事物
關 parallel (v.t) 與之匹敵
同 equal, match

一般正常速度 [`pærəˌlɛl]
ETS全真速度 [`pærəˌlɛl]
➡ 1) 名詞與動詞的唸法相同
　 2) 字尾 [l] 請勿唸成 [ɔ]（台式發音）

考古題應用 They asked the <u>contestants</u> to wear swimsuits in the pageant.
他們要求參賽者在選美比賽中穿著泳裝。

試練習題 What did they ask the contestants to do in the beauty pageant?

考生回答處 _____

考古題應用 They are giving out pamphlets about global warming.
他們在發送有關全球暖化的小冊子。

試練習題 What are the environmentalists doing in the park?

考生回答處 _____

考古題應用 The technicians are still working on the control panel.
技術人員還在操作控制面板。

試練習題 Why are all the lights on in the lab?

考生回答處 _____

P

考古題應用 Many people have gathered to watch the Rose Parade in L.A.
許多人聚集在洛杉磯觀賞玫瑰花車遊行。

試練習題 Why are so many tourists going to L.A. at this time of the year?

考生回答處 _____

考古題應用 His <u>popularity</u> has no parallel in this business.
他的人氣在這行是無人能比的。

試練習題 Mr. Hunter is very popular in this business, isn't he?

考生回答處 _____

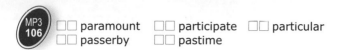
paramount (adj.) 首要的

同 chief, first, main, primary, superior

一般正常速度 [ˋpærəˌmaʊnt]
ETS全真速度 [ˋpærəˌmaʊnt]

➡ ou 的發音是 [aʊ] 而不是 [ɑ]（請仔細聽 MP3 示範）

participate (v.i) 參與

關 participation (n.) 參與
participant (n.) 參加者
同 join, attend, take part in

一般正常速度 [parˋtɪsəˌpet]
ETS全真速度 [parˋtɪsəˌbe(t)]

➡ 1) participate 與 participant 裡的第二個 [p] 均須唸成 [b]
2) 動詞字尾 [t] 輕唸即可

particular (adj.) 特別的

關 particularity (n.) 特殊性
同 special, peculiar, distinct

一般正常速度 [pəˋtɪkjələ]
ETS全真速度 [pəˋtɪgjələ]

➡ 1) 形容詞與名詞的 [k] 都要唸成 [g]
2) 名詞字尾 [t] 須變音為 [đ]

passerby (n.) 路人

關 pass (v.t) 經過
passage (n.) 通道
同 pedestrian, walker

一般正常速度 [ˋpæsəˌbaɪ]
ETS全真速度 [ˋpæsəˌbaɪ]

➡ 所有詞性的重音都在第一音節

pastime (n.) 娛樂

同 entertainment, recreation

一般正常速度 [ˋpæsˌtaɪm]
ETS全真速度 [ˋpæsˌtaɪm]

考古題應用 The <u>welfare of workers</u> should be paramount.
員工的福利應該是最重要的。

試練習題 Do you think sales figures should be paramount?
考生回答處 _____

考古題應用 They asked me to participate in an emergency meeting.
他們要求我參加一場緊急會議。

試練習題 Why are you staying after work today?
考生回答處 _____

考古題應用 There is nothing in this file of particular importance.
這份檔案裡沒有什麼特別重要的地方。

試練習題 Is this file strictly confidential?
考生回答處 _____

P

考古題應用 Many passersby were there when the accident happened.
意外發生時有很多路人在場。

試練習題 Did anyone see the car accident?
考生回答處 _____

考古題應用 Singing is his most favorite pastime.
唱歌是他最喜歡的娛樂。

試練習題 What does Jeffery like to do in his spare time?
考生回答處 _____

patience (n.) 耐性

關 patient (n.) 病人
patient (adj.) 有耐心的
同 tolerance, calmness, composure

一般正常速度 [ˋpeʃəns]
ETS全真速度 [ˋpeʃən(s)]

➡ 1) 所有詞性的第一個 t 都要唸成 [ʃ]
2) patience 的字尾 [s] 及 patient 的字尾 [t] 均輕唸即可

pay (v.i) 付錢

關 pay (n.) 薪水
payment (n.) 付款
payable (adj.) 需付費的
同 give, offer, liquidate

一般正常速度 [pe]
ETS全真速度 [pe]

Pe-

peak (n.) 最高點

關 peak (v.i) 攀升到最高點
peak (adj.) 最高點的
同 point, top, tip, apex, summit

一般正常速度 [pik]
ETS全真速度 [pik]

➡ 所有詞性的唸法相同

peculiar (adj.) 奇怪的

關 peculiarity (n.) 特殊性
peculiarly (adv.) 特別地
同 strange, uncommon, unusual

一般正常速度 [prˋkjuljɚ]
ETS全真速度 [prˋkjuljɚ]

➡ 1) 形容詞與副詞的重音都在第二音節，名詞的重音則在第四音節 (-ar-)
2) 名詞的 [t] 須變音為 [ɖ]

penalty (n.) 罰款

關 penalize (v.t) 處罰
同 punishment, fine

一般正常速度 [ˋpɛnltɪ]
ETS全真速度 [ˋpɛnɖɪ]

➡ 1) 名詞與動詞的重音都在第一音節
2) 名詞的 [t] 須變音為 [ɖ]

考古題應用 Our director has no patience with lazy workers.
我們主管對於懶惰的員工沒有耐性。

試練習題 Who does your director have no patience with?
考生回答處 _____

考古題應用 We have to pay in advance.
我們得預先付款。

試練習題 Do we pay for tickets on the day of the show?
考生回答處 _____

考古題應用 Demand for oil is at its peak in March.
石油的市場需求在三月份達到最高點。

試練習題 In which month is demand for oil at its peak?
考生回答處 _____

P

考古題應用 It really is peculiar that she wanted us to keep it as a secret.
她要我們保守這個祕密真的很奇怪。

試練習題 Why doesn't Teresa want us to discuss the deal?
考生回答處 _____

考古題應用 He had to pay a penalty for jaywalking.
他因為非法橫越馬路得付罰款。

試練習題 Do you know why Jerry looked so upset this morning?
考生回答處 _____

pending (adj.) 還沒解決的

同 undecided, undetermined, awaiting, up in the air

一般正常速度 [`pɛndɪŋ]

ETS全真速度 [`pɛnđɪŋ]

➡ [d] 須變音為 [đ]

penetrate (v.t) 滲透

關 penetration (n.) 滲透，穿透
同 enter, get in, pierce, go through

一般正常速度 [`pɛnə͵tret]

ETS全真速度 [`pɛnə͵tre(t)]

➡ 動詞字尾 [t] 輕唸即可

perceive (v.t) 察覺

關 perception (n.) 觀感
perceptible (adj.) 能觀察得到的
perceptive (adj.) 觀察力強的
同 see, notice, observe, recognize

一般正常速度 [pə`siv]

ETS全真速度 [pə`si(v)]

➡ 1) 所有詞性的重音都在第二音節
2) 動詞字尾 [v] 輕唸即可

performance (n.) 表演

關 perform (v.t) 表演
同 show, presentation, production, play

一般正常速度 [pə`fɔrməns]

ETS全真速度 [pə`fɔrmən(s)]

➡ 1) 名詞與動詞的重音都在第二音節
2) 名詞字尾 [s] 輕唸即可

period (n.) 期間

關 periodic (adj.) 週期性的
同 time, stage, term

一般正常速度 [`pɪrɪəd]

ETS全真速度 [`pɪrɪə(d)]

➡ 1) 名詞的重音在第一音節，形容詞的
重音在第三音節 (-od-)
2) 名詞字尾的 [d] 輕唸即可
3) 形容詞的 [d] 須變音為 [đ]

考古題應用 He has to take care of some pending issues.
他得去處理一些還沒解決的事情。

口試練習題 Why is Mark staying in Australia longer than expected?
考生回答處 _____

考古題應用 Our latest product successfully penetrated the European market.
我們最新的產品成功地打進了歐洲市場。

口試練習題 Why has your sales team's morale been so high lately?
考生回答處 _____

考古題應用 They failed to perceive where the problem was.
他們沒能看出問題出在哪裡。

口試練習題 Why didn't they come up with a solution to the problem?
考生回答處 _____

P

考古題應用 She is giving a performance at the national concert hall tonight.
她今晚會在國家音樂廳演出。

口試練習題 Where is the soloist from the Icelandic Orchestra giving a performance?

考生回答處 _____

考古題應用 There were long periods when our sales figures were down.
我們有很長一段時間的銷售量很差。

口試練習題 Has your company always done so well?
考生回答處 _____

permanent (adj.) 永久的

關 permanence (n.) 耐久度
permanently (adv.) 永久不變地
同 unchanging, constant, enduring,
invariable, lasting

一般正常速度 [ˋpɝmənənt]
ETS全真速度 [ˋpɝmənən(t)]

→ 1) 所有詞性的重音都在第一音節
2) 形容詞字尾的 [t] 輕唸即可；副詞
的 [t] 必須消音

permission (n.) 許可

關 permit (v.t) 允許
permissible (adj.) 可允許的
同 admission, agreement, approval,
allowance, authorization,
consent

一般正常速度 [pəˋmɪʃən]
ETS全真速度 [pəˋmɪʃən]

→ 1) 所有詞性的重音都在第二音節
2) 動詞字尾的 [t] 輕唸即可

personalize (v.i) 個人化

關 personality (n.) 個性
personal (adj.) 個人的
personally (adv.) 親自
同 make personal

一般正常速度 [ˋpɝsṇəˌlaɪz]
ETS全真速度 [ˋpɝsṇəˌlaɪ(z)]

→ 1) 動詞字尾 [z] 輕唸即可
2) 名詞字尾 [t] 須變音為 [đ]

personnel (n.) 工作人員

關 person (n.) 個人
personal (adj.) 個人的
personally (adv.) 親自
同 staff, employees, members,
workers, workforce

一般正常速度 [ˌpɝsṇˋɛl]
ETS全真速度 [ˌpɝsṇˋɛl]

→ 1) 只有 personnel 的重音在最後一音
節，其他詞性的重音都在第一音節
2) 字尾 [l] 請勿唸成 [ɔ]（台式發音）

perspective (n.) 觀點

同 viewpoint, attitude, overview

一般正常速度 [pəˋspɛktɪv]
ETS全真速度 [pəˋsbɛ__dɪv]

→ 1) 第二個 [p] 須變音為 [b]
2) [k] 停一拍即可，無須發音
3) [t] 須變音為 [d]

考古題應用 Just <u>fill in</u> your name, title, and permanent address.
只要<u>填寫</u>你的姓名、職稱以及永久住址。

口試練習題 What personal information is needed for this registration form?

考生回答處 _____

考古題應用 We can't <u>cut the budget</u> without the supervisor's permission.
沒有主管的許可我們不能<u>砍預算</u>。

口試練習題 Is it permissible for you to cut the budget?

考生回答處 _____

考古題應用 <u>Gift certificates</u> are personalized with the <u>recipient</u>'s name.
<u>禮券</u>寫上<u>受贈者</u>的名字使它個人化。

口試練習題 Can people other than the recipient use our gift certificates?

考生回答處 _____

P

考古題應用 Our main problem is a shortage in experienced personnel.
我們主要的問題在於缺乏有經驗的工作人員。

口試練習題 What is your sales team's main problem?

考生回答處 _____

考古題應用 His reports present two totally different perspectives on this issue.
他的報告對這個議題呈現出兩種截然不同的觀點。

口試練習題 Why are you so impressed with Jake's reports?

考生回答處 _____

persuade (v.t) 說服
關 persuasion (n.) 說服
persuasive (adj.) 有說服力的
同 cause to believe, convince, influence, talk into

一般正常速度 [pəˋswed]
ETS全真速度 [pəˋswe(d)]
➔ 動詞字尾 [d] 輕唸即可

petition (v.t) 請願
關 petition (n.) 請願
同 ask, beg, call upon, appeal

一般正常速度 [pəˋtɪʃən]
ETS全真速度 [pəˋtɪʃən]
➔ 動詞與名詞的唸法相同

Ph-

phase (n.) 階段
關 phase (v.t) 分段實行
同 stage, time, period

一般正常速度 [fez]
ETS全真速度 [fe(z)]
➔ 字尾 [z] 請勿唸成 [s]

phenomenon (n.) 現象
關 phenomenal (adj.) 卓越的
同 happening, occurrence, incident, fact, event

一般正常速度 [fəˋnamə͵nan]
ETS全真速度 [fəˋnamə͵nan]
➔ 名詞與形容詞的重音都在第二音節

physical (n.) 體檢
關 physician (n.) 內科醫生
physical (adj.) 身體的
同 medical examination

一般正常速度 [ˋfɪzɪkl]
ETS全真速度 [ˋfɪzɪgl]
➔ 1) physical 的 [k] 須變音為 [g]
2) physician 重音在第二音節

214

考古題應用　We'll make every effort to persuade her to <u>renew the contract</u>.
我們會盡一切努力來說服她續約。

口試練習題　Do you think Mrs. Hernandez will renew our contract?

考生回答處　_____

考古題應用　The residents are petitioning the government to repair the <u>riverbank</u>.
居民向政府請願修復河堤。

口試練習題　Why are the local residents petitioning the government?

考生回答處　_____

考古題應用　Our <u>end of season sales</u> have entered their final phase.
我們的季末出清已進入最後階段。

口試練習題　How much longer will the end of season sales last?

考生回答處　_____

P

考古題應用　The slump in our stock prices is not just a recent phenomenon.
我們股價下跌不是最近才發生的事。

口試練習題　Why has there been a sudden slump in our stock prices?

考生回答處　_____

考古題應用　He insists that everyone being <u>transferred to</u> Africa has a complete physical.
他堅持每個調到非洲的人都要做徹底的健康檢查。

口試練習題　What has the CEO asked us to do before transferring to Africa?

考生回答處　_____

Pi-

pile (v.t) 堆起來

關 pile (n.) 一堆

同 stack, load up, collect, accumulate, gather, store

一般正常速度 [paɪl]

ETS全真速度 [paɪl]

➡ 1) 動詞與名詞的唸法相同
2) 字尾 [l] 請勿唸成 [ɔ]（台式發音）

pinnacle (n.) 頂點

同 top, summit, peak, apex, apogee

一般正常速度 [`pɪnəkḷ]

ETS全真速度 [`pɪnəgḷ]

➡ 字尾 [k] 須唸成 [g]

pioneer (n.) 領先者

關 pioneer (v.t) 開拓

同 leader, founder, developer

一般正常速度 [ˌpaɪə`nɪr]

ETS全真速度 [ˌpaɪə`nɪr]

➡ 名詞與動詞的唸法相同

Pi-

place (v.t) 放置

關 place (n.) 地方
placement (n.) 安置

同 put, settle, set, install, lay, deposit, locate

一般正常速度 [ples]

ETS全真速度 [ple(s)]

➡ place 當動、名詞時唸法相同

plain (adj.) 清楚的

關 plain (n.) 平原
plain (adv.) 明白地

同 obvious, apparent, understandable, evident

一般正常速度 [plen]

ETS全真速度 [plen]

➡ 所有詞性的唸法相同

考古題應用　All the <u>bowls</u> are piled up on the shelf.
所有的<u>碗</u>都被堆放在架子上。

口試練習題　Where do you keep the bowls?
考生回答處　_____

考古題應用　The <u>violinist</u> reached his pinnacle of fame after his European tour.
那名<u>小提琴家</u>的名聲在歐洲之旅後達到顛峰。

口試練習題　How did the violinist become so well-known worldwide?
考生回答處　_____

考古題應用　Our company is a pioneer in LCD <u>development</u>.
我們公司是 LCD <u>研發</u>的領先者。

口試練習題　Why is everyone looking forward to seeing your latest model of LCDs?
考生回答處　_____

P

考古題應用　Please place the pears carefully in the <u>crates</u>.
請小心地將梨子放在<u>木箱</u>裡。

口試練習題　Where do I put those imported pears?
考生回答處　_____

考古題應用　It was plain to everyone that she had <u>tried her best</u>.
每個人都很清楚她已經<u>盡全力</u>了。

口試練習題　Why didn't the manager blame Ms. Roxwell for the loss of the contract?
考生回答處　_____

platform (n.) 講臺

回 stage, podium

一般正常速度 [ˋplæt͵fɔrm]
ETS全真速度 [ˋplæ__͵fɔrm]

➡ [t] 停一拍即可，無須發音

pledge (v.t) 保證

關 pledge (n.) 誓約；擔保品
回 promise, give one's word, vow, give one's oath

一般正常速度 [plɛdʒ]
ETS全真速度 [plɛ(dʒ)]

➡ 1) 動詞與名詞的唸法相同
   2) 字尾 [dʒ] 輕唸即可

plummet (v.i) 下滑

回 drop, down, fall, decrease, descend

一般正常速度 [ˋplʌmɪt]
ETS全真速度 [ˋplʌmɪ(t)]

➡ 字尾 [t] 輕唸即可

plunge (v.i) 暴跌

關 plunge (n.) 暴跌
回 descend, drop, fall, decrease, slump

一般正常速度 [plʌndʒ]
ETS全真速度 [plʌndʒ]

➡ 動詞與名詞的唸法相同

plus (n.) 加分

關 plus (adj.) 有益的
回 advantage, gain, benefit, extra

一般正常速度 [plʌs]
ETS全真速度 [plʌs]

➡ 名詞與形容詞的唸法相同

考古題應用　Yoji was asked to <u>receive an award</u> on the platform.
Yoji 被要求上講臺<u>領獎</u>。

試練習題　What was Yoji doing on the platform?

考生回答處

___

考古題應用　The law firm has pledged that its clients' files will remain <u>confidential</u>.
律師事務所已保證所有客戶的檔案將保持<u>機密</u>。

試練習題　Has the law firm pledged the confidentiality of its clients' files?

考生回答處

___

考古題應用　Their stock price has plummeted to an <u>all-time low</u> in just two weeks.
他們的股價僅在兩週內就下滑至<u>空前的新低</u>。

試練習題　Why did they have to call two emergency meetings in one day?

考生回答處

P

___

考古題應用　Our stock price has plunged to a new low.
我們股價已經暴跌至新低。

試練習題　What has happened since word of your financial crisis leaked out?

考生回答處

___

考古題應用　His experience in marketing is a huge plus for this job.
他在行銷方面的經驗為這份工作大大加分。

試練習題　Is Rob the right person to be our District Sales Manager?

考生回答處

Check List 5

到目前為止，字彙量又增加了不少，繼續學新單字之前，我們先來複習一下，看看是不是都記起來了！

☐ nationality	☐ obstruct	☐ outlook
☐ native	☐ obtain	☐ overall
☐ neat	☐ obvious	☐ overcast
☐ necessity	☐ occasion	☐ overcome
☐ negatively	☐ occupational	☐ overdue
☐ neutral	☐ occupy	☐ overlook
☐ normal	☐ occur	☐ overseas
☐ notable	☐ offer	☐ oversee
☐ notify	☐ official	☐ overview
☐ novelty	☐ omit	☐ overwhelming
☐ nullify	☐ operation	☐ owe
☐ obedience	☐ oppose	☐ own
☐ object	☐ option	☐ pack
☐ objective	☐ ordinary	☐ paddle
☐ obligation	☐ organize	☐ pageant
☐ obliged	☐ orient	☐ pamphlet
☐ observation	☐ ornament	☐ panel
☐ obstacle	☐ outline	☐ parade

- [ ] parallel
- [ ] paramount
- [ ] participate
- [ ] particular
- [ ] passerby
- [ ] pastime

- [ ] patience
- [ ] pay
- [ ] peak
- [ ] peculiar
- [ ] penalty
- [ ] pending

- [ ] penetrate
- [ ] perceive
- [ ] performance
- [ ] period
- [ ] permanent
- [ ] permission

- [ ] personalize
- [ ] personnel
- [ ] perspective
- [ ] persuade
- [ ] petition
- [ ] phase

- [ ] phenomenon
- [ ] physical
- [ ] pile
- [ ] pinnacle
- [ ] pioneer
- [ ] place

- [ ] plain
- [ ] platform
- [ ] pledge
- [ ] plummet
- [ ] plunge
- [ ] plus

Po-

pole (n.) 桿子
同 rod, stick

一般正常速度 [pol]
ETS全真速度 [pol]

➡ 字尾 [l] 請勿唸成 [ɔ]（台式發音）

policy (n.) 政策
關 policy (n.) 保險單
同 rule, guideline, regulation

一般正常速度 [`paləsɪ]
ETS全真速度 [`paləsɪ]

poll (n.) 民調
關 poll (v.t) 做民調
同 survey, vote, ballot, count

一般正常速度 [pol]
ETS全真速度 [pol]

➡ 1) 名詞與動詞的唸法相同
2) 字尾 [l] 請勿唸成 [ɔ]（台式發音）

pool (v.t) 匯集（想法、資金）
關 pool (n.) 游泳池
同 bring together, combine, merge

一般正常速度 [pul]
ETS全真速度 [pul]

➡ 1) 動詞與名詞的唸法相同
2) 字尾 [l] 請勿唸成 [ɔ]（台式發音）

portable (adj.) 可攜式的
關 port (n.) 港口
同 movable, light, easily carried

一般正常速度 [`portəbl]
ETS全真速度 [`porɖəbl]

➡ 1) 形容詞的 [t] 須變音為 [ɖ]
2) 名詞字尾 [t] 輕唸即可

考古題應用　There is a flag pole in front of the City Hall.
市政府前有一支旗桿。

口試練習題　Is there a fountain or a flag pole in front of the City Hall?
考生回答處

考古題應用　The government has to <u>adopt</u> new economic policies.
政府得<u>採用</u>新的經濟政策。

口試練習題　Is there any way to reduce unemployment figures?
考生回答處

考古題應用　We'll be conducting a poll on our latest product.
我們將針對最新的產品進行市調。

口試練習題　What are you conducting a poll on?
考生回答處

P

考古題應用　All staff members will have to pool their ideas.
所有的工作人員得一起集思廣益。

口試練習題　Will the manager work out a solution on his own?
考生回答處

考古題應用　He's got a portable television in the <u>kitchenette</u>.
他的小廚房裡有一部可提式電視。　/ˈKItʃ(ə)nˌɛt/

口試練習題　Can Mr. Blake watch the evening news while he is cooking?
考生回答處

portion (n.) 部分

關 portion (v.t) 分配
同 part, section, share, allocation, division

一般正常速度 [`porʃən]
ETS全真速度 [`porʃən]

➡ 名詞與動詞的唸法相同

pose (v.i) 擺姿勢

關 pose (n.) 姿勢
同 position, posture

一般正常速度 [poz]
ETS全真速度 [po(z)]

➡ 1) 動詞與名詞的唸法相同
2) 字尾 s 唸成 [z]
3) 字尾 [z] 輕唸即可

position (n.) 職位

關 position (v.t) 就定位
同 job, place, rank, status

一般正常速度 [pə`zɪʃən]
ETS全真速度 [pə`zɪʃən]

➡ 名詞與動詞的唸法相同

positive (adj.) 確定的

關 positiveness (n.) 確定
positively (adv.) 確定地
同 sure, certain, confident, convinced

一般正常速度 [`pazətɪv]
ETS全真速度 [`pazəɖɪ(v)]

➡ 1) 所有詞性的 [t] 都要唸成 [ɖ]
2) 形容詞字尾 [v] 輕唸即可

possess (v.t) 持有

關 possession (n.) 持有物
possessor (n.) 持有者
同 own, have, hold, acquire, control, dominate

一般正常速度 [pə`zɛs]
ETS全真速度 [pə`zɛ(s)]

➡ 1) 所有詞性的重音都在第二音節
2) 動詞字尾 [s] 輕唸即可

考古題應用　The pharmaceutical plant represents a small portion of my company's assets.
這家藥廠只是我公司資產的一小部分。

試練習題　Is this pharmaceutical plant your only asset?

考生回答處

考古題應用　The <u>attendees</u> to the workshop have posed for a photograph.
研習會的<u>參加人員</u>已擺好姿勢準備拍照。

試練習題　Are the attendees to the workshop ready for us to take a photograph?

考生回答處

考古題應用　I've sent a <u>resume</u> to apply for a position in a law firm.
我已經寄出<u>履歷表</u>申請律師事務所的工作。

試練習題　Have you started looking for a new job?

考生回答處

P

考古題應用　His supervisor seemed absolutely positive about it.
他的主管好像非常確定。

試練習題　Was Rob really the one who embezzled 20,000 dollars from the bank?
ɪmˈbɛzl̩

考生回答處

考古題應用　Anyone who possesses plant seeds has to <u>forfeit</u> them to customs officials.
任何持有植物種子的人都要將它們<u>交出來</u>給海關官員。

試練習題　Why can't Peter bring me some plant seeds from Thailand?

考生回答處

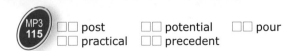
post (v.t) 張貼

關 poster (n.) 海報
同 put up, stick up, make known

一般正常速度 [post]
ETS全真速度 [po(st)]

→ 1) 動詞字尾 [st] 輕唸即可
   2) 名詞的 [t] 須變音為 [d]

potential (adj.) 潛在的

關 potential (n.) 潛力
potentially (adv.) 潛在地
同 possible, likely, promising, future

一般正常速度 [pə`tɛnʃəl]
ETS全真速度 [pə`tɛnʃəl]

→ 1) 所有詞性的重音都在第二音節
   2) 字尾 [l] 請勿唸成 [ɔ]（台式發音）

pour (v.i) 下大雨

關 pour (n.) 傾倒
同 rain hard, rain heavily

一般正常速度 [por]
ETS全真速度 [por]

→ 動詞與名詞的唸法相同

practical (adj.) 實際的

關 practice (n.) 實行
practicality (n.) 實用性
同 useful, doable, feasible, workable

一般正常速度 [`præktɪkl]
ETS全真速度 [`præ(k)tɪgl]

→ 1) 只有 practical 第二個 c 要發 [g]
   2) 除 practicality 的重音在第三音節
      (-cal-) 外，其他詞性的重音都在第
      一音節

precedent (n.) 先例

關 precede (v.t) 發生在前
precedence (n.) 領先；優先權
同 antecedent, previous example

一般正常速度 [`prɛsədənt]
ETS全真速度 [`prɛsədən(t)]

→ 只有 precede 重音在第二音節 (-cede)，
   兩個名詞的重音都在第一音節

考古題應用 We'll post the names of the <u>winners</u> on the <u>bulletin board</u> tomorrow.
我們明天會把<u>得主</u>的名字張貼在<u>公布欄</u>上。

試練習題 How do we know who won the items in the auction?
考生回答處 _____

考古題應用 We are still <u>weighing</u> its potential impact on the local economy.
我們還在<u>考量</u>其對當地經濟可能造成的衝擊。

試練習題 Are you sure you want to close one of your Vietnamese factories?
越南人 (形)
/vɪˌɛtnəˈmiz/
考生回答處 _____

考古題應用 The rain was pouring down.
雨下得很大。

試練習題 Why did they call off the company picnic?
考生回答處 _____

P

考古題應用 We don't hire people who <u>lack</u> practical experience.
我們不雇用<u>缺乏</u>實際經驗的人。

試練習題 Why did you reject my application?
考生回答處 _____

考古題應用 His successful career is without precedent.
他的事業成就是<u>史無前例的</u>。

試練習題 It's amazing that Edward has become a president at such a young age.
考生回答處

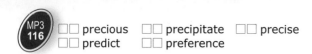
precious (adj.) 珍貴的

關 preciousness (n.) 珍貴性

同 valuable, important, costly, priceless

一般正常速度 [`prɛʃəs]

ETS全真速度 [`prɛʃə(s)]

➡ 1) 兩個詞性的重音都在第一音節
2) 形容詞字尾 [s] 輕唸即可

precipitate (v.t) 加速

關 precipitation (n.) 降雨

同 fasten, hasten, speed up, accelerate

一般正常速度 [prɪ`sɪpə.tet]

ETS全真速度 [prɪ`sɪbə.te(t)]

➡ 1) 兩個詞性的第二個 [p] 都唸 [b]
2) 動詞字尾 [t] 輕唸即可

precise (adj.) 精確的

關 precision (n.) 精確性
precisely (adv.) 精準地

同 accurate, right, correct, specific, actual, definite, exact

一般正常速度 [prɪ`saɪs]

ETS全真速度 [prɪ`saɪ(s)]

➡ 1) 所有詞性的重音都在第二音節
2) 只有名詞的重音節母音唸 [ɪ]，其他都唸 [aɪ]
3) 形容詞字尾 [s] 輕唸即可

predict (v.t) 預測

關 prediction (n.) 預測
predictable (adj.) 可預測的

同 foresee, foretell

一般正常速度 [prɪ`dɪkt]

ETS全真速度 [prɪ`dɪ(kt)]

➡ 1) 所有詞性的重音都在第二音節
2) predictable 的 [t] 要唸 [d]
3) 動詞字尾 [kt] 輕唸即可

preference (n.) 優先權

關 prefer (v.t) 偏好
preferable (adj.) 較偏好的

同 advantage, favor, precedence

一般正常速度 [`prɛfərəns]

ETS全真速度 [`prɛfərən(s)]

➡ 1) 除動詞的重音在第二音節 (-fer) 外，名詞與形容詞的重音都在第一音節
2) 名詞字尾 [s] 輕唸即可

考古題應用　He kept some precious objects in the safe.
他在保險箱裡放了一些貴重物品。

試練習題　What did Mr. Wilson keep in the safe?
考生回答處　_____

考古題應用　Lack of morale among its employees precipitated its downfall.
員工間缺乏士氣加速了它的衰落。

試練習題　What precipitated the company's downfall?
考生回答處　_____

考古題應用　The engineer gave us very precise specifications.
工程師給我們的規格非常精確。

試練習題　Are you sure these are the correct specifications for the model?
考生回答處　_____

P

考古題應用　Our advisors predict an increase in this quarter's sales figures.
我們的顧問預測本季營業數字會增加。

試練習題　What did your advisors say about this quarter's sales figures?
考生回答處　_____

考古題應用　We give preference to bilingual applicants.
我們把優先權給會講兩種語言的申請人。

試練習題　Who do you give preference to when hiring people?
考生回答處　_____

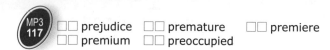
prejudice (n.) 偏見

關 prejudice (v.t) 有偏見
同 unfairness, bias, discrimination

一般正常速度 [ˋprɛdʒədɪs]

ETS全真速度 [ˋprɛdʒədɪs]

➡ 1) 名詞與動詞的唸法相同
   2) [d] 須變音為 [ɖ]

---

premature (adj.) 過早的

關 prematurely (adv.) 過早
同 early, green, incomplete, raw, undeveloped, untimely

一般正常速度 [ˌprimǝˋtjʊr]

ETS全真速度 [ˌprimǝˋtjʊr]

➡ 形容詞與副詞的重音都在第二音節

---

premiere (n.) 首映

關 premiere (v.t) 首映
同 first show, debut, opening

一般正常速度 [prɪˋmjɛr]

ETS全真速度 [prɪˋmjɛr]

➡ 名詞與動詞的唸法相同

---

premium (n.) 保險費

同 payment to buy insurance, fee

一般正常速度 [ˋprimɪǝm]

ETS全真速度 [ˋprimɪǝm]

➡ 重音在第一音節

---

preoccupied
(adj.) 心事重重的

關 preoccupy (v.t) 全神貫注
   preoccupation (n.) 專注
同 caught up in, taken up, lost in

一般正常速度 [priˋɑkjǝˌpaɪd]

ETS全真速度 [priˋɑgjǝˌbaɪ(d)]

➡ 1) 形容詞與動詞的重音都在第二音節
   2) 所有詞性的 [k] 均可變音為 [g]，第二個 [p] 可變音為 [b]
   3) 形容詞字尾 [d] 輕唸即可

考古題應用　He <u>was accused of</u> having a prejudice against foreign workers.
他被指控對外籍勞工有偏見。

□試練習題　Why was Mr. Tanaka demoted?
考生回答處　_____

考古題應用　I think it's a bit premature to ask him for a raise.
我覺得跟他要求加薪有點過早。

□試練習題　Is it the right time to ask Mr. Jimenez for a raise?
考生回答處　_____

考古題應用　Our president was invited to last week's premiere.
我們總經理應邀參加上週的首映。

□試練習題　Who was invited to last week's movie premiere?
考生回答處　_____

P

考古題應用　I paid the employment insurance premium by check.
我用支票付勞工保險費。

□試練習題　Did you pay for the employment insurance premium by cash or check?
考生回答處　_____

考古題應用　He is preoccupied with tomorrow's presentation.
他為了明天的報告而顯得心事重重的。

□試練習題　Why is Mr. Miller so quiet today?
考生回答處　_____

prescribe (v.t) 開藥

關 prescription (n.) 處方籤
prescriptive (adj.) 規定的
同 appoint, assign, define, specify

一般正常速度 [prɪˋskraɪb]
ETS全真速度 [prɪˋsgraɪ(b)]

➡ 1) 所有詞性的 [k] 均須變音為 [g]
2) 動詞字尾 [b] 輕唸即可

prestige (n.) 威信

關 prestigious (adj.) 有聲望的
同 fame, credit, honor, importance,
weight, regard, status

一般正常速度 [prɛsˋtiʒ]
ETS全真速度 [prɛsˋdiʒ]

➡ 1) 兩個詞性的重音都在第二音節
2) 名詞的 ge 唸 [ʒ]，形容詞的 gi 唸
[dʒ]
3) 兩個詞性的 [t] 均須變音為 [d]

presume (v.t) 猜想

關 presumption (n.) 推測
presumable (adj.) 可能的
presumably (adv.) 想必
同 guess, assume, suppose, think,
take it

一般正常速度 [prɪˋzjum]
ETS全真速度 [prɪˋzjum]

➡ 1) 所有詞性的重音都在第二音節
2) 所有詞性的 s 都要唸成 [z]
3) 只有名詞的重音節母音要唸成
[ʌ]，其他詞性都唸 [ju]

pretend (v.t) 假裝

關 pretension (n.) 假裝
同 fake, act, make believe

一般正常速度 [prɪˋtɛnd]
ETS全真速度 [prɪˋtɛn(d)]

➡ 1) 動詞與名詞的重音都在第二音節
2) 動詞字尾 [d] 輕唸即可

prevalent (adj.) 普遍的

關 prevail (v.i) 普遍
prevalence (n.) 普遍性
同 common, accepted, general,
popular, universal, widespread

一般正常速度 [ˋprɛvələnt]
ETS全真速度 [ˋprɛvələn(t)]

➡ 1) 形容詞與名詞的重音都在第一音
節，動詞的重音在第二音節
2) 只有動詞的重音節母音唸 [e]，其他
詞性的重音節母音皆唸 [ɛ]

考古題應用　His <u>physician</u> has prescribed medication for the flu.
他的<u>醫生</u>已經為他開藥治療流感。

試練習題　Did Daniel do anything about his flu?
考生回答處　_____

考古題應用　The invention of the new machine gained him international prestige.
他發明的新機器替他贏得國際間的聲望。

試練習題　How did Mr. Wang gain international prestige in this field?
考生回答處　_____

考古題應用　I presume she was there for business.
我猜她應該是去那裡洽公。

試練習題　Do you know why Sasha went to Frankfurt?
考生回答處　_____

P

考古題應用　We can <u>dive into the pool</u> pretending we are in Hawaii.
我們可以<u>潛入泳池裡</u>，假裝人在夏威夷。

試練習題　It's really frustrating that we can't go on vacation to Hawaii, isn't it?
考生回答處　_____

考古題應用　Going to work on a bike suddenly became prevalent.
騎機車上班突然變得盛行起來。

試練習題　Why have the sales of motorbikes doubled over the last five months?
考生回答處　_____

prevent (v.t) 阻止

關 prevention (n.) 預防
　 preventive (adj.) 預防的
同 stop, block, inhibit, impede

一般正常速度 [prɪˋvɛnt]
ETS全真速度 [prɪˋvɛn(t)]

➡ 1) 所有詞性的重音都在第二音節
　 2) 動詞字尾 [t] 輕唸即可
　 3) preventive 的 [t] 要變音為 [d]

previous (adj.) 先前的

關 previously (adv.) 之前
同 earlier, former, prior, preceding, antecedent, anterior

一般正常速度 [ˋprivɪəs]
ETS全真速度 [ˋprivɪə(s)]

➡ 1) 形容詞與副詞的重音都在第　音節
　 2) 形容詞字尾 [s] 輕唸即可

price (v.t) 定價

關 price (n.) 價格
同 cost, charge, rate, value

一般正常速度 [praɪs]
ETS全真速度 [praɪ(s)]

➡ 1) 動詞與名詞的唸法相同
　 2) 字尾 [s] 輕唸即可

prime (adj.) 首要的

關 prime (n.) 全盛期
同 top, best, principal, superior, highest

一般正常速度 [praɪm]
ETS全真速度 [praɪm]

➡ 形容詞與名詞的唸法相同

principle (n.) 原則

關 principles (n.) 原理
同 rule, standard, formula, criterion

一般正常速度 [ˋprɪnsəpl]
ETS全真速度 [ˋprɪnsəbl]

➡ 1) 第二個 [p] 均可變音為 [b]
　 2) 字尾 [l] 請勿唸成 [ɔ]（台式發音）

234

考古題應用　<u>Lack of funds</u> prevented us from expanding our factory.
資金的缺乏阻礙我們擴建工廠。

口試練習題　What made you give up on the expansion of the factory?
考生回答處　_____

考古題應用　She gained extensive experience from her previous job.
她從上一個工作得到很豐富的經驗。

口試練習題　Why does Jessie fit in so well at her new job?
考生回答處　_____

考古題應用　Their products are always reasonably priced.
他們的產品向來價格公道。

口試練習題　Why are their products always so popular?
考生回答處　_____

P

考古題應用　<u>Environmental issues</u> will be their prime concern.
環保議題會是他們首要的顧慮。

口試練習題　Will the city council vote against a new oil refinery?
考生回答處　_____

考古題應用　We won't accept any offer that goes against our principles.
我們不會接受任何違反原則的條件。

口試練習題　Will you take any offer they make?
考生回答處　_____

priority (n.) 優先

關 prioritize (v.t) 按優先順序處理
同 greater importance, first concern, preference

一般正常速度 [praɪ`ɔrətɪ]
ETS全真速度 [praɪ`ɔrəɖɪ]

➡ 1) 名詞與動詞的重音都在第二音節
2) 名詞的 [t] 可變音為 [ɖ]

private (adj.) 私人的

關 privacy (n.) 隱私權
privately (adv.) 私下地
同 own, personal, individual

一般正常速度 [`praɪvɪt]
ETS全真速度 [`praɪvɪ(t)]

➡ 形容詞字尾 [t] 輕唸即可，副詞的 [t] 必須消音

privilege (n.) 特權

關 privileged (adj.) 有特權的
同 right, advantage, benefit, entitlement

一般正常速度 [`prɪvɪlɪdʒ]
ETS全真速度 [`prɪvɪlɪdʒ]

➡ 名詞與形容詞的重音都在第一音節

prize (n.) 獎品

關 prize (adj.) 得獎的
同 award, honor, reward

一般正常速度 [praɪz]
ETS全真速度 [praɪz]

➡ 名詞與形容詞的唸法相同

probability (n.) 可能性

關 probable (adj.) 可能的
probably (adv.) 或許
同 possibility, chance, odds, presumption, prospect

一般正常速度 [ˌprɑbə`bɪlətɪ]
ETS全真速度 [ˌprɑbə`bɪləɖɪ]

➡ 1) 只有名詞的重音在第三音節，其他詞性的重音都在第一音節
2) 名詞字尾的 [t] 須變音為 [ɖ]

考古題應用　Our top priority is the arrangement of our <u>accommodations</u>.
我們的第一優先是安排<u>住宿</u>。

試練習題　What is the top priority for our travel arrangements?
考生回答處　_____

考古題應用　This garden is private property.
這座花園是私人土地。

試練習題　Is this garden open to the public?
考生回答處　_____

考古題應用　To dine in the <u>garden courtyard</u> is a member's only privilege.
在<u>中庭花園</u>用餐是會員的特權。

試練習題　Who can dine in the garden courtyard?
考生回答處　_____

P

考古題應用　She won first prize in a <u>writing competition</u>.
她在<u>作文比賽</u>中得到第一名。

試練習題　Why is Lucia in such a good mood?
考生回答處　_____

考古題應用　There is a strong probability that our team will win.
我們團隊贏的可能性很大。

試練習題　Which team will win the design contest?
考生回答處　_____

proceed (v.i) 繼續進行

関 proceeds [ˋprosidz] (n.) 所得
同 carry on, move on, progress, continue

一般正常速度 [prəˋsid]
ETS全真速度 [prəˋsi(d)]

➔ 1) 注意動詞與名詞的發音
   2) 動詞字尾 [d] 輕唸即可

process (v.t) 處理

関 process (n.) 過程
同 handle, take care of, deal with

一般正常速度 [ˋprasεs]
ETS全真速度 [ˋprasε(s)]

➔ 1) 動詞與名詞的唸法相同
   2) 字尾 [s] 輕唸即可

produce (n.) 農產品

関 produce [prəˋdju(s)] (v.t) 生產
   productivity (n.) 生產力
   production (n.) 生產
   productive (adj.) 多產的
同 crop, harvest

一般正常速度 [ˋpradjus]
ETS全真速度 [ˋpradju(s)]

➔ 1) produce 當動、名詞時唸法不同
   2) productive 與 productivity 裡第一個
      [t] 均須變音為 [d]

professional (adj.) 專業的

関 profession (n.) 職業
同 occupational, trained, expert, skilled, competent

一般正常速度 [prəˋfεʃənl]
ETS全真速度 [prəˋfεʃənl]

➔ 1) 形容詞與名詞的重音都在第二音節
   2) 形容詞字尾 [l] 請勿唸成 [ɔ]（台式
      發音）

profile (n.) 簡介

関 profile (v.t) 描寫
同 description, outline, sketch

一般正常速度 [ˋprofaɪl]
ETS全真速度 [ˋprofaɪl]

➔ 1) 名詞與動詞的唸法相同
   2) 字尾 [l] 請勿唸成 [ɔ]（台式發音）

考古題應用 After a short break, we'll proceed with the discussion.
在短暫休息之後，我們會繼續進行討論。

口試練習題 What will we do after a short break?

考生回答處 _____

考古題應用 Your application is still being processed.
你的申請還在處理中。

口試練習題 Did you accept my application for the job?

考生回答處 _____

考古題應用 The only produce we got were some fresh picked potatoes.
我們唯一買的農產品是一些現採馬鈴薯。

口試練習題 What produce did you get from the market this morning?

考生回答處 _____

P

考古題應用 Those workshops were conducted by professional instructors.
這些研習會是由專業的老師指導的。

口試練習題 Who conducted those computer workshops?

考生回答處 _____

考古題應用 There is a profile of the founder in the brochure.
小冊子裡有創辦人的簡介。

口試練習題 What is in the brochure?

考生回答處 _____

profit (n.) 利潤

關 profitable (adj.) 有賺錢的
同 gain, proceeds, earnings

一般正常速度 [ˋprafɪt]
ETS全真速度 [ˋprafɪ(t)]

➡ 1) 名詞字尾 [t] 輕唸即可
   2) 形容詞的 [t] 須變音為 [đ]

profound (adj.) 深遠的

關 profoundly (adv.) 深遠地
同 deep, lasting, great, intense

一般正常速度 [prəˋfaʊnd]
ETS全真速度 [prəˋfaʊn(d)]

➡ 1) 形容詞與副詞的重音都在第二音節
   2) 形容詞字尾 [d] 輕唸即可,副詞的
      [d] 必須消音

progress (n.) 進行

關 progress [prəˋgrɛ(s)] (v.i) 進展

一般正常速度 [ˋpragrɛs]
ETS全真速度 [ˋpragrɛ(s)]

➡ 名詞的重音在第一音節,動詞的重音
   則在第二音節

prohibit (v.t) 禁止

關 prohibition (n.) 禁令
同 ban, forbid, stop, disallow

一般正常速度 [proˋhɪbɪt]
ETS全真速度 [proˋhɪbɪ(t)]

➡ 動詞字尾 [t] 輕唸即可

project (v.t) 預計

關 project [ˋpradʒɛ(kt)] (n.) 計畫
同 plan, calculate, estimate, predict

一般正常速度 [prəˋdʒɛkt]
ETS全真速度 [prəˋdʒɛ(kt)]

➡ 1) 動詞的重音在第二音節,名詞的重
      音在第一音節
   2) 動詞字尾 [kt] 輕唸即可

考古題應用　The company's net profit for 2007 was eight million dollars.
公司 2007 年的淨利是八百萬美元。

試練習題　How much was the company's net profit in 2007?
考生回答處 _____

考古題應用　His invention had a profound impact on the development of food technology.
他的發明對食品科技的發展有深遠的影響。

試練習題　Why is Mr. Carter an important figure in the development of food technology?
考生回答處 _____

考古題應用　You have to <u>turn off</u> your cell phones while the meeting is in progress.
會議進行時請將手機<u>關掉</u>。

試練習題　What are we asked to do while the meeting is in progress?
考生回答處 _____

P

考古題應用　Smoking is prohibited in the entire building.
整棟大樓皆禁止吸菸。

試練習題　Is there a smoking area in this building?
考生回答處 _____

考古題應用　Our <u>gross profit</u> is projected to reach six million dollars next year.
我們的<u>毛利</u>預計明年可達到六百萬美元。

試練習題　What does the financial report say about our gross profit?
考生回答處 _____

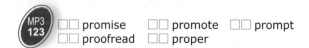
promise (v.i) 保證

關 promise (n.) 承諾

同 assure, give one's word, pledge, guarantee

一般正常速度 [ˋpramɪs]

ETS全真速度 [ˋpramɪ(s)]

➡ 1) 動詞與名詞的唸法相同
2) 字尾 [s] 輕唸即可

promote (v.t) 拔擢

關 promotion (n.) 升遷

同 move up, upgrade, elevate, advance, rise

一般正常速度 [prəˋmot]

ETS全真速度 [prəˋmo(t)]

➡ 1) 動詞與名詞的重音都在第二音節
2) 動詞字尾 [t] 輕唸即可

prompt (adj.) 即時的

關 prompt (v.t) 促使
promptly (adv.) 快速地

同 rapid, quick, immediate, instant, on time, speedy

一般正常速度 [prampt]

ETS全真速度 [pram(pt)]

➡ 形容詞的 [pt] 輕唸即可，副詞的 [t] 必須消音

proofread (v.t) 校閱

關 proofreader (n.) 校閱人員

同 double-check, revise

一般正常速度 [ˋpruf͵rid]

ETS全真速度 [ˋpruf͵ri(d)]

➡ 動詞字尾 [d] 輕唸即可

proper (adj.) 適當的

關 properly (adv.) 適當地

同 right, appropriate, suitable, fitting

一般正常速度 [ˋprapɚ]

ETS全真速度 [ˋprabɚ]

➡ 兩個詞性的第二個 [p] 均須變音為 [b]

242

考古題應用　He has promised not to leak the news to <u>the press</u>.
他保證不會把消息洩露給媒體。

口試練習題　Are you sure it's appropriate to tell Ross the news?

考生回答處　_____

考古題應用　She has been promoted to the position of <u>regional manager</u>.
她已被升遷至區經理的職位。

口試練習題　Why did Nicole move into a bigger office?

考生回答處　_____

考古題應用　Prompt payment is recommended.
我們建議即時付款。

口試練習題　Would you prefer we pay the bill in installments?

考生回答處　_____

P

考古題應用　He asked me to proofread two <u>status reports</u>.
他要我校閱兩份進度報告。

口試練習題　What did Thomas ask you to do?

考生回答處　_____

考古題應用　He is feeling much better after proper treatments.
在適當的治療後他覺得好多了。

口試練習題　How is Joe feeling after being hospitalized?

考生回答處　_____

property (n.) 房地產

同 assets, belongings, wealth, possessions, estate, capital

一般正常速度 [ˋprɑpətɪ]
ETS全真速度 [ˋprɑbəɖɪ]

➡ 1) 第二個 [p] 須變音為 [b]
2) 字尾 [t] 須變音為 [ɖ]

proportion (n.) 比例

關 proportional (adj.) 比例上的
同 distribution, ration, relative amount, ratio

一般正常速度 [prəˋporʃən]
ETS全真速度 [prəˋporʃən]

➡ 1) 名詞與形容詞的重音都在第二音節
2) 形容詞字尾 [l] 請勿唸成 [ɔ]（台式發音）

propose (v.t) 提出

關 proposal (n.) 提案
同 suggest, come up with

一般正常速度 [prəˋpoz]
ETS全真速度 [prəˋpo(z)]

➡ 1) 動詞與名詞的重音都在第二音節
2) 名詞字尾 [l] 請勿唸成 [ɔ]（台式發音）

proprietor (n.) 所有人

關 proprietorial (adj.) 所有者的
同 owner, possessor, holder, keeper, manager

一般正常速度 [prəˋpraɪətə]
ETS全真速度 [prəˋpraɪəɖə]

➡ 1) 名詞的重音在第二音節，形容詞的重音則在第四音節 (-tor-)
2) 名詞的 [t] 須變音為 [ɖ]

prosecute (v.t) 起訴

關 prosecution (n.) 起訴
prosecutor (n.) 檢察官
同 sue, bring suit against, take to court

一般正常速度 [ˋprɑsɪ‚kjut]
ETS全真速度 [ˋprɑsɪ‚kju(t)]

➡ 1) prosecute 與 prosecutor 的重音都在第一音節
2) 動詞字尾 [t] 輕唸即可
3) prosecutor 字尾 [t] 須變音為 [ɖ]

考古題應用　The property downtown is getting more expensive.
市區的房地產變得愈來愈貴。

試練習題　Why are you considering buying a house in the suburbs?
考生回答處　_____

考古題應用　The proportion of Asian workers has risen to 30%.
亞裔員工的比例已經上升到 30% 了。

試練習題　Are less than 10% of your workers Asian?
考生回答處　_____

考古題應用　Our company has proposed a plan to develop rural areas.
我們公司提出了一項開發郊區的計畫。

試練習題　Which area will your company develop?
考生回答處　_____

P

考古題應用　The proprietor of the restaurant wants to discuss its garden expansion.
餐廳的所有人想討論擴建花園的事。

試練習題　Why is the landscape designer on his way to the restaurant?
考生回答處　_____

考古題應用　He was prosecuted for embezzling.
他因為盜用公款被起訴。

試練習題　Why was Mr. Kim prosecuted?
考生回答處　_____

prospect (n.) 前途

關 prospect (v.t) 探勘
prospective (adj.) 有希望的
同 future, potential, possibility, plan, outlook, chances

一般正常速度 [`praspɛkt]
ETS全真速度 [`prasbɛ(kt)]

➡ 1) 名詞與動詞的唸法相同
2) 第二個 [p] 須變音為 [b]
3) 字尾 [kt] 輕唸即可

protest (v.i) 抗議

關 protest [`protɛs(t)] (n.) 抗議
同 disapprove, complain, demonstrate, disagree

一般正常速度 [prə`tɛst]
ETS全真速度 [prə`tɛ(st)]

➡ 1) 動詞的重音在第二音節，名詞的重音在第一音節
2) 動詞字尾 [st] 輕唸即可

proud (adj.) 引以為傲的

關 pride (n.) 驕傲
proudly (adv.) 驕傲地
同 honored, self-respecting

一般正常速度 [praud]
ETS全真速度 [prau(d)]

➡ 形容詞與名詞的字尾 [d] 均輕唸即可，副詞的 [d] 則必須消音

provide (v.t) 提供

關 provision (n.) 供應
provider (n.) 供應者
同 offer, give, afford

一般正常速度 [prə`vaɪd]
ETS全真速度 [prə`vaɪd]

➡ 1) 所有詞性的重音都在第二音節
2) 動詞的 i 唸 [aɪ]，名詞的 i 唸 [ɪ]
3) provider 的 [d] 須變音為 [ɖ]

provided (conj.) 如果

同 if

一般正常速度 [prə`vaɪdɪd]
ETS全真速度 [prə`vaɪɖɪd]

➡ 第一個 [d] 須變音為 [ɖ]

考古題應用 She has found a job with excellent prospects.
她找到了一份前途看好的工作。

試練習題 Why is Ariel in such a good mood?

考生回答處 _____

考古題應用 The employees are protesting against his decision.
員工對他的決定提出抗議。

試練習題 How are the employees reacting to Ronald's decision of cutting salaries?

考生回答處 _____

考古題應用 We are very proud of his achievement.
我們對他的成就感到非常驕傲。

試練習題 How do you feel about your son's promotion?

考生回答處 _____

考古題應用 The new caterer will provide us with better service.
新的外燴業者會提供我們更好的服務。

試練習題 Why are we switching caterers?

考生回答處 _____

考古題應用 Provided they cut wages, the workers will go on strike.
如果他們調降薪資，工人就會罷工。

試練習題 What will happen if the board decides to cut wages?

考生回答處 _____

P

provisional (adj.) 臨時的

關 provision (n.) 提供的物品；法律條款
provisions (n.) 食物的供應
同 temporary, for now

一般正常速度 [prə`vɪʒənḷ]
ETS全真速度 [prə`vɪʒənḷ]

➡ 所有詞性的重音都在第二音節

prudent (adj.) 謹慎的

關 prudence (n.) 謹慎
prudently (adv.) 謹慎地
同 careful, cautious, discreet, circumspect

一般正常速度 [`prudn̩t]
ETS全真速度 [`pru__n̩(t)]

➡ 1) 形容詞與副詞的 [d] 均停一拍即可
2) 形容詞的 [t] 輕唸即可，副詞的 [t] 須消音

prune (v.t) 修剪

同 cut, trim, clip, shorten, reduce

一般正常速度 [prun]
ETS全真速度 [prun]

Pu-

public (adj.) 大眾的

關 public (n.) 民眾
publicly (adv.) 公開地
同 common, civil, general

一般正常速度 [`pʌblɪk]
ETS全真速度 [`pʌblɪ(k)]

➡ 1) 三個詞性的重音都在第一音節
2) 形容詞字尾 [k] 輕唸即可，副詞的 [k] 必須消音

publicity (n.) 宣傳

關 publicize (v.t) 宣傳
publicist (n.) 宣傳人員
同 attention, public notice

一般正常速度 [pʌb`lɪsətɪ]
ETS全真速度 [pʌb`lɪsəɗɪ]

➡ 1) 只有 publicity 的重音在第二音節，其他兩個詞性的重音都在第一音節
2) publicity 的 [t] 須變音為 [ɗ]

考古題應用 You need to get a provisional parking pass first.
你得先取得臨時停車證。

試練習題 May I park here without a parking permit?
考生回答處 _____

考古題應用 It would be more prudent to consult a <u>financial expert</u> first.
先諮詢<u>財務專家</u>是比較謹慎的做法。

試練習題 Should we join the retirement savings plan?
考生回答處 _____

考古題應用 The gardeners are out pruning roses.
園丁在外面修剪玫瑰。

試練習題 What are the gardeners doing in the courtyard?
考生回答處 _____

P

考古題應用 Denise goes to work by public transport.
Denise 搭乘大眾運輸工具上班。

試練習題 Does Denise go to work by car or public transport?
考生回答處 _____

考古題應用 The publicity campaign for our spring collection is coming up soon.
我們春裝系列的宣傳活動就快開始了。

試練習題 Why have our publicists been so busy lately?
考生回答處 _____

MP3 127

□□ publish □□ punch □□ punctual
□□ punish □□ purchase

publish (v.t) 出版

關 publisher (n.) 出版社
publication (n.) 出版品
同 issue, produce, bring about, put out

一般正常速度 [ˋpʌblɪʃ]
ETS全真速度 [ˋpʌlɪ(ʃ)]

➡ 1) 所有詞性的 u 均唸 [ʌ] 而不是 [ɑ]（台式發音）
2) 動詞字尾 [ʃ] 輕唸即可

punch (v.i) 打下印記

關 punch (n.) 拳打
同 hit, strike

一般正常速度 [pʌntʃ]
ETS全真速度 [pʌn(tʃ)]

➡ 1) 動詞與名詞的唸法相同
2) 字尾 [tʃ] 輕唸即可，請勿過度噘嘴（否則聽起來會變成中文的「區」）

punctual (adj.) 準時的

關 punctually (adv.) 準時地
同 on time, on the dot, exact, timely

一般正常速度 [ˋpʌŋktʃʊəl]
ETS全真速度 [ˋpʌŋ(k)tʃʊəl]

➡ 1) 形容詞與副詞的重音都在第一音節
2) [k] 均輕唸即可

punish (v.t) 處罰

關 punishment (n.) 處罰
punitive (adj.) 懲罰性的
同 correct, penalize, give a lesson to

一般正常速度 [ˋpʌnɪʃ]
ETS全真速度 [ˋpʌnɪ(ʃ)]

➡ 1) 所有詞性的重音都在第一音節
2) punitive 裡的 [t] 須變音為 [đ]
3) 只有 punitive 的 u 發 [ju]

purchase (v.t) 購買

關 purchase (n.) 購買
同 buy, acquire, get, obtain, pay for, shop for

一般正常速度 [ˋpɜtʃəs]
ETS全真速度 [ˋpɜtʃə(s)]

➡ 1) 動詞與名詞的唸法相同
2) 字尾 [s] 輕唸即可

考古題應用 They publish <u>children's literature</u>.
他們出版兒童文學。

試練習題 What sort of books do they publish?
考生回答處 _____

考古題應用 We punch in at 9 a.m. every day.
我們每天早上九點打卡。

試練習題 What time do you punch in at work every day?
考生回答處 _____

考古題應用 He is always very punctual.
他一向非常準時。

試練習題 Will Luke be here on time tomorrow?
考生回答處 _____

P

考古題應用 Motorists should be harshly punished for <u>drunk driving</u>.
駕駛人該為酒醉駕車受到嚴厲的懲罰。

試練習題 Should we punish motorists for drunk driving?
考生回答處 _____

考古題應用 We are purchasing tickets for the concert.
我們在買音樂會的票。

試練習題 What are you doing at the ticket booth?
考生回答處 _____

purpose (n.) 目的

關 purpose (v.t) 決心要做
purposeful (adj.) 有決心的
同 goal, intention, object

一般正常速度 [ˋpɝpəs]

ETS全真速度 [ˋpɝbə(s)]

➡ 1) 所有詞性的重音都在第一音節
2) 所有詞性的第二個 [p] 均須變音為 [b]
3) purpose 字尾 [s] 輕唸即可

pursuit (n.) 追求

關 pursue (v.t) 追求
同 search, hunting, seeking

一般正常速度 [pəˋsjut]

ETS全真速度 [pəˋsju(t)]

➡ 1) 名詞與動詞的重音都在第二音節
2) 名詞字尾 [t] 輕唸即可

qualification (n.) 資格

關 qualify (v.t) 符合資格
qualified (adj.) 合格的
同 ability, quality, capability,
suitability

一般正常速度 [͵kwaləfəˋkeʃən]

ETS全真速度 [͵kwaləfəˋkeʃən]

➡ 除了名詞的重音在第四音節外，其他
兩個詞性的重音都在第一音節

quantity (n.) 數量

同 number, amount, sum, portion

一般正常速度 [ˋkwantətɪ]

ETS全真速度 [ˋkwanđəđɪ]

➡ 兩個 [t] 都可變音為 [đ]

quarter (n.) 一季

關 quarterly (adj.) 一季的
同 a period of three months

一般正常速度 [ˋkwɔrtɚ]

ETS全真速度 [ˋkwɔrđɚ]

➡ [t] 須變音為 [đ]

考古題應用 I am traveling in Paris for business purposes.
我在巴黎旅行是爲了公務上的目的。

試練習題 Are you traveling in Paris for sightseeing or business purposes?

考生回答處 _____

考古題應用 He never feels tired in his pursuit of excellence.
在追求卓越的過程中他從未感覺疲憊。

試練習題 Why is Mr. Scott such a well-known scholar?

考生回答處 _____

考古題應用 He's got the right qualifications to be my <u>successor</u>.
他具備了成爲我的<u>接班人</u>所應有的資格。

試練習題 Why was Mr. Gordon appointed to be your successor?

考生回答處 _____

P

Q

考古題應用 We can produce the latest models in large quantities.
我們能大量生產最新的機種。

試練習題 You can only produce the latest models in small quantities, right?

考生回答處 _____

考古題應用 Our profits have increased by twenty percent this quarter.
我們的利潤在本季增加了20%。

試練習題 By how much have our profits increased this quarter?

考生回答處 _____

question (v.t) 質疑

關 question (n.) 問題
  questionnaire (n.) 問卷
同 doubt, challenge, disbelieve, call
  into question

一般正常速度 [`kwɛstʃən]
ETS全真速度 [`kwɛsʤən]

➡ 1) 只有 questionnaire 的重音在最後
   一音節 (-naire)
  2) 所有詞性的 [tʃ] 均可變音為 [ʤ]

quota (n.) 額度

同 amount, allocation, proportion,
  share, portion

一般正常速度 [`kwotə]
ETS全真速度 [`kwoɖə]

➡ [t] 可變音為 [ɖ]

quote (v.t) 引述

關 quotation (n.) 引言
同 cite, retell

一般正常速度 [kwot]
ETS全真速度 [kwo(t)]

➡ 動詞字尾 [t] 輕唸即可

考古題應用　No one has ever questioned her honesty.
沒有人質疑過她的誠實。

口試練習題　Do you think Ms. Donovan lied to us?
考生回答處　_____

考古題應用　The factory failed to <u>fulfill</u> its production quota for this month.
工廠沒有達<u>到</u>這個月的生產額度。

口試練習題　Why is the production manager so worried?
考生回答處　_____

考古題應用　The article didn't quote her <u>comments</u> correctly.
那篇文章沒有正確引述她的<u>評論</u>。

口試練習題　Why was Ms. Myers so upset about the newspaper article?
考生回答處　_____

Q

Check List 6

到目前為止，字彙量又增加了不少，繼續學新單字之前，我們先來複習一下，看看是不是都記起來了！

☐ pole	☐ predict	☐ private
☐ policy	☐ preference	☐ privilege
☐ poll	☐ prejudice	☐ prize
☐ pool	☐ premature	☐ probability
☐ portable	☐ premiere	☐ proceed
☐ portion	☐ premium	☐ process
☐ pose	☐ preoccupied	☐ produce
☐ position	☐ prescribe	☐ professional
☐ positive	☐ prestige	☐ profile
☐ possess	☐ presume	☐ profit
☐ post	☐ pretend	☐ profound
☐ potential	☐ prevalent	☐ progress
☐ pour	☐ prevent	☐ prohibit
☐ practical	☐ previous	☐ project
☐ precedent	☐ price	☐ promise
☐ precious	☐ prime	☐ promote
☐ precipitate	☐ principle	☐ prompt
☐ precise	☐ priority	☐ proofread

- [ ] proper
- [ ] property
- [ ] proportion
- [ ] propose
- [ ] proprietor
- [ ] prosecute

- [ ] prospect
- [ ] protest
- [ ] proud
- [ ] provide
- [ ] provided
- [ ] provisional

- [ ] prudent
- [ ] prune
- [ ] public
- [ ] publicity
- [ ] publish
- [ ] punch

- [ ] punctual
- [ ] punish
- [ ] purchase
- [ ] purpose
- [ ] pursuit
- [ ] qualification

- [ ] quantity
- [ ] quarter
- [ ] question
- [ ] quota
- [ ] quote

race (v.i) 加速

關 race (n.) 比賽
同 hurry, hasten, speed up

一般正常速度 [res]
ETS全真速度 [re(s)]

➡ 1) 動詞與名詞的唸法相同
2) 字尾 [s] 輕唸即可

radical (adj.) 徹底的

關 radically (adv.) 徹底地;激進地
同 thorough, complete, entire, extreme

一般正常速度 [`rædɪkḷ]
ETS全真速度 [`ræɖɪgḷ]

➡ 1) 兩個詞性的 [d] 均須變音為 [ɖ]
2) 字尾 [k] 均可變音為 [g]

raffle (n.) 彩券

關 raffle (v.t) 用對獎方式銷售
同 lottery, draw

一般正常速度 [`ræfḷ]
ETS全真速度 [`ræfḷ]

➡ 1) 名詞與動詞的唸法相同
2) 字尾的 [l] 請勿唸成 [ɔ]（台式發音）

raise (n.) 加薪

關 raise (v.t) 舉起
同 increase, advance, improvement

一般正常速度 [rez]
ETS全真速度 [rez]

➡ 名詞與動詞的唸法相同

rally (v.i) 集合

關 rally (n.) 集合;集會
同 gather, assemble, meet

一般正常速度 [`rælɪ]
ETS全真速度 [`rælɪ]

➡ 動詞與名詞的唸法相同

考古題應用 He needed to race to finish a project by the deadline.
他得在截止日期前加速完成企畫案。

試練習題 Why did Andy stay up so late last night?

考生回答處 _____

考古題應用 Her company needs a radical change in management.
她公司的管理需要徹底的改變。

試練習題 What does Stacey need to do to overcome her company's crisis?

考生回答處 _____

考古題應用 He purchased two raffle tickets.
他買了兩張彩券。

試練習題 What did Brian do with the rest of the money?

考生回答處 _____

R

考古題應用 He received a raise along with his promotion.
他升遷時也一起加薪了。

試練習題 Is Tony getting a raise or just a promotion?

考生回答處 _____

考古題應用 The workers rallied in the plaza to protest against the new policy.
工人們在廣場聚集抗議新的政策。

試練習題 Why did the workers rally in the plaza?

考生回答處 _____

randomly (adv.) 隨便地

關 random (adj.) 隨便的，任意的
同 casually, aimlessly, by chance

一般正常速度 [`rændəmlɪ]
ETS全真速度 [`rændəmlɪ]

rapidly (adv.) 快速地

關 rapid (adj.) 快速的
同 fast, quickly, in a hurry, hurriedly

一般正常速度 [`ræpɪdlɪ]
ETS全真速度 [`ræbɪ__lɪ]

➡ 1) 兩個詞性的 [p] 均須變音為 [b]
2) 形容詞字尾 [d] 輕唸即可，副詞的 [d] 則必須消音

rate (n.) 比率

關 rate (v.t) 評比
同 ratio, percentage, degree

一般正常速度 [ret]
ETS全真速度 [re(t)]

➡ 1) 名詞與動詞的唸法相同
2) 字尾 [t] 輕唸即可

rational (adj.) 合理的

關 ration (n.) 配額
同 logical, wise, reasonable

一般正常速度 [`ræʃənļ]
ETS全真速度 [`ræʃənļ]

➡ 形容詞與名詞的重音都在第一音節

raw (adj.) 未加工的

關 rawness (n.) 未成熟
同 natural, unprocessed, unprepared

一般正常速度 [rɔ]
ETS全真速度 [rɔ]

考古題應用 The folders have been <u>piled up</u> randomly on the desk.
檔案夾被隨便堆放在書桌上。

試練習題 Have the folders been piled up neatly or randomly on the desk?

考生回答處 _____

考古題應用 The population of the city has grown rapidly.
這個都市的人口成長得很快。

試練習題 How has the population of the city grown?

考生回答處 _____

考古題應用 He borrowed money from the bank at a very high interest rate.
他以很高的利率向銀行借錢。

試練習題 How did he raise enough capital to start a new company?

考生回答處 _____

考古題應用 <u>Shutting down</u> the plant in Panama would be a rational decision.
關掉在巴拿馬的工廠是很合理的決定。

試練習題 Do you think we should shut down the plant in Panama?

考生回答處 _____

考古題應用 We imported the raw materials from Argentina.
我們從阿根廷進口原料。

試練習題 Where did you obtain the raw materials for your products?

考生回答處 _____

R

reach (v.t) 抵達

關 reach (n.) 範圍
同 arrive at, get to

一般正常速度 [ritʃ]
ETS全真速度 [ri(tʃ)]

➡ 1) 動詞與名詞的唸法相同
2) 字尾 [tʃ] 輕唸即可

---

reaction (n) 反應

關 react (v.i) 回應

一般正常速度 [rɪˋækʃən]
ETS全真速度 [rɪˋækʃən]

➡ 動詞字尾 [kt] 輕唸即可

---

realize (v.t) 明白

關 realization (n.) 領悟
同 understand, recognize

一般正常速度 [ˋrɪəˌlaɪz]
ETS全真速度 [ˋrɪəˌlaɪz]

➡ 動詞的重音在第一音節，名詞的重音
則在第四音節 (-za-)

---

reap (v.t) 收割

關 reaper (n.) 收割者
同 harvest, collect, gather, get,
acquire

一般正常速度 [rip]
ETS全真速度 [ri(p)]

➡ 1) 動詞字尾 [p] 輕唸即可
2) 名詞的 [p] 須變音為 [b]

---

reasonably (adv.) 合理地

關 reason (n.) 理由
reasonable (adj.) 合理的
同 logically, practically, rationally

一般正常速度 [ˋrizənəblɪ]
ETS全真速度 [ˋrizənəblɪ]

➡ 1) 所有詞性的重音都在第一音節
2) 形容詞字尾 [l] 請勿唸成 [ɔ]（台式
發音）

考古題應用　They will reach Munich on Thursday morning.
他們將在週四早上抵達慕尼黑。

口試練習題　When will our representatives reach Munich?
考生回答處　_____

考古題應用　We called a <u>press conference</u> in reaction to the strike.
我們召開記者會來回應這場罷工活動。

口試練習題　What did you do to react to the strike?
考生回答處　_____

考古題應用　The director didn't realize the effort I've been putting forth.
主管對我所做的努力並不知情。

口試練習題　Why didn't you get the merit raise?
考生回答處　_____

R

考古題應用　The farmers will reap their crops before the typhoon comes.
農夫會在颱風來襲前收割他們的農作物。

口試練習題　What will the farmers do before the typhoon comes?
考生回答處　_____

考古題應用　Because of <u>production costs</u>, I believe they are reasonably priced.
我相信就製作成本來說，價格是相當公道的。

口試練習題　Don't you think your products are too expensive?
考生回答處　_____

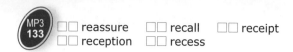
reassure (v.t) 令人安心

關 reassuringly (adv.) 令人安心地
同 encourage, cheer up, comfort

一般正常速度 [ˌriəˋʃʊr]
ETS全真速度 [ˌriəˋʃʊr]

➡ 動詞與副詞的重音都在第三音節

recall (v.t) 回收

關 recall [ˋrɪkɔl] (n.) 回收
同 call back, take back, withdraw, retract

一般正常速度 [rɪˋkɔl]
ETS全真速度 [rɪˋkɔl]

➡ 動詞的重音在第二音節，名詞的重音在第一音節

receipt (n.) 收據

關 receive (v.t) 收到
同 sales slip, voucher

一般正常速度 [rɪˋsit]
ETS全真速度 [rɪˋsi(t)]

➡ 名詞的 p 不須發音，字尾 [t] 輕唸即可

reception (n.) 接待

關 receive (v.t) 收到
同 acceptance, receiving, admission

一般正常速度 [rɪˋsɛpʃən]
ETS全真速度 [rɪˋsɛ(p)ʃən]

➡ 1) 名詞重音節母音 e 要唸成 [ɛ]
　 2) 名詞的 [p] 輕唸即可

recess (n.) 休息

關 recess [rɪˋsɛ(s)] (v.i) 休假
同 break, holiday, rest

一般正常速度 [ˋrɪsɛs]
ETS全真速度 [ˋrɪsɛ(s)]

➡ 名詞的重音在第一音節，動詞的重音在第二音節

考古題應用 We felt very reassured after his briefing.
在他的簡報後我們就覺得相當安心了。

試練習題 How did you feel after Mr. Lin's briefing?
考生回答處 _____

考古題應用 The company said it will recall all of the unsafe baby strollers.
公司表示會回收所有不安全的嬰兒推車。

試練習題 How has the company dealt with their unsafe baby strollers?
考生回答處 _____

考古題應用 You can ask the sales clerk to write another receipt.
你可以要求售貨員再開一張收據。

試練習題 What if I couldn't find the receipt for the reimbursement?
考生回答處 _____

R

考古題應用 You can get a brochure from the reception area.
你可以在接待區拿到宣傳手冊。

試練習題 Where can I get a brochure for this museum?
考生回答處 _____

考古題應用 We will take a thirty-minute recess.
我們將休息 30 分鐘。

試練習題 How long will the recess be?
考生回答處 _____

recipe (n.) 配方

同 formula, directions, instructions

一般正常速度 [ˋrɛsəpɪ]

ETS全真速度 [ˋrɛsəbɪ]

➡ 1) [p] 可變音為 [b]
2) 字尾 e 須發 [ɪ] 的音

reciprocal (adj.) 互惠的

關 reciprocate (v.t) 回報
同 mutual, exchanged, complementary

一般正常速度 [rɪˋsɪprəkl]

ETS全真速度 [rɪˋsɪprəgl]

➡ 1) 形容詞與動詞的重音都在第二音節
2) 形容詞的 [k] 可變音為 [g]

reckon (v.t) 估計

關 reckoning (n.) 估計
同 guess, estimate, calculate, add up, total

一般正常速度 [ˋrɛkən]

ETS全真速度 [ˋrɛgən]

➡ 1) 動詞與名詞的重音都在第一音節
2) 兩個詞性的 [k] 均須變音為 [g]

recognize (v.t) 認可

關 recognition (n.) 認可
recognizable (adj.) 可辨識的
同 acknowledge, admit, accept, appreciate

一般正常速度 [ˋrɛkəɡˏnaɪz]

ETS全真速度 [ˋrɛkə(g)ˏnaɪz]

➡ 所有詞性的 [g] 均輕唸即可

recommend (v.t) 建議

關 recommendation (n.) 推薦
同 propose, suggest, advise, advocate

一般正常速度 [ˏrɛkəˋmɛnd]

ETS全真速度 [ˏrɛkəˋmɛn(d)]

➡ 動詞字尾 [d] 輕唸即可

考古題應用　She <u>accidentally</u> leaked our recipe to a competitor.
她<u>不小心</u>把我們的配方洩露給一家競爭對手。

試練習題　Why is the company filing a lawsuit against Ms. Choi?
考生回答處

考古題應用　They have signed a reciprocal <u>trade agreement</u>.
他們已經簽定了一項互惠的<u>商務協定</u>。

試練習題　Have they accomplished anything after the meeting?
考生回答處

考古題應用　They reckoned our assets are worth ten million dollars.
他們估計我們的資產值一千萬美元。

試練習題　How much did the experts reckon our assets are worth?
考生回答處

R

考古題應用　Mr. Fletcher's success is widely recognized.
Fletcher 先生的成就是大家所公認的。

試練習題　Why did you ask Mr. Fletcher to deliver the opening speech?
考生回答處

考古題應用　He recommended that we wear <u>protective gear</u>.
他建議我們穿上<u>護具</u>。

試練習題　What did the tour guide recommend we do before canoeing?
考生回答處

recover (v.t) 取回

圞 recovery (n.) 恢復
同 take back, regain, retake

一般正常速度 [rɪˋkʌvɚ]
ETS全真速度 [rɪˋkʌvɚ]

➡ 動詞與名詞的重音都在第二音節

recruit (v.t) 招募

圞 recruit (n.) 新進人員
同 raise, muster

一般正常速度 [rɪˋkrut]
ETS全真速度 [rɪˋkru(t)]

➡ 1) 動詞與名詞的唸法相同
   2) 字尾 [t] 輕唸即可

redeem (v.t) 贖回

圞 redemption (n.) 贖回
同 regain, recover, buy back,
   repossess, win back

一般正常速度 [rɪˋdim]
ETS全真速度 [rɪˋdim]

➡ 1) 動詞與名詞的重音都在第二音節
   2) 名詞重音節母音 e 唸 [ɛ]
   3) 名詞的 [p] 必須消音

reduce (v.t) 減少

圞 reduction (n.) 減少
同 lower, decrease, cut down,
   downsize

一般正常速度 [rɪˋdjus]
ETS全真速度 [rɪˋdju(s)]

➡ 1) 動詞與名詞的重音都在第二音節
   2) 動詞字尾 [s] 輕唸即可
   3) 名詞重音節母音 u 唸 [ʌ]

redundant (adj.) 多餘的

圞 redundancy (n.) 多餘
同 extra, unnecessary, unwanted

一般正常速度 [rɪˋdʌndənt]
ETS全真速度 [rɪˋdʌn__ən(t)]

➡ 1) 形容詞與名詞的重音都在第二音節
   2) 第二個 [d] 均可消音
   3) 形容詞字尾 [t] 輕唸即可

考古題應用 　We <u>filed a report</u> with the police to recover our stolen money.
我們向<u>警方報案</u>以取回我們被偷的那筆錢。

口試練習題 　Why did you file a report with the police?

考生回答處 　_____

考古題應用 　We are recruiting well-trained <u>volunteers</u>.
我們在招募訓練有素的<u>志工</u>。

口試練習題 　Why are we interviewing people?

考生回答處 　_____

考古題應用 　He redeemed his car from the <u>pawnshop</u>.
他把車子從<u>當鋪</u>贖回來了。

口試練習題 　Did Mike get his car back?

考生回答處 　_____

考古題應用 　We have taken <u>preventative measures</u> to reduce <u>occupational hazards</u>.
我們已經採取了<u>預防措施</u>來降低<u>職業傷害</u>。

口試練習題 　Have you done anything to reduce occupational hazards?

考生回答處 　_____

考古題應用 　We store our redundant <u>machine parts</u> in the <u>warehouse</u>.
我們把多餘的<u>機器零件</u>存放在<u>倉庫</u>裡。

口試練習題 　What do you store in the warehouse?

考生回答處 　_____

R

refer (v.i) 提及

關 reference (n.) 參考
同 concern, relate, be relevant to

一般正常速度 [rɪ`fɝ]
ETS全真速度 [rɪ`fɝ]

➡ 動詞的重音在第二音節，名詞的重音在第一音節

refinance (v.t) 轉貸

一般正常速度 [ˌrifɪ`næns]
ETS全真速度 [ˌrifɪ`næns]

refine (v.t) 提煉

關 refinement (n.) 提煉
refinery (n.) 提煉廠
refined (adj.) 精製的
同 process, purify, clarify

一般正常速度 [rɪ`faɪn]
ETS全真速度 [rɪ`faɪn]

➡ 所有詞性的重音節都在第二音節

reflection (n.) 倒影

關 reflect (v.t) 反映
同 image

一般正常速度 [rɪ`flɛkʃən]
ETS全真速度 [rɪ`flɛ__ʃən]

➡ 1) 名詞與動詞的重音都在第二音節
2) 名詞的 [k] 停一拍即可，無須發音

reform (v.t) 改革

關 reform (n.) 改革
同 change, improve, correct, reconstruct

一般正常速度 [rɪ`fɔrm]
ETS全真速度 [rɪ`fɔrm]

➡ 動詞與名詞的唸法相同

考古題應用 She was referring to the <u>pharmaceutical plant</u> workers.
她說的是藥廠的員工。

試練習題 Who was Ms. Jackson referring to as the most hard-working type of employees?

考生回答處 _____

考古題應用 We refinanced the house for lower interest rates.
我們爲了較低的利率將房子轉貸。

試練習題 Why did you refinance your house?

考生回答處 _____

考古題應用 Oil must be refined before it is used.
石油在使用前要先提煉過。

試練習題 What do we do with oil before it is used?

考生回答處 _____

R

考古題應用 The reflection of the mountain on the lake is very beautiful.
那座山在湖面上的倒影非常漂亮。

試練習題 Why is everyone photographing the lake?

考生回答處 _____

考古題應用 Our manager decided to reform the <u>merit system</u>.
我們經理決定要改革績效制度。

試練習題 What has your manager decided to do first thing next quarter?

考生回答處 _____

refund (n.) 退款

關 refund [rɪˋfʌnd] (v.t) 退款
同 return, reimbursement, repayment

一般正常速度 [ˋriˏfʌnd]
ETS全真速度 [ˋriˏfʌn(d)]

➜ 1) 名詞的重音在第一音節，動詞的重音在第二音節
2) 名詞字尾 [d] 輕唸即可

refuse (v.i) 拒絕

關 refusal (n.) 拒絕
同 turn down, deny, reject

一般正常速度 [rɪˋfjuz]
ETS全真速度 [rɪˋfjuz]

➜ 動詞與名詞的重音都在第二音節

regional (adj.) 地區性的

關 region (n.) 地區
同 sectional, district, local

一般正常速度 [ˋridʒənl]
ETS全真速度 [ˋridʒənl]

➜ 1) 形容詞與名詞重音都在第一音節
2) 形容詞字尾 [l] 請勿唸成 [ɔ]（台式發音）

register (v.t) 註冊

關 register (n.) 登記
registration (n.) 掛號
registered (adj.) 掛號的
同 sign up, check in, enter

一般正常速度 [ˋrɛdʒɪstə]
ETS全真速度 [ˋrɛdʒɪsdə]

➜ 1) register 當動、名詞時唸法相同
2) 所有詞性的 [st] 均須變音為 [sd]

regret (v.t) 後悔

關 regret (n.) 遺憾
同 feel sorry for, be upset, miss

一般正常速度 [rɪˋgrɛt]
ETS全真速度 [rɪˋgrɛ(t)]

➜ 1) 動詞與名詞的唸法相同
2) 字尾 [t] 輕唸即可

272

考古題應用 Any customer with a <u>defective product</u> can demand a full refund.
買到瑕疵品的顧客皆可要求全額退款。

試練習題 Who can demand a full refund from your outlet?
考生回答處 _____

考古題應用 He refused to comment further on this issue.
他拒絕針對這個話題做進一步的評論。

試練習題 Did the CEO make any further comments on the lay-offs?
考生回答處 _____

考古題應用 This report <u>outlines</u> regional differences in our sales figures.
這份報告概述了我們銷售數字的地區性差異。

試練習題 What kind of information does this annual report provide?
考生回答處 _____

R

考古題應用 You need to register the product online to get the <u>extended guarantee</u>.
你必須爲產品線上註冊以延長保固期。

試練習題 How do I get the extended guarantee?
考生回答處 _____

考古題應用 He regretted selling the plant to the competitor.
他後悔把工廠賣給競爭對手。

試練習題 Why was Mr. Kondo so upset with himself?
考生回答處 _____

regularly (adv.) 定期地
關 regular (adj.) 週期性的
同 periodically, constantly

一般正常速度 [ˋrɛgjələlɪ]
ETS全真速度 [ˋrɛgjələlɪ]
➡ 副詞與形容詞的重音都在第一音節

regulation (n.) 規定
關 regulate (v.t) 規定
同 rule, policy, law, order

一般正常速度 [͵rɛgjəˋleʃən]
ETS全真速度 [͵rɛgjəˋleʃən]
➡ 名詞的重音在第三音節，動詞的重音在第一音節

rehearse (v.i) 排練
關 rehearsal (n.) 排練
同 practice, drill, prepare, try out

一般正常速度 [rɪˋhɝs]
ETS全真速度 [rɪˋhɝ(s)]
➡ 1) 動詞與名詞的重音都在第二音節
2) 動詞字尾 [s] 輕唸即可

reinforce (v.t) 加強
關 reinforcement (n.) 強化
同 strengthen, harden, fortify, consolidate, toughen

一般正常速度 [͵riɪnˋfɔrs]
ETS全真速度 [͵riɪnˋfɔr(s)]
➡ 1) 動詞與名詞的重音都在第三音節
2) 動詞字尾 [s] 輕唸即可
3) 名詞字尾 [t] 輕唸即可

release (v.t) 發布
關 release (n.) 釋放
同 issue, make known, make public

一般正常速度 [rɪˋlis]
ETS全真速度 [rɪˋli(s)]
➡ 1) 動詞與名詞的唸法相同
2) 字尾 [s] 輕唸即可

[考古題應用] We conduct computer workshops regularly.
我們定期舉辦電腦研習會。

[□試練習題] How do you help employees improve their computer skills?
[考生回答處] _____

[考古題應用] We can't ignore the safety regulations.
我們不能忽視安全規定。

[□試練習題] Do we have to put on hard hats when entering the plant?
[考生回答處] _____

[考古題應用] Hundreds of dancers are rehearsing for the grand opening ceremony.
數百名舞者為了盛大開幕典禮正在排練。

[□試練習題] Why is the auditorium still open at this hour?
[考生回答處] _____

R

[考古題應用] We need to reinforce the exterior walls with steel bars.
我們必須用鋼筋來強化外牆。

[□試練習題] What does the engineer recommend we do with the exterior walls?
[考生回答處] _____

[考古題應用] He is ready to release the news to the press this afternoon.
他準備在下午對媒體發布這項消息。

[□試練習題] When will Mr. Hill make public his upcoming retirement?
[考生回答處] _____

relevant (adj.) 相關的

關 relate (v.t) 有關
　relation (n.) 關係
同 related

一般正常速度 [ˋrɛləvənt]

ETS全真速度 [ˋrɛləvən(t)]

➡ 1) 形容詞的重音在第一音節，動詞與
　　名詞的重音都在第二音節 (-lat-)
　2) 形容詞的第一個 e 要唸成 [ɛ]
　3) 形容詞與動詞字尾 [t] 均輕唸即可

relieved (adj.) 放心的

關 relieve (v.t) 釋放
　relief (n.) 安心
同 feeling unburdened, not feeling
　worried

一般正常速度 [rɪˋlivd]

ETS全真速度 [rɪˋliv(d)]

➡ 1) 所有詞性的重音都在第二音節
　2) 形容詞字尾 [d] 輕唸即可

relocate (v.t) 搬遷

關 relocation (n.) 搬遷
同 move

一般正常速度 [riˋloket]

ETS全真速度 [riˋloke(t)]

➡ 1) 動詞的重音在第二音節，名詞的重
　　音在第三音節 (-ca-)
　2) 動詞字尾 [t] 輕唸即可

remedy (n.) 補救（方法）

關 remedy (v.t) 補救
同 correction, solution

一般正常速度 [ˋrɛmədɪ]

ETS全真速度 [ˋrɛmədɪ]

➡ 1) 名詞與動詞的唸法相同
　2) [d] 須變音為 [ɖ]

remind (v.t) 提醒

關 reminder (n.) 催函
同 remember, put in mind, refresh
　one's memory

一般正常速度 [rɪˋmaɪnd]

ETS全真速度 [rɪˋmaɪn(d)]

➡ 1) 動詞與名詞的重音都在第二音節
　2) 動詞字尾 [d] 輕唸即可
　3) 名詞字尾 [d] 須變音為 [ɖ]

考古題應用 Carmen doesn't have much relevant experience.
Carmen 沒有太多的相關經驗。

試練習題 Who will represent us at the convention, Luisa or Carmen?
考生回答處 _____

考古題應用 She would be relieved to know that the <u>vineyards</u> are fine.
她若知道葡萄園沒事應該就會放心了。

試練習題 Does Mrs. Petit know our vineyards survived the storm?
考生回答處 _____

考古題應用 We've decided to relocate our <u>headquarters</u> to Atlanta.
我們已經決定將總部搬遷到亞特蘭大。

試練習題 Where are you relocating your headquarters?
考生回答處 _____

R

考古題應用 Mr. Willis has provided us with a remedy for our losses.
Willis 先生已經提供我們損失的補救方法。

試練習題 Have you asked Mr. Willis how we can make up for our losses?
考生回答處 _____

考古題應用 She reminded me that I hadn't filed the analysis report.
她提醒我還沒交分析報告。

試練習題 Why did Ms. O'Neil call you?
考生回答處 _____

☐☐ remittance　☐☐ remote　☐☐ remove
☐☐ renew　☐☐ renovate

remittance (n.) 匯款

關 remit (v.t) 匯款
同 payment

一般正常速度 [rɪˋmɪtn̩s]
ETS全真速度 [rɪˋmɪ＿n̩s]

➡ 1) 名詞與動詞的重音都在第二音節
　 2) 名詞的 [t] 停一拍即可，無須發音

remote (adj.) 遙遠的

關 remoteness (n.) 遙遠
同 distant, faraway

一般正常速度 [rɪˋmot]
ETS全真速度 [rɪˋmo(t)]

➡ 1) 形容詞字尾 [t] 輕唸即可
　 2) 名詞的 [t] 停一拍即可，無須發音

remove (v.t) 免職

關 removable (adj.) 可移除的
同 take away, dispose, expel

一般正常速度 [rɪˋmuv]
ETS全真速度 [rɪˋmuv]

➡ 1) 動詞與形容詞的重音都在第二音節
　 2) 形容詞字尾 [l] 請勿唸成 [ɔ]（台式發音）

renew (v.t) 繼續

關 renewal (n.) 更新
　 renewable (adj.) 可繼續的
同 continue, extend, prolong

一般正常速度 [rɪˋnju]
ETS全真速度 [rɪˋnju]

➡ 1) 所有詞性的重音都在第二音節
　 2) 名詞字尾 [l] 請勿唸成 [ɔ]（台式發音）

renovate (v.t) 翻修

關 renovation (n.) 翻修
同 remodel, renew, repair, refurbish

一般正常速度 [ˋrɛnəˌvet]
ETS全真速度 [ˋrɛnəˌve(t)]

➡ 動詞字尾 [t] 輕唸即可

Her secretary has called to confirm us of the remittance.
她的祕書已經打電話來確認過匯款。

Has Ms. Chen remitted the balance to us?
考生回答處
_____

The resort is located in a remote alpine village.
渡假區位於一個遙遠的阿爾卑斯山小村莊。

Where is the beautiful resort you visited last time?
考生回答處
_____

The corrupt officer has been removed from his position.
貪汙的官員已經被免職了。

What happened to the officer that was prosecuted for corruption?
考生回答處
_____

R

We've decided to just renew the lease.
我們決定只要續約。

Will you buy the property when the lease is up?
考生回答處
_____

The hotel is renovating its lobby.
飯店正在翻修大廳。

Why is the front entrance to the hotel blocked?
考生回答處
_____

rent (v.t) 租借

關 rent (n.) 租金
   rental (n.) 租借
同 borrow, lease, hire, let

一般正常速度 [rɛnt]
ETS全真速度 [rɛn(t)]

➡ 1) 動詞字尾 [t] 輕唸即可
   2) rental 的 [t] 須變音為 [d]

repair (n.) 修理

關 repair (v.t) 修理
   repairable (adj.) 可修理的
同 fixing, making good, patch

一般正常速度 [rɪ`pɛr]
ETS全真速度 [rɪ`pɛr]

➡ 所有詞性的重音都在第二音節

reply (v.t) 回覆

關 reply (n.) 回覆
同 answer, respond, react, return

一般正常速度 [rɪ`plaɪ]
ETS全真速度 [rɪ`plaɪ]

➡ 動詞與名詞的唸法相同

represent (v.t) 代表

關 representative (n.) 代表
同 act for, speak for, stand for

一般正常速度 [ˌrɛprɪ`zɛnt]
ETS全真速度 [ˌrɛbrɪ`zɛn(t)]

➡ 1) 動詞與名詞的第一個 e 都唸 [ɛ]
   2) [p] 均可變音為 [b]
   3) 動詞字尾 [t] 輕唸即可
   4) 名詞中的兩個 [t] 均須變音為 [d]

reputation (n.) 名聲

關 reputable (adj.) 名聲好的
同 fame, credit, honor, esteem

一般正常速度 [ˌrɛpjə`teʃən]
ETS全真速度 [ˌrɛbjə`teʃən]

➡ 1) 名詞的重音在第三音節，形容詞的
      重音在第一音節
   2) [p] 均可變音為 [b]
   3) 形容詞的 [t] 須變音為 [d]

考古題應用 He will rent a car at the airport.
他會在機場租車。

口試練習題 How will Mr. Gilmour get to the hotel from the airport?
考生回答處 _____

考古題應用 Our <u>minivan</u> is in the repair shop.
我們的<u>休旅車</u>在修車廠裡。

口試練習題 Why do we have to go to the airport by shuttle bus?
考生回答處 _____

考古題應用 She replied that she would accept our <u>offer</u>.
她回覆說會接受我們的<u>條件</u>。

口試練習題 Has Ms. Norman returned our E-mail?
考生回答處 _____

R

考古題應用 The <u>union leaders</u> will be there to represent us.
<u>工會領袖</u>會到場代表我們。

口試練習題 Will everyone in the union attend the meeting?
考生回答處 _____

考古題應用 Its services have given the hotel an excellent reputation.
飯店的服務讓它享有很好的名聲。

口試練習題 Why is this five-star hotel always among tourists' top
choices?
考生回答處 _____

request (v.t) 要求

關 request (n.) 要求
同 demand, call for, ask for

一般正常速度 [rɪˋkwɛst]
ETS全真速度 [rɪˋkwɛ(st)]

➡ 1) 動詞與名詞的唸法相同
2) 字尾 [st] 輕唸即可

requirement (n.) 需求

關 require (v.t) 需求
同 need, demand

一般正常速度 [rɪˋkwaɪrmənt]
ETS全真速度 [rɪˋkwaɪrmən(t)]

➡ 1) 名詞與動詞的重音都在第二音節
2) 名詞字尾 [t] 輕唸即可

rescue (v.t) 拯救

關 rescue (n.) 拯救
同 save, recover, get out

一般正常速度 [ˋrɛskju]
ETS全真速度 [ˋrɛsgju]

➡ 1) 動詞與名詞的唸法相同
2) [k] 可變音為 [g]

research (n.) 研究

關 research (v.t) 做研究
同 study, analysis, investigation

一般正常速度 [rɪˋsɝtʃ]
ETS全真速度 [rɪˋsɝ(tʃ)]

➡ 名詞與動詞的重音位置相同（在第一
音節或第二音節皆可）

reservation (n.) 訂位

關 reserve (v.t) 保留
同 preserve, arrangement

一般正常速度 [ˌrɛzəˋveʃən]
ETS全真速度 [ˌrɛzəˋveʃən]

➡ 名詞的重音在第三音節，動詞的重音
在第二音節 (-serve)

考古題應用　The new members are requested to pay <u>initiation fees</u>.
新會員被要求繳交<u>入會費</u>。

試練習題　What are the new members of the club requested to do?

考生回答處　＿＿＿＿＿＿＿＿＿＿＿＿＿＿＿＿＿＿＿＿＿＿

考古題應用　The <u>maintenance requirements</u> of these machines are the same.
這些機器的<u>維修需求</u>是一樣的。

試練習題　Are the maintenance requirements of these machines different?

考生回答處　＿＿＿＿＿＿＿＿＿＿＿＿＿＿＿＿＿＿＿＿＿＿

考古題應用　He rescued our company from <u>the brink of bankruptcy</u>.
他把我們的公司從<u>破產邊緣</u>救回來。

試練習題　Why are you so grateful for what Mr. Ryder did?

考生回答處　＿＿＿＿＿＿＿＿＿＿＿＿＿＿＿＿＿＿＿＿＿＿

R

考古題應用　We are still conducting research on the medicine's <u>side effects</u>.
我們還在進行此藥物的<u>副作用</u>研究。

試練習題　Is the new medicine ready to hit the market?

考生回答處　＿＿＿＿＿＿＿＿＿＿＿＿＿＿＿＿＿＿＿＿＿＿

考古題應用　I'll call the restaurant to <u>confirm</u> our reservation.
我會打電話向餐廳<u>確認</u>我們的訂位。

試練習題　Are you sure we'll have a table at the fancy restaurant tonight?

考生回答處　＿＿＿＿＿＿＿＿＿＿＿＿＿＿＿＿＿＿＿＿＿＿

reshuffle (v.t) 改組

關 reshuffle (n.) 改組；重新洗牌
同 change, rearrange

一般正常速度 [riˋʃʌfḷ]
ETS全真速度 [riˋʃʌfḷ]

➡ 1) 動詞與名詞的唸法相同
2) 字尾 [ḷ] 請勿唸成 [ɔ]（台式發音）

---

resident (n.) 居民

關 residence (n.) 居住地
residency (n.) 居留權
residential (adj.) 住宅的
同 inhabitant, local, occupant,
tenant

一般正常速度 [ˋrɛzədənt]
ETS全真速度 [ˋrɛzəđən(t)]

➡ 1) 名詞的重音都在第一音節，形容詞
的重音在第三音節 (-den-)
2) resident 字尾 [t] 輕唸即可
3) 形容詞字尾 [ḷ] 請勿唸成 [ɔ]

---

resign (v.i) 辭職

關 resignation (n.) 辭職
同 quit, leave, step down, give up

一般正常速度 [rɪˋzaɪn]
ETS全真速度 [rɪˋzaɪn]

➡ 動詞的重音在第二音節，名詞的重音
在第三音節 (-na-)

---

resist (v.t) 抗拒

關 resistance (n.) 抵制
resistant (adj.) 有抵抗力的
同 refuse, turn down

一般正常速度 [rɪˋzɪst]
ETS全真速度 [rɪˋzɪ(st)]

➡ 1) 動詞字尾 [st] 輕唸即可
2) 形容詞與名詞的第一個 [t] 要唸成
[d]

---

resolve (v.t) 解決

關 resolution (n.) 決心
同 settle, solve, fix, work out

一般正常速度 [rɪˋzalv]
ETS全真速度 [rɪˋzal(v)]

➡ 1) 動詞的重音在第二音節，名詞的重
音在第三音節 (-lu-)
2) 兩個詞性的 s 都要唸成 [z]

考古題應用 The president has decided to reshuffle the congress.
總統決定將國會改組。

試練習題 Why is everyone so surprised at the president's latest announcement?

考生回答處 _____

考古題應用 The local residents prefer a park to a factory.
當地居民比較想要公園而非工廠。

試練習題 Which one do the local residents prefer, a park or a factory?

考生回答處 _____

考古題應用 He resigned from the board because of health concerns.
他因健康上的顧慮辭掉董事會的職務。

試練習題 Why did Mr. Chen resign?

考生回答處 _____

R

考古題應用 The director resisted their salary demands.
主管反對他們的薪資要求。

試練習題 How did the director react to his staff's salary demands?

考生回答處 _____

考古題應用 We have come up with a way to resolve the labor dispute.
我們已想出辦法來解決勞資糾紛。

試練習題 Can your company deal with the labor dispute?

考生回答處 _____

resource (n.) 資源

關 resourceful (adj.) 豐富的
同 source, supply

一般正常速度 [`rɪsors]
ETS全真速度 [`rɪsor(s)]

➡ 1) 名詞的重音在第一音節，形容詞的重音在第二音節 (-source-)
2) 形容詞字尾 [l] 請勿唸成 [ɔ]（台式發音）

respond (v.i) 回應

關 response (n.) 回覆
同 answer, reply, return, react

一般正常速度 [rɪ`spand]
ETS全真速度 [rɪ`sban(d)]

➡ 1) [p] 均須變音為 [b]
2) 動詞字尾 [d] 及名詞字尾 [s] 均輕唸即可

respondent (n.) 受訪者

關 respond (v.i) 回應
respondence (n.) 回應
同 answerer, responder

一般正常速度 [rɪ`spandənt]
ETS全真速度 [rɪ`sban__n(t)]

➡ 1) 所有詞性的重音都在第二音節
2) 所有詞性的 [p] 均須變音為 [b]
3) 名詞的 [d] 停一拍即可，無須發音

responsible (adj.) 負責的

關 responsibility (n.) 責任
同 reliable, dependable, conscientious

一般正常速度 [rɪ`spansəbl]
ETS全真速度 [rɪ`sbansəbl]

➡ 1) [p] 均須變音為 [b]
2) 形容詞字尾 [l] 請勿唸成 [ɔ]（台式發音）
3) 名詞字尾 [t] 須變音為 [d]

restore (v.t) 恢復

關 restoration (n.) 恢復
restorable (adj.) 可恢復的
同 fix, repair, reconstruct, rebuild, renew, recover

一般正常速度 [rɪ`stor]
ETS全真速度 [rɪ`sdor]

➡ 1) [t] 均須變音為 [d]
2) 形容詞字尾 [l] 請勿唸成 [ɔ]

考古題應用 | Germany is a country rich in mineral resources.
德國是一個礦物資源豐富的國家。

試練習題 | What kind of natural resources does Germany have?
考生回答處 | _____

考古題應用 | The government has not responded to our protest.
政府尚未回應我們的抗議。

試練習題 | Has the government responded to your protest?
考生回答處 | _____

考古題應用 | The respondents will finish the questionnaires in no time.
受訪者馬上就可以填好問卷。

試練習題 | Do the respondents need more time for the questionnaires?
考生回答處 | _____

R

考古題應用 | They held him responsible for the company's losses.
他們覺得公司損失要由他負責。

試練習題 | Why did the committee blame the PR manager?
考生回答處 | _____

考古題應用 | We've successfully restored our competitiveness.
我們已成功恢復我們的競爭力。

試練習題 | What has happened since the labor dispute came to an end?
考生回答處 | _____

restrict (v.t) 限制

關 restriction (n.) 限制
restricted (adj.) 有限制的
同 limit, confine, regulate

一般正常速度 [rɪˋstrɪkt]
ETS全真速度 [rɪˋsdrɪ(kt)]

➔ 1) [st] 均須變音為 [sd]
2) 動詞字尾的 [kt] 輕唸即可

result (n.) 結果

關 result (v.i) 造成
同 outcome, end, conclusion,
consequence

一般正常速度 [rɪˋzʌlt]
ETS全真速度 [rɪˋzʌl(t)]

➔ 1) 名詞與動詞的唸法相同
2) 字尾 [t] 輕唸即可

resume (v.t) 重新開始

同 restart, continue, carry on, begin
again

一般正常速度 [rɪˋzjum]
ETS全真速度 [rɪˋzjum]

➔ 1) 重音在第二音節
2) u 唸 [ju] 或 [u] 皆可

résumé (n.) 履歷表

同 summary, curriculum vitae

一般正常速度 [͵zɛzjʊˋme]
ETS全真速度 [͵zɛzjʊˋme]

retail (n.) 零售

關 retail (v.t) 零售
retailer (n.) 零售商
retail (adv.) 零售地

一般正常速度 [ˋritel]
ETS全真速度 [ˋritel]

➔ 1) 所有詞性的重音都在第一音節
2) 字尾 [l] 請勿唸成 [ɔ] (台式發音)

考古題應用 The government has decided to restrict the number of foreign workers in the country.
政府已決定要限制國內外籍勞工的數量。

口試練習題 Are there any new policies on foreign workers?

考生回答處 _____

考古題應用 They missed their flight as a result of heavy traffic.
他們因為塞車而錯過了班機。

口試練習題 Why were the consultants late for the convention?

考生回答處 _____

考古題應用 After resigning, he will resume his teaching job.
辭職後，他會重返教職的工作。

口試練習題 What will Mr. Higgins do after his resignation as a consultant?

考生回答處 _____

R

考古題應用 Remember to correct spelling mistakes in your résumé.
記得訂正履歷表上的拼字錯誤。

口試練習題 What do you recommend I do before sending out my résumé?

考生回答處 _____

考古題應用 I bought this mobile phone at a retail store.
我在零售店買了這支手機。

口試練習題 Where did you buy your new mobile phone?

考生回答處 _____

retain (v.t) 保留

關 retention (n.) 保留
同 keep, hold, remain, maintain

一般正常速度 [rɪˋten]
ETS全真速度 [rɪˋten]

➡ 動詞與名詞的重音都在第二音節

retire (v.i) 退休

關 retirement (n.) 退休
retiree (n.) 退休人員

一般正常速度 [rɪˋtaɪr]
ETS全真速度 [rɪˋtaɪr]

➡ 除 retiree 重音在最後一音節 (-ee) 外，
其他詞性的重音都在第二音節

retrieve (v.t) 取回

關 retrieval (n.) 取回
同 get back, restore, regain,
recover, redeem, win back

一般正常速度 [rɪˋtriv]
ETS全真速度 [rɪˋtri(v)]

➡ 1) 動詞與名詞的重音都在第二音節
2) 名詞字尾 [l] 請勿唸成 [ɔ]（台式發
音）

reveal (v.t) 透露

關 revelation (n.) 揭露
同 leak, make known, make public,
tell

一般正常速度 [rɪˋvil]
ETS全真速度 [rɪˋvil]

➡ 1) 動詞的重音在第二音節，名詞的重
音在第三音節 (-la-)
2) 動詞的第一個 e 唸 [ɪ]，名詞則唸 [ɛ]
3) 動詞字尾 [l] 請勿唸成 [ɔ]

reverse (v.t) 徹底改變

關 reverse (n.) 相反
reverse (adj.) 相反的
同 undo, overturn, invalidate,
cancel, change, alter

一般正常速度 [rɪˋvɜs]
ETS全真速度 [rɪˋvɜ(s)]

➡ 1) 所有詞性的唸法相同
2) 字尾 [s] 輕唸即可

考古題應用　The mansion still retains its 18th-century <u>elegance</u>.
這棟豪宅仍保有它 18 世紀的<u>高雅</u>。

試練習題　Why are there so many bidders for this old mansion?
考生回答處 _____

考古題應用　He'll be retiring at the end of the year.
他將在年底退休。

試練習題　When will Mr. Tyson retire from city hall?
考生回答處 _____

考古題應用　He retrieved his briefcase at the airport's <u>lost-and-found</u>.
他在機場的<u>失物招領處</u>取回公事包。

試練習題　Where did he retrieve his briefcase?
考生回答處 _____

R

考古題應用　We are <u>not authorized</u> to reveal the winners.
我們<u>沒有權利</u>透露得主。

試練習題　Can you tell us the winners of the auction?
考生回答處 _____

考古題應用　The government won't reverse its decision to <u>raise taxes</u>.
政府不會改變它提高稅金的決定。

試練習題　Will the government reverse its decision to raise taxes?
考生回答處 _____

review (n.) 考核

關 review (v.t) 複習
同 assessment, evaluation, judge

一般正常速度 [rɪ`vju]
ETS全真速度 [rɪ`vju]

➡ 名詞與動詞的唸法相同

revision (n.) 修正

關 revise (v.t) 訂正
同 correction, proofreading, alteration, change

一般正常速度 [rɪ`vɪʒən]
ETS全真速度 [rɪ`vɪʒən]

➡ 1) 名詞與動詞的重音都在第二音節
　 2) 名詞的第一個 i 唸成 [ɪ]，動詞的 i 唸成 [aɪ]

revive (v.t) 振興

同 restore, renew, recover, renovate, refresh, bring around

一般正常速度 [rɪ`vaɪv]
ETS全真速度 [rɪ`vaɪ(v)]

➡ 1) 重音在第二音節
　 2) 字尾 [v] 輕唸即可

rewarding (adj.) 有報酬的

關 reward (n.) 獎賞
同 worthy, worthwhile, gainful, gratifying

一般正常速度 [rɪ`wɔrdɪŋ]
ETS全真速度 [rɪ`wɔrdɪŋ]

➡ 1) 形容詞的 [d] 須變音為 [đ]
　 2) 名詞字尾 [d] 輕唸即可

Ri-

right (n.) 權利

關 right (adj.) 正確的
　 right (adv.) 正確地
同 power, authority

一般正常速度 [raɪt]
ETS全真速度 [raɪ(t)]

➡ 1) 所有詞性的唸法相同
　 2) 字尾 [t] 輕唸即可

考古題應用　We'll be giving Carl his <u>performance</u> review soon.
我們很快將考核 Carl 的<u>工作表現</u>。

□試練習題　Why does Carl look so nervous?

考生回答處　_____

考古題應用　He made <u>a number of</u> revisions to the draft.
這份草稿他做了<u>許多</u>修正。

□試練習題　Mr. Temple has proofread this draft, hasn't he?

考生回答處　_____

考古題應用　The government has been trying to revive <u>the local economy</u>.
政府一直努力振興<u>地方經濟</u>。

□試練習題　Has the government done anything to revive the local economy?

考生回答處　_____

考古題應用　1998 was a very successful and rewarding year for us.
1998 年對我們來說是非常成功且相當賺錢的一年。

□試練習題　How was your business in the year of 1998?

考生回答處　_____

考古題應用　They have no right to park in our staff garage.
他們沒有權利停在我們的員工停車場。

□試練習題　Can customers park in your staff garage?

考生回答處　_____

R

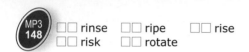

rinse (v.t) 洗滌

關 rinse (n.) 洗滌
同 wash, clean, bathe

一般正常速度 [rɪns]
ETS全真速度 [rɪn(s)]

➡ 1) 動詞與名詞的唸法相同
　 2) 字尾 [s] 輕唸即可

---

ripe (adj.) 成熟的

關 ripen (v.i) 成熟
同 mature, ripened, ready, fully grown

一般正常速度 [raɪp]
ETS全真速度 [raɪ(p)]

➡ 1) 形容詞字尾 [p] 輕唸即可
　 2) 動詞的 [p] 須變音為 [b]

---

rise (n.) 上漲

關 rise (v.i) 升起
同 increase

一般正常速度 [raɪz]
ETS全真速度 [raɪ(z)]

➡ 1) 名詞與動詞的唸法相同
　 2) 字尾 [z] 輕唸即可

---

risk (v.t) 冒險

關 risk (n.) 風險
　 risky (adj.) 危險的
同 take a chance on, hazard, venture

一般正常速度 [rɪsk]
ETS全真速度 [rɪs(k)]

➡ 1) 動詞與名詞的唸法相同
　 2) 字尾 [k] 輕唸即可
　 3) 形容詞的 [k] 可變音為 [g]

Ro-

rotate (v.i) 輪流

關 rotation (n.) 循環
同 alternate, take turns, switch, interchange

一般正常速度 [ˋrotet]
ETS全真速度 [ˋrote(t)]

➡ 1) 動詞的重音在第一音節，名詞的重音在第二音節 (-ta-)
　 2) 動詞字尾 [t] 輕唸即可

考古題應用　It's very important for us to rinse the vegetables before cooking.
烹飪前清洗蔬菜是很重要的。

口試練習題　What preparations should we make before cooking?
考生回答處　_____

考古題應用　The truck is loaded with ripe apples.
卡車裝滿了熟蘋果。

口試練習題　What is the truck loaded with?
考生回答處　_____

考古題應用　There's a sharp rise in power consumption during the summer.
夏天用電量激增。

口試練習題　Why has the government asked us to conserve electricity?
考生回答處　_____

考古題應用　Those who park illegally may risk a big fine.
違規停車的人要冒著高額罰金的風險。

口試練習題　What will happen to those who park in the tow-away zone?
考生回答處　_____

考古題應用　The host of the award ceremony rotates annually.
頒獎典禮的主持人每年輪流。

口試練習題　Will you also be hosting the year's award ceremony?
考生回答處　_____

R

rough (adj.) 粗暴的

關 rough (v.t) 粗暴對待
roughly (adv.) 大致上
同 quick, raw, unrefined, hasty, rude

一般正常速度 [rʌf]
ETS全真速度 [rʌ(f)]

➡ 1) 形容詞與動詞的唸法相同
2) 母音 [ʌ] 請勿唸成 [ɑ] （台式發音）
3) 字尾 [f] 輕唸即可

route (n.) 路線

關 route (v.t) 走…路線
同 way, direction, road, passage,
course

一般正常速度 [rut]
ETS全真速度 [ru(t)]

➡ 1) 名詞與動詞的唸法相同
2) 母音 ou 可唸 [u] 或 [aʊ]
3) 字尾 [t] 輕唸即可

routine (adj.) 例行的

關 routine (n.) 例行公事
同 typical, usual, habitual, normal

一般正常速度 [ruˋtin]
ETS全真速度 [ruˋtin]

➡ 形容詞與名詞的唸法相同

Ru-

rule (v.t) 判定

關 rule (n.) 統治
ruler (n.) 管理者
ruling (adj.) 管理的
同 judge, decide, determine, find

一般正常速度 [rul]
ETS全真速度 [rul]

➡ 1) rule 當動、名詞時唸法相同
2) 字尾的 [l] 請勿唸成 [ɔ] （台式發音）

rush (v.t) 趕緊處理

關 rush (n.) 匆忙
同 speed up, hurry, accelerate,
hasten, quicken, race

一般正常速度 [rʌʃ]
ETS全真速度 [rʌ(ʃ)]

➡ 1) 動詞與名詞的唸法相同
2) 字尾 [ʃ] 輕唸即可

考古題應用 The warranty doesn't cover damage caused by rough handling.
保固不包含使用不當造成的損壞。

試練習題 Does the warranty cover damage caused by rough handling?

考生回答處 _____

考古題應用 They've decided to take a different route.
他們決定要改走別的路線。

試練習題 Are your parents aware that Route 20 is currently under construction?

考生回答處 _____

考古題應用 Our security officers are conducting a routine examination.
我們的安全人員正在進行例行檢查。

試練習題 Why is the east wing of the building closed at this time?

考生回答處 _____

R

考古題應用 The court has ruled it unlawful.
法庭判定它不合法。

試練習題 Why do they have to abort the merger?
使中止
(ə'bɔrt)

考生回答處 _____

考古題應用 You'd better ask the shipping department to rush her order.
你最好請出貨部門趕緊處理她的訂單。

試練習題 Ms. Martinez was very upset about the delay, wasn't she?

考生回答處 _____

Check List 7

到目前為止，字彙量又增加了不少，繼續學新單字之前，我們先來複習一下，
看看是不是都記起來了！

☐ race	☐ reception	☐ refuse
☐ radical	☐ recess	☐ regional
☐ raffle	☐ recipe	☐ register
☐ raise	☐ reciprocal	☐ regret
☐ rally	☐ reckon	☐ regularly
☐ randomly	☐ recognize	☐ regulation
☐ rapidly	☐ recommend	☐ rehearse
☐ rate	☐ recover	☐ reinforce
☐ rational	☐ recruit	☐ release
☐ raw	☐ redeem	☐ relevant
☐ reach	☐ reduce	☐ relieved
☐ reaction	☐ redundant	☐ relocate
☐ realize	☐ refer	☐ remedy
☐ reap	☐ refinance	☐ remind
☐ reasonably	☐ refine	☐ remittance
☐ reassure	☐ reflection	☐ remote
☐ recall	☐ reform	☐ remove
☐ receipt	☐ refund	☐ renew

- ☐ renovate
- ☐ rent
- ☐ repair
- ☐ reply
- ☐ represent
- ☐ reputation

- ☐ request
- ☐ requirement
- ☐ rescue
- ☐ research
- ☐ reservation
- ☐ reshuffle

- ☐ resident
- ☐ resign
- ☐ resist
- ☐ resolve
- ☐ resource
- ☐ respond

- ☐ respondent
- ☐ responsible
- ☐ restore
- ☐ restrict
- ☐ result
- ☐ resume

- ☐ résumé
- ☐ retail
- ☐ retain
- ☐ retire
- ☐ retrieve
- ☐ reveal

- ☐ reverse
- ☐ review
- ☐ revision
- ☐ revive
- ☐ rewarding
- ☐ right

- ☐ rinse
- ☐ ripe
- ☐ rise
- ☐ risk
- ☐ rotate
- ☐ rough

- ☐ route
- ☐ routine
- ☐ rule
- ☐ rush

S
Sa-

sabotage (v.t) 破壞

關 sabotage (n.) 破壞
同 damage, disable, destroy

一般正常速度 [ˋsæbəˌtɑʒ]
ETS全真速度 [ˋsæbəˌtɑʒ]

➡ 1) 動詞與名詞的唸法相同
　　2) 字尾 ge 須唸成 [ʒ]

safety (n.) 安全

關 safe (n.) 保險箱
　　safe (adj.) 安全的
同 security, protection

一般正常速度 [ˋseftɪ]
ETS全真速度 [ˋsefdɪ]

➡ safety 字尾的 [t] 須變音為 [d]

sale (n.) 拍賣

關 sell (v.t) 販賣
同 vending, dealing, selling

一般正常速度 [sel]
ETS全真速度 [sel]

➡ 名詞與動詞的字尾 [l] 請勿唸成 [ɔ]
　　（台式發音）

salute (n.) 致敬

關 salute (v.t) 敬禮
同 recognition, tribute

一般正常速度 [səˋlut]
ETS全真速度 [səˋlu(t)]

➡ 1) 名詞與動詞的唸法相同
　　2) 字尾 [t] 輕唸即可

sample (v.t) 品嚐

關 sample (n.) 樣品
同 taste, try, test

一般正常速度 [ˋsæmpl]
ETS全真速度 [ˋsæmbl]

➡ 1) 動詞與名詞的唸法相同
　　2) [p] 可變音為 [b]
　　3) 字尾 [l] 請勿唸成 [ɔ]（台式發音）

考古題應用 Our competitors may try to sabotage our new campaign.
我們的競爭者會企圖破壞我們的新活動。

□試練習題 Why did the CEO ask us to take preventative measures?

考生回答處 _____

考古題應用 Safety checks are carried out in all international airports.
所有的國際機場都實施安全檢查。

□試練習題 What safety measures does the U.S. government take in its airports?

考生回答處 _____

考古題應用 They are having a clearance sale.
他們在舉辦清倉拍賣。

□試練習題 Why are there more customers than usual at the Wilson Office Depot?

考生回答處 _____

考古題應用 We will give our salute to the retiring Product Manager.
我們要向即將退休的產品經理致敬。

□試練習題 Why is the office throwing a party this weekend?

考生回答處 _____

考古題應用 We have invited experts to sample the wine.
我們邀請專家來品酒。

□試練習題 Who did you invite to sample your award-winning red wine?

考生回答處 _____

8

sanction (n.) 許可

關 sanction (v.t) 許可

同 approval, permission, allowance, confirmation, endorsement, entitlement

一般正常速度 [`sæŋkʃən]

ETS全真速度 [`sæŋ(k)ʃən]

➡ 1) 名詞與動詞的唸法相同
2) [k] 輕唸即可

sand (v.t) 用沙紙磨

關 sand (n.) 沙子

同 rub, make smooth

一般正常速度 [sænd]

ETS全真速度 [sæn(d)]

➡ 1) 動詞與名詞的唸法相同
2) 字尾 [d] 輕唸即可

sanitary (adj.) 衛生的

關 sanitation (n.) 衛生

同 clean, healthy

一般正常速度 [`sænə‚tɛrɪ]

ETS全真速度 [`sænə‚tɛrɪ]

➡ 形容詞的重音在第一音節，名詞的重音在第三音節 (-ta-)

satisfactory
(adj.) 令人滿意的

關 satisfy (v.t) 滿意
satisfaction (n.) 滿足

同 good enough, acceptable, adequate

一般正常速度 [‚sætɪs`fæktərɪ]

ETS全真速度 [‚sædɪs`fæ(k)dərɪ]

➡ 1) 所有詞性的第一個 [t] 均須變音為 [đ]
2) 形容詞的 [k] 輕唸即可
3) 形容詞第二個 [t] 可變音為 [d]

scan (v.t) 瀏覽

關 scan (n.) 掃瞄
scanner (n.) 掃瞄器

同 check, look through, run over, skim

一般正常速度 [skæn]

ETS全真速度 [sgæn]

➡ 1) scan 當動、名詞唸法相同
2) [k] 可變音為 [g]

[考古題應用] The medicine <u>hit the market</u> without the sanction of the FDA.
那個藥品沒有食品藥物管理局的許可就<u>上市</u>了。

[口試練習題] Why are they recalling the medicine?
[考生回答處] _____

[考古題應用] The furniture maker is sanding a shelf board.
家具師傅正用沙紙磨層板。

[口試練習題] What is the furniture maker working on?
[考生回答處] _____

[考古題應用] It's sanitary to wear gloves when processing food.
戴手套處理食物是衛生的。

[口試練習題] What is a sanitary thing to do when processing food?
[考生回答處] _____

[考古題應用] His performance is satisfactory.
他的表現令人滿意。

[口試練習題] Mr. Carter is a very competent employee, isn't he?
[考生回答處] _____

[考古題應用] Heather has been scanning the <u>classified ads</u> for hours.
Heather 已經瀏覽<u>分類廣告</u>好幾個小時了。

[口試練習題] What has Heather been doing with the newspapers?
[考生回答處] _____

scarcely (adv.) 幾乎沒有

關 scarcity (n.) 缺乏
同 hardly, barely, almost not

一般正常速度 [`skɛrslɪ]
ETS全真速度 [`skɛrslɪ]

➡ 1) 副詞與名詞的重音都在第一音節
2) 名詞的 [t] 須變音為 [d]

scenery (n.) 風景

關 scene (n.) 景色
同 view, landscape, surroundings

一般正常速度 [`sinərɪ]
ETS全真速度 [`sinərɪ]

schedule (v.t) 預定

關 schedule (n.) 行程表
同 program, arrange, plan, organize

一般正常速度 [`skɛdʒʊl]
ETS全真速度 [`skɛdʒʊl]

➡ 1) 動詞與名詞的唸法相同
2) 字尾 [l] 請勿唸成 [ɔ]（台式發音）

scheme (n.) 方案

關 scheme (v.t) 策畫
同 plan, plot, project, proposal

一般正常速度 [skim]
ETS全真速度 [sgim]

➡ 1) 名詞與動詞的唸法相同
2) [k] 須變音為 [g]

scholarship (n.) 獎學金

關 scholar (n.) 學者
scholarly (adj.) 學術的
同 fellowship

一般正常速度 [`skɑlɚˏʃɪp]
ETS全真速度 [`sgɑlɚˏʃɪp]

➡ 所有詞性中的 [k] 均須變音為 [g]

考古題應用 I scarcely see him work overtime.
我幾乎沒看過他加班。

試練習題 Ronald always punches out on time, doesn't he?
考生回答處 _____

考古題應用 She is taking pictures of the beautiful scenery.
她正在拍攝美麗的風景。

試練習題 What is Diana doing out there by the lake?
考生回答處 _____

考古題應用 Our guest speaker is scheduled to arrive at 10 o'clock.
我們的演講來賓預定在十點抵達。

試練習題 When is our guest speaker scheduled to arrive?
考生回答處 _____

考古題應用 The mayor has worked out a scheme to lower unemployment figures.
市長已經想出降低失業數字的方案。

試練習題 What has the mayor done to lower unemployment figures?
考生回答處 _____

考古題應用 She won a scholarship to Yale.
她拿到耶魯大學的獎學金。

試練習題 Why is Gemma quitting her job?
考生回答處 _____

□□ scope　□□ scrape　□□ screen
□□ script　□□ scrub

scope (n.) 範圍

回 range, extent, area

一般正常速度 [skop]

ETS全真速度 [sgo⁽ᵖ⁾]

➡ 1) [k] 可變音為 [g]
　　2) 字尾 [p] 輕唸即可

scrape (v.t) 刮掉

關 scrape (n.) 刮痕
　　scraper (n.) 刮刀
回 scratch, rub, skin

一般正常速度 [skrep]

ETS全真速度 [sgre⁽ᵖ⁾]

➡ 1) 所有詞性的 [k] 均須變音為 [g]
　　2) scrape 的 [p] 輕唸即可，scraper
　　　的 [p] 須變音為 [b]

screen (v.t) 過濾

關 screen (n.) 螢幕
回 filter, scan, examine

一般正常速度 [skrin]

ETS全真速度 [sgrin]

➡ 1) 動詞與名詞的唸法相同
　　2) [k] 可變音為 [g]

script (n.) 稿子

回 writing, text

一般正常速度 [skrɪpt]

ETS全真速度 [sgrɪ⁽ᵖᵗ⁾]

➡ 1) [k] 可變音為 [g]
　　2) 字尾 [pt] 輕唸即可

scrub (v.t) 刷洗

關 scrub (n.) 刷洗
回 clean, cleanse, rub

一般正常速度 [skrʌb]

ETS全真速度 [sgrʌ⁽ᵇ⁾]

➡ 1) 動詞與名詞的唸法相同
　　2) [k] 可變音為 [g]
　　3) 字尾 [b] 輕唸即可

MP3
153

考古題應用 The side effects of the new drug are beyond our scope of study.
新藥物的副作用不在我們的研究範圍。

口試練習題 Why aren't the side effects of the new drug in your research report?

考生回答處 _____

考古題應用 The farmer is scraping the mud off of his boots.
農夫正把靴子上的泥巴刮掉。

口試練習題 What is the farmer doing to his boots?

考生回答處 _____

考古題應用 The security officers are screening the guests of the governor's party.
安全人員在過濾州長派對上的來賓。

口試練習題 What are the security officers doing with the metal detectors?

考生回答處 _____

考古題應用 She is proofreading the script of my speech.
她正在幫我校閱演講稿。

口試練習題 Has Ms. Rivera gone to lunch yet?

考生回答處 _____

S

考古題應用 I'll ask the <u>maids</u> to scrub the floor.
我會請傭人刷洗地板。

口試練習題 Don't you think you should do some cleaning before the guests arrive?

考生回答處 _____

scrutinize (v.t) 仔細檢查

關 scrutiny (n.) 監視；細看
同 examine, inspect, investigate, study

一般正常速度 [ˋskrutn̩͵aɪz]
ETS全真速度 [ˋsgru__n̩͵aɪz]

➜ 1) 動詞與名詞的 [k] 均須變音為 [g]
　 2) [t] 停一拍即可，無須發音

sculpture (n.) 雕像

關 sculpture (v.t) 雕刻
　 sculptor (n.) 雕刻家
同 statue

一般正常速度 [ˋskʌlptʃɚ]
ETS全真速度 [ˋsgʌl__tʃɚ]

➜ 1) 所有詞性的 [k] 均須變音為 [g]
　 2) 所有詞性的 [p] 均無須唸出
　 3) sculptor 的 [t] 須變音為 [d]

seal (v.t) 密封

關 seal (n.) 封印
同 close, shut, secure

一般正常速度 [sil]
ETS全真速度 [sil]

➜ 動詞與名詞的唸法相同

seam (n.) 接縫處

關 seamless (adj.) 無縫的
同 joint, closure

一般正常速度 [sim]
ETS全真速度 [sim]

➜ 形容詞重音在第一音節

season (n.) 季節

關 season (v.t) 調味
　 seasonable (adj.) 合時宜的
同 time of year, period

一般正常速度 [ˋsizn̩]
ETS全真速度 [ˋsizn̩]

➜ 1) 所有詞性的重音都在第一音節
　 2) 形容詞字尾 [l] 請勿唸成 [ɔ]（台式發音）

考古題應用 They are still scrutinizing the results of the experiment.
他們還在仔細檢查實驗結果。

□試練習題 Has the R&D Department written up a report for the experiment?

考生回答處 _____

考古題應用 We added another sculpture in the foyer.
我們在前廳多加了一座雕像。

□試練習題 What did you do to make your foyer more attractive?

考生回答處 _____

考古題應用 He is sealing the cardboard box with tape.
他正在用膠帶把紙箱封起來。

□試練習題 What is Brandon doing with the cardboard box?

考生回答處 _____

考古題應用 The shirt ripped along a seam.
這件襯衫從接縫處裂開了。

□試練習題 Why is the customer returning this shirt?

考生回答處 _____

考古題應用 Spring is the high season for tourism in Japan.
春天是日本旅遊業的旺季。

□試練習題 Which time of the year is the high season for tourism in Japan?

考生回答處 _____

seat (n.) 座位

關 seat (v.t) 可容納…座位
同 chair

一般正常速度 [sit]
ETS全真速度 [si(t)]

➡ 1) 名詞與動詞的唸法相同
　 2) 字尾 [t] 輕唸即可

secondary (adj.) 次要的

關 second (adj.) 第二的
同 minor, lower, unimportant

一般正常速度 [ˋsɛkənˌdɛrɪ]
ETS全真速度 [ˋsɛgənˌdɛrɪ]

➡ [k] 均須變音為 [g]

secure (adj.) 牢固的

關 secure (v.t) 確保
　 security (n.) 安全
同 fixed, immovable, fastened

一般正常速度 [sɪˋkjur]
ETS全真速度 [sɪˋkjur]

➡ 1) 所有詞性的重音都在第二音節
　 2) 名詞裡的 [t] 須變音為 [d]

seemingly (adv.) 表面看來

關 seeming (adj.) 表面上的
同 on the surface

一般正常速度 [ˋsimɪŋlɪ]
ETS全真速度 [ˋsimɪŋlɪ]

segment (n.) 部分

關 segment (v.t) 切割
同 part, section, region, division,
　 portion

一般正常速度 [ˋsɛgmənt]
ETS全真速度 [ˋsɛ(g)mən(t)]

➡ 1) 名詞與動詞的唸法相同
　 2) [g] 輕唸即可
　 3) 字尾 [t] 輕唸即可

考古題應用 We reserved the front seats for the mayor and his staff.
我們保留前排的座位給市長跟他的幕僚。

試練習題 Why are the front seats of the lecture hall unoccupied?
考生回答處 _____

考古題應用 All other concerns are secondary to environmental protection.
跟環境保護比起來，其他顧慮都是次要的。

試練習題 Is environmental protection our top priority?
考生回答處 _____

考古題應用 Just make sure all windows and signboards are secure.
要確認一下所有的窗戶跟招牌都是牢固的。

試練習題 What preparations do we have to make before the storm comes?
考生回答處 _____

考古題應用 The lawyer needs to examine any seemingly unrelated evidence.
律師要檢視每一項表面看來不相關的證據。

試練習題 What is the lawyer doing with those regular files?
考生回答處 _____

考古題應用 The experts analyze consumers' preferences in terms of market segments.
專家以市場區隔的觀點分析消費者喜好。

試練習題 How do the experts analyze consumers' preferences?
考生回答處 _____

S

seize (v.t) 抓住

關 seizure (n.) 抓住
同 hold, take, fasten, catch

一般正常速度 [siz]
ETS全真速度 [si(z)]

➡ 動詞字尾 [z] 輕唸即可

select (v.t) 選擇

關 selection (n.) 選擇
　 selective (adj.) 小心選擇的
同 choose, pick, prefer

一般正常速度 [sə`lɛkt]
ETS全真速度 [sə`lɛ(kt)]

➡ 1) 所有詞性的重音都在第二音節
　 2) 動詞字尾 [kt] 輕唸即可
　 3) 形容詞的 [t] 須變音為 [d]

seniority (n.) 年資

關 senior (adj.) 年長的；較高階的
同 rank, eldership

一般正常速度 [sin`jɔrɛtɪ]
ETS全真速度 [sin`jɔrədɪ]

➡ 1) 名詞的重音在第二音節，形容詞的
　　 重音在第一音節
　 2) 名詞的 [t] 須變音為 [d]

sensible (adj.) 合理的

關 senses (n.) 理智
　 sensibility (n.) 感性
同 practical, reasonable, rational,
　 realistic

一般正常速度 [`sɛnsəbḷ]
ETS全真速度 [`sɛnsəbḷ]

➡ 1) 只有 sensibility 的重音在第三音節
　　 (-bil-)，其他詞性的重音都在第一音
　　 節
　 2) sensibility 的 [t] 須變音為 [d]

separate (adj.) 分開的

關 separate (v.t) 隔開
　 separation (n.) 分開
　 separately (adv.) 分開地
同 divided, unconnected, isolated

一般正常速度 [`sɛpərɪt]
ETS全真速度 [`sɛbərɪ(t)]

➡ 1) 形容詞字尾 [t] 輕唸即可，副詞的
　　 [t] 則必須消音
　 2) 所有詞性的 [p] 均須變音為 [b]

考古題應用 The police officer seized the boy's arm before he fell.
警察在男孩跌倒前抓住他的手臂。

□試練習題 Who saved the little boy from falling?
考生回答處 _____

考古題應用 We took a vote to select the committee chairman.
我們投票選出委員會的主席。

□試練習題 How did you select the committee chairman?
考生回答處 _____

考古題應用 The director gives raises based on seniority.
主管根據年資來加薪。

□試練習題 Does the director give raises based on merit or seniority?
考生回答處 _____

考古題應用 It's sensible to ask for an invoice when shopping at an outlet store.
在大賣場購物索取發票是合理的。

□試練習題 Could I ask for an invoice when shopping at an outlet store?
考生回答處 _____

考古題應用 The VIP lounge and cafeteria are on separate floors.
貴賓休息室跟自助餐廳在不同的樓層。

□試練習題 Are both the VIP lounge and cafeteria on the same floor?
考生回答處 _____

sequence (n.) 連續

關 sequel (n.) 續集
同 procession, progression, series

一般正常速度 [ˋsikwəns]
ETS全真速度 [ˋsigwən(s)]
➜ [k] 均須變音為 [g]

service (n.) 服務

關 serve (v.t) 為…服務
同 help, assistance

一般正常速度 [ˋsɝvɪs]
ETS全真速度 [ˋsɝvɪ(s)]
➜ 名詞字尾 [s] 輕唸即可

session (n.) 期間

同 period, term

一般正常速度 [ˋsɛʃən]
ETS全真速度 [ˋsɛʃən]

settlement (n.) 解決

關 settle (v.t) 解決
同 agreement, arrangement, working out

一般正常速度 [ˋsɛtlmənt]
ETS全真速度 [ˋsɛđlmən(t)]
➜ 1) 名詞與動詞字的第一個 [t] 均須變
　　音為 [đ]
　　2) 名詞字尾 [t] 輕唸即可

severance (n.) 中斷

關 sever (v.t) 切斷
同 cut, break off, termination

一般正常速度 [ˋsɛvərəns]
ETS全真速度 [ˋsɛvərən(s)]
➜ 1) 名詞與動詞的重音都在第一音節
　　2) 字尾 [s] 輕唸即可

考古題應用 A sequence of good investments made him a billionaire.
一連串的正確投資使他成為億萬富翁。

試練習題 What made Mr. Sloan a billionaire?
考生回答處 _____

考古題應用 That electronics store provides very poor after-sale service.
那個電器賣場提供的售後服務很差。

試練習題 Why didn't you buy the printer at the electronics store across
the street?
考生回答處 _____

考古題應用 There will be a question-and-answer session following the
speech.
演講結束後會有一段問答時間。

試練習題 When can we ask the keynote speaker some questions?
考生回答處 _____

考古題應用 The management has worked out a pay settlement.
主管們已經想出薪資解決方案了。

試練習題 Has the management worked out anything to settle the
strike?
考生回答處 _____

考古題應用 At least his employer has given him severance pay.
至少他的雇主已經給了他遣散費。

試練習題 Isn't it horrible that Frank was laid off?
考生回答處 _____

severe (adj.) 嚴重的

關 severely (adv.) 嚴重地
同 serious, hard, grave, intense

一般正常速度 [sə`vɪr]
ETS全真速度 [sə`vɪr]

➡ 兩個詞性的重音都在第二音節

sew (v.t) 縫合

同 join, fasten

一般正常速度 [so]
ETS全真速度 [so]

➡ 母音唸成 [o] 而不是 [ɔ]（台式發音）

Sh-

shadow (n.) 影子

關 shadow (v.t) 遮蔽
同 cover, shade

一般正常速度 [`ʃædo]
ETS全真速度 [`ʃædo]

➡ 名詞與動詞的唸法相同

shallow (adj.) 膚淺的

關 shallow (v.t) 變淺
同 skin-deep, ignorant, empty,
foolish

一般正常速度 [`ʃælo]
ETS全真速度 [`ʃælo]

➡ 形容詞與動詞的唸法相同

shame (n.) 丟臉

關 shame (v.t) 令人蒙羞
shameful (adj.) 可恥的
同 disgrace, dishonor, discredit

一般正常速度 [ʃem]
ETS全真速度 [ʃem]

➡ 所有詞性的母音 a 都唸 [e] 而不是 [ɛ]

考古題應用 Losing the contract was a severe setback to our company.
失去這份合約對我們公司來說是很嚴重的挫敗。

試練習題 How has your company been affected after losing the contract?

考生回答處 _____

考古題應用 We're still waiting for a part to fix the sewing machine.
我們還在等零件以修理縫紉機。

試練習題 Why isn't the sewing machine working?

考生回答處 _____

考古題應用 The workers are taking a break in the shadow of the office tower.
工人在辦公大樓的陰影下休息。

試練習題 What are the construction workers doing in the shadow of the office tower?

考生回答處 _____

考古題應用 No one wants to share his shallow thoughts.
沒人想分享他膚淺的想法。

試練習題 Why isn't anyone taking notes on Mr. Choi's lecture?
演講
/ˈlɛktʃɚ/

考生回答處 _____

考古題應用 There's no shame in asking for help.
請人幫忙沒有什麼好丟臉的。

試練習題 Do you think I should ask my colleagues for help?

考生回答處 _____

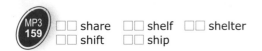

share (n.) 市占率

關 share (v.t) 分享
同 part, portion, proportion, allotment

一般正常速度 [ʃɛr]
ETS全真速度 [ʃɛr]

➡ 1) 名詞與動詞的唸法相同
2) 字首的 [ʃ] 請輕輕噘嘴即可

shelf (n.) 架子

關 shelve (v.t) 上架
同 ledge

一般正常速度 [ʃɛlf]
ETS全真速度 [ʃɛl(f)]

➡ 名詞字尾 [f] 輕唸即可

shelter (n.) 避難所

關 shelter (v.t) 庇護
同 cover, defense, protection

一般正常速度 [ˋʃɛltɚ]
ETS全真速度 [ˋʃɛlɖɚ]

➡ 1) 名詞與動詞的唸法相同
2) [t] 須變音為 [ɖ]

shift (n.) 值班

關 shift (v.t) 替換
同 change, switch, alteration, move

一般正常速度 [ʃɪft]
ETS全真速度 [ʃɪ(ft)]

➡ 1) 名詞與動詞的唸法相同
2) 字尾 [ft] 輕唸即可

ship (v.t) 送貨

關 ship (n.) 船
shipment (n.) 出貨
同 deliver, send, carry

一般正常速度 [ʃɪp]
ETS全真速度 [ʃɪ(p)]

➡ 1) ship 當動、名詞時唸法相同
2) shipment 的 [p] 及 [t] 均輕唸即可

考古題應用　Our market share is growing <u>steadily</u>.
我們的市占率持續穩定成長。

口試練習題　What does the report say about our market share?
考生回答處 _____

考古題應用　They have removed all <u>expired</u> food from the shelves.
他們已經把所有過期的食品都從架子上移走了。

口試練習題　Is there still expired food on the shelves?
考生回答處 _____

考古題應用　All <u>villagers</u> will be transported to the emergency shelters.
所有的村民都會被送往緊急避難所。

口試練習題　What do we do with the villagers before the typhoon comes?
考生回答處 _____

考古題應用　She is working the <u>graveyard shift</u>.
她值大夜班。
['grev,jard]

口試練習題　What shift is Rita working?
考生回答處 _____

考古題應用　We ship our goods via UPS Standard service.
我們利用 UPS 的服務送貨。

口試練習題　How do you ship your goods?
考生回答處 _____

shock (v.t) 震驚

關 shock (n.) 震驚
同 horrify, shake, stun

一般正常速度 [ʃɑk]
ETS全真速度 [ʃɑ(k)]

➡ 1) 動詞與名詞的唸法相同
2) 字尾 [k] 輕唸即可

shop (v.i) 購買

關 shop (n.) 商店
shopper (n.) 購物者
同 buy, purchase

一般正常速度 [ʃɑp]
ETS全真速度 [ʃɑ(p)]

➡ 1) shop 的字尾 [p] 輕唸即可
2) shopper 的 [p] 須變音為 [b]

shorten (v.t) 縮短

關 short (adj.) 短的
同 cut, decrease, reduce, trim

一般正常速度 [ˋʃɔrtn̩]
ETS全真速度 [ˋʃɔr__n̩]

➡ 動詞的 [t] 停一拍即可，無須發音

shortfall (n.) 短缺

同 shortage, lack, deficit

一般正常速度 [ˋʃɔrt.fɔl]
ETS全真速度 [ˋʃɔr__.fɔl]

➡ [t] 停一拍即可，無須發音

shorthand (n.) 速記

同 fast writing

一般正常速度 [ˋʃɔrt.hænd]
ETS全真速度 [ˋʃɔr__.hæn(d)]

➡ 1) [t] 停一拍即可，無須發音
2) 字尾 [d] 輕唸即可

考古題應用 Everyone was shocked at the VP's sudden resignation.
大家都對副總突然辭職感到震驚。

口試練習題 How did the headquarters react to the VP's sudden resignation?

考生回答處 _____

考古題應用 I always shop for small appliances at the electronics store nearby.
我總是在附近的電器行購買小家電。

口試練習題 Where do you shop for small appliances?

考生回答處 _____

考古題應用 She will have to shorten her vacation by one day.
她得縮短一天休假。

口試練習題 Ms. Young will return to the office earlier than expected, won't she?

考生回答處 _____

考古題應用 We expect a shortfall of two million dollars.
我們預計會有兩百萬美元的短缺。

口試練習題 Do you think we can make our sales target for this quarter?

考生回答處 _____

8

考古題應用 I don't know how to take notes in shorthand.
我不會用速記的方式做筆記。

口試練習題 Do you know how to take notes in shorthand?

考生回答處 _____

shortsighted (adj.) 短視的

關 shortsightedness (n.) 短視
shortsightedly (adv.) 短視地
同 blind to, unenlightened, unwitting

一般正常速度 [`ʃɔrt`saɪtɪd]
ETS全真速度 [`ʃɔr__`saɪɾɪ(d)]

➡ 1) 所有詞性的第一個 [t] 均停一拍即
可，第二個 [t] 均須變音為 [ɾ]
2) 形容詞字尾 [d] 輕唸即可，副詞的
[d] 須消音

shred (v.t) 弄碎

關 shred (n.) 碎片
同 cut, tear

一般正常速度 [ʃrɛd]
ETS全真速度 [ʃrɛ(d)]

➡ 1) 動詞與名詞的唸法相同
2) 字尾 [d] 輕唸即可

shrink (v.i) 萎縮

關 shrinkage (n.) 萎縮
同 decrease, reduce, downsize,
drop off, diminish

一般正常速度 [ʃrɪŋk]
ETS全真速度 [ʃrɪŋ(k)]

➡ 1) 動詞字尾 [k] 輕唸即可
2) 名詞的 [k] 須唸成 [g]

shutdown (n.) 關閉

關 shut (v.t) 關閉
同 stop, close

一般正常速度 [`ʃʌt.daʊn]
ETS全真速度 [`ʃʌ__.daʊn]

➡ 名詞的 [t] 停一拍即可，無須發音

shuttle (n.) 接駁車

關 shuttle (v.t) 以接駁車運送
同 vehicle

一般正常速度 [`ʃʌtl]
ETS全真速度 [`ʃʌɾl]

➡ 1) 名詞與動詞的唸法相同
2) [t] 可變音為 [ɾ]

考古題應用　It's very shortsighted not to learn the local language.
不學當地的語言是很短視的。

試練習題　Should we encourage our staff in Brazil to learn the local language?

考生回答處　_____

考古題應用　Please put these documents into the shredding machine.
請將這些文件放進碎紙機裡。

試練習題　Do I need to file these documents before leaving the office?

考生回答處　_____

考古題應用　I don't know what to do with our shrinking market share.
我不知該如何處理我們萎縮的市占率。

試練習題　Why are you calling Mr. Chao for advice?

考生回答處　_____

考古題應用　The unannounced shutdown of the factory shocked us.
未宣布就關閉工廠讓我們很震驚。

試練習題　What made everyone at headquarters so shocked?

考生回答處　_____

S

考古題應用　There's a free 24-hour shuttle service between the airport and our hotel.
從機場到我們飯店有 24 小時免費接駁車服務。

試練習題　How do I get to your hotel from the airport at 2 a.m.?

考生回答處　_____

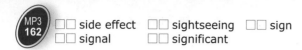
Si-

side effect (n.) 副作用

同 unexpected effect

一般正常速度 [saɪd ɪˋfɛkt]

ETS全真速度 [saɪɖ ɪˋfɛ(kt)]

➜ 1) [d] 須變音為 [ɖ]
2) [ɖ] 與 [ɪ] 須唸連音
3) 字尾 [kt] 輕唸即可

sightseeing (n.) 觀光

關 sightseer (n.) 觀光客
同 visiting places

一般正常速度 [ˋsaɪt.siɪŋ]

ETS全真速度 [ˋsaɪ__.siɪŋ]

➜ [t] 停一拍即可，無須發音

sign (v.t) 簽名

關 signature (n.) 簽名
sign (n.) 標誌
同 write, endorse, autograph

一般正常速度 [saɪn]

ETS全真速度 [saɪn]

➜ sign 的 i 唸 [aɪ]，signature 的 i 則唸 [ɪ]

signal (n.) 號誌

關 signal (v.i) 發射信號
signal (adj.) 顯著的
同 mark, sign, indicator

一般正常速度 [ˋsɪgn̩]

ETS全真速度 [ˋsɪ(g)n̩]

➜ [g] 輕唸即可

significant (adj.) 重要的

關 significance (n.) 重要性
同 important, meaningful,
noteworthy

一般正常速度 [sɪgˋnɪfəkənt]

ETS全真速度 [sɪ(g)ˋnɪfəgən(t)]

➜ 1) 形容詞與名詞的重音都在第二音節
2) [g] 均輕唸即可
3) [k] 均可變音為 [g]
4) 形容詞字尾 [t] 輕唸即可

考古題應用　They have proven this drug's side effects as harmful.
他們已經證明這項藥品的副作用有害。

試練習題　Why did the FDA ask you to recall the drug?
考生回答處　_____

考古題應用　We have scheduled two days of sightseeing in Rome.
我們有安排兩天時間在羅馬觀光。

試練習題　Will you visit Rome for strictly business purposes?
僅僅地
[strıktlı]
考生回答處　_____

考古題應用　Please sign the guestbook at the reception area.
請在接待區的訪客簿上簽名。

試練習題　Where do I sign the guestbook?
考生回答處　_____

考古題應用　The traffic signals are currently out of order.
交通號誌目前故障中。

試練習題　What's causing the traffic jam?
考生回答處　_____

考古題應用　This is our most significant product debut.
這是我們最重要的產品的首次發表。

試練習題　Why did you launch so many advertising campaigns for the product's debut?

考生回答處　_____

☐☐ similarity　☐☐ simplify　☐☐ simultaneously
☐☐ single　☐☐ sink

similarity (n.) 相同點

關 similar (adj.) 相似的
similarly (adv.) 相同地
同 sameness, likeness

一般正常速度 [ˌsɪməˈlærətɪ]
ETS全真速度 [ˌsɪməˈlærədɪ]

➡ 1) 形容詞與副詞的重音在第一音節，
名詞的重音在第三音節
2) 名詞字尾 [t] 須變音為 [d]

simplify (v.t) 簡化

關 simplification (n.) 簡化
simplicity (n.) 單純
simple (adj.) 簡單的
同 make easier, streamline

一般正常速度 [ˈsɪmpləˌfaɪ]
ETS全真速度 [ˈsɪmbləˌfaɪ]

➡ 1) 所有詞性的 [p] 均須變音為 [b]
2) simplicity 的 [t] 須變音為 [d]

simultaneously
(adv.) 同時地

關 simultaneous (adj.) 同時的
同 at the same time, together

一般正常速度 [ˌsaɪməlˈtenɪəslɪ]
ETS全真速度 [ˌsaɪməlˈtenɪəslɪ]

➡ 副詞與形容詞的重音都在第三音節

single (adj.) 單一的

同 one, only

一般正常速度 [ˈsɪŋgl̩]
ETS全真速度 [ˈsɪŋgl̩]

➡ 字尾 [l] 請勿唸成 [ɔ]（台式發音）

sink (n.) 水槽

關 sink (v.t) 下沉

一般正常速度 [sɪŋk]
ETS全真速度 [sɪŋ(k)]

➡ 1) 名詞與動詞的唸法相同
2) 字尾 [k] 輕唸即可

考古題應用　There's no similarity between the two proposals.
這兩份企畫案之間沒有相同點。

□試練習題　Are these two proposals identical?

adj 完全相同的
/aɪˈdɛntɪkl/

考生回答處 _____

考古題應用　We need to simplify the operating system, that's all.
我們只需要簡化這個操作系統。

□試練習題　Do we need to change the entire operating system?

考生回答處 _____

考古題應用　His book and CD will be released simultaneously.
他的書跟 CD 會同時發行。

□試練習題　Will Peter's book and CD be released separately?

考生回答處 _____

考古題應用　Over three thousand people visit the exhibition every single day.
每一天都有超過三千人參觀這個展覽。

□試練習題　How many people visit the exhibition in a single day?

考生回答處 _____

考古題應用　The dirty plates are piled up in the sink.
髒盤子堆放在水槽裡。

□試練習題　Where are the dirty plates?

考生回答處 _____

situated (adj.) 位於⋯的

關 situate (v.t) 放置
同 located

一般正常速度 [ˋsɪtʃʊˌetɪd]
ETS全真速度 [ˋsɪtʃʊˌeđɪd]

➡ 1) 形容詞與動詞的重音都在第一音節
2) 形容詞字尾 [t] 須變音為 [đ]

Sk-

sketch (v.i) 概略描述

關 sketch (n.) 素描
同 outline, depict

一般正常速度 [skɛtʃ]
ETS全真速度 [skɛ(tʃ)]

➡ 1) 動詞與名詞的唸法相同
2) 字尾 [tʃ] 輕唸即可

skim (v.t) 瀏覽

同 scan, skip, leaf through

一般正常速度 [skɪm]
ETS全真速度 [sgɪm]

➡ [k] 須變音為 [g]

skip (v.i) 跳過

同 leave out, omit

一般正常速度 [skɪp]
ETS全真速度 [sgɪ(p)]

➡ 1) [k] 須變音為 [g]
2) 字尾 [p] 輕唸即可

Sl-

slacken (v.i) 減弱

關 slack (adj.) 鬆懈的
同 decrease, slow down, drop off,
diminish, lessen

一般正常速度 [ˋslækən]
ETS全真速度 [ˋslægən]

➡ 動詞的 [k] 須變音為 [g]

考古題應用　Our office complex is conveniently situated near all major banks.
我們辦公大樓的位置便利，鄰近各大銀行。

口試練習題　Where is your office complex situated?
考生回答處　_____

考古題應用　The interior designer only sketched out the plan.
室內設計師只概述了一下計畫。

口試練習題　Did the interior designer describe the plan in detail?
考生回答處　_____

考古題應用　I only have five minutes left to skim the report.
我只剩五分鐘可以瀏覽報告。

口試練習題　How much time is left for you to review the report?
考生回答處　_____

考古題應用　We'd better skip to the last item.
我們最好直接跳到最後一項。

口試練習題　There is not much time left for us to go through everything on the agenda.
考生回答處　_____

考古題應用　The demand for imported fruit has slackened.
進口水果的市場需求已經減少了。

口試練習題　How do you account for our recent drop in imported fruit business?
考生回答處　_____

8

329

slice (v.t) 切片

關 slice (n.) 一片
同 cut, divide

一般正常速度 [slaɪs]
ETS全真速度 [slaɪ(s)]

➡ 1) 動詞與名詞的唸法相同
2) 字尾 [s] 輕唸即可

slide (v.i) 下滑

關 slide (n.) 溜滑梯
同 drop, decline, diminish, descend, fall, lower

一般正常速度 [slaɪd]
ETS全真速度 [slaɪ(d)]

➡ 1) 動詞與名詞的唸法相同
2) 字尾 [d] 輕唸即可

slightly (adv.) 輕微地

關 slight (adj.) 輕微的
同 little, somewhat

一般正常速度 [`slaɪtlɪ]
ETS全真速度 [`slaɪ__lɪ]

➡ 副詞字尾 [t] 停一拍即可，無須發音

slip (v.i) 滑落

關 slip (n.) 小紙條
同 decrease, slacken, drop off, diminish

一般正常速度 [slɪp]
ETS全真速度 [slɪ(p)]

➡ 1) 動詞與名詞的唸法相同
2) 字尾 [p] 輕唸即可

slope (n.) 斜坡

關 slope (v.i) 使傾斜

一般正常速度 [slop]
ETS全真速度 [slo(p)]

➡ 1) 名詞與動詞的唸法相同
2) 字尾 [p] 輕唸即可

考古題應用 The chef is slicing some salmon.
主廚正在將一些鮭魚切片。

口試練習題 What is the chef doing over the kitchen counter?
考生回答處 _____

考古題應用 He seemed to be very surprised at the product's sliding popularity.
對於產品的人氣下滑他似乎很驚訝。

口試練習題 How does our manager feel about the product's sliding popularity?
考生回答處 _____

考古題應用 The current carpeting is slightly worn.
目前地毯有些磨損。

口試練習題 Why are they replacing the carpet in the lobby?
考生回答處 _____

考古題應用 Our earnings per share have slipped 1% since June.
我們的每股盈餘自六月以來滑落了一個百分點。

口試練習題 How much have our earnings per share slipped since June?
考生回答處 _____

考古題應用 The resort is located on a gentle slope.
渡假村位於一處和緩的斜坡上。

口試練習題 Is the resort located on a beach or on a slope?
考生回答處 _____

S

slot (n.) 投幣口

關 slot (v.t) 投幣
同 opening, slit

一般正常速度 [slɑt]

ETS全真速度 [slɑ(t)]

➡ 1) 名詞與動詞的唸法相同
2) 字尾 [t] 輕唸即可

slump (n.) 暴跌

關 slump (v.i) 暴跌
同 decline, drop, fall

一般正常速度 [slʌmp]

ETS全真速度 [slʌm(p)]

➡ 1) 名詞與動詞的唸法相同
2) 字尾 [p] 輕唸即可

smooth (adj.) 光滑的

關 smooth (v.t) 弄平
同 even, plain

一般正常速度 [smuð]

ETS全真速度 [smuð]

➡ 形容詞與動詞的唸法相同

smuggle (v.t) 走私

關 smuggling (n.) 走私
smuggler (n.) 走私者
同 ship goods illegally

一般正常速度 [ˋsmʌgl]

ETS全真速度 [ˋsmʌgl]

➡ 所有詞性的重音都在第一音節

考古題應用　You have to put a coin in the slot first.
你得先把一枚硬幣投進投幣口。

試練習題　How do I use the Xerox machine?
考生回答處　_____

考古題應用　There will be a slump in our stock prices.
我們的股價會暴跌。

試練習題　Will the recall of defective products affect our stock prices?
考生回答處　_____

考古題應用　This silk scarf feels very smooth.
這條絲巾摸起來很光滑。

試練習題　How does the silk scarf feel?
考生回答處　_____

考古題應用　He was charged with smuggling cigars into the U.S.
他因走私雪茄到美國而被告。

試練習題　What crime was Juan charged for in Texas?
考生回答處　_____

S

Check List 8

到目前為止，字彙量又增加了不少，繼續學新單字之前，我們先來複習一下，看看是不是都記起來了！

☐ sabotage	☐ script	☐ service
☐ safety	☐ scrub	☐ session
☐ sale	☐ scrutinize	☐ settlement
☐ salute	☐ sculpture	☐ severance
☐ sample	☐ seal	☐ severe
☐ sanction	☐ seam	☐ sew
☐ sand	☐ season	☐ shadow
☐ sanitary	☐ seat	☐ shallow
☐ satisfactory	☐ secondary	☐ shame
☐ scan	☐ secure	☐ share
☐ scarcely	☐ seemingly	☐ shelf
☐ scenery	☐ segment	☐ shelter
☐ schedule	☐ seize	☐ shift
☐ scheme	☐ select	☐ ship
☐ scholarship	☐ seniority	☐ shock
☐ scope	☐ sensible	☐ shop
☐ scrape	☐ separate	☐ shorten
☐ screen	☐ sequence	☐ shortfall

- [ ] shorthand
- [ ] shortsighted
- [ ] shred
- [ ] shrink
- [ ] shutdown
- [ ] shuttle

- [ ] side effect
- [ ] sightseeing
- [ ] sign
- [ ] signal
- [ ] significant
- [ ] similarity

- [ ] simplify
- [ ] simultaneously
- [ ] single
- [ ] sink
- [ ] situated
- [ ] sketch

- [ ] skim
- [ ] skip
- [ ] slacken
- [ ] slice
- [ ] slide
- [ ] slightly

- [ ] slip
- [ ] slope
- [ ] slot
- [ ] slump
- [ ] smooth
- [ ] smuggle

So-

soar (v.i) 飆漲

關 soar (n.) 飆漲
同 rise, increase, escalate

一般正常速度 [sor]
ETS全真速度 [sor]

➡ 動詞與名詞的唸法相同

---

socialize (v.i) 應酬

關 social (n.) 聯誼會
　　socialization (n.) 社會化
同 entertain, get together

一般正常速度 [ˋsoʃə͵laɪz]
ETS全真速度 [ˋsoʃə͵laɪ(z)]

➡ 1) 動詞的重音在第一音節，名詞
　　socialization 的重音在第四音節
　2) social 的 [l] 請勿唸成 [ɔ]（台式發音）
　3) 動詞字尾 [z] 輕唸即可

---

soften (v.t) 減輕

關 soft (adj.) 軟的
同 ease, calm, lessen, diminish

一般正常速度 [ˋsɔfn̩]
ETS全真速度 [ˋsɔfn̩]

➡ 動詞的 [t] 不可發音，形容詞的 [t] 輕
　唸即可

---

sole (adj.) 唯一的

關 solely (adv.) 唯一地
同 only, one, exclusive

一般正常速度 [sol]
ETS全真速度 [sol]

➡ 字尾 [l] 請勿唸成 [ɔ]（台式發音）

---

solicit (v.t) 索取

關 solicitation (n.) 懇求
同 ask, beg, seek

一般正常速度 [səˋlɪsɪt]
ETS全真速度 [səˋlɪsɪ(t)]

➡ 1) 動詞的重音在第二音節，名詞的重
　　音在第四音節 (-ta-)
　2) 動詞字尾 [t] 輕唸即可

考古題應用 Vegetable prices have soared since the typhoon.
颱風過後蔬菜的價格飆漲。

口試練習題 Why are you taking veggie burgers off today's menu?
考生回答處 _____

考古題應用 I often socialize with clients after work.
我常在下班之後跟客戶應酬。

口試練習題 Why do you go home late so often?
考生回答處 _____

考古題應用 I have worked out a way to soften the impact.
我已經想出辦法來減輕衝擊。

口試練習題 The staff will be shocked by the upcoming downsizing, won't they?
考生回答處 _____

考古題應用 Your sole responsibility is to <u>entertain</u> the European clients.
你唯一的職責就是<u>招待</u>歐洲客戶。

s

口試練習題 Do I need to help you restructure our department?
考生回答處 _____

考古題應用 She'd better call their manager to solicit compensation.
她最好打電話給他們的經理索取賠償。

口試練習題 How will Sandra be refunded for the poor courier service?
考生回答處 _____

soothing (adj.) 令人放鬆的

關 soothe (v.t) 撫慰
同 calming, relaxing, easeful

一般正常速度 [`suðɪŋ]
ETS全真速度 [`suðɪŋ]

➡ 兩個詞性的 [ð] 均須含舌發音

sophisticated

(adj.) 成熟的

關 sophistication (n.) 成熟
同 refined, highly-developed

一般正常速度 [sə`fɪstɪˌketɪd]
ETS全真速度 [sə`fɪsdɪˌkeðɪ(d)]

➡ 1) 形容詞的第一個 [t] 發 [d]，第二個
    [t] 發 [d]
    2) 形容詞字尾 [d] 輕唸即可

sort (v.t) 分類

關 sort (n.) 種類
同 grade, group, categorize, classify

一般正常速度 [sɔrt]
ETS全真速度 [sɔr(t)]

➡ 1) 動詞與名詞的唸法相同
    2) 字尾 [t] 輕唸即可

sound (adj.) 明智的

關 sound (n.) 聲音
同 reasonable, wise, correct,
   rational, logical

一般正常速度 [saʊnd]
ETS全真速度 [saʊn(d)]

➡ 1) 形容詞與名詞的唸法相同
    2) 字尾 [d] 輕唸即可

source (n.) 來源

同 origin

一般正常速度 [sors]
ETS全真速度 [sor(s)]

➡ 字尾 [s] 輕唸即可

考古題應用 The atmosphere in the VIP lounge is very soothing.
貴賓休息室的氣氛很令人放鬆。

試練習題 How is the VIP lounge at Heathrow Airport?
考生回答處 _____

考古題應用 Yacht manufacturing in Taiwan is highly sophisticated.
台灣的遊艇製造相當成熟。

試練習題 Why are so many yachts in Monaco imported from Taiwan?
[jɑt]
考生回答處 _____

考古題應用 These potatoes have been carefully sorted according to size.
這些馬鈴薯已依照大小仔細分類過。

試練習題 How are these potatoes sorted?
考生回答處 _____

考古題應用 To acquire that particular apartment is a sound investment.
買下那棟公寓是明智的投資。

試練習題 Is it wise for Teresa to acquire the apartment near Central Park?
考生回答處 _____

考古題應用 We'd better find a new source of raw materials soon.
我們最好趕緊找新的原料來源。

試練習題 Our biggest supplier is going out of business.
考生回答處 _____

Sp-

spare (v.t) 撥出

關 spare (adj.) 多餘的
同 give, grant

一般正常速度 [spɛr]
ETS全真速度 [sbɛr]

→ 1) 動詞與形容詞的唸法相同
   2) [p] 須變音為 [b]

specialize (v.i) 專精於

關 specialty (n.) 專長
同 be good at, focus on

一般正常速度 [ˋspɛʃəl.aɪz]
ETS全真速度 [ˋsbɛʃəl.aɪz]

→ 1) 動詞與名詞的 [p] 均須變音為 [b]
   2) 名詞字尾 [t] 須變音為 [đ]

specific (adj.) 明確的

關 specification (n.) 規格
   specifically (adv.) 明確地
同 clear-cut, precise, definite,
   explicit

一般正常速度 [sprˋsɪfɪk]
ETS全真速度 [sbrˋsɪfɪ(k)]

→ 1) 所有詞性的 [p] 均須變音為 [b]
   2) 形容詞字尾 [k] 輕唸即可

speculate (v.t) 推測

關 speculation (n.) 推測
   speculative (adj.) 推測性的
同 guess, suppose

一般正常速度 [ˋspɛk jə.let]
ETS全真速度 [ˋsbɛg jə.le(t)]

→ 1) 所有詞性的 [p] 均須變音為 [b]
   2) [k] 均可變音為 [g]
   3) 動詞字尾 [t] 輕唸即可
   4) 形容詞的 [t] 須變音為 [đ]

speed (v.i) 加快

關 speed (n.) 速度
同 hurry, hasten, accelerate

一般正常速度 [spid]
ETS全真速度 [sbi(d)]

→ 1) 動詞與名詞的唸法相同
   2) [p] 須變音為 [b]
   3) 字尾 [d] 輕唸即可

考古題應用　She can only spare half an hour for the interview.
她只能為訪問撥出半小時。

□試練習題　How much time has the deputy chairman given you for the interview?

考生回答處　_____

考古題應用　We've <u>consulted</u> an expert who specializes in fabrics.
我們已<u>請教</u>過一名專精於布料的專家。

□試練習題　Have you figured out a way to enhance the durability of your fabrics?

考生回答處　_____

考古題應用　He needs to be more specific about giving <u>instructions</u>.
他下<u>指令</u>時需要更明確一點。

□試練習題　No one seems to know how to follow the manager's instructions.

考生回答處　_____

考古題應用　Everyone is speculating that he will be promoted soon.
所有人都推測他很快就會被升職。

□試練習題　Mr. Jones has brought in a lot of customers, hasn't he?

考生回答處　_____

考古題應用　You'd better speed up to meet the deadline.
你最好加快速度以趕上截止日期。

□試練習題　Do you think I can make the deadline for shipment?

考生回答處　_____

split (v.t) 分裂

關 split (n.) 裂痕
同 diverge, come apart, disunite

一般正常速度 [splɪt]
ETS全真速度 [sblɪ(t)]

➡ 1) 動詞與名詞的唸法相同
2) [p] 可變音為 [b]
3) 字尾 [t] 輕唸即可

spoil (v.t) 毀壞

關 spoilage (n.) 毀壞
同 ruin, upset, damage, destroy, harm

一般正常速度 [spɔɪl]
ETS全真速度 [sbɔɪl]

➡ 動詞與名詞的 [p] 均須變音為 [b]

sponsor (v.t) 贊助

關 sponsor (n.) 贊助者
同 fund, finance, back

一般正常速度 [ˋspɑnsɚ]
ETS全真速度 [ˋsbɑnsɚ]

➡ 1) 動詞與名詞唸法相同
2) [p] 須變音為 [b]
3) [n] 請勿唸成 [ŋ]（台式發音）

spontaneously

(adv.) 自動地

關 spontaneous (adj.) 自動的
同 automatically, voluntarily, instinctively

一般正常速度 [spɑnˋtenɪəslɪ]
ETS全真速度 [sbɑnˋtenɪəslɪ]

➡ 1) 副詞與形容詞的重音都在第二音節
2) [p] 均須變音為 [b]

spread (v.t) 散播

關 spread (n.) 散播
同 make public, make known, broadcast, cast

一般正常速度 [sprɛd]
ETS全真速度 [sbrɛ(d)]

➡ 1) 動詞與名詞的唸法相同
2) [p] 須變音為 [b]
3) 字尾 [d] 輕唸即可

考古題應用 Our board is deeply split on this issue.
我們董事會對此事的意見嚴重分歧。

口試練習題 Does everyone on your board agree with the merger?
考生回答處 _____

考古題應用 The unwise investment spoiled the future of his company.
錯誤的投資毀掉了他公司的前途。

口試練習題 Dr. Phil's company didn't invest wisely in real estate, did it?
考生回答處 _____

考古題應用 Our research has been sponsored by the government.
我們的研究有政府贊助。

口試練習題 Are there any sponsors for your research?
考生回答處 _____

考古題應用 The audience spontaneously stood up and cheered.
觀眾們自動站起來歡呼。

口試練習題 Did the audience enjoy the performance last night?
考生回答處 _____

考古題應用 His main competitors are spreading rumors about him.
他主要的競爭者在散播有關他的謠言。

口試練習題 Why has Roger decided to call a press conference?
考生回答處 _____

S

Sq-

square (n.) 廣場

關 square (adj.) 正方形的
同 plaza

一般正常速度 [skwɛr]
ETS全真速度 [sgwɛr]

➔ 1) 名詞與形容詞的唸法相同
2) [k] 須變音為 [g]

squeeze (v.i) 擠壓

關 squeeze (n.) 擠壓
同 force, press

一般正常速度 [skwiz]
ETS全真速度 [sgwi(z)]

➔ 1) 動詞與名詞的唸法相同
2) [k] 均須變音為 [g]
3) 字尾 [z] 輕唸即可

St-

stack (v.t) 堆放

關 stack (n.) 一堆
同 pile, load

一般正常速度 [stæk]
ETS全真速度 [sdæ(k)]

➔ 1) 動詞與名詞的唸法相同
2) [t] 須變音為 [d]
3) 字尾 [k] 輕唸即可

stage (n.) 階段

關 stage (v.t) 上演
同 period, phase, point

一般正常速度 [stedʒ]
ETS全真速度 [sde(dʒ)]

➔ 1) 名詞與動詞的唸法相同
2) [t] 須變音為 [d]
3) 字尾 [dʒ] 輕唸即可

stagnant (adj.) 停滯不前的

關 stagnate (v.t) 停滯
同 inactive, still

一般正常速度 [`stægnənt]
ETS全真速度 [`sdægnən(t)]

➔ 1) 兩個詞性字首的 [t] 均須變音為 [d]
2) 字尾 [t] 均輕唸即可

考古題應用　There are some food stands near the square.
廣場附近有一些小吃攤。

口試練習題　Where can I find something to eat in this neighborhood?
考生回答處　_____

考古題應用　There's still room for you to squeeze in.
還有位子可以讓你擠進來。

口試練習題　Is every seat on the bus occupied?
考生回答處　_____

考古題應用　Please stack the cartons against the wall.
請把紙箱靠著牆堆放。

口試練習題　Where do I put these cartons, Mr. Chen?
考生回答處　_____

考古題應用　Our product was quite popular in its early stages.
我們的產品在初期相當受歡迎。

口試練習題　How did you accumulate enough capital for branch stores?
考生回答處　_____

考古題應用　Our business has remained stagnant since she retired.
自她退休後，我們的業績就停滯不前。

口試練習題　How has your business been since the chief designer retired?
考生回答處　_____

stain (v.i) 弄髒

關 stain (n.) 汙點
同 dirty, soil, tarnish

一般正常速度 [sten]
ETS全真速度 [sden]

➡ 1) 動詞與名詞的唸法相同
　 2) [t] 須變音為 [d]

stake (v.t) 押注

關 stake (n.) 賭注
同 take risks

一般正常速度 [stek]
ETS全真速度 [sde(k)]

➡ 1) 動詞與名詞的唸法相同
　 2) [t] 須變音為 [d]
　 3) 字尾 [k] 輕唸即可

stall (v.i) 熄火

關 stall (n.) 熄火
同 stop

一般正常速度 [stɔl]
ETS全真速度 [sdɔl]

➡ 1) 動詞與名詞的唸法相同
　 2) [t] 須變音為 [d]

stamp (v.i) 蓋章

關 stamp (n.) 戳記
同 mark, imprint

一般正常速度 [stæmp]
ETS全真速度 [sdæm(p)]

➡ 1) 動詞與名詞的唸法相同
　 2) [t] 須變音 [d]
　 3) 字尾 [p] 輕唸即可

stand (n.) 攤位

關 stand (v.i) 站著

一般正常速度 [stænd]
ETS全真速度 [sdæn(d)]

➡ 1) 名詞與動詞的唸法相同
　 2) [t] 須變音 [d]
　 3) 字尾 [d] 輕唸即可

考古題應用 Plastic <u>tablecloths</u> don't stain easily.
塑膠桌巾不容易弄髒。

口試練習題 Why did you replace the lace tablecloths with plastic ones?

考生回答處

考古題應用 Teddy staked his final hopes on this election.
Teddy 把最後的希望押注在這次的選舉上。

口試練習題 Has Teddy given up on running for mayor?

考生回答處

考古題應用 A sedan has stalled on the steep slope.
一部轎車在陡峭的斜坡上熄火了。

口試練習題 What stalled on the steep slope?

考生回答處

考古題應用 The clerk forgot to stamp the guarantee.
售貨員忘了在保證書上面蓋章。

口試練習題 Why are you returning to the electronics store with the computer's guarantee?

考生回答處

S

考古題應用 I got the *Chicago Tribune* at a newspaper stand.
我在書報攤買到這份《芝加哥論壇報》。

口試練習題 Where did you get the *Chicago Tribune*?

考生回答處

standard (adj.) 標準的

關 standardize (v.t) 標準化
standard (n.) 標準
同 set, typical, acceptable, customary

一般正常速度 [`stændəd]
ETS全真速度 [`sdændə(d)]

➡ 1) 所有詞性的重音都在第一音節
2) [t] 均須變音為 [d]
3) 形容詞與名詞的字尾 [d] 輕唸即可

standby (adj.) 備用的

同 spare, backup

一般正常速度 [`stænd.baɪ]
ETS全真速度 [`sdæn__.baɪ]

➡ 1) [t] 須變音為 [d]
2) [d] 停一拍即可，無須發音

staple (adj.) 主要的

關 staple (n.) 日常的必需品
同 basic, main, essential, key, primary, principal, fundamental

一般正常速度 [`stepḷ]
ETS全真速度 [`sdebḷ]

➡ 1) 形容詞與名詞的唸法相同
2) [t] 須變音為 [d]
3) [p] 須變音為 [b]
4) 字尾 [ḷ] 請勿唸成 [ɔ]（台式發音）

stare (v.i) 凝視

關 stare (n.) 凝視
同 look, watch, gaze

一般正常速度 [stɛr]
ETS全真速度 [sdɛr]

➡ 1) 動詞與名詞的唸法相同
2) [t] 須變音為 [d]

starve (v.t) 缺乏

同 lack, be short of

一般正常速度 [stɑrv]
ETS全真速度 [sdɑr(v)]

➡ 1) [t] 須變音為 [d]
2) 字尾 [v] 輕唸即可

| 考古題應用 | We have Standard Operating Procedures to follow.
我們有標準作業程序可依循。 |

| 口試練習題 | What do you do to work safely? |
| 考生回答處 | |

| 考古題應用 | I often bring a standby battery with me.
我總是隨身攜帶備用電池。 |

| 口試練習題 | Aren't you worried that your cell phone may run low on power? |
| 考生回答處 | |

| 考古題應用 | Corn is the staple food in many African countries.
玉米是許多非洲國家的主食。 |

| 口試練習題 | What is one of the main staple foods in Africa? |
| 考生回答處 | |

| 考古題應用 | I stared out the window.
我凝視窗外。 |

| 口試練習題 | Did you take a nap on the tour bus? |
| 考生回答處 | |

| 考古題應用 | The lab has been starved of experienced technicians.
實驗室缺乏有經驗的技術人員。 |

| 口試練習題 | Why are you constantly interviewing people? |
| 考生回答處 | |

S

state (n.) 狀態

關 state (v.t) 說明

同 condition, situation, position

一般正常速度 [stet]

ETS全真速度 [sde(t)]

➡ 1) 名詞與動詞的唸法相同
2) 第一個 [t] 須變音為 [d]
3) 字尾 [t] 輕唸即可

statement (n.) 聲明

關 state (v.t) 說明

同 announcement, declaration

一般正常速度 [`stetmənt]

ETS全真速度 [`sde__mən(t)]

➡ 1) 第一個 [t] 須變音為 [d]
2) 第二個 [t] 停一拍即可，無須發音
3) 字尾 [t] 輕唸即可

statistics (n.) 數據

關 statistical (adj.) 數據上的
statistically (adv.) 數據上

同 numbers

一般正常速度 [stə`tɪstɪks]

ETS全真速度 [sdə`tɪsdɪ(ks)]

➡ 1) 所有詞性的重音都在第二音節
2) 第一個與第三個 [t] 均須變音為
[d]，第二個 [t] 發音不變
3) 名詞字尾 [ks] 輕唸即可

staunch (adj.) 忠實的

同 loyal, firm, steadfast, faithful,
devoted

一般正常速度 [stɔntʃ]

ETS全真速度 [sdɔntʃ]

➡ [t] 須變音為 [d]

steady (adj.) 穩定的

關 steadily (adv.) 穩定地

同 stable, firm, safe, constant

一般正常速度 [`stɛdɪ]

ETS全真速度 [`sdɛdɪ]

➡ 形容詞與副詞的第一個 [t] 均須變音為
[d]，第二個 [d] 均須變音為 [ð]

考古題應用 She is still in a state of anger.
她還在生氣。

試練習題 Has Ms. Ramos forgiven what you did?
考生回答處 _____

考古題應用 Our President issued a statement on the joint venture.
我們總經理發表了合資經營的聲明。

試練習題 What kind of statement did your President issue this morning?
考生回答處 _____

考古題應用 These statistics show that our sales are up by 25%.
這些數據顯示我們的業績成長了 25%。

試練習題 What do these statistics say about our sales?
考生回答處 _____

考古題應用 She is a staunch supporter of environmental protection.
她是環保的忠實支持者。

S

試練習題 Bridget voted against plastic packaging, right?
考生回答處 _____

考古題應用 We have had a steady increase in the number of clients.
我們的客戶數量有穩定的成長。

試練習題 Has there been a steady decline in the number of your clients?
考生回答處 _____

sticky (adj.) 有黏性的

關 stick (v.i) 黏住
同 adhesive, gluey

一般正常速度 [ˋstɪkɪ]
ETS全真速度 [ˋsdɪgɪ]

➜ 1) [t] 均須變音為 [d]
2) 形容詞的 [k] 須變音為 [g]

stimulate (v.t) 刺激

關 stimulation (n.) 刺激
stimulus (n.) 刺激物
stimulating (adj.) 令人振奮的
同 motivate, encourage, provoke

一般正常速度 [ˋstɪmjəˌlet]
ETS全真速度 [ˋsdɪmjəˌle(t)]

➜ 1) 除 stimulation 的重音在第三音節
外，其他詞性的重音都在第一音節
2) 字首 [t] 均須變音為 [d]
3) 動詞字尾 [t] 輕唸即可

stipulation (n.) 規定

關 stipulate (v.t) 規定
同 term, agreement, requirement,
condition, specification

一般正常速度 [ˌstɪpjəˋleʃən]
ETS全真速度 [ˌsdɪbjəˋleʃən]

➜ 1) 名詞的重音在第三音節，動詞的重
音在第一音節
2) [t] 均須變音為 [d]
3) [p] 均須變音為 [b]

stir (v.t) 攪拌

關 stir (n.) 攪拌
同 beat, shake, mix

一般正常速度 [stɝ]
ETS全真速度 [sdɝ]

➜ 1) 動詞與名詞的唸法相同
2) [t] 須變音為 [d]

stock (n.) 存貨

關 stock (v.t) 儲存
同 supply, store, goods, inventory

一般正常速度 [stɑk]
ETS全真速度 [sdɑ(k)]

➜ 1) 名詞與動詞的唸法相同
2) [t] 須變音為 [d]
3) 字尾 [k] 輕唸即可

考古題應用 Just write the names on sticky labels.
把名稱寫在貼紙上。

試練習題 How should I mark the contents of the jars?
考生回答處 _____

考古題應用 Low <u>mortgage rates</u> stimulate the real estate market.
低<u>房貸利率</u>能刺激房地產市場。

試練習題 Why do local banks lower mortgage rates?
考生回答處 _____

考古題應用 You'd better obey the stipulations set for shipping items.
你最好遵守貨運規定。

試練習題 Do I really have to ship the orders within a month?
考生回答處 _____

考古題應用 Please stir the soup while it's being <u>boiled</u>.
請在<u>煮</u>湯時一邊攪拌。

試練習題 What should I do with the soup while it's being boiled?
考生回答處 _____

考古題應用 We don't have any more <u>beige</u> shirts in stock.
我們的庫存已經沒有<u>米黃色</u>襯衫了。

試練習題 We still have ten beige shirts in stock, don't we?
考生回答處 _____

store (v.t) 存放

關 store (n.) 商店
　storage (n.) 儲存
同 save, stock, reserve, accumulate,
　deposit, hoard, put aside

一般正常速度 [stor]
ETS全真速度 [sdor]

➡ 1) store 當動、名詞時唸法相同
　2) [t] 均須變音為 [d]

stow (v.t) 堆放

關 stowage (n.) 堆放
同 stack, load, put away, stash,
　store, deposit

一般正常速度 [sto]
ETS全真速度 [sdo]

➡ [t] 均須變音為 [d]

straighten (v.i) 釐清

關 straight (adj.) 直的
　straight (adv.) 清楚地
同 correct, rectify, clear up, become
　clear, settle, work out

一般正常速度 [`stretn̩]
ETS全真速度 [`sdre__n̩]

➡ 1) 第一個 [t] 均須變音為 [d]
　2) 動詞的第二個 [t] 停一拍即可，無
　　須發音

strategic (adj.) 策略性的

關 strategy (n.) 策略
同 planned, calculated, deliberate

一般正常速度 [strə`tidʒɪk]
ETS全真速度 [sdrə`tidʒɪ(k)]

➡ 1) 形容詞的重音在第二音節，名詞的
　　重音在第一音節
　2) 第一個 [t] 均須變音為 [d]
　3) 名詞的第二個 [t] 要變音為 [đ]

strengthen (v.t) 強化

關 strength (n.) 力量
同 reinforce, consolidate, back up,
　fortify, toughen

一般正常速度 [`strɛŋθən]
ETS全真速度 [`sdrɛŋθən]

➡ [t] 均須變音為 [d]

考古題應用　We've rented a <u>warehouse</u> to store the machinery.
我們租了一個倉庫來存放機器。

口試練習題　Where do you keep the machinery?

考生回答處　_____

考古題應用　He stowed his backpack in the <u>overhead compartment</u>.
他把背包放在<u>頂上置物櫃</u>內。

口試練習題　Did Zach put his backpack underneath the seat or stow it in the overhead compartment?

考生回答處　_____

考古題應用　You should straighten out any misunderstanding between you two.
你們兩個應該把誤會釐清。

口試練習題　Mr. Walter thinks I am spreading rumors about him.

考生回答處　_____

考古題應用　She thinks the strategic alliance can help our business.
她認為策略聯盟對我們生意有幫助。

口試練習題　What's Julia's advice on improving your business?

考生回答處　_____

考古題應用　Earlier frustrations only strengthened my <u>resolve</u> to succeed.
過去的挫敗只會強化我成功的<u>決心</u>。

口試練習題　Were you discouraged by earlier frustrations?

考生回答處　_____

S

stress (v.t) 強調

關 stress (n.) 壓力
同 emphasize, accentuate, underline

一般正常速度 [strɛs]
ETS全真速度 [sdrɛs]

➤ 1) 動詞與名詞的唸法相同
2) [t] 須變音為 [d]

strict (adj.) 嚴格的

關 strictly (adv.) 嚴格地
同 harsh, stern, rigid

一般正常速度 [strɪkt]
ETS全真速度 [sdrɪ(kt)]

➤ 1) 第一個 [t] 均須變音為 [d]
2) 形容詞字尾 [t] 輕唸即可，副詞的 [t] 則必須消音

strike (n.) 罷工

關 strike (v.i) 罷工
同 stop working

一般正常速度 [straɪk]
ETS全真速度 [sdraɪ(k)]

➤ 1) 名詞與動詞的唸法相同
2) [t] 須變音為 [d]
3) 字尾 [k] 輕唸即可

string (n.) 繩子

關 string (v.t) 用繩子綁
同 cord

一般正常速度 [strɪŋ]
ETS全真速度 [sdrɪŋ]

➤ 1) 名詞與動詞的唸法相同
2) [t] 須變音為 [d]

stroll (v.i) 散步

關 stroller (n.) 推車
同 take a walk

一般正常速度 [strol]
ETS全真速度 [sdrol]

➤ 1) 動詞與名詞的 [t] 均須變音為 [d]
2) 動詞字尾 [l] 請勿唸成 [ɔ]（台式發音）

考古題應用 Our director always stresses the importance of teamwork.
我們主任一向強調團隊合作的重要性。

試練習題 What does your director always stress?
考生回答處 _____

考古題應用 Mr. McQueen is always very strict with new recruits.
McQueen 先生對新進人員向來十分嚴格。

試練習題 Why are the new recruits complaining about Mr. McQueen?
考生回答處 _____

考古題應用 The drivers went on strike against their extended working hours.
司機以罷工來反對延長工時。

試練習題 Why did the drivers go on strike?
考生回答處 _____

考古題應用 She wants us to tie the documents together with string.
她要我們用繩子把文件綁在一起。

試練習題 Does Ms. Chu want us to staple the documents?
考生回答處 _____

考古題應用 We strolled along the famous Champs Elysees Avenue.
我們沿著著名的香榭麗舍大道散步。

試練習題 What did you first do in Paris?
考生回答處 _____

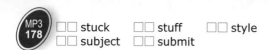
stuck (adj.) 卡住

關 stick (v.i) 卡住
同 fixed, firm, fastened

一般正常速度 [stʌk]
ETS全真速度 [sdʌ(k)]

➡ 1) 形容詞與動詞的 [t] 均須變音為 [d]
   2) 形容詞字尾 [k] 輕唸即可

stuff (n.) 東西

關 stuff (v.t) 填塞
同 things, materials, belongings, goods

一般正常速度 [stʌf]
ETS全真速度 [sdʌ(f)]

➡ 1) 名詞與動詞的唸法相同
   2) [t] 須變音為 [d]
   3) 字尾 [f] 輕唸即可

style (n.) 風格

關 style (v.t) 做造型
   stylish (adj.) 時尚的
同 mode, form, manner

一般正常速度 [staɪl]
ETS全真速度 [sdaɪl]

➡ 1) style 當動、名詞時唸法相同
   2) [t] 均須變音為 [d]
   3) 名詞與動詞的字尾 [l] 請勿唸成 [ɔ]
     （台式發音）

Su-

subject (n.) 對象

關 subject (adj.) 易受…影響的
   subjective (adj.) 主觀的
同 point, issue, theme, topic, matter, object

一般正常速度 [ˋsʌbdʒɪkt]
ETS全真速度 [ˋsʌ(b)dʒɪ(kt)]

➡ 1) subject 的重音在第一音節，
   subjective 的重音在第二音節
   2) [b] 均輕唸即可
   3) subjective 的 [t] 須變音為 [d]

submit (v.t) 繳交

關 submission (n.) 繳交
同 file, hand in, present

一般正常速度 [səbˋmɪt]
ETS全真速度 [sə(b)ˋmɪ(t)]

➡ 1) 動詞與名詞的重音都在第二音節
   2) [b] 均輕唸即可
   3) 動詞字尾 [t] 輕唸即可

考古題應用 She was stuck in traffic.
她被困在車陣中。

試練習題 Why was Ms. Marshall late for the convention?
考生回答處 _____

考古題應用 He kept a calculator and other stuff in the <u>drawer</u>.
他把計算機跟其他東西放在<u>抽屜</u>裡。

試練習題 What is in Victor's drawer?
考生回答處 _____

考古題應用 His personal style of <u>leadership</u> is very popular.
他的個人<u>領導</u>風格很受歡迎。

試練習題 Mr. Dayton has been a very supportive director, hasn't he?
考生回答處 _____

考古題應用 His arrogance has become the subject of criticism among employees.
他的傲慢已經成為員工批評的對象。

試練習題 Have you heard anything about the new PR manager?
考生回答處 _____

S

考古題應用 He has submitted the <u>budget projections</u> for the director to approve.
他已經繳交<u>預算編列書</u>給主管審核。

試練習題 Is Andrew still working on the budget projections?
考生回答處 _____

subscribe (v.i) 訂閱

關 subscription (n.) 訂閱
　　subscriber (n.) 訂戶
同 order, pay

一般正常速度 [səb`skraɪb]
ETS全真速度 [sə(b)`sgraɪ(b)]

➡ 1) 所有詞性的重音都在第二音節
　　2) [b] 均輕唸即可
　　3) [k] 均可變音為 [g]
　　4) 動詞字尾 [b] 輕唸即可

subsidize (v.t) 補助

關 subsidiary (n.) 補助物
　　subsidy (n.) 補助金
　　subsidiary (adj.) 次要的
同 fund, support, sponsor, finance

一般正常速度 [`sʌbsə͵daɪz]
ETS全真速度 [`sʌ(b)sə͵ɖaɪ(z)]

➡ 1) [b] 均輕唸即可
　　2) [d] 均可變音為 [ɖ]
　　3) 動詞字尾 [z] 輕唸即可
　　4) subsidiary 重音在第二音節

substantially
(adv.) 實質上

關 substantial (adj.) 實質的
同 essentially

一般正常速度 [səb`stænʃəlɪ]
ETS全真速度 [sə(b)`sdænʃəlɪ]

➡ 1) 副詞與形容詞的重音都在第二音節
　　2) [b] 均輕唸即可
　　3) 重音節 [t] 均須變音為 [d]

substitute (n.) 替代品

關 substitute (v.t) 替代
　　substitution (n.) 替代
同 replacement, change, alternate,
　　fill-in

一般正常速度 [`sʌbstə͵tjut]
ETS全真速度 [`sʌ(b)sdə͵tjut]

➡ 1) substitute 的重音在第一音節，
　　　substitution 的重音在第三音節 (-tu-)
　　2) [b] 均輕唸即可
　　3) 第一個 [t] 均可變音為 [d]

suburb (n.) 郊區

關 suburban (adj.) 郊區的
同 outskirts

一般正常速度 [`sʌbɝb]
ETS全真速度 [`sʌbɝ(b)]

➡ 1) 名詞的重音在第一音節，形容詞的
　　　重音在第二音節 (-ur-)
　　2) 名詞的第一個 u 唸 [ʌ]，形容詞則
　　　唸 [ə]

[考古題應用] I subscribed at that time in order to receive 30% off of the regular rate.
我當時訂閱是爲了享有一般價格的七折。

[試練習題] Why did you subscribe to *National Geographic* in January?

[考生回答處] _____

[考古題應用] Our <u>product development</u> is partially subsidized by the government.
我們的產品研發部分由政府補助。

[試練習題] Who subsidizes your product development?

[考生回答處] _____

[考古題應用] The new <u>courier service</u> can provide us with substantially lower rates.
新的宅配服務可提供我們實質上較低的費率。

[試練習題] Why are we switching our courier service provider?

[考生回答處] _____

[考古題應用] We can use butter as a substitute.
我們可以用奶油來當替代品。

[試練習題] What should we do if we run out of olive oil?

[考生回答處] _____

[考古題應用] The President's mansion is located in the suburbs.
總經理的豪宅位於郊區。

[試練習題] Did the President acquire a downtown mansion?

[考生回答處] _____

succeed (v.t) 繼任

關 successor (n.) 繼承者
同 come next, follow

一般正常速度 [sək`sid]

ETS全真速度 [sə(k)`si(d)]

➡ 1) 動詞與名詞的重音都在第二音節
2) 動詞的重音節母音唸 [i]，名詞的重音節母音唸成 [ɛ]
3) 動詞的 [k] 及字尾 [d] 均輕唸即可

sue (v.t) 控告

同 accuse, charge, blame

一般正常速度 [su]

ETS全真速度 [su]

suffer (v.t) 遭受

關 sufferer (n.) 患者；受害者
同 bear, endure, go through, undergo

一般正常速度 [`sʌfɚ]

ETS全真速度 [`sʌfɚ]

➡ 1) 動詞與名詞的重音都在第一音節
2) 重音節母音均為 [ʌ]，請勿唸成 [ɑ]（台式發音）

sum (v.i) 總結

關 sum (n.) 總和
同 conclude, epitomize, recapitulate

一般正常速度 [sʌm]

ETS全真速度 [sʌm]

➡ 動詞與名詞的唸法相同

summit (n.) 高峰會

同 top, point, peak, apex, pinnacle

一般正常速度 [`sʌmɪt]

ETS全真速度 [`sʌmɪ(t)]

➡ 1) 重音節母音 [ʌ] 請勿唸成 [ɑ]（台式發音）
2) 字尾 [t] 輕唸即可

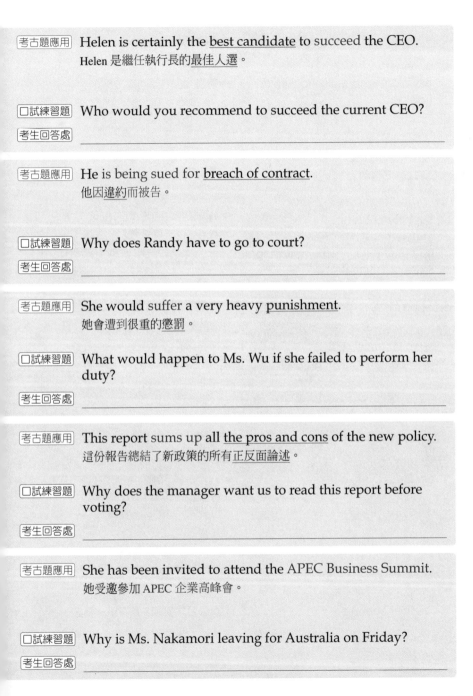

考古題應用 Helen is certainly the best candidate to succeed the CEO.
Helen 是繼任執行長的最佳人選。

試練習題 Who would you recommend to succeed the current CEO?
考生回答處 _____

考古題應用 He is being sued for breach of contract.
他因違約而被告。

試練習題 Why does Randy have to go to court?
考生回答處 _____

考古題應用 She would suffer a very heavy punishment.
她會遭到很重的懲罰。

試練習題 What would happen to Ms. Wu if she failed to perform her duty?
考生回答處 _____

考古題應用 This report sums up all the pros and cons of the new policy.
這份報告總結了新政策的所有正反面論述。

試練習題 Why does the manager want us to read this report before voting?
考生回答處 _____

考古題應用 She has been invited to attend the APEC Business Summit.
她受邀參加 APEC 企業高峰會。

試練習題 Why is Ms. Nakamori leaving for Australia on Friday?
考生回答處 _____

8

superior (adj.) 高級的

關 superior (n.) 上司
同 excellent, good, distinguished, first-class

一般正常速度 [sə`pɪrɪə]
ETS全真速度 [sə`pɪrɪə]

➡ 形容詞與名詞的唸法相同

supplementary (adj.) 補充的

關 supplement (v.t) 補充
supplement (n.) 補充品
同 complementary, accompanying, extra, additional

一般正常速度 [ˌsʌplə`mɛntərɪ]
ETS全真速度 [ˌsʌblə`mɛndərɪ]

➡ 1) 動詞與名詞的唸法相同
2) [p] 可變音為 [b]
3) 字母 u 均唸音為 [ʌ]，請勿唸成 [ɑ]（台式發音）

supply (v.t) 供應

關 supply (n.) 供應
supplier (n.) 供應商
同 provide, offer, give, grant

一般正常速度 [sə`plaɪ]
ETS全真速度 [sə`plaɪ]

➡ 所有詞性的重音都在第二音節

suppose (v.t) 猜想

關 supposedly (adv.) 據稱
同 assume, think, guess

一般正常速度 [sə`poz]
ETS全真速度 [sə`po(z)]

➡ 1) 動詞與副詞的重音都在第二音節
2) 動詞字尾 [z] 輕唸即可
3) 副詞的 [d] 必須消音

surgery (n.) 手術

關 surgeon (n.) 外科醫師
同 medical operation

一般正常速度 [`sɝdʒərɪ]
ETS全真速度 [`sɝdʒərɪ]

➡ 兩個名詞的重音都在第一音節

考古題應用 We are capable of making superior quality flour.
我們有辦法生產高品質的麵粉。

試練習題 What can you make with our newly acquired equipment?
考生回答處 _____

考古題應用 He recommended I find more supplementary information.
他建議我多找一些補充資料。

試練習題 What does professor Almquist think about your research paper?
考生回答處 _____

考古題應用 We supply the shelters with clean water and food.
我們供應乾淨的水跟食物給避難所。

試練習題 What do you supply the shelters with?
考生回答處 _____

考古題應用 I suppose Jake will get a raise.
我猜 Jake 會加薪。

試練習題 Who do you think will get a raise, Jake or Arthur?
考生回答處 _____

考古題應用 His knee requires surgery.
他膝蓋需要動手術。

試練習題 How is Randy's knee injury?
考生回答處 _____

surround (v.t) 圍繞

關 surroundings (n.) 環境
surrounding (adj.) 附近的
同 enclose, encircle

一般正常速度 [sə`raʊnd]
ETS全真速度 [sə`raʊn(d)]

➜ 1) 所有詞性的重音都在第二音節
2) 重音節母音均唸 [aʊ]，請勿唸成 [ɑ]
（台式發音）
3) 動詞字尾 [d] 輕唸即可

survey (n.) 調查

關 survey [sə`ve] (v.t) 調查
同 investigation, study, review, inspection, examination

一般正常速度 [`sɜve]
ETS全真速度 [`sɜve]

➜ 名詞的重音在第一音節，動詞的重音在第二音節

survive (v.t) 克服

關 survival (n.) 生存
survivor (n.) 倖存者
同 pull through, last, exist, endure

一般正常速度 [sə`vaɪv]
ETS全真速度 [sə`vaɪ(v)]

➜ 1) 所有詞性的重音都在第二音節
2) survival 的字尾 [l] 請勿唸成 [ɔ]（台式發音）

suspend (v.t) 暫停

關 suspension (n.) 暫停
同 cease, stop, interrupt, put off

一般正常速度 [sə`spɛnd]
ETS全真速度 [sə`sbɛn(d)]

➜ 1) 動詞與名詞的重音都在第二音節
2) [p] 均須變音為 [b]
3) 動詞字尾 [d] 輕唸即可

sustain (v.t) 支撐

關 sustenance (n.) 支持
sustaining (adj.) 有幫助的
同 support, keep, maintain, aid, provide for

一般正常速度 [sə`sten]
ETS全真速度 [sə`sden]

➜ 1) 動詞與形容詞的重音都在第二音節，名詞的重音在第一音節
2) [t] 均須變音為 [d]

考古題應用 This spring resort is surrounded by <u>maple trees</u>.
這座溫泉會館被<u>楓樹</u>圍繞著。

試練習題 What's so special about this particular spring resort?
考生回答處 _____

考古題應用 We are going to conduct a survey of the product's popularity.
我們將針對產品的人氣進行調查。

試練習題 What are these questionnaires for?
考生回答處 _____

考古題應用 I am glad that he survived the <u>sharp competition</u>.
我很高興他克服了<u>激烈的競爭</u>。

試練習題 Did you know that Kenji finally won the scholarship?
考生回答處 _____

考古題應用 The union decided to suspend the strike.
工會決定暫停罷工。

S

試練習題 What was the union's decision after yesterday's negotiation?
考生回答處 _____

考古題應用 Our store can't be sustained if the landlord <u>raises the rent</u>.
如果房東<u>漲租</u>我們的店就無法維持下去。

試練習題 What financial crisis is your store facing?
考生回答處 _____

Sw-

sweep (v.t) 掃地

關 sweep (n.) 掃地
同 clean, brush, clear, remove

一般正常速度 [swip]
ETS全真速度 [swi(p)]

➤ 1) 動詞與名詞的唸法相同
　2) 字尾 [p] 輕唸即可

swift (adj.) 迅速的

關 swiftness (n.) 迅速
　swiftly (adv.) 迅速地
同 fast, quick, express, hurried

一般正常速度 [swɪft]
ETS全真速度 [swɪ(ft)]

➤ 副詞與名詞的 [t] 均無須發音，形容詞
　字尾 [ft] 輕唸即可

swing (v.t) 揮動

關 swing (n.) 鞦韆
同 move back and forth

一般正常速度 [swɪŋ]
ETS全真速度 [swɪŋ]

➤ 動詞與名詞的唸法相同

swipe (v.t)（用力）刷

關 swipe (n.) 用力揮擊

一般正常速度 [swaɪp]
ETS全真速度 [swaɪ(p)]

➤ 1) 動詞與名詞的唸法相同
　2) 字尾 [p] 輕唸即可

switch (v.i) 轉換

關 switch (n.) 開關
同 change, exchange

一般正常速度 [swɪtʃ]
ETS全真速度 [swɪ(tʃ)]

➤ 1) 動詞與名詞的唸法相同
　2) 字尾 [tʃ] 輕唸即可

考古題應用　The waiter is still sweeping the floor.
服務生還在掃地。

口試練習題　Why can't we dine in that restaurant right now?

考生回答處　_____

考古題應用　We've received a swift reply from the Customer Relations Representative.
我們已經收到客服代表的立即回應。

口試練習題　What happened after you filed a complaint to the telephone company?

考生回答處　_____

考古題應用　The player swung the bat and hit the ball over the fence.
球員揮棒將球擊出牆外。

口試練習題　Why is the crowd cheering and applauding?

考生回答處　_____

考古題應用　You have to swipe your card before entering the room.
你要先刷卡才能進房間。

口試練習題　How do I get into the room?

考生回答處　_____

考古題應用　Our merchandise will switch from detergents to cosmetics.
我們的商品將從清潔劑轉換成化妝品。

口試練習題　What will be the major change in your corporate policy?

考生回答處　_____

Sy-

symbol (n.) 標示

關 symbolize (v.t) 象徵
　symbolic (adj.) 象徵性的
同 representation, image, mark,
　sign, logo

一般正常速度 [`sɪmbl̩]
ETS全真速度 [`sɪmbl̩]

➡ 1) 名詞與動詞的重音都在第一音節，
　　形容詞的重音在第二音節 (-bol-)
　2) 名詞字尾 [l] 請勿唸成 [ɔ]（台式發音）

sympathize (v.i) 贊同

關 sympathy (n.) 同理心
同 agree, go along with, understand

一般正常速度 [`sɪmpə.θaɪz]
ETS全真速度 [`sɪmbə.θaɪz]

➡ 1) 動詞與名詞的重音都在第一音節
　2) [p] 均可變音為 [b]

symptom (n.) 症狀

同 sign, warning, indication

一般正常速度 [`sɪmptəm]
ETS全真速度 [`sɪm(p)dəm]

➡ 1) [p] 輕唸即可
　2) [t] 須變音為 [d]

syndicate (n.) 集團

關 syndicate [`sɪndɪ.ket] (v.t) 聯合
同 company, organization, group

一般正常速度 [`sɪndɪkɪt]
ETS全真速度 [`sɪndɪkɪ(t)]

➡ 1) syndicate 當動、名詞時唸法不同
　2) [d] 可變音為 [ɖ]

synthetic (adj.) 合成的

關 synthesize (v.t) 合成
同 man-made, artificial

一般正常速度 [sɪn`θɛtɪk]
ETS全真速度 [sɪn`θɛɖɪ(k)]

➡ 1) 形容詞的重音在第二音節，動詞的
　　重音在第一音節
　2) 形容詞的 [t] 可變音為 [ɖ]
　3) 形容詞字尾 [k] 輕唸即可

考古題應用 Please read the washing symbols carefully.
請仔細閱讀清洗標示。

口試練習題 What do I do before dry cleaning this chiffon skirt?
考生回答處 _____

考古題應用 It's hard to sympathize with his decision.
他的決定很難讓人贊同。

口試練習題 Don't you find Mr. Gonzales's retirement too unexpected?
考生回答處 _____

考古題應用 A stuffy nose may also be a symptom of the flu.
鼻塞也可能是流行性感冒的症狀。

口試練習題 What other symptoms of the flu are there except coughing?
考生回答處 _____

考古題應用 Another syndicate is bidding against us for the same contract.
另一個集團跟我們在競標同一份合約。

口試練習題 Why are you so apprehensive about winning the contract?
考生回答處 _____

考古題應用 These shoes are made of synthetic leather.
這些鞋子是合成皮做的。

口試練習題 Are these shoes made of authentic leather?
考生回答處 _____

S

Check List 9

到目前為止，字彙量又增加了不少，繼續學新單字之前，我們先來複習一下，看看是不是都記起來了！

- ☐ soar
- ☐ socialize
- ☐ soften
- ☐ sole
- ☐ solicit
- ☐ soothing

- ☐ sophisticated
- ☐ sort
- ☐ sound
- ☐ source
- ☐ spare
- ☐ specialize

- ☐ specific
- ☐ speculate
- ☐ speed
- ☐ split
- ☐ spoil
- ☐ sponsor

- ☐ spontaneously
- ☐ spread
- ☐ square
- ☐ squeeze
- ☐ stack
- ☐ stage

- ☐ stagnant
- ☐ stain
- ☐ stake
- ☐ stall
- ☐ stamp
- ☐ stand

- ☐ standard
- ☐ standby
- ☐ staple
- ☐ stare
- ☐ starve
- ☐ state

- ☐ statement
- ☐ statistics
- ☐ staunch
- ☐ steady
- ☐ sticky
- ☐ stimulate

- ☐ stipulation
- ☐ stir
- ☐ stock
- ☐ store
- ☐ stow
- ☐ straighten

- ☐ strategic
- ☐ strengthen
- ☐ stress
- ☐ strict
- ☐ strike
- ☐ string

- ☐ stroll
- ☐ stuck
- ☐ stuff
- ☐ style
- ☐ subject
- ☐ submit

- ☐ subscribe
- ☐ subsidize
- ☐ substantially
- ☐ substitute
- ☐ suburb
- ☐ succeed

- ☐ sue
- ☐ suffer
- ☐ sum
- ☐ summit
- ☐ superior
- ☐ supplementary

- ☐ supply
- ☐ suppose
- ☐ surgery
- ☐ surround
- ☐ survey
- ☐ survive

- ☐ suspend
- ☐ sustain
- ☐ sweep
- ☐ swift
- ☐ swing
- ☐ swipe

- ☐ switch
- ☐ symbol
- ☐ sympathize
- ☐ symptom
- ☐ syndicate
- ☐ synthetic

□□ table □□ tactic □□ tag
□□ talent □□ tally

T

Ta-

table (n.) 表格

關 table (v.t) 製表
同 chart, diagram

一般正常速度 [`tebl]
ETS全真速度 [`tebl]

➡ 1) 名詞與動詞的唸法相同
2) 字尾 [l] 請勿唸成 [ɔ]（台式發音）

tactic (n.) 策略

關 tactical (adj.) 策略性的
同 strategy, method, policy, scheme

一般正常速度 [`tæktɪk]
ETS全真速度 [`tæ__dɪ(k)]

➡ 1) 名詞與形容詞的重音都在第一音節
2) 第一個 [k] 停一拍即可，無須發音
3) 第二個 [t] 均須變音為 [d]
4) 名詞字尾 [k] 輕唸即可

tag (n.) 標籤

關 tag (v.t) 加標籤
同 mark, label

一般正常速度 [tæg]
ETS全真速度 [tæ(g)]

➡ 名詞與動詞的唸法相同

talent (n.) 天份

關 talented (adj.) 有天份的
同 ability, gift, aptitude, capacity

一般正常速度 [`tælənt]
ETS全真速度 [`tælən(t)]

➡ 1) 名詞與形容詞重音都在第一音節
2) 形容詞的第二個 [t] 可變音為 [d]
3) 名詞字尾 [t] 輕唸即可

tally (n.) 紀錄

關 tally (v.t) 計算
同 count, computation, mark, record

一般正常速度 [`tælɪ]
ETS全真速度 [`tælɪ]

➡ 名詞與動詞的唸法相同

考古題應用 The sales figures in Table 2 need to be <u>revised</u>.
表格二的銷售數字需要修正。

口試練習題 Are the sales figures in this report correct?

考生回答處 _____

考古題應用 She uses very special selling tactics.
她運用很特別的銷售策略。

口試練習題 Why is Akiko such a successful sales representative?

考生回答處 _____

考古題應用 The sales clerk forgot to attach the price tag to the merchandise.
售貨員忘了將商品貼上價格標籤。

口試練習題 The price tag is missing, isn't it?

考生回答處 _____

考古題應用 He had a very special artistic talent.
他有非常特殊的藝術天份。

口試練習題 How did Bellini become such a well-known Italian painter?

考生回答處 _____

T

考古題應用 The janitor has kept a careful tally of the visitors.
管理員對訪客人數有很詳細的紀錄。

口試練習題 How do you know the exact number of visitors?

考生回答處 _____

target (n.) 目標

關 target (v.t) 瞄準
同 aim, goal, object, objective

一般正常速度 [`targɪt]
ETS全真速度 [`targɪ(t)]

➡ 1) 名詞與動詞的唸法相同
2) 字尾 [t] 輕唸即可

task (n.) 任務

關 task (v.t) 派予任務
同 job, mission, duty, assignment, work

一般正常速度 [tæsk]
ETS全真速度 [tæ(sk)]

➡ 1) 名詞與動詞的唸法相同
2) 字尾 [sk] 輕唸即可

Te-

tear (v.i) 撕破

關 tear [tɪr] (n.) 眼淚
同 pull apart, rip, split

一般正常速度 [tɛr]
ETS全真速度 [tɛr]

➡ 動詞的母音唸 [ɛ]，名詞的母音唸 [ɪ]

technical (adj.) 技術的

關 technology (n.) 技術
technique (n.) 技巧

一般正常速度 [`tɛknɪkl]
ETS全真速度 [`tɛ__nɪgl]

➡ 1) 形容詞的重音在第一音節，名詞的
重音在第二音節 (-nol-), (-nique)
2) 第一個 [k] 停一拍即可，無須發音
3) 形容詞第二個 [k] 須變音為 [g]

teller (n.) 出納人員

同 clerk, cashier

一般正常速度 [`tɛlə]
ETS全真速度 [`tɛlə]

考古題應用 We've successfully met the monthly sales target.
我們已成功達到本月的銷售目標。

試練習題 Have you fallen short of the monthly sales target?
考生回答處 _____

考古題應用 The manager's prime task is to <u>restore our competitiveness</u>.
經理的首要之務是<u>重建我們的競爭力</u>。

試練習題 What is the manager's prime task?
考生回答處 _____

考古題應用 They are tearing down the old museum.
他們正在拆除舊博物館。

試練習題 Why are there so many bulldozers and cranes in front of the museum?
考生回答處 _____

考古題應用 They have <u>encountered</u> some technical problems.
他們<u>遭遇</u>到一些技術問題。

T

試練習題 Why do they have to put off the product launch?
考生回答處 _____

考古題應用 The tellers at that bank are very helpful to their customers.
那家銀行的出納人員對客戶很幫忙。

試練習題 Why did you open an account at M&T bank?
考生回答處 _____

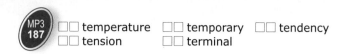
temperature (n.) 溫度

關 temperate (adj.) 溫度適中的
同 degree of heat or coldness

一般正常速度 [`tɛmprətʃə]
ETS全真速度 [`tɛmbrətʃə]

➡ 1) 名詞與形容詞的重音都在第一音節
2) [p] 均須變音為 [b]
3) 形容詞字尾 [t] 輕唸即可

temporary (adj.) 臨時的

關 temporarily (adv.) 臨時地
同 brief, provisional, momentary

一般正常速度 [`tɛmpə.rɛrɪ]
ETS全真速度 [`tɛmbə.rɛrɪ]

➡ 1) 形容詞與副詞的重音都在第一音節
2) [p] 均可變音為 [b]

tendency (n.) 趨勢

關 tend (v.i) 傾向
同 inclination

一般正常速度 [`tɛndənsɪ]
ETS全真速度 [`tɛndənsɪ]

tension (n.) 緊張

關 tense (adj.) 緊張的
同 pressure, stress

一般正常速度 [`tɛnʃən]
ETS全真速度 [`tɛnʃən]

terminal (n.) 航廈

關 terminal (adj.) 終點的
同 station

一般正常速度 [`tɝmənl]
ETS全真速度 [`tɝmənl]

➡ 1) 名詞與形容詞的唸法相同
2) 字尾 [l] 請勿唸成 [ɔ]（台式發音）

考古題應用 The average temperature in England during the summer is 60°F.
英國夏天的平均溫度是華氏 60 度。

試練習題 Is England very hot during the summer?
考生回答處 _____

考古題應用 Temporary tents have been set up for the book fair.
書展需要的臨時帳篷已經架好了。

試練習題 Are you still working on the temporary tents?
考生回答處 _____

考古題應用 Our stock prices have a tendency to fluctuate.
我們的股價有波動的趨勢。

試練習題 Are your stock prices relatively stable?
考生回答處 _____

考古題應用 The tension between the two departments remains.
這兩個部門間的緊張仍持續著。

試練習題 Have the Sales Department and the R&D Department worked out their disagreement?
考生回答處 _____

T

考古題應用 This is a domestic terminal.
這裡是國內航廈。

試練習題 Is this an international terminal or a domestic terminal?
考生回答處 _____

territory (n.) 領域

回 area, district, region, terrain

一般正常速度 [ˋtɛrəˌtorɪ]

ETS全真速度 [ˋtɛrəˌɖorɪ]

➔ 第二個 [t] 須變音為 [ɖ]

text (n.) 文字

回 words, contents, passage

一般正常速度 [tɛkst]

ETS全真速度 [tɛ(kst)]

➔ 字尾 [kst] 輕唸即可

textile (n.) 紡織品

關 textile (adj.) 紡織的
回 woven material, fabrics, cloth

一般正常速度 [ˋtɛkstaɪl]

ETS全真速度 [ˋtɛ(ks)daɪl]

➔ 1) 名詞與形容詞的唸法相同
2) [ks] 輕唸即可
3) 第二個 [t] 可變音為 [d]
4) 字尾 [l] 請勿唸成 [ɔ] (台式發音)

theory (n.) 理論

Th-

關 theoretical (adj.) 理論上的
回 assumption, guess, speculation

一般正常速度 [ˋθiərɪ]

ETS全真速度 [ˋθiərɪ]

➔ 1) 名詞的重音在第一音節，形容詞的
重音在第三音節 (-ret-)
2) 形容詞的 [t] 須變音為 [ɖ]

therapy (n.) 治療

關 therapeutic (adj.) 治療的；有療效
的
回 cure, treatment, healing, remedy

一般正常速度 [ˋθɛrəpɪ]

ETS全真速度 [ˋθɛrəbɪ]

➔ 1) 名詞的重音在第一音節，形容詞的
重音在第三音節 (-peu-)
2) 名詞的 [p] 須變音為 [b]
3) 形容詞的 [t] 須變音為 [ɖ]

考古題應用 We shouldn't have rushed into unfamiliar territory.
我們不該急著進入不熟悉的領域。

試練習題 Was it unwise for us to switch our focus to food manufacturing?

考生回答處 ＿＿＿＿＿＿＿＿＿＿＿＿＿＿＿＿＿＿＿＿＿

考古題應用 She is carefully examining the text on her computer screen.
她在仔細檢視電腦螢幕上的文字。

試練習題 What is the editor doing at her desk?

考生回答處 ＿＿＿＿＿＿＿＿＿＿＿＿＿＿＿＿＿＿＿＿＿

考古題應用 The interior designer is selecting home textiles.
室內設計師正在挑選傢飾布。

試練習題 What is the interior designer getting from the home improvement outlet?

考生回答處 ＿＿＿＿＿＿＿＿＿＿＿＿＿＿＿＿＿＿＿＿＿

考古題應用 He can't tell the difference between theory and practice.
他分不出理論跟實際的差異。

T

試練習題 Don't you think Jonathan's proposal is too unrealistic?

考生回答處 ＿＿＿＿＿＿＿＿＿＿＿＿＿＿＿＿＿＿＿＿＿

考古題應用 Latest research indicates that music therapy might help.
最新研究指出音樂治療可能有幫助。

試練習題 Do I need to see a doctor for my sleep disorder?

考生回答處 ＿＿＿＿＿＿＿＿＿＿＿＿＿＿＿＿＿＿＿＿＿

thorough (adj.) 詳盡的

一般正常速度 [ˋθɝo]
ETS全真速度 [ˋθɝo]

關 thoroughly (adv.) 詳盡地
同 full, complete, comprehensive, careful, exhaustive

Ti-

tie (v.t) 繫緊

一般正常速度 [taɪ]
ETS全真速度 [taɪ]

關 tie (n.) 領帶
同 fasten, secure, bind

➡ 動詞與名詞的唸法相同

title (n.) 職稱

一般正常速度 [ˋtaɪtl]
ETS全真速度 [ˋtaɪđl]

關 title (v.t) 命名
同 name

➡ 1) 名詞與動詞的唸法相同
   2) 第二個 [t] 須變音為 [đ]
   3) 字尾 [l] 請勿唸成 [ɔ] (台式發音)

To-

token (n.) 代幣

一般正常速度 [ˋtokən]
ETS全真速度 [ˋtogən]

關 token (adj.) 象徵性的

➡ 1) 名詞與形容詞的唸法相同
   2) [k] 須變音為 [g]

tolerate (v.t) 忍受

一般正常速度 [ˋtɑləˏret]
ETS全真速度 [ˋtɑləˏre(t)]

關 tolerance (n.) 忍耐
   tolerant (adj.) 寬容的
   tolerable (adj.) 可忍受的
同 endure, bear, stand, put up with, accept, suffer, undergo

➡ 1) 所有詞性的重音都在第一音節
   2) 動詞字尾 [t] 輕唸即可

考古題應用 The police conducted a thorough investigation.
警察做了詳細的調查。

試練習題 What happened after someone broke into your office?
考生回答處 _____

考古題應用 Please tie the labels to your <u>check-in luggage</u>.
請將<u>這些</u>標籤繫在你的<u>托運行李</u>上。

試練習題 Where do I tie these labels?
考生回答處 _____

考古題應用 Please <u>fill in</u> your name, address and title.
請<u>填寫</u>你的姓名、地址和職稱。

試練習題 What personal information should I put on this entry form?
考生回答處 _____

考古題應用 I already <u>inserted</u> the tokens into the machine.
我已經把代幣<u>投進</u>機器裡。

T

試練習題 Where are the tokens I gave you?
考生回答處 _____

考古題應用 The staff can no longer tolerate his <u>incompetence</u>.
員工們再也忍受不了他的<u>無能</u>。

試練習題 Why are staff members filing complaints against the Product Manager?

考生回答處 _____

tour (n.) 遊覽

關 tour (v.t) 遊覽
同 visit, journey, trip

一般正常速度 [tur]
ETS全真速度 [tur]

➡ 名詞與動詞的唸法相同

Tr-

trace (v.t) 找出

關 trace (n.) 痕跡
traceable (adj.) 找得到的
同 search for, find, track, seek

一般正常速度 [tres]
ETS全真速度 [tre(s)]

➡ 1) trace 當動、名詞時唸法相同
2) 動詞與名詞的字尾 [s] 均輕唸即可

trade (n.) 貿易

關 trade (v.i) 做生意
同 dealing, business, transaction

一般正常速度 [tred]
ETS全真速度 [tre(d)]

➡ 1) 名詞與動詞的唸法相同
2) 字尾 [d] 輕唸即可

traditional (adj.) 傳統的

關 tradition (n.) 傳統
traditionally (adv.) 傳統地
同 accustomed, customary, fixed,
established, usual

一般正常速度 [trə`dɪʃənl]
ETS全真速度 [trə`dɪʃənl]

➡ 1) 所有詞性的重音都在第二音節
2) 形容詞字尾 [l] 請勿唸成 [ɔ]（台式
發音）

transaction (n.) 交易

關 transact (v.t) 交易
同 negotiation

一般正常速度 [træn`zækʃən]
ETS全真速度 [træn`zækʃən]

➡ 1) 名詞與動詞的重音都在第二音節
2) 動詞字尾 [kt] 輕唸即可

考古題應用 | We went on a free guided tour of the Prado Museum.
我們參加普拉度博物館的免費導覽。

試練習題 | What did you do on your vacation in Madrid?
考生回答處 | _____

考古題應用 | It's hard to trace the source of a rumor.
要找出謠言的來源很難。

試練習題 | Have you found the source of the rumor?
考生回答處 | _____

考古題應用 | We will be holding a trade show this month.
我們這個月即將舉辦貿易展。

試練習題 | Why have you been working so hard lately?
考生回答處 | _____

考古題應用 | The main objective is to <u>preserve</u> our traditional craft.
主要目的是在保存我們的傳統工藝。

T

試練習題 | What is the main objective of your cultural foundation?
考生回答處 | _____

考古題應用 | You can't cancel the transaction aften making the payment.
付款後你就無法取消交易。

試練習題 | May I cancel a transaction?
考生回答處 | _____

transition (n.) 過渡時期

關 transit (v.i) 過渡
　 transitional (adj.) 過渡期的
同 changeover, passing, transit,
　 shift, progression

一般正常速度 [trænˋzɪʃən]
ETS全真速度 [trænˋzɪʃən]

➡ 1) 所有詞性的 s 均要唸成 [z]
　 2) 形容詞字尾 [l] 請勿唸成 [ɔ]（台式
　　　發音）

translate (v.t) 翻譯

關 translation (n.) 翻譯
　 translator (n.) 翻譯人員
同 interpret

一般正常速度 [trænsˋlet]
ETS全真速度 [trænsˋle(t)]

➡ 1) 所有詞性的重音都在第二音節
　 2) 動詞字尾 [t] 輕唸即可
　 3) translator 的第二個 [t] 須變音為 [d]

transport (v.t) 運送

關 transport (n.) 運輸
　 transportation (n.) 運輸
同 carry, transfer, move, ship

一般正常速度 [trænsˋpɔrt]
ETS全真速度 [trænsˋbɔr(t)]

➡ 1) transport 當動詞時重音在第二音
　　　節，當名詞時重音在第一音節
　 2) [p] 均須變音為 [b]
　 3) 動詞字尾 [t] 輕唸即可

tray (n.) 托盤

同 platter

一般正常速度 [tre]
ETS全真速度 [tre]

trial (n.) 試用

同 test, check, examination

一般正常速度 [traɪl]
ETS全真速度 [traɪl]

➡ 字尾 [l] 請勿唸成 [ɔ]（台式發音）

考古題應用 We had a very smooth leadership transition.
我們領導權的轉移非常順利。

試練習題 Did the change in leadership negatively affect your company?

考生回答處 _____

考古題應用 Please translate this article from English to Japanese.
請將這篇文章從英文翻譯成日文。

試練習題 What do you want me to do with this article?

考生回答處 _____

考古題應用 The truck will transport the goods to the harbor on Monday.
卡車會在週一把貨運送到港口。

試練習題 When will you transport the goods to the harbor?

考生回答處 _____

考古題應用 The waiter is serving <u>refreshments</u> on a tray.
服務生用托盤上小點心。

T

試練習題 Is the waiter serving refreshments on a dish?

考生回答處 _____

考古題應用 There's a 10-day free trial period for this product.
這個產品有十天的免費鑑賞期。

試練習題 How long is the free trial period for this product?

考生回答處 _____

tribute (n.) 致敬

同 respect, honor, recognition, acknowledgment, applause, gratitude, compliment

一般正常速度 [ˋtrɪbjut]

ETS全真速度 [ˋtrɪbju(t)]

➡ 字尾 [t] 輕唸即可

trim (v.t) 修剪

關 trim (adj.) 整齊的
同 cut, clip, shave, prune

一般正常速度 [trɪm]

ETS全真速度 [trɪm]

➡ 動詞與形容詞的唸法相同

trivial (adj.) 瑣碎的

關 triviality (n.) 瑣事
同 unimportant, small, insignificant, minor, petty, slight

一般正常速度 [ˋtrɪvɪəl]

ETS全真速度 [ˋtrɪvɪəl]

➡ 1) 名詞的重音在第三音節 (-al-)
2) 名詞字尾 [t] 須變音為 [đ]
3) 形容詞字尾 [l] 請勿唸成 [ɔ]（台式發音）

tropical (adj.) 熱帶的

關 tropically (adv.) 熱帶地
同 hot, humid, torrid

一般正常速度 [ˋtrɑpɪkl]

ETS全真速度 [ˋtrɑbɪgl]

➡ 1) 兩個詞性的重音都在第一音節
2) [p] 均須變音為 [b]
3) [k] 均須變音為 [g]
4) 形容詞字尾 [l] 請勿唸成 [ɔ]（台式發音）

trust (n.) 信託

關 trust (v.t) 託付
　　trustee (n.) 受信託人
同 custody, guard, protection, trusteeship

一般正常速度 [trʌst]

ETS全真速度 [trʌs(t)]

➡ 1) trustee 重音在第二音節 (-ee)
2) trust 字尾 [t] 輕唸即可，trustee 第二個 [t] 須變音為 [d]

考古題應用 Over 200 people paid tribute to him at the <u>memorial service</u>.
有超過兩百個人在<u>告別式</u>上向他致敬。

口試練習題 Were there many people at the late minister's memorial service?
考生回答處 _____

考古題應用 We've hired <u>gardeners</u> to trim the <u>hedges</u>.
我們雇用<u>園丁</u>來修剪<u>樹叢</u>。

口試練習題 How do you keep this garden so attractive?
考生回答處 _____

考古題應用 He tends to <u>lose his temper</u> over trivial matters.
他容易因爲小事而<u>發脾氣</u>。

口試練習題 Mr. Kim is always in a bad mood, isn't he?
考生回答處 _____

考古題應用 They <u>went scuba diving</u> near a tropical island.
他們到一個熱帶小島附近<u>浮潛</u>。

口試練習題 Where did your family go scuba diving?
考生回答處 _____

考古題應用 The charitable trust is set up for <u>abused children</u>.
這個慈善信託基金是爲了<u>受虐兒</u>設置的。

口試練習題 For whom did you set up this charitable trust?
考生回答處 _____

T

Tu-

turn (n.) 轉換

關 turn (v.t) 轉換
同 change, cycle, rotation

一般正常速度 [tɜn]
ETS全真速度 [tɜn]
➡ 名詞與動詞的唸法相同

turnaround (n.) 突然好轉

同 reversal

一般正常速度 [ˋtɜnəˌraʊnd]
ETS全真速度 [ˋtɜnəˌraʊn(d)]
➡ 字尾 [d] 輕唸即可

turnout (n.) 出席人數

同 attendance

一般正常速度 [ˋtɜnˌaʊt]
ETS全真速度 [ˋtɜnˌaʊ(t)]
➡ 1) turn 與 out 須唸連音
2) 字尾 [t] 輕唸即可

turnover (n.) 營業額

同 business

一般正常速度 [ˋtɜnˌovə]
ETS全真速度 [ˋtɜnˌovə]
➡ [n] 與 [o] 必須連音

tutor (n.) 家教

關 tutor (v.t) 教家教
同 teacher, instructor, trainer

一般正常速度 [ˋtjutə]
ETS全真速度 [ˋtjuɖə]
➡ 1) 名詞與動詞的唸法相同
2) 第二個 [t] 須變音為 [ɖ]

考古題應用 We would take turns using the copier on the first floor.
我們會輪流使用一樓的影印機。

試練習題 What would you do if the copier on the third floor was broken?
考生回答處 _____

考古題應用 Wise investments have brought him to a sudden financial turnaround.
正確投資讓他的經濟突然好轉。

試練習題 I thought Mr. Kinski was broke!
考生回答處 _____

考古題應用 We expect a large turnout despite the rain.
我們預計就算下雨出席人數仍會很多。

試練習題 Will the rain affect the art fair's turnout?
考生回答處 _____

考古題應用 We have a turnover of 5,000 dollars a week there.
我們那邊一週有五千美元的營業額。

試練習題 How much money does your branch store in London make a week?
考生回答處 _____

考古題應用 I've asked Julio to be her Spanish tutor.
我已經請 Julio 當她的西班牙語家教。

試練習題 Don't you think Sally should hire a Spanish tutor?
考生回答處 _____

T

Ty-

typical (adj.) 典型的

關 typically (adv.) 通常
同 standard, usual, normal, average, characteristic

一般正常速度 [ˋtɪpɪkl̩]

ETS全真速度 [ˋtɪbɪgl̩]

➡ 1) 形容詞與副詞的重音都在第一音節
2) [p] 均須變音為 [b]
3) [k] 均須變音為 [g]

U

Ul-

ultimate (adj.) 最終的

關 ultimately (adv.) 最終地
同 last, final, terminal

一般正常速度 [ˋʌltəmɪt]

ETS全真速度 [ˋʌlđəmɪ(t)]

➡ 1) 形容詞與副詞的重音都在第一音節
2) 形容詞字尾 [t] 輕唸即可，副詞的 [t] 則須消音

Un-

unanimous (adj.) 一致的

關 unanimously (adv.) 一致地
同 agreed, in agreement, united

一般正常速度 [juˋnænəməs]

ETS全真速度 [juˋnænəmə(s)]

➡ 兩個詞性的重音都在第二音節

underestimate (v.t) 低估

同 underrate, belittle

一般正常速度 [ˋʌndəˋɛstəˌmet]

ETS全真速度 [ˋʌndəˋɛsdəˌme(t)]

➡ 1) 第一個 [t] 須變音為 [d]
2) 字尾 [t] 輕唸即可

undergo (v.t) 經歷

同 experience, bear, endure, stand

一般正常速度 [ˌʌndəˋgo]

ETS全真速度 [ˌʌndəˋgo]

考古題應用 This desk is very typical of the Victorian era.
這張桌子有非常典型的維多利亞時代風格。

試練習題 What style of furniture is this antique desk?

考生回答處 _____

考古題應用 Their ultimate goal is to open a branch store in every Asian country.
他們的最終目標是在每個亞洲國家都開設分店。

試練習題 What is the ultimate goal of the PSM Enterprise?

考生回答處 _____

考古題應用 The committee was unanimous in their decision to hire him.
委員會一致決定雇用他。

試練習題 Did anyone vote against hiring Mr. Lawrence?

考生回答處 _____

考古題應用 You underestimated the importance of teamwork.
你們低估了團隊合作的重要性。

T
U

試練習題 Why did we lose the contract to such a small company?

考生回答處 _____

考古題應用 Our department has undergone many changes.
我們部門經歷過許多變化。

試練習題 Your staff has changed a lot over the last three years, hasn't it?

考生回答處 _____

✓ **underline** (v.t) 強調
同 emphasize, stress

一般正常速度 [ˌʌndəˋlaɪn]
ETS全真速度 [ˌʌndəˋlaɪn]

undertake (v.t) 承擔
同 take on

一般正常速度 [ˌʌndəˋtek]
ETS全真速度 [ˌʌndəˋte(k)]
➡ 字尾 [k] 輕唸即可

✓ **uniform** (adj.) 不變的
關 uniform (n.) 制服
　uniformly (adv.) 不變地
同 unchanging, consistent, constant

一般正常速度 [ˋjunəˌfɔrm]
ETS全真速度 [ˋjunəˌfɔrm]
➡ 所有詞性的重音都在第一音節

unique (adj.) 獨一無二的
關 uniquely (adv.) 獨特地
同 one and only, uncomparable,
　unequalled

一般正常速度 [juˋnik]
ETS全真速度 [juˋni(k)]
➡ 形容詞字尾 [k] 輕唸即可

unity (n.) 團結
關 unite (v.t) 聯合
同 entity, union, undividedness

一般正常速度 [ˋjunətɪ]
ETS全真速度 [ˋjunəɾɪ]
➡ 1) 名詞的重音在第一音節，動詞的重
　　音在第二音節 (-nite)
　2) 名詞的 [t] 須變音為 [ɾ]

考古題應用 Our director has always underlined the importance of teamwork.
我們主管一直強調團隊合作的重要性。

試練習題 Our department doesn't encourage us to work alone, does it?

考生回答處 _____

考古題應用 She undertook the job of settling labor disputes.
她負責解決勞資糾紛的工作。

試練習題 What was Mrs. Wang's position in the union?

考生回答處 _____

考古題應用 We must maintain a uniform temperature in the greenhouse all day.
我們必須讓溫室整天保持在恆溫的狀態。

試練習題 Did you reset the greenhouse temperature this afternoon?

考生回答處 _____

考古題應用 He's got a very unique style of painting.
他有非常獨特的繪畫風格。

試練習題 What made Jason Pollok a celebrated artist?

考生回答處 _____

U

考古題應用 She stressed the importance of departmental unity.
她強調部門間團結的重要性。

試練習題 What did the CEO say in the opening speech of the ceremony?

考生回答處 _____

unload (v.t) 卸下

同 unpack, empty, discharge, off-load

一般正常速度 [ʌn`lod]

ETS全真速度 [ʌn`lo(d)]

➜ 字尾 [d] 輕唸即可

Up-

update (v.t) 更新

關 update [`ʌpde(t)] (n.) 更新
同 renew, bring up to date

一般正常速度 [ʌp`det]

ETS全真速度 [ʌp`de(t)]

➜ 1) 動詞的重音在第二音節，名詞的重音在第一音節
   2) 字尾 [t] 均輕唸即可

Ur-

urge (v.t) 催促

關 urge (n.) 衝動
同 push, force, hasten, encourage, stimulate

一般正常速度 [ɜdʒ]

ETS全真速度 [ɜdʒ]

➜ 動詞與名詞的唸法相同

Ut-

utilities (n.) 水電

關 utilize (v.t) 利用

一般正常速度 [ju`tɪlətɪz]

ETS全真速度 [ju`tɪlədɪz]

➜ 1) 名詞的重音在第二音節，動詞的重音在第一音節
   2) 名詞的第二個 [t] 須變音為 [d]

---

utterly (adv.) 完全地

關 utter (adj.) 全然的
同 totally, completely, absolutely, entirely, thoroughly, fully

一般正常速度 [`ʌtəlɪ]

ETS全真速度 [`ʌdəlɪ]

➜ 兩個詞性的 [t] 均須變音為 [d]

考古題應用 The bellboy is unloading the luggage from the <u>limo</u>.
飯店服務生正將行李從<u>加長型轎車</u>上卸下來。

試練習題 What is the bellboy doing by the limo?
考生回答處

考古題應用 The VP will update her on the progress of negotiations.
副總經理會向她更新談判的最新進度。

試練習題 Who will update the CEO on the progress of negotiations?
考生回答處

考古題應用 The union has urged its members to <u>take action</u>.
工會已經催促會員<u>採取行動</u>。

試練習題 Will the union put off the strike again?
考生回答處

考古題應用 The <u>tenants</u> have to pay for their own utilities.
<u>承租人</u>得自己付水電費。

試練習題 Will the landlord cover part of the utility bill?
考生回答處

U

考古題應用 They are utterly different.
它們完全不同。

試練習題 What do these two models have in common?
考生回答處

vacancy (n.) 空位

關 vacate (v.t) 清空
vacant (adj.) 空的
同 opening, room, space, void

一般正常速度 [ˋvekənsɪ]
ETS全真速度 [ˋvegənsɪ]

➡ 除動詞外，其他兩個詞性的 [k] 均須變音為 [g]

vaccinate (v.t) 預防注射

關 vaccine (n.) 疫苗
vaccination (n.) 預防注射

一般正常速度 [ˋvæksən.et]
ETS全真速度 [ˋvæ(k)sən.e(t)]

➡ 1) [k] 均輕唸即可
2) 動詞字尾 [t] 輕唸即可

vague (adj.) 模糊的

關 vaguely (adv.) 模糊地
同 unclear, obscure, blurred,
imprecise, doubtful

一般正常速度 [veg]
ETS全真速度 [ve(g)]

➡ 字尾 [g] 輕唸即可

valid (adj.) 有效的

關 validate (v.t) 使…有效
validity (n.) 有效性
同 lawful, legal, legitimate

一般正常速度 [ˋvælɪd]
ETS全真速度 [ˋvælɪ(d)]

➡ 1) 名詞的重音在第二音節
2) 動詞與名詞的 [d] 均須變音為 [ð]

valuable (n.) 貴重物品

關 value (n.) 價值
同 treasure

一般正常速度 [ˋvæljuəbl]
ETS全真速度 [ˋvæljuəbl]

➡ 1) 兩個名詞的重音都在第一音節
2) valuable 字尾 [l] 請勿唸成 [ɔ]（台式發音）

398

[考古題應用] This hotel seldom has vacancies even in the <u>low season</u>.
這家飯店即使在<u>淡季</u>都很少有空房。

[口試練習題] This five-star hotel is really popular, isn't it?
[考生回答處] _____

[考古題應用] We have to be vaccinated against some diseases.
我們必須打疫苗來預防某些疾病。

[口試練習題] What do you have to do before going on your trip to India?
[考生回答處] _____

[考古題應用] The witness gave us too vague of a description.
目擊者提供給我們的描述太過模糊了。

[口試練習題] Why didn't you find the person who smashed the car window?
[考生回答處] _____

[考古題應用] Your passport is valid for another five years.
你護照的有效期還有五年。

[口試練習題] Has my passport expired?
[考生回答處] _____

V

[考古題應用] I <u>deposited</u> my valuables in the bank safe.
我把貴重物品<u>存放</u>在銀行保險箱。

[口試練習題] Where did you deposit your valuables?
[考生回答處] _____

variable (adj.) 易變的

關 vary (v.t) 改變
variation (n.) 改變
variety (n.) 多樣性；種類
同 changeable, shifting, unsteady, unstable

一般正常速度 [ˋvɛrɪəbḷ]
ETS全真速度 [ˋvɛrɪəbḷ]

➡ variety 字尾 [t] 須變音為 [d]

Ve-

vehicle (n.) 交通工具

同 means

一般正常速度 [ˋviɪkḷ]
ETS全真速度 [ˋviɪgḷ]

➡ [k] 須變音為 [g]

ventilation (n.) 通風

關 vent (n.) 通風口

一般正常速度 [ˌvɛntḷˋeʃən]
ETS全真速度 [ˌvɛndḷˋeʃən]

➡ ventilation 的 [t] 須變音為 [d]

venture (v.t) 冒險

關 venture (n.) 冒險
同 take risks, risk, stake

一般正常速度 [ˋvɛntʃɚ]
ETS全真速度 [ˋvɛntʃɚ]

➡ 動詞與名詞的唸法相同

verge (n.) 邊緣

關 verge (v.i) 瀕臨
同 edge, border, boundary

一般正常速度 [vɝdʒ]
ETS全真速度 [vɝ(dʒ)]

➡ 名詞與動詞的唸法相同

考古題應用 The price of fresh fruits is variable <u>as well</u>.
新鮮水果的價格也<u>一樣</u>不定。

試練習題 The price of fresh vegetables varies according to season, doesn't it?

考生回答處 _____

考古題應用 Our government encourages the development of <u>fuel-efficient</u> vehicles.
我們政府鼓勵研發<u>省油</u>的交通工具。

試練習題 Why is your company developing fuel-efficient vehicles?

考生回答處 _____

考古題應用 The ventilation in the <u>greenhouse</u> needs to be improved.
<u>溫室</u>裡的通風要改善。

試練習題 What do you think of the ventilation in the greenhouse?

考生回答處 _____

考古題應用 Brandon ventures the most <u>capital</u> on his new restaurant.
Brandon 把大部分的<u>資金</u>押注在他的新餐廳上。

試練習題 What does Brandon venture the most capital on?

考生回答處 _____

V

考古題應用 Our research is on the verge of a major <u>breakthrough</u>.
我們的研究已經接近重大<u>突破</u>了。

試練習題 How is your research going?

考生回答處 _____

☐☐ verify　　☐☐ version　　☐☐ vessel
☐☐ vestige　　☐☐ veteran

verify (v.t) 核對

關 verification (n.) 驗證
　　verifiable (adj.) 可證實的
同 confirm, check, validate

一般正常速度 [ˋvɛrə͵faɪ]
ETS全真速度 [ˋvɛrə͵faɪ]

➡ 動詞與形容詞的重音都在第一音節，
　名詞的重音在第四音節 (-ca-)

version (n.) 版本

同 style, type, model

一般正常速度 [ˋvɝʒən]
ETS全真速度 [ˋvɝʒən]

vessel (n.) 船隻

同 ship

一般正常速度 [ˋvɛsl]
ETS全真速度 [ˋvɛsl]

➡ 字尾 [l] 請勿唸成 [ɔ]（台式發音）

vestige (n.) 遺跡

同 trace, sign, residue, remains

一般正常速度 [ˋvɛstɪdʒ]
ETS全真速度 [ˋvɛsdɪ(dʒ)]

➡ 1) [t] 須變音為 [d]
　 2) 字尾 [dʒ] 輕唸即可

veteran (n.) 老手

關 veteran (adj.) 老練的
同 old hand

一般正常速度 [ˋvɛtərən]
ETS全真速度 [ˋvɛđərən]

➡ 1) 名詞與形容詞的唸法相同
　 2) [t] 均須變音為 [đ]

考古題應用　They have to verify your <u>identity</u>.
他們得核對你的<u>身分</u>。

□試練習題　Why do I have to present two photo IDs to get a new bank account?
考生回答處 _____

考古題應用　The later version was the one we finally <u>adopted</u>.
我們最終<u>採用</u>的是後來的版本。

□試練習題　Which version of the manual did you adopt, the first version or the later one?
考生回答處 _____

考古題應用　It's no wonder many fishing vessels <u>are docked at</u> the harbor.
難怪許多漁船<u>停泊</u>在港口。

□試練習題　I heard the storm is coming soon.
考生回答處 _____

考古題應用　The earthquake has destroyed the last vestige of the old temple.
地震已經把老寺廟最後的遺跡都摧毀了。

□試練習題　Where is the famous old temple in this neighborhood?
考生回答處 _____

V

考古題應用　Mr. Marshall is a veteran salesman.
Marshall 先生是業務方面的老手。

□試練習題　Does Mr. Marshall have any relevant sales experience?
考生回答處 _____

Vi-

victim (n.) 受害者

關 victimize (v.t) 傷害
同 sufferer

一般正常速度 [`vɪktɪm]
ETS全真速度 [`vɪ(k)dɪm]

→ 1) 名詞與動詞的重音都在第一音節
2) [k] 均輕唸即可
3) [t] 均須變音成 [d]

virtually (adv.) 事實上

關 virtual (adj.) 事實上的
同 practically, in fact

一般正常速度 [`vɜtʃuəlɪ]
ETS全真速度 [`vɜtʃuəlɪ]

vision (n.) 願景

關 visionary (adj.) 夢想的
同 perception, insight, foresight

一般正常速度 [`vɪʒən]
ETS全真速度 [`vɪʒən]

→ 兩個詞性的 s 均唸成 [ʒ]

Vo-

volatile (adj.) 不穩定的

關 volatility (n.) 反覆無常
同 unstable, unsteady, changeable, inconstant

一般正常速度 [`valətaɪl]
ETS全真速度 [`valədaɪl]

→ [t] 須變音為 [d]

volume (n.) 份量

關 voluminous (adj.) 龐大的
同 quantity

一般正常速度 [`valjəm]
ETS全真速度 [`valjəm]

→ 名詞的重音在第一音節，形容詞的重音在第二音節 (-lu-)

考古題應用 The laid-off workers would certainly end up being victims.
被解雇的員工會變成受害者。

試練習題 What would happen if the company couldn't afford the severance pay?

考生回答處 _____

考古題應用 Virtually some guests have complained about their uncomfortable bedding.
事實上有些客人抱怨寢具不舒服。

試練習題 Our guests haven't filed any complaints about their rooms, right?

考生回答處 _____

考古題應用 Our shared vision is to create the best hotel in the world.
我們共同的願景就是創造一個全球最好的飯店。

試練習題 What is the shared vision amongst your staff?

考生回答處 _____

考古題應用 We help investors make sound judgments in volatile markets.
我們幫助投資者在市場不穩定時做正確的判斷。

試練習題 What does your consulting firm do for investors?

考生回答處 _____

V

考古題應用 Our volume of trade with the Middle East has decreased.
我們與中東的貿易量減少了。

試練習題 How has the political instability in the Middle East affected your business?

考生回答處 _____

☐☐ volunteer　☐☐ vote　☐☐ voucher
☐☐ voyage　☐☐ wage

---

volunteer (v.i) 自願

關 volunteer (n.) 自願者
voluntary (adj.) 自願的
voluntarily (adv.) 自願地
同 offer

一般正常速度 [ˌvɑlən`tɪr]
ETS全真速度 [ˌvɑlən`tɪr]

➡ 動詞與名詞的重音都在第三音節，形容詞跟副詞的重音在第一音節

---

vote (v.i) 投票

關 vote (n.) 選票
voter (n.) 投票人
同 elect

一般正常速度 [vot]
ETS全真速度 [vo(t)]

➡ 1) 動詞字尾 [t] 輕唸即可
　 2) voter 的 [t] 須變音為 [d]

---

voucher (n.) 憑證

關 vouch (v.t) 擔保
同 receipt, ticket

一般正常速度 [`vautʃɚ]
ETS全真速度 [`vautʃɚ]

---

voyage (n.) 航行

關 voyage (v.i) 航行
voyager (n.) 航行者
同 sailing, cruise, journey, travel, trip

一般正常速度 [`vɔɪɪdʒ]
ETS全真速度 [`vɔɪɪ(dʒ)]

➡ 1) 所有詞性的重音都在第一音節
　 2) voyage 字尾 [dʒ] 輕唸即可

---

wage (n.) 工資

同 pay, earnings, payment, fee

一般正常速度 [wedʒ]
ETS全真速度 [we(dʒ)]

➡ 字尾 [dʒ] 輕唸即可

考古題應用　Tony volunteered to take her to the mall.
Tony 自願開車送她到購物中心。

試練習題　Did you ask Tony to give Teresa a ride to the mall?
考生回答處　_____

考古題應用　The residents voted unanimously against the <u>demolition</u>.
居民們一致投票反對<u>拆除</u>。

試練習題　Did the residents vote for the demolition of the park?
考生回答處　_____

考古題應用　I forgot to bring my parking vouchers.
我忘了帶停車券。

試練習題　Why didn't you park in your usual parking lot?
考生回答處　_____

考古題應用　The <u>cruise liner</u> hit heavy fog on its first voyage.
這艘<u>遊輪</u>在首航就碰上濃霧。

試練習題　Did the cruise liner have a smooth first voyage?
考生回答處　_____

V

W

考古題應用　He demands a raise in wages of 20%.
他要求工資調升 20%。

試練習題　What is Mr. Carreras' wage demand?
考生回答處　_____

wander (v.t) 漫步

同 stroll, drift, cruise

一般正常速度 [ˋwandɚ]

ETS全真速度 [ˋwandɚ]

➡ 重音節母音 a 須唸成 [a]

wardrobe (n.) 衣服

同 clothes, apparel, outfit

一般正常速度 [ˋwɔrd‚rob]

ETS全真速度 [ˋwɔrd‚ro(b)]

➡ 字尾 [b] 輕唸即可

warn (v.t) 警告

關 warning (n.) 警告
同 alert, inform, advise, admonish, notify

一般正常速度 [wɔrn]

ETS全真速度 [wɔrn]

warranty (n.) 保證書

關 warrant (v.t) 擔保
同 guarantee, assurance

一般正常速度 [ˋwɔrəntɪ]

ETS全真速度 [ˋwɔrənɖɪ]

➡ 1) 名詞與動詞的重音都在第一音節
2) 名詞的 [t] 可變音為 [ɖ]

waste (v.t) 浪費

關 waste (n.) 浪費
wasteful (adj.) 浪費的
同 misuse

一般正常速度 [west]

ETS全真速度 [we(st)]

➡ 1) 動詞字尾 [st] 輕唸即可，形容詞字尾 [t] 須消音
2) 形容詞字尾 [l] 請勿唸成 [ɔ]（台式發音）

考古題應用 The tourists are wandering around the famous Michigan Avenue.
觀光客漫步在著名的密西根大道上。

口試練習題 What are the tourists doing in downtown Chicago?

考生回答處 _____

考古題應用 Her summer wardrobe is mostly clothing made from <u>cotton</u>.
她夏天的衣服大多是<u>棉</u>製的。

口試練習題 What does Martha's summer wardrobe mostly consist of?

考生回答處 _____

考古題應用 He warned us against the <u>credibility</u> of the applicant.
他警告過我們有關那名申請者的<u>可信度</u>。

口試練習題 What did Dr. Murphy warn you against?

考生回答處 _____

考古題應用 All of our products come with a two-year warranty.
我們所有的產品都附有兩年的保證書。

口試練習題 Does your product come with a warranty?

考生回答處 _____

W

考古題應用 You are wasting your time <u>bargaining</u> with him.
你跟他<u>討價還價</u>是在浪費時間。

口試練習題 Do you think Mr. Miyata will give me a huge discount?

考生回答處 _____

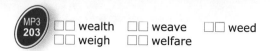

We-

wealth (n.) 財富

關 wealthy (adj.) 富有的
同 fortune, riches, possessions, property

一般正常速度 [wɛlθ]
ETS全真速度 [wɛl(θ)]
➔ 名詞字尾 [θ] 輕唸即可

weave (v.t) 編織

關 weave (n.) 織法
同 knit

一般正常速度 [wiv]
ETS全真速度 [wi(v)]
➔ 動詞與名詞的唸法相同

weed (v.t) 除草

關 weed (n.) 雜草
同 mow the lawn, uproot

一般正常速度 [wid]
ETS全真速度 [wi(d)]
➔ 1) 動詞與名詞的唸法相同
   2) 字尾 [d] 輕唸即可

weigh (v.i) 有…重量

關 weight (n.) 重量

一般正常速度 [we]
ETS全真速度 [we]

welfare (n.) 福利

同 benefit, favor

一般正常速度 [`wɛl.fɛr]
ETS全真速度 [`wɛl.fɛr]

考古題應用　He accumulated great wealth from the stock market trade.
他在股市累積了龐大的財富。

試練習題　How did Mr. Ozawa become so rich?
考生回答處　＿＿＿＿＿＿＿＿＿＿＿＿＿＿＿＿＿＿＿＿＿＿

考古題應用　She wove me a pair of mittens.
她織給我一雙手套。

試練習題　What did your aunt give you for Christmas?
考生回答處　＿＿＿＿＿＿＿＿＿＿＿＿＿＿＿＿＿＿＿＿＿＿

考古題應用　The farmers are weeding the cornfield.
農夫在玉米田裡除草。

試練習題　What are the farmers doing in the cornfield?
考生回答處　＿＿＿＿＿＿＿＿＿＿＿＿＿＿＿＿＿＿＿＿＿＿

考古題應用　His new laptop computer weighs less than expected.
他的新筆記型電腦比預期的輕。

試練習題　How much does his new laptop computer weigh?
考生回答處　＿＿＿＿＿＿＿＿＿＿＿＿＿＿＿＿＿＿＿＿＿＿

W

考古題應用　We provided employees with better benefits and welfare.
我們提供員工更好的福利。

試練習題　How did your company successfully reduce its turnover rate?
考生回答處　＿＿＿＿＿＿＿＿＿＿＿＿＿＿＿＿＿＿＿＿＿＿

MP3
204

□□ will　　□□ wipe　　□□ withdraw
□□ witness　□□ workforce

Wi-

will (n.) 意願

關 will (n.) 遺囑
同 intention, purpose, aim

一般正常速度 [wɪl]
ETS全真速度 [wɪl]

➡ 字尾 [l] 請勿唸成 [ɔ]（台式發音）

---

wipe (v.t) 擦拭

關 wipe (n.) 擦拭
同 rub, clean, mop, erase

一般正常速度 [waɪp]
ETS全真速度 [waɪ(p)]

➡ 1) 動詞與名詞唸法相同
　 2) 字尾 [p] 輕唸即可

---

withdraw (v.t) 提款

關 withdrawal (n.) 提款
同 extract, take away

一般正常速度 [wɪð`drɔ]
ETS全真速度 [wɪð`drɔ]

➡ 1) 兩個詞性的重音都在第二音節
　 2) 名詞字尾 [l] 請勿唸成 [ɔ]（台式發音）

---

witness (n.) 證人

關 witness (v.t) 目擊
同 observer, watcher, viewer

一般正常速度 [`wɪtnɪs]
ETS全真速度 [`wɪ__nɪ(s)]

➡ 1) 名詞與動詞的唸法相同
　 2) [t] 停一拍即可，無須發音

Wo-

workforce (n.) 員工

一般正常速度 [`wɜkfors]
ETS全真速度 [`wɜ(k)for(s)]

➡ [k] 與字尾 [s] 均輕唸即可

考古題應用 He signed the papers by his own free will.
他自願簽署那些文件。

試練習題 Did anyone force Brian to sign the papers?
考生回答處 _____

考古題應用 She is wiping the kitchen counter with a <u>sponge</u>.
她正在用海綿擦拭廚房流理台。

試練習題 What is Samantha wiping the kitchen counter with?
考生回答處 _____

考古題應用 I withdrew 100 dollars from the ATM.
我從自動提款機領了一百塊美元。

試練習題 How much money did you withdraw from the ATM?
考生回答處 _____

考古題應用 He is the key witness in a case.
他是一椿案件中的關鍵證人。

試練習題 Why does Mr. Watson have to go to the police station?
考生回答處 _____

W

考古題應用 This company has a workforce of 2,000 people.
這家公司的員工有兩千人。

試練習題 How large is the company's workforce?
考生回答處 _____

MP3 205

□□ workshop　　□□ worth　　□□ wrap
□□ yield　　□□ youth

---

workshop (n.) 研習會

同 seminar, study group

一般正常速度 [`wɜk.ʃap]
ETS全真速度 [`wɜ(k)ˌʃa(p)]

➡ [k] 與字尾 [p] 均輕唸即可

---

worth (prep.) 值得

關 worth (n.) 價值
worthy (adj.) 有價值的
同 having the value

一般正常速度 [wɜθ]
ETS全真速度 [wɜ(θ)]

➡ 1) worth 字尾 th 唸 [θ]，worthy 字尾
　 th 則唸 [ð]
　 2) worth 字尾 [θ] 輕唸即可

---

wrap (v.t) 包起來

關 wrapping (n.) 包裝
同 enclose, pack, package, encase,
enfold

一般正常速度 [ræp]
ETS全真速度 [ræ(p)]

➡ 動詞字尾 [p] 輕唸即可，名詞的 [p]
　 則須變音為 [b]

---

yield (v.t) 生產

關 yield (n.) 產量
同 produce, provide, give, supply

一般正常速度 [jild]
ETS全真速度 [jil(d)]

➡ 1) 動詞與名詞的唸法相同
　 2) 字中 [l] 請勿唸成 [ɔ]（台式發音）
　 3) 字尾 [d] 輕唸即可

---

youth (n.) 年輕

關 young (adj.) 年輕的
同 early days

一般正常速度 [juθ]
ETS全真速度 [ju(θ)]

➡ 1) 名詞母音為 [u]，形容詞母音則是
　 [ʌ]（請勿唸成 [a]）
　 2) 名詞字尾 [θ] 輕唸即可

考古題應用 Most employees participated in the computer workshop.
大部分的員工都參加了電腦研習會。

試練習題 Were there many participants in the computer workshop?
考生回答處 _____

考古題應用 He inherited a house worth two billion dollars.
他繼承了一棟價值 20 億美元的房子。

試練習題 Did Mr. Morrison inherit a house of little worth?
考生回答處 _____

考古題應用 The clerk wrapped it up in printed paper.
售貨員用有圖案的紙把它包起來。

試練習題 What did the clerk gift-wrap the sweater with?
考生回答處 _____

考古題應用 This land yielded crops worth one million dollars last year.
這塊土地去年生產的農作物價值一百萬美元。

試練習題 Did this land have a rich harvest last year?
考生回答處 _____

W
Y

考古題應用 In my youth, I wanted to be a landscape designer.
我年輕時想當景觀設計師。

試練習題 Did you have a great interest in designing at a young age?
考生回答處 _____

zealous (adj.) 熱衷的

關 zeal (n.) 熱忱
同 eager, enthusiastic, devoted

一般正常速度 [ˋzɛləs]
ETS全真速度 [ˋzɛlə(s)]

➡ 1) 形容詞的重音節母音發 [ɛ]，名詞的
母音發 [i]
2) 形容詞字尾 [s] 輕唸即可

zip (v.t) 拉上

關 zipper (n.) 拉鍊

一般正常速度 [zɪp]
ETS全真速度 [zɪ(p)]

➡ 動詞字尾 [p] 輕唸即可，名詞的 [p]
則須變音為 [b]

416

考古題應用　Carla has long been a zealous environmentalist.
Carla 一直是個熱衷的環保人士。

口試練習題　I didn't know Carla was so concerned about environmental issues.

考生回答處　_____

考古題應用　Please put the cheese in the bag and zip it shut.
請把起司放進袋子封緊。

口試練習題　Should I put the cheese on the plate?

考生回答處　_____

Z

Check List 10

恭喜，你已經背完所有 TOEIC 最熱門的頻考字彙了！我們再來複習一下，讓這些單字能記得更牢、認得更快！

☐ table	☐ theory	☐ trim
☐ tactic	☐ therapy	☐ trivial
☐ tag	☐ thorough	☐ tropical
☐ talent	☐ tie	☐ trust
☐ tally	☐ title	☐ turn
☐ target	☐ token	☐ turnaround
☐ task	☐ tolerate	☐ turnout
☐ tear	☐ tour	☐ turnover
☐ technical	☐ trace	☐ tutor
☐ teller	☐ trade	☐ typical
☐ temperature	☐ traditional	☐ ultimate
☐ temporary	☐ transaction	☐ unanimous
☐ tendency	☐ transition	☐ underestimate
☐ tension	☐ translate	☐ undergo
☐ terminal	☐ transport	☐ underline
☐ territory	☐ tray	☐ undertake
☐ text	☐ trial	☐ uniform
☐ textile	☐ tribute	☐ unique

☐ unity	☐ vessel	☐ wealth
☐ unload	☐ vestige	☐ weave
☐ update	☐ veteran	☐ weed
☐ urge	☐ victim	☐ weigh
☐ utilities	☐ virtually	☐ welfare
☐ utterly	☐ vision	☐ will
☐ vacancy	☐ volatile	☐ wipe
☐ vaccinate	☐ volume	☐ withdraw
☐ vague	☐ volunteer	☐ witness
☐ valid	☐ vote	☐ workforce
☐ valuable	☐ voucher	☐ workshop
☐ variable	☐ voyage	☐ worth
☐ vehicle	☐ wage	☐ wrap
☐ ventilation	☐ wander	☐ yield
☐ venture	☐ wardrobe	☐ youth
☐ verge	☐ warn	☐ zealous
☐ verify	☐ warranty	☐ zip
☐ version	☐ waste	

TOEIC

TOEIC

國家圖書館出版品預行編目資料

趙御笙 TOEIC 字彙資優班：一次學會字彙、聽力、口語 / 趙御笙
作. – 初版. – 臺北市：眾文圖書, 民97. 05
　　　面：公分

ISBN 978-957-532-340-0

1.　多益測驗　2.　詞彙

805.1894　　　　　　　　　　　　　　97001379

定價 480 元

趙御筌 TOEIC® 字彙資優班
一次學會字彙、聽力、口語

2011 年 9 月 初版五刷

作　　者	趙御筌
英文校閱	D. Corey Sanderson
主　　編	陳瑠琍
編　　輯	黃炯睿
美術設計	嚴國綸
發 行 人	黃建和
發 行 所	眾文圖書股份有限公司
	台北市重慶南路一段 9 號
網路書店	http://www.jwbooks.com.tw
電　　話	(02) 2311-8168
傳　　真	(02) 2311-9683
劃撥帳號	01048805

局版台業字第 1593 號　　　　　　　　　　　　　　版權所有・請勿翻印

本書若有缺頁、破損或裝訂錯誤，請寄回下列地址更換。
新北市 23145 新店區寶橋路 235 巷 6 弄 2 號 4 樓